# Enrollment Form

☐ **Yes!** I WANT TO BE A *Privileged* *Woman.*

Enclosed is one *PAGES & PRIVILEGES*™ Proof of Purchase from any Harlequin or Silhouette book currently for sale in stores (Proofs of Purchase are found on the back pages of books) and the store cash register receipt. Please enroll me in *PAGES & PRIVILEGES*™. Send my Welcome Kit and FREE Gifts -- and activate my FREE benefits -- immediately.

*More great gifts and benefits to come like these luxurious Truly Lace and L'Effleur gift baskets.*

NAME (please print)

ADDRESS                                    APT. NO

CITY                    STATE              ZIP/POSTAL CODE

---

**PROOF OF PURCHASE**
SAMPLE ONLY
Pages & Privileges™

**NO CLUB!
NO COMMITMENT!**
*Just one purchase brings you great Free Gifts and Benefits!*
(More details in back of this book.)

Please allow 6-8 weeks for delivery. Quantities are limited. We reserve the right to substitute items. Enroll before October 31, 1995 and receive one full year of benefits.

Name of store where this book was purchased_____

Date of purchase_____

Type of store:

☐ Bookstore    ☐ Supermarket    ☐ Drugstore

☐ Dept. or discount store (e.g. K-Mart or Walmart)

☐ Other (specify)_____

Which Harlequin or Silhouette series do you usually read?

_____

---

**Complete and mail with one Proof of Purchase and store receipt to:**

**U.S.:** *PAGES & PRIVILEGES*™, P.O. Box 1960, Danbury, CT 06813-1960

**Canada:** *PAGES & PRIVILEGES*™, 49-6A The Donway West, P.O. 813, North York, ON M3C 2E8        **PRINTED IN U.S.A**

Dear Readers,

One of the Long, Tall Texans books in this second omnibus has led to a sequel. In *Sutton's Way,* the leader of Amanda Corrie Callaway's rock group, "Desperado," is a huge Texan named Hank Shoeman. I have had an ongoing request from one special reader for several years to write about Hank, and I am delighted to tell her that he has his own story in "Redbird," which Silhouette released in a collection of short stories called *Abduction & Seduction* in March, 1995.

The second book here, *Ethan,* is a favorite of mine because the heroine is a concert pianist— a dream of mine which gave way to writing fever. (Actually, I play a computer keyboard a lot better than I play a piano keyboard, and people who have heard me play will agree wholeheartedly!)

The third book in this omnibus is *Connal,* the first of the Tremayne brothers to have his own book. (The others are Harden and Evan, both mentioned in this one.)

I hope you enjoy these three books, and thanks again for the friendship all of you have given me over the years, and for your wonderful response to the Long, Tall Texans series.

All my love,

Diana Palmer

# DIANA PALMER

got her start in writing as a newspaper reporter and
published her first romance novel for Silhouette Books
in 1982. In 1993, she celebrated the publication of her
fiftieth novel for Silhouette Books. *Affaire de Coeur*
lists her as one of the top ten romance authors in the
country. Beloved by fans worldwide, Diana Palmer is
the winner of five national Waldenbooks Romance
Bestseller awards and two national B. Dalton Books
Bestseller awards.

# Diana Palmer

## Long, Tall Texans II

Silhouette Books

Published by Silhouette Books

America's Publisher of Contemporary Romance

SILHOUETTE BOOKS

ISBN 0-373-20112-5

by Request

LONG, TALL TEXANS II

Copyright © 1995 by Harlequin Books S.A.

The publisher acknowledges the copyright holders of the individual works as follows:

SUTTON'S WAY
Copyright © 1989 by Diana Palmer
ETHAN
Copyright © 1990 by Diana Palmer
CONNAL
Copyright © 1990 by Diana Palmer

**Printed in U.S.A.**

# *CONTENTS*

# SUTTON'S WAY

## Diana Palmer

To Barry Call
of Charbons in Gainesville, GA

Many thanks

# Chapter One

The noise outside the cabin was there again, and Amanda shifted restlessly with the novel in her lap, curled up in a big armchair by the open fireplace in an Indian rug. Until now, the cabin had been paradise. There was three feet of new snow outside, she had all the supplies she needed to get her through the next few wintery weeks of Wyoming weather, and there wasn't a telephone in the place. Best of all, there wasn't a neighbor.

Well, there was, actually. But nobody in their right mind would refer to that man on the mountain as a neighbor. Amanda had only seen him once and once was enough.

She'd met him, if their head-on encounter could be referred to as a meeting, on a snowy Saturday last week. Quinn Sutton's majestic ranch house overlooked this cabin nestled against the mountainside.

He'd been out in the snow on a horse-drawn sled that contained huge square bales of hay, and he was heaving them like feather pillows to a small herd of red-and-white cattle. The sight had touched Amanda, because it indicated concern. The tall, wiry rancher out in a blizzard feeding his starving cattle. She'd even smiled at the tender picture it made.

And then she'd stopped her four-wheel-drive vehicle and stuck her blond head out the window to ask directions to the Blalock Durning place, which was the cabin one of her aunt's friends was loaning her. And the tender picture dissolved into stark hostility.

The tall rancher turned toward her with the coldest black eyes and the hardest face she'd ever seen in her life. He had a day's growth of stubble, but the stubble didn't begin to cover up the frank homeliness of his lean face. He had amazingly high cheekbones, a broad forehead and a jutting chin, and he looked as if someone had taken a straight razor to one side of his face, which had a wide scratch. None of that bothered Amanda because Hank Shoeman and the other three men who made music with her group were even uglier than Quinn Sutton. But at least Hank and the boys could smile. This man looked as if he invented the black scowl.

"I said," she'd repeated with growing nervousness, "can you tell me how to get to Blalock Durning's cabin?"

Above the sheepskin coat, under the battered gray ranch hat, Quinn Sutton's tanned face didn't move a muscle. "Follow the road, turn left at the lodgepoles," he'd said tersely, his voice as deep as a rumble of thunder.

"Lodgepoles?" she'd faltered. "You mean Indian lodgepoles? What do they look like?"

"Lady," he said with exaggerated patience, "a lodgepole is a pine tree. It's tall and piney, and there are a stand of them at the next fork in the road."

"You don't need to be rude, Mr. . . ?"

"Sutton," he said tersely. "Quinn Sutton."

"Nice to meet you," she murmured politely. "I'm Amanda." She wondered if anyone might accidentally recognize her here in the back of beyond, and on the off chance, she gave her mother's maiden name instead of her own last name. "Amanda Corrie," she added untruthfully. "I'm going to stay in the cabin for a few weeks."

"This isn't the tourist season," he'd said without the slightest pretense at friendliness. His black eyes cut her like swords.

"Good, because I'm not a tourist," she said.

"Don't look to me for help if you run out of wood or start hearing things in the dark," he added coldly. "Somebody will tell you eventually that I have no use whatsoever for women."

While she was thinking up a reply to that, a young boy of about twelve had come running up behind the sled.

"Dad!" he called, amazingly enough to Quinn Sutton. "There's a cow in calf down in the next pasture. I think it's a breech!"

"Okay, son, hop on," he told the boy, and his voice had become fleetingly soft, almost tender. He looked back at Amanda, though, and the softness left him. "Keep your door locked at night," he'd said. "Unless you're expecting Durning to join you," he added with a mocking smile.

She'd stared at him from eyes as black as his own and started to tell him that she didn't even know Mr. Durning, who was her aunt's friend, not hers. But she bit her tongue. It wouldn't do to give this man an opening. "I'll do that little thing," she agreed. She glanced at the boy, who was eyeing her curiously from his perch on the sled. "And it seems that you do have at least one use for women," she added with a vacant smile. "My condolences to your wife, Mr. Sutton."

She'd rolled up the window before he could speak and she'd whipped the four-wheel-drive down the road with little regard for safety, sliding all over the place on the slick and rutted country road.

She glared into the flames, consigning Quinn Sutton to them with all her angry heart. She hoped and prayed that there wouldn't ever be an accident or a reason she'd have to seek out his company. She'd rather have asked help from a passing timber wolf. His son hadn't seemed at all like him, she recalled. Sutton was as dangerous looking as a timber wolf, with a face like the side of a bombed mountain and eyes that were coal-black and cruel. In the sheepskin coat he'd been wearing with that raunchy Stetson that day, he'd looked like one of the old mountain men might have back in Wyoming's early days. He'd given Amanda some bad moments and she'd hated him after that uncomfortable confrontation. But the boy had been kind. He was redheaded and blue-eyed, nothing like his father, not a bit of resemblance.

She knew the rancher's name only because her aunt had mentioned him, and cautioned Amanda about going near the Sutton ranch. The ranch was called Ricochet, and Amanda had immediately thought of a bullet going awry. Probably one of Sutton's ancestors had thrown some lead now and again. Mr. Sutton looked a lot more like a bandit than he did a rancher, with his face unshaven, that wide, awful scrape on his cheek and his crooked nose. It was an unforgettable face all around, especially those eyes. . . .

She pulled the Indian rug closer and gave the book in her slender hand a careless glance. She wasn't really in the mood to read. Memories kept tearing her heart. She leaned her blond head back against the chair and her dark eyes studied the flames with idle appreciation of their beauty.

The nightmare of the past few weeks had finally caught up with her. She'd stood onstage, with the lights beating down on her long blond hair and outlining the beige leather dress that was her trademark, and her voice had simply refused to cooperate. The shock of being unable to produce a single note had caused her to faint, to the shock and horror of the audience.

She came to in a hospital, where she'd been given what seemed to be every test known to medical science. But nothing would produce her singing voice, even though she could talk. It was, the doctor told her, purely a psychological problem, caused by the trauma of what had happened. She needed rest.

So Hank, who was the leader of the group, had called her Aunt Bess and convinced her to arrange for Amanda to get away from it all. Her aunt's rich boyfriend had this holiday cabin in Wyoming's Grand Teton Mountains and was more than willing to let

Amanda recuperate there. Amanda had protested, but
Hank and the boys and her aunt had insisted. So here
she was, in the middle of winter, in several feet of
snow, with no television, no telephone and facilities
that barely worked. Roughing it, the big, bearded
bandleader had told her, would do her good.

She smiled when she remembered how caring and
kind the guys had been. Her group was called Desperado, and her leather costume was its trademark.
The four men who made up the rest of it were fine
musicians, but they looked like the Hell's Angels on
stage in denim and leather with thick black beards and
mustaches and untrimmed hair. They were really
pussycats under that rough exterior, but nobody had
ever been game enough to try to find out if they were.

Hank and Deke and Jack and Johnson had been
trying to get work at a Virginia night spot when they'd
run into Amanda Corrie Callaway, who was also trying to get work there. The club needed a singer and a
band, so it was a match made in heaven, although
Amanda with her sheltered upbringing had been a little afraid of her new backup band. They, on the other
hand, had been nervous around her because she was
such a far cry from the usual singers they'd worked
with. The shy, introverted young blonde made them
self-conscious about their appearance. But their first
performance together had been a phenomenal hit, and
they'd been together four years now.

They were famous, now. Desperado had been on the
music videos for two years, they'd done television
shows and magazine interviews, and they were recognized everywhere they went. Especially Amanda, who
went by the stage name of Mandy Callaway. It wasn't

a bad life, and it was making them rich. But there wasn't much rest or time for a personal life. None of the group was married except Hank, and he was already getting a divorce. It was hard for a homebound spouse to accept the frequent absences that road tours required.

She still shivered from the look Quinn Sutton had given her, and now she was worried about her Aunt Bess, though the woman was more liberal minded and should know the score. But Sutton had convinced Amanda that she wasn't the first woman to be at Blalock's cabin. She should have told that arrogant rancher what her real relationship with Blalock Durning was, but he probably wouldn't have believed her.

Of course, she could have put him in touch with Jerry and proved it. Jerry Allen, their road manager, was one of the best in the business. He'd kept them from starving during the beginning, and they had an expert crew of electricians and carpenters who made up the rest of the retinue. It took a huge bus to carry the people and equipment, appropriately called the "Outlaw Express."

Amanda had pleaded with Jerry to give them a few weeks rest after the tragedy that had cost her her nerve, but he'd refused. Get back on the horse, he'd advised. And she'd tried. But the memories were just too horrible.

So finally he'd agreed to Hank's suggestion and she was officially on hiatus, as were the other members of the group, for a month. Maybe in that length of time she could come to grips with it, face it.

It had been a week and she felt better already. Or she would, if those strange noises outside the cabin would just stop! She had horrible visions of wolves breaking in and eating her.

"Hello?"

The small voice startled her. It sounded like a boy's. She got up, clutching the fire poker in her hand and went to the front door. "Who's there?" she called out tersely.

"It's just me. Elliot," he said. "Elliot Sutton."

She let out a breath between her teeth. Oh, no, she thought miserably, what was he doing here? His father would come looking for him, and she couldn't bear to have that . . . that savage anywhere around!

"What do you want?" she groaned.

"I brought you something."

It would be discourteous to refuse the gift, she guessed, especially since he'd apparently come through several feet of snow to bring it. Which brought to mind a really interesting question: where was his father?

She opened the door. He grinned at her from under a thick cap that covered his red hair.

"Hi," he said. "I thought you might like to have some roasted peanuts. I did them myself. They're nice on a cold night."

Her eyes went past him to a sled hitched to a sturdy draft horse. "Did you come in that?" she asked, recognizing the sled he and his father had been riding the day she'd met them.

"Sure," he said. "That's how we get around in winter, what with the snow and all. We take hay out to the livestock on it. You remember, you saw us. Well, we usually take hay out on it, that is. When Dad's not laid up," he added pointedly, and his blue eyes said more than his voice did.

She knew she was going to regret asking the question before she opened her mouth. She didn't want to ask. But no young boy came to a stranger's house in the middle of a snowy night just to deliver a bag of roasted peanuts.

"What's wrong?" she asked with resigned perception.

He blinked. "What?"

"I said, what's wrong?" She made her tone gentler. He couldn't help it that his father was a savage, and he was worried under that false grin. "Come on, you might as well tell me."

He bit his lower lip and looked down at his snow-covered boots. "It's my dad," he said. "He's bad sick and he won't let me get the doctor."

So there it was. She knew she shouldn't have asked. "Can't your mother do something?" she asked hopefully.

"My mom ran off with Mr. Jackson from the livestock association when I was just a little feller," he replied, registering Amanda's shocked expression. "She and Dad got divorced and she died some years ago, but Dad doesn't talk about her. Will you come, miss?"

"I'm not a doctor," she said, hesitating.

"Oh, sure, I know that," he agreed eagerly, "but you're a girl. And girls know how to take care of sick folks, don't they?" The confidence slid away and he looked like what he was—a terrified little boy with nobody to turn to. "Please, lady," he added. "I'm scared. He's hot and shaking all over and—!"

"I'll get my boots on," she said. She gathered them from beside the fireplace and tugged them on, and then she went for a coat and stuffed her long blond hair under a stocking cap. "Do you have cough syrup, aspirins, throat lozenges—that sort of thing?"

"Yes, ma'am," he said eagerly, then sighed. "Dad won't take them, but we have them."

"Is he suicidal?" Amanda asked angrily as she went out the door behind him and locked the cabin before she climbed on the sled with the boy.

"Well sometimes things get to him," he ventured. "But he doesn't ever get sick, and he won't admit that he is. But he's out of his head and I'm scared. He's all I got."

"We'll take care of him," she promised, and hoped she could deliver on the promise. "Let's go."

"Do you know Mr. Durning well?" he asked as he called to the draft horse and started him back down the road and up the mountain toward the Sutton house.

"He's sort of a friend of a relative of mine," she said evasively. The sled ride was fun, and she was enjoying the cold wind and snow in her face, the delicious mountain air. "I'm only staying at the cabin for a few weeks. Just time to...get over something."

"Have you been sick, too?" he asked curiously.

"In a way," she said noncommittally.

The sled went jerkily up the road, around the steep hill. She held on tight and hoped the big draft horse had steady feet. It was a harrowing ride at the last, and then they were up, and the huge redwood ranch house came into sight, blazing with light from its long, wide front porch to the gabled roof.

"It's a beautiful house," Amanda said.

"My dad added on to it for my mom, before they married," he told her. He shrugged. "I don't remember much about her, except she was redheaded. Dad sure hates women." He glanced at her apologetically. "He's not going to like me bringing you...."

"I can take care of myself," she returned, and smiled reassuringly. "Let's go see how bad it is."

"I'll get Harry to put up the horse and sled," he said, yelling toward the lighted barn until a grizzled old man appeared. After a brief introduction to Amanda, Harry left and took the horse away.

"Harry's been here since Dad was a boy," Elliot told her as he led her down a bare-wood hall and up a steep staircase to the second storey of the house. "He does most everything, even cooks for the men." He paused outside a closed door, and gave Amanda a worried look. "He'll yell for sure."

"Let's get it over with, then."

She let Elliot open the door and look in first, to make sure his father had something on.

"He's still in his jeans," he told her, smiling as she blushed. "It's okay."

She cleared her throat. So much for pretended sophistication, she thought, and here she was twenty-four years old. She avoided Elliot's grin and walked into the room.

Quinn Sutton was sprawled on his stomach, his bare muscular arms stretched toward the headboard. His back gleamed with sweat, and his thick, black hair was damp with moisture. Since it wasn't hot in the room, Amanda decided that he must have a high fever. He was moaning and talking unintelligibly.

"Elliot, can you get me a basin and some hot water?" she asked. She took off her coat and rolled up the sleeves of her cotton blouse.

"Sure thing," Elliot told her, and rushed out of the room.

"Mr. Sutton, can you hear me?" Amanda asked softly. She sat down beside him on the bed, and lightly touched his bare shoulder. He was hot, all right—burning up. "Mr. Sutton," she called again.

"No," he moaned. "No, you can't do it . . . !"

"Mr. Sutton . . ."

He rolled over and his black eyes opened, glazed with fever, but Amanda barely noticed. Her eyes were on the rest of him, male perfection from shoulder to narrow hips. He was darkly tanned, too, and thick, black hair wedged from his chest down his flat stomach to the wide belt at his hips. Amanda, who was remarkably innocent not only for her age, but for her profession as well, stared like a star-struck girl. He was beautiful, she thought, amazed at the elegant lines of his body, at the ripple of muscle and the smooth, glistening skin.

"What the hell do you want?" he rasped.

So much for hero worship, she thought dryly. She lifted her eyes back to his. "Elliot was worried," she said quietly. "He came and got me. Please don't fuss at him. You're raging with fever."

"Damn the fever, get out," he said in a tone that might have stopped a charging wolf.

"I can't do that," she said. She turned her head toward the door where Elliot appeared with a basin full of hot water and a towel and washcloth over one arm.

"Here you are, lady," he said. "Hi, Dad," he added with a wan smile at his furious father. "You can beat me when you're able again."

"Don't think I won't," Quinn growled.

"There, there, you're just feverish and sick, Mr. Sutton," Amanda soothed.

"Get Harry and have him throw her off my land," Quinn told Elliot in a furious voice.

"How about some aspirin, Elliot, and something for him to drink? A small whiskey and something hot—"

"I don't drink whiskey," Quinn said harshly.

"He has a glass of wine now and then," Elliot ventured.

"Wine, then." She soaked the cloth in the basin. "And you might turn up the heat. We don't want him to catch a chill when I sponge him down."

"You damned well aren't sponging me down!" Quinn raged.

She ignored him. "Go and get those things, please, Elliot, and the cough syrup, too."

"You bet, lady!" he said grinning.

"My name is Amanda," she said absently.

"Amanda," the boy repeated, and went back downstairs.

"God help you when I get back on my feet," Quinn said with fury. He laid back on the pillow, shivering when she touched him with the cloth. "Don't...!"

"I could fry an egg on you. I have to get the fever down. Elliot said you were delirious."

"Elliot's delirious to let you in here," he shuddered. Her fingers accidentally brushed his flat stom-

ach and he arched, shivering. "For God's sake,
don't," he groaned.

"Does your stomach hurt?" she asked, concerned.
"I'm sorry." She soaked the cloth again and rubbed
it against his shoulders, his arms, his face.

His black eyes opened. He was breathing roughly,
and his face was taut. The fever, she imagined. She
brushed back her long hair, and wished she'd tied it
up. It kept flowing down onto his damp chest.

"Damn you," he growled.

"Damn you, too, Mr. Sutton." She smiled sweetly.
She finished bathing his face and put the cloth and
basin aside. "Do you have a long-sleeved shirt?"

"Get out!"

Elliot came back with the medicine and a small glass
of wine. "Harry's making hot chocolate," he said
with a smile. "He'll bring it up. Here's the other
stuff."

"Good," she said. "Does your father have a pajama jacket or something long-sleeved?"

"Sure!"

"Traitor," Quinn groaned at his son.

"Here you go." Elliot handed her a flannel top,
which she proceeded to put on the protesting and very
angry Mr. Sutton.

"I hate you," Quinn snapped at her with his last
ounce of venom.

"I hate you, too," she agreed. She had to reach
around him to get the jacket on, and it brought her
into much too close proximity to him. She could feel
the hair on his chest rubbing against her soft cheek,
she could feel her own hair smoothing over his bare
shoulder and chest. Odd, that shivery feeling she got

from contact with him. She ignored it forcibly and got
his other arm into the pajama jacket. She fastened it,
trying to keep her fingers from touching his chest any
more than necessary because the feel of that pelt of
hair disturbed her. He shivered violently at the touch
of her hands and her long, silky hair, and she assumed it was because of his fever.

"Are you finished?" Quinn asked harshly.

"Almost." She pulled the covers over him, found
the electric-blanket control and turned it on. Then she
ladled cough syrup into him, gave him aspirin and had
him take a sip of wine, hoping that she wasn't over-
dosing him in the process. But the caffeine in the hot
chocolate would probably counteract the wine and
keep it from doing any damage in combination with
the medicine. A sip of wine wasn't likely to be that
dangerous anyway, and it might help the sore throat
she was sure he had.

"Here's the cocoa," Harry said, joining them with
a tray of mugs filled with hot chocolate and topped
with whipped cream.

"That looks delicious. Thank you so much,"
Amanda said, and smiled shyly at the old man.

He grinned back. "Nice to be appreciated." He
glared at Quinn. "Nobody else ever says so much as a
thank-you!"

"It's hard to thank a man for food poisoning,"
Quinn rejoined weakly.

"He ain't going to die," Harry said as he left. "He's
too damned mean."

"That's a fact," Quinn said and closed his eyes.

He was asleep almost instantly. Amanda drew up a
chair and sat down beside him. He'd still need look-

ing after, and presumably the boy went to school. It was past the Christmas holidays.

"You go to school, don't you?" she asked Elliot.

He nodded. "I ride the horse out to catch the bus and then turn him loose. He comes to the barn by himself. You're staying?"

"I'd better, I guess," she said. "I'll sit with him. He may get worse in the night. He's got to see a doctor tomorrow. Is there one around here?"

"There's Dr. James in town, in Holman that is," he said. "He'll come out if Dad's bad enough. He has a cancer patient down the road and he comes to check on her every few days. He could stop by then."

"We'll see how your father is feeling. You'd better get to bed," she said and smiled at him.

"Thank you for coming, Miss...Amanda," Elliot said. He sighed. "I don't think I've ever been so scared."

"It's okay," she said. "I didn't mind. Good night, Elliot."

He smiled at her. "Good night."

He went out and closed the door. Amanda sat back in her chair and looked at the sleeping face of the wild man. He seemed vulnerable like this, with his black eyes closed. He had the thickest lashes she'd ever seen, and his eyebrows were thick and well shaped above his deep-set eyes. His mouth was rather thin, but it was perfectly shaped, and the full lower lip was sensuous. She liked that jutting chin, with its hint of stubbornness. His nose was formidable and straight, and he wasn't that bad looking...asleep. Perhaps it was the coldness of his eyes that made him seem so much rougher when he was awake. Not that he looked that unintimidating even now. He had so many coarse edges. . . .

She waited a few minutes and touched his forehead. It was a little cooler, thank God, so maybe he was going to be better by morning. She went into the bathroom and washed her face and went back to sit by him. Somewhere in the night, she fell asleep with her blond head pillowed on the big arm of the chair. Voices woke her.

"Has she been there all night, Harry?" Quinn was asking.

"Looks like. Poor little critter, she's worn out."

"I'll shoot Elliot!"

"Now, boss, that's no way to treat the kid. He got scared, and I didn't know what to do. Women know things about illness. Why, my mama could doctor people and she never had no medical training. She used herbs and things."

Amanda blinked, feeling eyes on her. She found Quinn Sutton gazing steadily at her from a sitting position on the bed.

"How do you feel?" she asked without lifting her sleepy head.

"Like hell," he replied. "But I'm a bit better."

"Would you like some breakfast, ma'am?" Harry asked with a smile. "And some coffee?"

"Coffee. Heavenly. But no breakfast, thanks, I won't impose," she said drowsily, yawning and stretching uninhibitedly as she sat up, her full breasts beautifully outlined against the cotton blouse in the process.

Quinn felt his body tautening again, as it had the night before so unexpectedly and painfully when her hands had touched him. He could still feel them, and the brush of her long, silky soft hair against his skin. She smelled of gardenias and the whole outdoors, and he hated her more than ever because he'd been briefly vulnerable.

"Why did you come with Elliot?" Quinn asked her when Harry had gone.

She pushed back her disheveled hair and tried not to think how bad she must look without makeup and with her hair uncombed. She usually kept it in a tight braid on top of her head when she wasn't performing. It made her feel vulnerable to have its unusual length on display for a man like Quinn Sutton.

"Your son is only twelve," she answered him belatedly. "That's too much responsibility for a kid," she added. "I know. I had my dad to look after at that age, and no mother. My dad drank," she added with a bitter smile. "Excessively. When he drank he got into trouble. I can remember knowing how to call a bail bondsman at the age of thirteen. I never dated, I never took friends home with me. When I was eighteen, I ran away from home. I don't even know if he's still alive, and I don't care."

"That's one problem Elliot won't ever have," he replied quietly. "Tough girl, aren't you?" he added, and his black eyes were frankly curious.

She hadn't meant to tell him so much. It embarrassed her, so she gave him her most belligerent glare. "Tough enough, thanks," she said. She got out of the chair. "If you're well enough to argue, you ought to be able to take care of yourself. But if that fever goes up again, you'll need to see the doctor."

"I'll decide that," he said tersely. "Go home."

"Thanks, I'll do that little thing." She got her coat and put it on without taking time to button it. She pushed her hair up under the stocking cap, aware of his eyes on her the whole time.

"You don't fit the image of a typical hanger-on," he said unexpectedly.

She glanced at him, blinking with surprise. "I beg your pardon?"

"A hanger-on," he repeated. He lifted his chin and studied her with mocking thoroughness. "You're Durning's latest lover, I gather. Well, if it's money you're after, he's the perfect choice. A pretty little tramp could go far with him... Damn!"

She stood over him with the remains of his cup of hot chocolate all over his chest, shivering with rage.

"I'm sorry," she said curtly. "That was a despicable thing to do to a sick man, but what you said to me was inexcusable."

She turned and went to the door, ignoring his muffled curses as he threw off the cover and sat up.

"I'd cuss, too," she said agreeably as she glanced back at him one last time, her eyes running helplessly over the broad expanse of hair-roughened skin. "All that sticky hot chocolate in that thicket on your chest," she mused. "It will probably take steam cleaning to remove it. Too bad you can't attract a 'hanger-on' to help you bathe it out. But, then, you aren't as rich as Mr. Durning, are you?" And she walked out, her nose in the air. As she went toward the stairs, she imagined that she heard laughter. But of course, that couldn't have been possible.

# *Chapter Two*

Amanda regretted the hot-chocolate incident once she was back in the cabin, even though Quinn Sutton had deserved every drop of it. How dare he call her such a name!

Amanda was old-fashioned in her ideas. A real country girl from Mississippi who'd had no example to follow except a liberated aunt and an alcoholic parent, and she was like neither of them. She hardly even dated these days. Her working gear wasn't the kind of clothing that told men how conventional her ideals were. They saw the glitter and sexy outfit and figured that Amanda, or just "Mandy" as she was known onstage, lived like her alter ego looked. There were times when she rued the day she'd ever signed on with Desperado, but she was too famous and making too much money to quit now.

She put her hair in its usual braid and kept it there for the rest of the week, wondering from time to time about Quinn Sutton and whether or not he'd survived his illness. Not that she cared, she kept telling herself. It didn't matter to her if he turned up his toes.

There was no phone in the cabin, and no piano. She couldn't play solitaire, she didn't have a television. There was only the radio and the cassette player for company, and Mr. Durning's taste in music was really extreme. He liked opera and nothing else. She'd have died for some soft rock, or just an instrument to practice on. She could play drums as well as the synthesizer and piano, and she wound up in the kitchen banging on the counter with two stainless-steel knives out of sheer boredom.

When the electricity went haywire in the wake of two inches of freezing rain on Sunday night, it was almost a relief. She sat in the darkness laughing. She was trapped in a house without heat, without light, and the only thing she knew about fireplaces was that they required wood. The logs that were cut outside were frozen solid under the sleet and there were none in the house. There wasn't even a pack of matches.

She wrapped up in her coat and shivered, hating the solitude and the weather and feeling the nightmares coming back in the icy night. She didn't want to think about the reason her voice had quit on her, but if she spent enough time alone, she was surely going to go crazy reliving that night onstage.

Lost in thought, in nightmarish memories of screams and her own loss of consciousness, she didn't hear the first knock on the door until it came again.

"Miss Corrie!" a familiar angry voice shouted above the wind.

She got up, feeling her way to the door. "Keep your shirt on," she muttered as she threw it open.

Quinn Sutton glared down at her. "Get whatever you'll need for a couple of days and come on. The power's out. If you stay here you'll freeze to death. It's going below zero tonight. My ranch has an extra generator, so we've still got the power going."

She glared back. "I'd rather freeze to death than go anywhere with you, thanks just the same."

He took a slow breath. "Look, your morals are your own business. I just thought—"

She slammed the door in his face and turned, just in time to have him kick in the door and come after her.

"I said you're coming with me, lady," he said shortly. He bent and picked her up bodily and started out the door. "And to hell with what you'll need for a couple of days."

"Mr. . . . Sutton!" she gasped, stunned by the unexpected contact with his hard, fit body as he carried her easily out the door and closed it behind them.

"Hold on," he said tautly and without looking at her. "The snow's pretty heavy right through this drift."

In fact, it was almost waist deep. She hadn't been outside in two days, so she hadn't noticed how high it had gotten. Her hands clung to the old sheepskin coat he was wearing. It smelled of leather and tobacco and whatever soap he used, and the furry collar was warm against her cold cheek. He made her feel small and helpless, and she wasn't sure she liked it.

"I don't like your tactics," she said through her teeth as the wind howled around them and sleet bit into her face like tiny nails.

"They get results. Hop on." He put her up on the sled, climbed beside her, grasped the reins and turned the horse back toward the mountain.

She wanted to protest, to tell him to take his offer and go to hell. But it was bitterly cold and she was shivering too badly to argue. He was right, and that was the hell of it. She could freeze to death in that cabin easily enough, and nobody would have found her until spring came or until her aunt persuaded Mr. Durning to come and see about her.

"I don't want to impose," she said curtly.

"We're past that now," he replied. "It's either this or bury you."

"I'm sure I know which you'd prefer," she muttered, huddling in her heavy coat.

"Do you?" he asked, turning his head. In the daylight glare of snow and sleet, she saw an odd twinkle in his black eyes. "Try digging a hole out there."

She gave him a speaking glance and resigned herself to going with him.

He drove the sled right into the barn and left her to wander through the aisle, looking at the horses and the two new calves in the various stalls while he dealt with unhitching and stalling the horse.

"What's wrong with these little things?" she asked, her hands in her pockets and her ears freezing as she nodded toward the two calves.

"Their mamas starved out in the pasture," he said quietly. "I couldn't get to them in time."

He sounded as if that mattered to him. She looked up at his dark face, seeing new character in it. "I didn't think a cow or two would matter," she said absently.

"I lost everything I had a few months back," he said matter-of-factly. "I'm trying to pull out of bankruptcy, and right now it's a toss-up as to whether I'll even come close. Every cow counts." He looked down at her. "But it isn't just the money. It disturbs me to see anything die from lack of attention. Even a cow."

"Or a mere woman?" she said with a faint smile. "Don't worry, I know you don't want me here. I'm ... grateful to you for coming to my rescue. Most of the firewood was frozen and Mr. Durning apparently doesn't smoke, because there weren't a lot of matches around."

He scowled faintly. "No, Durning doesn't smoke. Didn't you know?"

She shrugged. "I never had reason to ask," she said, without telling him that it was her aunt, not herself, who would know about Mr. Durning's habits. Let him enjoy his disgusting opinion of her.

"Elliot said you'd been sick."

She lifted a face carefully kept blank. "Sort of," she replied.

"Didn't Durning care enough to come with you?"

"Mr. Sutton, my personal life is none of your business," she said firmly. "You can think whatever you want to about me. I don't care. But for what it's worth, I hate men probably as much as you hate women, so you won't have to hold me off with a stick."

His face went hard at the remark, but he didn't say anything. He searched her eyes for one long moment and then turned toward the house, gesturing her to follow.

Elliot was overjoyed with their new house guest. Quinn Sutton had a television and all sorts of tapes, and there was, surprisingly enough, a brand-new keyboard on a living-room table.

She touched it lovingly, and Elliot grinned at her. "Like it?" he asked proudly. "Dad gave it to me for Christmas. It's not an expensive one, you know, but it's nice to practice on. Listen."

He turned it on and flipped switches, and gave a pretty decent rendition of a tune by Genesis.

Amanda, who was formally taught in piano, smiled at his efforts. "Very good," she praised. "But try a B-flat instead of a B at the end of that last measure and see if it doesn't give you a better sound."

Elliot cocked his head. "I play by ear," he faltered.

"Sorry." She reached over and touched the key she wanted. "That one." She fingered the whole chord. "You have a very good ear."

"But I can't read music," he sighed. His blue eyes searched her face. "You can, can't you?"

She nodded, smiling wistfully. "I used to long for piano lessons. I took them in spurts and then begged a ... friend to let me use her piano to practice on. It took me a long time to learn just the basics, but I do all right."

"All right" meant that she and the boys had won a Grammy award for their last album and it had been one of her own songs that had headlined it. But she couldn't tell Elliot that. She was convinced that Quinn

Sutton would have thrown her out the front door if he'd known what she did for a living. He didn't seem like a rock fan, and once he got a look at her stage costume and her group, he'd probably accuse her of a lot worse than being his neighbor's live-in lover. She shivered. Well, at least she didn't like Quinn Sutton, and that was a good thing. She might get out of here without having him find out who she really was, but just in case, it wouldn't do to let herself become interested in him.

"I don't suppose you'd consider teaching me how to read music?" Elliot asked. "For something to do, you know, since we're going to be snowed in for a while, the way it looks."

"Sure, I'll teach you," she murmured, smiling at him. "If you dad doesn't mind," she added with a quick glance at the doorway.

Quinn Sutton was standing there, in jeans and red-checked flannel shirt with a cup of black coffee in one hand, watching them.

"None of that rock stuff," he said shortly. "That's a bad influence on kids."

"Bad influence?" Amanda was almost shocked, despite the fact that she'd gauged his tastes very well.

"Those raucous lyrics and suggestive costumes, and satanism," he muttered. "I confiscated his tapes and put them away. It's indecent."

"Some of it is, yes," she agreed quietly. "But you can't lump it all into one category, Mr. Sutton. And these days, a lot of the groups are even encouraging chastity and going to war on drug use..."

"You don't really believe that bull, do you?" he asked coldly.

"It's true, Dad," Elliot piped up.

"You can shut up," he told his son. He turned. "I've got a lot of paperwork to get through. Don't turn that thing on high, will you? Harry will show you to your room when you're ready to bed down, Miss Corrie," he added, and looked as if he'd like to have shown her to a room underwater. "Or Elliot can."

"Thanks again," she said, but she didn't look up. He made her feel totally inadequate and guilty. In a small way, it was like going back to that night...

"Don't stay up past nine, Elliot," Quinn told his son.

"Okay, Dad."

Amanda looked after the tall man with her jaw hanging loose. "What did he say?" she asked.

"He said not to stay up past nine," Elliot replied. "We all go to bed at nine," he added with a grin at her expression. "There, there, you'll get used to it. Ranch life, you know. Here, now, what was that about a B-flat? What's a B-flat?"

She was obviously expected to go to bed with the chickens and probably get up with them, too. Absently she picked up the keyboard and began to explain the basics of music to Elliot.

"Did he really hide all your tapes?" she asked curiously.

"Yes, he did," Elliot chuckled, glancing toward the stairs. "But I know where he hid them." He studied her with pursed lips. "You know, you look awfully familiar somehow."

Amanda managed to keep a calm expression on her face, despite her twinge of fear. Her picture, along with that of the men in the group, was on all their al-

bums and tapes. God forbid that Elliot should be a fan
and have one of them, but they were popular with
young people his age. "They say we all have a coun-
terpart, don't they?" she asked and smiled. "Maybe
you saw somebody who looked like me. Here, this is
how you run a C scale. . . ."

She successfully changed the subject and Elliot
didn't bring it up again. They went upstairs a half hour
later, and she breathed a sigh of relief. Since the autocratic Mr. Sutton hadn't given her time to pack, she
wound up sleeping in her clothes under the spotless
white sheets. She only hoped that she wasn't going to
have the nightmares here. She couldn't bear the
thought of having Quinn Sutton ask her about them.
He'd probably say that she'd gotten just what she deserved.

But the nightmares didn't come. She slept with delicious abandon and didn't dream at all. She woke up
the next morning oddly refreshed just as the sun was
coming up, even before Elliot knocked on her door to
tell her that Harry had breakfast ready downstairs.

She combed out her hair and rebraided it, wrapping it around the crown of her head and pinning it
there as she'd had it last night. She tidied herself after
she'd washed up, and went downstairs with a lively
step.

Quinn Sutton and Elliot were already making great
inroads into huge, fluffy pancakes smothered in syrup
when she joined them.

Harry brought in a fresh pot of coffee and grinned
at her. "How about some hotcakes and sausage?" he
asked.

"Just a hotcake and a sausage, please," she said and grinned back. "I'm not much of a breakfast person."

"You'll learn if you stay in these mountains long," Quinn said, sparing her a speaking glance. "You need more meat on those bones. Fix her three, Harry."

"Now, listen..." she began.

"No, you listen," Quinn said imperturbably, sipping black coffee. "My house, my rules."

She sighed. It was just like old-times at the orphanage, during one of her father's binges when she'd had to live with Mrs. Brim's rules. "Yes, sir," she said absently.

He glared at her. "I'm thirty-four, and you aren't young enough to call me 'sir.'"

She lifted startled dark eyes to his. "I'm twenty-four," she said. "Are you really just thirty-four?" She flushed even as she said it. He did look so much older, but she hadn't meant to say anything. "I'm sorry. That sounded terrible."

"I look older than I am," he said easily. "I've got a friend down in Texas who thought I was in my late thirties, and he's known me for years. No need to apologize." He didn't add that he had a lot of mileage on him, thanks to his ex-wife. "You look younger than twenty-four," he did add.

He pushed away his empty plate and sipped coffee, staring at her through the steam rising from it. He was wearing a blue-checked flannel shirt this morning, buttoned up to his throat, with jeans that were well fitting but not overly tight. He didn't dress like the men in Amanda's world, but then, the men she knew weren't the same breed as this Teton man.

"Amanda taught me all about scales last night," Elliot said excitedly. "She really knows music."

"How did you manage to learn?" Quinn asked her, and she saw in his eyes that he was remembering what she'd told him about her alcoholic father.

She lifted her eyes from her plate. "During my dad's binges, I stayed at the local orphanage. There was a lady there who played for her church. She taught me."

"No sisters or brothers?" he asked quietly.

She shook her head. "Nobody in the world, except an aunt." She lifted her coffee cup. "She's an artist, and she's been living with her latest lover—"

"You'd better get to school, son," Quinn interrupted tersely, nodding at Elliot.

"I sure had, or I'll be late. See you!"

He grabbed his books and his coat and was gone in a flash, and Harry gathered the plates with a smile and vanished into the kitchen.

"Don't talk about things like that around Elliot," Quinn said shortly. "He understands more than you think. I don't want him corrupted."

"Don't you realize that most twelve-year-old boys know more about life than grown-ups these days?" she asked with a faint smile.

"In your world, maybe. Not in mine."

She could have told him that she was discussing the way things were, not the way she preferred them, but she knew it would be useless. He was so certain that she was wildly liberated. She sighed. "Maybe so," she murmured.

"I'm old-fashioned," he added. His dark eyes narrowed on her face. "I don't want Elliot exposed to the liberated outlook of the so-called modern world until he's old enough to understand that he has a choice. I don't like a society that ridicules honor and fidelity and innocence. So I fight back in the only way I can. I go to church on Sunday, Miss Corrie," he mused, smiling at her curious expression. "Elliot goes, too. You might not know it from watching television or going to movies, but there are still a few people in America who also go to church on Sunday, who work hard all week and find their relaxation in ways that don't involve drugs, booze or casual sex. How's that for a shocking revelation?"

"Nobody ever accused Hollywood of portraying real life," she replied with a smile. "But if you want my honest opinion, I'm pretty sick of gratuitous sex, filthy language and graphic violence in the newer movies. In fact, I'm so sick of it that I've gone back to watching the old-time movies from the 1940s." She laughed at his expression. "Let me tell you, these old movies had real handicaps—the actors all had to keep their clothes on and they couldn't swear. The writers were equally limited, so they created some of the most gripping dramas ever produced. I love them. And best of all, you can even watch them with kids."

He pursed his lips, his dark eyes holding hers. "I like George Brent, George Sanders, Humphrey Bogart, Bette Davis and Cary Grant best," he confessed. "Yes, I watch them, too."

"I'm not really all that modern myself," she confessed, toying with the tablecloth. "I live in the city, but not in the fast lane." She put down her coffee cup. "I can understand why you feel the way you do, about taking Elliot to church and all. Elliot told me a little about his mother..."

He closed up like a plant. "I don't talk to outsiders about my personal life," he said without apology and got up, towering over her. "If you'd like to watch television or listen to music, you're welcome. I've got work to do."

"Can I help?" she asked.

His heavy eyebrows lifted. "This isn't the city."

"I know how to cut open a bale of hay," she said. "The orphanage was on a big farm. I grew up doing chores. I can even milk a cow."

"You won't milk the kind of cows I keep," he returned. His dark eyes narrowed. "You can feed those calves in the barn, if you like. Harry can show you where the bottle is."

Which meant that he wasn't going to waste his time on her. She nodded, trying not to feel like an unwanted guest. Just for a few minutes she'd managed to get under that hard reserve. Maybe that was good enough for a start. "Okay."

His black eyes glanced over her hair. "You haven't worn it down since the night Elliot brought you here," he said absently.

"I don't ever wear it down at home, as a rule," she said quietly. "It...gets in my way." It got recognized, too, she thought, which was why she didn't dare let it loose around Elliot too often.

His eyes narrowed for an instant before he turned and shouldered into his jacket.

"Don't leave the perimeter of the yard," he said as he stuck his weather-beaten Stetson on his dark, thick hair. "This is wild country. We have bears and wolves, and a neighbor who still sets traps."

"I know my limitations, thanks," she said. "Do you have help, besides yourself?"

He turned, thrusting his big, lean hands into work gloves. "Yes, I have four cowboys who work around the place. They're all married."

She blushed. "Thank you for your sterling assessment of my character."

"You may like old movies," he said with a penetrating stare. "But no woman with your kind of looks is a virgin at twenty-four," he said quietly, mindful of Harry's sharp ears. "And I'm a backcountry man, but I've been married and I'm not stupid about women. You won't play me for a fool."

She wondered what he'd say if he knew the whole truth about her. But it didn't make her smile to reflect on that. She lowered her eyes to the thick white mug. "Think what you like, Mr. Sutton. You will anyway."

"Damned straight."

He walked out without looking back, and Amanda felt a vicious chill even before he opened the door and went out into the cold white yard.

She waited for Harry to finish his chores and then went with him to the barn, where the little calves were curled up in their stalls of hay.

"They're only days old," Harry said, smiling as he brought the enormous bottles they were fed from. In fact, the nipples were stretched across the top of buckets and filled with warm mash and milk. "But they'll grow. Sit down, now. You may get a bit dirty..."

"Clothes wash," Amanda said easily, smiling. But this outfit was all she had. She was going to have to get the elusive Mr. Sutton to take her back to the cabin to get more clothes, or she'd be washing out her things in the sink tonight.

She knelt down in a clean patch of hay and coaxed the calf to take the nipple into its mouth. Once it got a taste of the warm liquid, it wasn't difficult to get it to drink. Amanda loved the feel of its silky red-and-white coat under her fingers as she stroked it. The animal was a Hereford, and its big eyes were pink rimmed and soulful. The calf watched her while it nursed.

"Poor little thing," she murmured softly, rubbing between its eyes. "Poor little orphan."

"They're tough critters, for all that," Harry said as he fed the other calf. "Like the boss."

"How did he lose everything, if you don't mind me asking?"

He glanced at her and read the sincerity in her expression. "I don't guess he'd mind if I told you. He was accused of selling contaminated beef."

"Contaminated . . . how?"

"It's a long story. The herd came to us from down in the Southwest. They had measles. Not," he added when he saw her puzzled expression, "the kind humans get. Cattle don't break out in spots, but they do develop cysts in the muscle tissue and if it's bad enough, it means that the carcasses have to be destroyed." He shrugged. "You can't spot it, because there are no definite symptoms, and you can't treat it because there isn't a drug that cures it. These cattle had it and contaminated the rest of our herd. It was like the end of the world. Quinn had sold the beef cattle to the packing-plant operator. When the meat was ordered destroyed, he came back on Quinn to recover his money, but Quinn had already spent it to buy new cattle. We went to court... Anyway, to make a long story short, they cleared Quinn of any criminal charges and gave him the opportunity to make restitution. In turn, he sued the people who sold him the contaminated herd in the first place.'' He smiled ruefully. ''We just about broke even, but it meant starting over from scratch. That was last year. Things are still rough, but Quinn's a tough customer and he's got a good business head. He'll get through it. I'd bet on him.''

Amanda pondered that, thinking that Quinn's recent life had been as difficult as her own. At least he had Elliot. That must have been a comfort to him. She said as much to Harry.

He gave her a strange look. ''Well, yes, Elliot's special to him,'' he said, as if there were things she didn't know. Probably there were.

''Will these little guys make it?'' she asked when the calf had finished his bottle.

''I think so,'' Harry said. ''Here, give me that bottle and I'll take care of it for you.''

She sighed, petting the calf gently. She liked farms and ranches. They were so real, compared to the artificial life she'd known since she was old enough to leave home. She loved her work and she'd always enjoyed performing, but it seemed sometimes as if she lived in another world. Values were nebulous, if they even existed, in the world where she worked. Old-fashioned ideas like morality, honor, chastity were laughed at or ignored. Amanda kept hers to herself, just as she kept her privacy intact. She didn't discuss her inner feelings with anyone. Probably her friends and associates would have died laughing if they'd known just how many hang-ups she had, and how distant her outlook on life was from theirs.

"Here's another one," Quinn said from the front of the barn.

Amanda turned her head, surprised to see him because he'd ridden out minutes ago. He was carrying another small calf, but this one looked worse than the younger ones did.

"He's very thin," she commented.

"He's got scours." He laid the calf down next to her. "Harry, fix another bottle."

"Coming up, boss."

Amanda touched the wiry little head with its rough hide. "He's not in good shape," she murmured quietly.

Quinn saw the concern on her face and was surprised by it. He shouldn't have been, he reasoned. Why would she have come with Elliot in the middle of the night to nurse a man she didn't even like, if she wasn't a kind woman?

"He probably won't make it," he agreed, his dark eyes searching hers. "He'd been out there by himself for a long time. It's a big property, and he's a very small calf," he defended when she gave him a meaningful look. "It wouldn't be the first time we missed one, I'm sorry to say."

"I know." She looked up as Harry produced a third bottle, and her hand reached for it just as Quinn's did.

She released it, feeling odd little tingles at the brief contact with his lean, sure hand.

"Here goes," he murmured curtly. He reached under the calf's chin and pulled its mouth up to slide the nipple in. The calf could barely nurse, but after a minute it seemed to rally and then it fed hungrily.

"Thank goodness," Amanda murmured. She smiled at Quinn, and his eyes flashed as they met hers, searching, dark, full of secrets. They narrowed and then abruptly fell to her soft mouth, where they lingered with a kind of questioning irritation, as if he wanted very much to kiss her and hated himself for it. Her heart leaped at the knowledge. She seemed to have a new, built-in insight about this standoffish man, and she didn't understand either it or her attitude toward him. He was domineering and hardheaded and unpredictable and she should have disliked him. But she sensed a sensitivity in him that touched her heart. She wanted to get to know him.

"I can do this," he said curtly. "Why don't you go inside?"

She was getting to him, she thought with fascination. He was interested in her, but he didn't want to be. She watched the way he avoided looking directly at her again, the angry glance of his eyes.

Well, it certainly wouldn't do any good to make him furious at her, especially when she was going to be his unwanted houseguest for several more days, from the look of the weather.

"Okay," she said, giving in. She got to her feet slowly. "I'll see if I can find something to do."

"Harry might like some company while he works in the kitchen. Wouldn't you, Harry?" he added, giving the older man a look that said he'd damned sure better like some company.

"Of course I would, boss," Harry agreed instantly.

Amanda pushed her hands into her pockets with a last glance at the calves. She smiled down at them. "Can I help feed them while I'm here?" she asked gently.

"If you want to," Quinn said readily, but without looking up.

"Thanks." She hesitated, but he made her feel shy and tongue-tied. She turned away nervously and walked back to the house.

Since Harry had the kitchen well in hand, she volunteered to iron some of Quinn's cotton shirts. Harry had the ironing board set up, but not the iron, so she went into the closet and produced one. It looked old, but maybe it would do, except that it seemed to have a lot of something caked on it.

She'd just started to plug it in when Harry came into the room and gasped.

"Not that one!" he exclaimed, gently taking it away from her. "That's Quinn's!"

She opened her mouth to make a remark, when Harry started chuckling.

"It's for his skis," he explained patiently.

She nodded. "Right. He irons his skis. I can see that."

"He does. Don't you know anything about skiing?"

"Well, you get behind a speedboat with them on..."

"Not waterskiing. *Snow* skiing," he emphasized.

She shrugged. "I come from southern Mississippi." She grinned at him. "We don't do much business in snow, you see."

"Sorry. Well, Quinn was an Olympic contender in giant slalom when he was in his late teens and early twenties. He would have made the team, but he got married and Elliot was on the way, so he gave it up. He still gets in plenty of practice," he added, shuddering. "On old Ironside peak, too. Nobody, but nobody, skis it except Quinn and a couple of other experts from Larry's Lodge over in Jackson Hole."

"I haven't seen that one on a map..." she began, because she'd done plenty of map reading before she came here.

"Oh, that isn't its official name, it's what Quinn calls it." He grinned. "Anyway, Quinn uses this iron to put wax on the bottom of his skis. Don't feel bad, I didn't know any better, either, at first, and I waxed a couple of shirts. Here's the right iron."

He handed it to her, and she plugged it in and got started. The elusive Mr. Sutton had hidden qualities, it seemed. She'd watched the winter Olympics every four years on television, and downhill skiing fascinated her. But it seemed to Amanda that giant slalom called for a kind of reckless skill and speed that would require ruthlessness and single-minded determination. Considering that, it wasn't at all surprising to her that Quinn Sutton had been good at it.

# Chapter Three

Amanda helped Harry do dishes and start a load of clothes in the washer. But when she took them out of the dryer, she discovered that several of Quinn's shirts were missing buttons and had loose seams.

Harry produced a needle and some thread, and Amanda set to work mending them. It gave her something to do while she watched a years-old police drama on television.

Quinn came in with Elliot a few hours later.

"Boy, the snow's bad," Elliot remarked as he rubbed his hands in front of the fire Harry had lit in the big stone fireplace. "Dad had to bring the sled out to get me, because the bus couldn't get off the main highway."

"Speaking of the sled," Amanda said, glancing at Quinn, "I've got to have a few things from the cabin.

I'm really sorry, but I'm limited to what I'm wearing...."

"I'll run you down right now, before I go out again."

She put the mending aside. "I'll get my coat."

"Elliot, you can come, too. Put your coat back on," Quinn said unexpectedly, ignoring his son's surprised glance.

Amanda didn't look at him, but she understood why he wanted Elliot along. She made Quinn nervous. He was attracted to her and he was going to fight it to the bitter end. She wondered why he considered her such a threat.

He paused to pick up the shirt she'd been working on, and his expression got even harder as he glared at her. "You don't need to do that kind of thing," he said curtly.

"I've got to earn my keep somehow." She sighed. "I can feed the calves and help with the housework, at least. I'm not used to sitting around doing nothing," she added. "It makes me nervous."

He hesitated. An odd look rippled over his face as he studied the neat stitches in his shirtsleeve where the rip had been. He held it for a minute before he laid it gently back on the sofa. He didn't look at Amanda as he led the way out the door.

It didn't take her long to get her things together. Elliot wandered around the cabin. "There are knives all over the counter," he remarked. "Want me to put them in the sink?"

"Go ahead. I was using them for drumsticks," she called as she closed her suitcase.

"They don't look like they'd taste very good." Elliot chuckled.

She came out of the bedroom and gave him an
amused glance. "Not that kind of drumsticks, you
turkey. Here." She put down the suitcase and took the
blunt stainless-steel knives from him. She glanced
around to make sure Quinn hadn't come into the
house and then she broke into an impromptu drum
routine that made Elliot grin even more.

"Say, you're pretty good," he said.

She bowed. "Just one of my minor talents," she
said. "But I'm better with a keyboard. Ready to go?"

"Whenever you are."

She started to pick up her suitcase, but Elliot
reached down and got it before she could, a big grin on
his freckled face. She wondered again why he looked
so little like his father. She knew that his mother had
been a redhead, too, but it was odd that he didn't re-
semble Quinn in any way at all.

Quinn was waiting on the sled, his expression unreadable, impatiently smoking his cigarette. He let
them get on and turned the draft horse back toward
his own house. It was snowing lightly and the wind
was blowing, not fiercely but with a nip in it. Amanda
sighed, lifting her face to the snow, not caring that her
hood had fallen back to reveal the coiled softness of
her blond hair. She felt alive out here as she never had
in the city, or even back East. There was something
about the wilderness that made her feel at peace with
herself for the first time since the tragedy that had sent
her retreating here.

"Enjoying yourself?" Quinn asked unexpectedly.

"More than I can tell you," she replied. "It's like no other place on earth."

He nodded. His dark eyes slid over her face, her cheeks flushed with cold and excitement, and they lingered there for one long moment before he forced his gaze back to the trail. Amanda saw that look and it brought a sense of foreboding. He seemed almost angry.

In fact, he was. Before the day was out, it was pretty apparent that he'd withdrawn somewhere inside himself and had no intention of coming out again. He barely said two words to Amanda before bedtime.

"He's gone broody," Elliot mused before he and Amanda called it a night. "He doesn't do it often, and not for a long time, but when he's got something on his mind, it's best not to get on his nerves."

"Oh, I'll do my best," Amanda promised, and crossed her heart.

But that apparently didn't do much good, in her case, because he glared at her over breakfast the next morning and over lunch, and by the time she finished mending a window curtain in the kitchen and helped Harry bake a cake for dessert, she was feeling like a very unwelcome guest.

She went out to feed the calves, the nicest of her daily chores, just before Quinn was due home for supper. Elliot had lessons and he was holed up in his room trying to get them done in time for a science-fiction movie he wanted to watch after supper. Quinn insisted that homework came first.

She fed two of the three calves and Harry volunteered to feed the third, the little one that Quinn had brought home with scours, while she cut the cake and laid the table. She was just finishing the place settings when she heard the sled draw up outside the door.

Her heart quickened at the sound of Quinn's firm, measured stride on the porch. The door opened and he came in, along with a few snowflakes.

He stopped short at the sight of her in an old white apron with wisps of blond hair hanging around her flushed face, a bowl of whipped potatoes in her hands.

"Don't you look domestic?" he asked with sudden, bitter sarcasm.

The attack was unexpected, although it shouldn't have been. He'd been irritable ever since the day before, when he'd noticed her mending his shirt.

"I'm just helping Harry," she said. "He's feeding the calves while I do this."

"So I noticed."

She put down the potatoes, watching him hang up his hat and coat with eyes that approved his tall, fit physique, the way the red-checked flannel shirt clung to his muscular torso and long back. He was such a lonely man, she thought, watching him. So alone, even with Elliot and Harry here. He turned unexpectedly, catching her staring and his dark eyes glittered.

He went to the sink to wash his hands, almost vibrating with pent-up anger. She sensed it, but it only piqued her curiosity. He was reacting to her. She felt it, knew it, as she picked up a dish towel and went close to him to wrap it gently over his wet hands. Her big black eyes searched his, and she let her fingers linger on his while time seemed to end in the warm kitchen.

His dark eyes narrowed, and he seemed to have stopped breathing. He was aware of so many sensations. Hunger. Anger. Loneliness. Lust. His head spun with them, and the scent of her was pure, soft woman, drifting up into his nostrils, cocooning him in the smell of cologne and shampoo. His gaze fell helplessly to her soft bow of a mouth and he wondered how it would feel to bend those few inches and take it roughly under his own. It had been so long since he'd kissed a woman, held a woman. Amanda was particularly feminine, and she appealed to everything that was masculine in him. He almost vibrated with the need to reach out to her.

But that way lay disaster, he told himself firmly. She was just another treacherous woman, probably bored with confinement, just keeping her hand in with attracting men. He probably seemed like a pushover, and she was going to use her charms to make a fool of him. He took a deep, slow breath and the glitter in his eyes became even more pronounced as he jerked the towel out of her hands and moved away.

"Sorry," she mumbled. She felt her cheeks go hot, because there had been a cold kind of violence in the action that warned her his emotions weren't quite under control. She moved away from him. Violence was the one thing she did expect from men. She'd lived with it for most of her life until she'd run away from home.

She went back to the stove, stirring the sauce she'd made to go with the boiled dumpling.

"Don't get too comfortable in the kitchen," he warned her. "This is Harry's private domain and he doesn't like trespassers. You're just passing through."

"I haven't forgotten that, Mr. Sutton," she replied, and her eyes kindled with dark fire as she looked at him. There was no reason to make her feel so unwelcome. "Just as soon as the thaw comes, I'll be out of your way for good."

"I can hardly wait," he said, biting off the words.

Amanda sighed wearily. It wasn't her idea of the perfect rest spot. She'd come away from the concert stage needing healing, and all she'd found was another battle to fight.

"You make me feel so at home, Mr. Sutton," she said wistfully. "Like part of the family. Thanks so much for your gracious hospitality, and do you happen to have a jar of rat poison...?"

Quinn had to bite hard to keep from laughing. He turned and went out of the kitchen as if he were being chased.

After supper, Amanda volunteered to wash dishes, but Harry shooed her off. Quinn apparently did book work every night, because he went into his study and closed the door, leaving Elliot with Amanda for company. They'd watched the science-fiction movie Elliot had been so eager to see and now they were working on the keyboard.

"I think I've got the hang of C major," Elliot announced, and ran the scale, complete with turned under thumb on the key of F.

"Very good," she enthused. "Okay, let's go on to G major."

She taught him the scale and watched him play it, her mind on Quinn Sutton's antagonism.

"Something bothering you?" Elliot asked suspiciously.

She shrugged. "Your dad doesn't want me here."

"He hates women," he said. "You knew that, didn't you?"

"Yes. But why?"

He shook his head. "It's because of my mother. She did something really terrible to him, and he never talks about her. He never has. I've got one picture of her, in my room."

"I guess you look like her," she said speculatively.

He handed her the keyboard. "I've got red hair and freckles like she had," he confessed. "I'm just sorry that I...well, that I don't look anything like Dad. I'm glad he cares about me, though, in spite of everything. Isn't it great that he likes me?"

What an odd way to talk about his father, Amanda thought as she studied him. She wanted to say something else, to ask about that wording, but it was too soon. She hid her curiosity in humor.

"'There are more things in heaven and earth, Horatio, than are dreamt of in your philosophy,'" she intoned deeply.

He chuckled. "Hamlet," he said. "Shakespeare. We did that in English class last month."

"Culture in the high country." She applauded. "Very good, Elliot."

"I like rock culture best," he said in a stage whisper. "Play something."

She glanced toward Quinn's closed study door with a grimace. "Something soft."

"No!" he protested, and grinned. "Come on, give him hell."

"Elliot!" she chided.

"He needs shaking up, I tell you, he's going to die an old maid. He gets all funny and red when unmarried ladies talk to him at church, and just look at how grumpy he's been since you've been around. We've got to save him, Amanda," he said solemnly.

She sighed. "Okay. It's your funeral." She flicked switches, turning on the auto rhythm, the auto chords, and moved the volume to maximum. With a mischievous glance at Elliot, she swung into one of the newest rock songs, by a rival group, instantly recognizable by the reggae rhythm and sweet harmony.

"Good God!" came a muffled roar from the study.

Amanda cut off the keyboard and handed it to Elliot.

"No!" Elliot gasped.

But it was too late. His father came out of the study and saw Elliot holding the keyboard and started smoldering.

"It was her!" Elliot accused, pointing his finger at her.

She peered at Quinn over her drawn-up knees. "Would I play a keyboard that loud in your house, after you warned me not to?" she asked in her best meek voice.

Quinn's eyes narrowed. They went back to Elliot.

"She's lying," Elliot said. "Just like the guy in those truck commercials on TV...!"

"Keep it down," Quinn said without cracking a smile. "Or I'll give that thing the decent burial it really needs. And no more damned rock music in my house! That thing has earphones. Use them!"

"Yes, sir," Elliot groaned.

Amanda saluted him. "We hear and obey, excellency!" she said with a deplorable Spanish accent.

"Your wish is our command. We live only to serve...!"

The slamming of the study door cut her off. She burst into laughter while Elliot hit her with a sofa cushion.

"You animal," he accused mirthfully. "Lying to Dad, accusing me of doing something I never did! How could you?"

"Temporary insanity," she gasped for breath. "I couldn't help myself."

"We're both going to die," he assured her. "He'll lie awake all night thinking of ways to get even and when we least expect it, pow!"

"He's welcome. Here. Run that G major scale again."

He let her turn the keyboard back on, but he was careful to move the volume switch down as far as it would go.

It was almost nine when Quinn came out of the study and turned out the light.

"Time for bed," he said.

Amanda had wanted to watch a movie that was coming on, but she knew better than to ask. Presumably they did occasionally watch television at night. She'd have to ask one of these days.

"Good night, Dad. Amanda," Elliot said, grinning as he went upstairs with a bound.

"Did you do your homework?" Quinn called up after him.

"Almost."

"What the hell does that mean?" he demanded.

"It means I'll do it first thing in the morning! 'Night, Dad!"

A door closed.

Quinn glared at Amanda. "That won't do," he said tersely. "His homework comes first. Music is a nice hobby, but it's not going to make a living for him."

Why not, she almost retorted, it makes a six-figure annual income for me, but she kept her mouth shut.

"I'll make sure he's done his homework before I offer to show him anything else on the keyboard. Okay?"

He sighed angrily. "All right. Come on. Let's go to bed."

She put her hands over her chest and gasped, her eyes wide and astonished. "Together? Mr. Sutton, really!"

His dark eyes narrowed in a veiled threat. "Hell will freeze over before I wind up in bed with you," he said icily. "I told you, I don't want used goods."

"Your loss," she sighed, ignoring the impulse to lay a lamp across his thick skull. "Experience is a valuable commodity in my world." She deliberately smoothed her hands down her waist and over her hips, her eyes faintly coquettish as she watched him watching her movements. "And I'm very experienced," she drawled. In music, she was.

His jaw tautened. "Yes, it does show," he said. "Kindly keep your attitudes to yourself. I don't want my son corrupted."

"If you really meant that, you'd let him watch movies and listen to rock music and trust him to make up his own mind about things."

"He's only twelve."

"You aren't preparing him to live in the real world," she protested.

"This," he said, "is the real world for him. Not some fancy apartment in a city where women like you lounge around in bars picking up men."

"Now you wait just a minute," she said. "I don't lounge around in bars to pick up men." She shifted her stance. "I hang out in zoos and flash elderly men in my trench coat."

He threw up his hands. "I give up."

"Good! Your room or mine?"

He whirled, his dark eyes flashing. Her smile was purely provocative and she was deliberately baiting him, he could sense it. His jaw tautened and he wanted to pick her up and shake her for the effect her teasing was having on him.

"Okay, I quit," Amanda said, because she could see that he'd reached the limits of his control and she wasn't quite brave enough to test the other side of it. "Good night. Sweet dreams."

He didn't answer her. He followed her up the stairs and watched her go into her room and close the door. After a minute, he went into his own room and locked the door. He laughed mirthlessly at his own rash action, but he hoped she could hear the bolt being thrown.

She could. It shocked her, until she realized that he'd done it deliberately, probably trying to hurt her. She laid back on her bed with a long sigh. She didn't know what to do about Mr. Sutton. He was beginning to get to her in a very real way. She had to keep her perspective. This was only temporary. It would help to keep it in mind.

Quinn was thinking the same thing. But when he turned out the light and closed his eyes, he kept feeling Amanda's loosened hair brushing down his chest, over his flat stomach, his loins. He shuddered and woke up sweating in the middle of the night. It was the worst and longest night of his life.

The next morning, Quinn glared at Amanda across the breakfast table after Elliot had left for school.

"Leave my shirts alone," he said curtly. "If you find any more tears, Harry can mend them."

Her eyebrows lifted. "I don't have germs," she pointed out. "I couldn't contaminate them just by stitching them up."

"Leave them alone," he said harshly.

"Okay. Suit yourself." She sighed. "I'll just busy myself making lacy pillows for your bed."

He said something expressive and obscene; her lips fell open and she gaped at him. She'd never heard him use language like that.

It seemed to bother him that he had. He put down his fork, left his eggs and went out the door as if leopards were stalking him.

Amanda stirred her eggs around on the plate, feeling vaguely guilty that she'd given him such a hard time that he'd gone without half his breakfast. She didn't know why she needled him. It seemed to be a new habit, maybe to keep him at bay, to keep him from noticing how attracted she was to him.

"I'm going out to feed the calves, Harry," she said after a minute.

"Dress warm. It's snowing again," he called from upstairs.

"Okay."

She put on her coat and hat and wandered out to the barn through the path Quinn had made in the deep snow. She'd never again grumble at little two- and three-foot drifts in the city, she promised herself. Now that she knew what real snow was, she felt guilty for all her past complaints.

The barn was warmer than the great outdoors. She pushed snowflakes out of her eyes and face and went to fix the bottles as Harry had shown her, but Quinn was already there and had it done.

"No need to follow me around trying to get my attention," Amanda murmured with a wicked smile. "I've already noticed how sexy and handsome you are."

He drew in a furious breath, but just as he was about to speak she moved closer and put her fingers against his cold mouth.

"You'll break my heart if you use ungentlemanly language, Mr. Sutton," she told him firmly. "I'll just feed the calves and admire you from afar, if you don't mind. It seems safer than trying to throw myself at you."

He looked torn between shaking her and kissing her. She stood very still where he towered above her, even bigger than usual in that thick shepherd's coat and his tall, gray Stetson. He looked down at her quietly, his narrowed eyes lingering on her flushed cheeks and her soft, parted mouth.

Her hands were resting against the coat, and his were on her arms, pulling. She could hardly breathe as she realized that he'd actually touched her voluntarily. He jerked her face up under his, and she could see anger and something like bitterness in the dark eyes that held hers until she blushed.

"Just what are you after, city girl?" he asked coldly.

"A smile, a kind word and, dare I say it, a round of hearty laughter?" she essayed with wide eyes, trying not to let him see how powerfully he affected her.

His dark eyes fell to her mouth. "Is that right? And nothing more?"

Her breath came jerkily through her lips. "I...have to feed the calves."

His eyes narrowed. "Yes, you do." His fingers on her arms contracted, so that she could feel them even through the sleeves of her coat. "Be careful what you offer me," he said in a voice as light and cold as the snow outside the barn. "I've been without a woman for one hell of a long time, and I'm alone up here. If you're not what you're making yourself out to be, you could be letting yourself in for some trouble."

She stared up at him only half comprehending what he was saying. As his meaning began to filter into her consciousness, her cheeks heated and her breath caught in her throat.

"You...make it sound like a threat," she breathed.

"It is a threat, Amanda," he replied, using her name for the first time. "You could start something you might not want to finish with me, even with Elliot and Harry around."

She bit her lower lip nervously. She hadn't considered that. He looked more mature and formidable than he ever had before, and she could feel the banked-down fires in him kindling even as he held her.

"Okay," she said after a minute.

He let her go and moved away from her to get the bottles. He handed them to her with a long, speculative look.

"It's all right," she muttered, embarrassed. "I won't attack you while your back is turned. I almost never rape men."

He lifted an eyebrow, but he didn't smile. "You crazed female sex maniac," he murmured.

"Goody Two Shoes," she shot back.

A corner of his mouth actually turned up. "You've got that one right," he agreed. "Stay close to the house while it's snowing like this. We wouldn't want to lose you."

"I'll just bet we wouldn't," she muttered and stuck her tongue out at his retreating back.

She knelt down to feed the calves, still shaken by her confrontation with Quinn. He was an enigma. She was almost certain that he'd been joking with her at the end of the exchange, but it was hard to tell from his poker face. He didn't look like a man who'd laughed often or enough.

The littlest calf wasn't responding as well as he had earlier. She cuddled him and coaxed him to drink, but he did it without any spirit. She laid him back down with a sigh. He didn't look good at all. She worried about him for the rest of the evening, and she didn't argue when the television was cut off at nine o'clock. She went straight to bed, with Quinn and Elliot giving her odd looks.

# Chapter Four

Amanda was subdued at the breakfast table, more so when Quinn started watching her with dark, accusing eyes. She knew she'd deliberately needled him for the past two days, and now she was sorry. He'd hinted that her behavior was about to start something, and she was anxious not to make things any worse than they already were.

The problem was that she was attracted to him. The more she saw of him, the more she liked him. He was different from the superficial, materialistic men in her own world. He was hardheaded and stubborn. He had values, and he spoke out for them. He lived by a rigid code of ethics, and honor was a word that had great meaning for him. Under all that, he was sensitive and caring. Amanda couldn't help the way she was beginning to feel about him. She only wished that she hadn't started off on the wrong foot with him.

She set out to win him over, acting more like her real self. She was polite and courteous and caring, but without the rough edges she'd had in the beginning. She still did the mending, despite his grumbling, and she made cushions for the sofa out of some cloth Harry had put away. But all her domestic actions only made things worse. Quinn glared at her openly now, and his lack of politeness raised even Harry's eyebrows.

Amanda had a sneaking hunch that it was attraction to her that was making him so ill humored. He didn't act at all like an experienced man, despite his marriage, and the way he looked at her was intense. If she could bring him out into the open, she thought, it might ease the tension a little.

She did her chores, including feeding the calves, worrying even more about the littlest one because he wasn't responding as well today as he had the day before. When Elliot came home, she refused to help him with the keyboard until he did his homework. With a rueful smile and a knowing glance at his dad, he went up to his room to get it over with.

Meanwhile, Harry went out to get more firewood and Amanda was left in the living room with Quinn watching an early newscast.

The news was, as usual, all bad. Quinn put out his cigarette half angrily, his dark eyes lingering on Amanda's soft face.

"Don't you miss the city?" he asked.

She smiled. "Sure. I miss the excitement and my friends. But it's nice here, too." She moved toward the big armchair he was sitting in, nervously contemplating her next move. "You don't mind all that much, do you? Having me around, I mean?"

He glared up at her. He was wearing a blue-checked flannel shirt, buttoned up to the throat, and the hard muscles of his chest strained against it. He looked twice as big as usual, his dark hair unruly on his broad forehead as he stared up into her eyes.

"I'm getting used to you, I guess," he said stiffly. "Just don't get too comfortable."

"You really don't want me here, do you?" she asked quietly.

He sighed angrily. "I don't like women," he muttered.

"I know." She sat down on the arm of his chair, facing him. "Why not?" she asked gently.

His body went taut at the proximity. She was too close. Too female. The scent of her got into his nostrils and made him shift restlessly in the chair. "It's none of your damned business why not," he said evasively. "Will you get up from there?"

She warmed at the tone of his voice. So she did disturb him! Amanda smiled gently as she leaned forward. "Are you sure you want me to?" she asked and suddenly threw caution to the wind and slid down into his lap, putting her soft mouth hungrily on his.

He stiffened. He jerked. His big hands bit into her arms so hard they bruised. But for just one long, sweet moment, his hard mouth gave in to hers and he gave her back the kiss, his lips rough and warm, the pressure bruising, and he groaned as if all his dreams had come true at once.

He tasted of smoke for the brief second that he allowed the kiss. Then he was all bristling indignation and cold fury. He slammed to his feet, taking her with him, and literally threw her away, so hard that she fell against and onto the sofa.

"Damn you," he ground out. His fists clenched at his sides. His big body vibrated with outrage. "You cheap little tart!"

She lay trembling, frightened of the violence in his now white face and blazing dark eyes. "I'm not," she defended feebly.

"Can't you live without it for a few days, or are you desperate enough to try to seduce me?" he hissed. His eyes slid over her with icy contempt. "It won't work. I've told you already, I don't want something that any man can have! I don't want any part of you, least of all your overused body!"

She got to her feet on legs that threatened to give way under her, backing away from his anger. She couldn't even speak. Her father had been like that when he drank too much, white-faced, icy hot, totally out of control. And when he got that way, he hit. She cringed away from Quinn as he moved toward her and suddenly, she whirled and ran out of the room.

He checked his instinctive move to go after her. So she was scared, was she? He frowned, trying to understand why. He'd only spoken the truth; did she not like hearing what she was? The possibility that he'd been wrong, that she wasn't a cheap little tart, he wouldn't admit even to himself.

He sat back down and concentrated on the television without any real interest. When Elliot came downstairs, Quinn barely looked up.

"Where's Amanda going?" he asked his father.

Quinn raised an eyebrow. "What?"

"Where's Amanda going in such a rush?" Elliot asked again. "I saw her out the window, tramping through waist-deep snow. Doesn't she remember what you told her about old McNaber's traps? She's headed straight for them if she keeps on the way she's headed... Where are you going?"

Quinn was already on his feet and headed for the back door. He got into his shepherd's coat and hat without speaking, his face pale, his eyes blazing with mingled fear and anger.

"She was crying," Harry muttered, sparing him a glance. "I don't know what you said to her, but—"

"Shut up," Quinn said coldly. He stared the older man down and went out the back door and around the house, following in the wake Amanda's body had made. She was already out of sight, and those traps would be buried under several feet of snow. Bear traps, and she wouldn't see them until she felt them. The thought of that merciless metal biting her soft flesh didn't bear thinking about, and it would be his fault because he'd hurt her.

Several meters ahead, into the woods now, Amanda was cursing silently as she plowed through the snowdrifts, her black eyes fierce even through the tears. Damn Quinn Sutton, she panted. She hoped he got eaten by moths during the winter, she hoped his horse stood on his foot, she hoped the sled ran over him and packed him into the snow and nobody found him until spring. It was only a kiss, after all, and he'd kissed her back just for a few seconds.

She felt the tears burning coldly down her cheeks as they started again. Damn him. He hadn't had to make her feel like such an animal, just because she'd kissed

him. She cared about him. She'd only wanted to get on
a friendlier footing with him. But now she'd done it.
He hated her for sure, she'd seen it in his eyes, in his
face, when he'd called her those names. Cheap little
tart, indeed! Well, Goody Two Shoes Sutton could
just hold his breath until she kissed him again, so
there!

She stopped to catch her breath and then plowed on.
The cabin was somewhere down here. She'd stay in it
even if she did freeze to death. She'd shack up with a
grizzly bear before she'd spend one more night under
Quinn Sutton's roof. She frowned. Were there grizzly
bears in this part of the country?

"Amanda, stop!"

She paused, wondering if she'd heard someone call
her name, or if it had just been the wind. She was in a
break of lodgepole pines now, and a cabin was just
below in the valley. But it wasn't Mr. Durning's cabin.
Could that be McNaber's...?

"Amanda!"

That was definitely her name. She glanced over her
shoulder and saw the familiar shepherd's coat and
dark worn Stetson atop that arrogant head.

"Eat snow, Goody Two Shoes!" she yelled back.
"I'm going home!"

She started ahead, pushing hard now. But he had
the edge, because he was walking in the path she'd
made. He was bigger and faster, and he had twice her
stamina. Before she got five more feet, he had her by
the waist.

She fought him, kicking and hitting, but he simply
wrapped both arms around her and held on until she
finally ran out of strength.

"I hate you," she panted, shivering as the cold and the exertion got to her. "I hate you!"

"You'd hate me more if I hadn't stopped you," he said, breathing hard. "McNaber lives down there. He's got bear traps all over the place. Just a few more steps, and you'd have been up to your knees in them, you little fool! You can't even see them in snow this deep!"

"What would you care?" she groaned. "You don't want me around. I don't want to stay with you anymore. I'll take my chances at the cabin!"

"No, you won't, Amanda," he said. His embrace didn't even loosen. He whipped her around, his big hands rough on her sleeves as he shook her. "You're coming back with me, if I have to carry you!"

She flinched, the violence in him frightening her. She swallowed, her lower lip trembling and pulled feebly against his hands.

"Let go of me," she whispered. Her voice shook, and she hated her own cowardice.

He scowled. She was paper white. Belatedly he realized what was wrong and his hands released her. She backed away as far as the snow would allow and stood like a young doe at bay, her eyes dark and frightened.

"Did he hit you?" he asked quietly.

She didn't have to ask who. She shivered. "Only when he drank," she said, her voice faltering. "But he always drank." She laughed bitterly. "Just...don't come any closer until you cool down, if you please."

He took a slow, steadying breath. "I'm sorry," he said, shocking her. "No, I mean it. I'm really sorry. I wouldn't have hit you, if that's what you're thinking.

Only a coward would raise his hand to a woman,'' he said with cold conviction.

She wrapped her arms around herself and stood, just breathing, shivering in the cold.

"We'd better get back before you freeze," he said tautly. Her very defensiveness disarmed him. He felt guilty and protective all at once. He wanted to take her to his heart and comfort her, but even as he stepped toward her, she backed away. He hadn't imagined how much that would hurt until it happened. He stopped and stood where he was, raising his hands in an odd gesture of helplessness. "I won't touch you," he promised. "Come on, honey. You can go first."

Tears filmed her dark eyes. It was the first endearment she'd ever heard from him and it touched her deeply. But she knew it was only casual. Her behavior had shocked him and he didn't know what to do. She let out a long breath.

Without a quip or comeback, she eased past him warily and started back the way they'd come. He followed her, giving thanks that he'd been in time, that she hadn't run afoul of old McNaber's traps. But now he'd really done it. He'd managed to make her afraid of him.

She went ahead of him into the house. Elliot and Harry took one look at her face and Quinn's and didn't ask a single question.

She sat at the supper table like a statue. She didn't speak, even when Elliot tried to bring her into the conversation. And afterward, she curled up in a chair in the living room and sat like a mouse watching television.

Quinn couldn't know the memories he'd brought back, the searing fear of her childhood. Her father had been a big man, and he was always violent when he drank. He was sorry afterward, sometimes he even cried when he saw the bruises he'd put on her. But it never stopped him. She'd run away because it was more than she could bear, and fortunately there'd been a place for runaways that took her in. She'd learned volumes about human kindness from those people. But the memories were bitter and Quinn's bridled violence had brought them sweeping in like storm clouds.

Elliot didn't ask her about music lessons. He excused himself a half hour early and went up to bed. Harry had long since gone to his own room.

Quinn sat in his big chair, smoking his cigarette, but he started when Amanda put her feet on the floor and glanced warily at him.

"Don't go yet," he said quietly. "I want to talk to you."

"We don't have anything to say to each other," she said quietly. "I'm very sorry for what I did this afternoon. It was impulsive and stupid, and I promise I'll never do it again. If you can just put up with me until it thaws a little, you'll never have to see me again."

He sighed wearily. "Is that what you think I want?" he asked, searching her face.

"Of course it is," she replied simply. "You've hated having me here ever since I came."

"Maybe I have. I've got more reason to hate and distrust women than you'll ever know. But that isn't what I want to talk about," he said, averting his gaze from her wan face. He didn't like thinking about that kiss and how disturbing it had been. "I want to know why you thought I might hit you."

She dropped her eyes to her lap. "You're big, like my father," she said. "When he lost his temper, he always hit."

"I'm not your father," Quinn pointed out, his dark eyes narrowing. "And I've never hit anyone in a temper, except maybe another man from time to time when it was called for. I never raised my hand to Elliot's mother, although I felt like it a time or two, in all honesty. I never lifted a hand to her even when she told me she was pregnant with Elliot."

"Why should you have?" she asked absently. "He's your son."

He laughed coldly. "No, he isn't."

She stared at him openly. "Elliot isn't yours?" she asked softly.

He shook his head. "His mother was having an affair with a married man and she got caught out." He shrugged. "I was twenty-two and grass green and she mounted a campaign to marry me. I guess I was pretty much a sitting duck. She was beautiful and stacked and she had me eating out of her hand in no time. We got married and right after the ceremony, she told me what she'd done. She laughed at how clumsy I'd been during the courtship, how she'd had to steel herself not to be sick when I'd kissed her. She told me about Elliot's father and how much she loved him, then she dared me to tell people the truth about how easy it had been to make me marry her." He blew out a cloud of smoke, his eyes cold with memory. "She had me over a barrel. I was twice as proud back then as I am now. I couldn't bear to have the whole community laughing at me. So I stuck it out. Until Elliot was born, and she and his father took off for parts unknown for a weekend of love. Unfortunately for them, he wrecked the car in his haste to get to a motel and killed both of them outright.''

"Does Elliot know?'' she asked, her voice quiet as she glanced toward the staircase.

"Sure,'' he said. "I couldn't lie to him about it. But I took care of him from the time he was a baby, and I raised him. That makes me his father just as surely as if I'd put the seed he grew from into his mother's body. He's my son, and I'm his father. I love him.''

She studied his hard face, seeing behind it to the pain he must have suffered. "You loved her, didn't you?''

"Calf love,'' he said. "She came up on my blind side and I needed somebody to love. I'd always been shy and clumsy around girls. I couldn't even get a date when I was in school because I was so rough edged. She paid me a lot of attention. I was lonely.'' His big shoulders shrugged. "Like I said, a sitting duck. She taught me some hard lessons about your sex,'' he added, his narrowed eyes on her face. "I've never forgotten them. And nobody's had a second chance at me.''

Her breath came out as a sigh. "That's what you thought this afternoon, when I kissed you,'' she murmured, reddening at her own forwardness. "I'm sorry. I didn't realize you might think I was playing you for a sucker.''

He frowned. "Why did you kiss me, Amanda?''

"Would you believe, because I wanted to?'' she asked with a quiet smile. "You're a very attractive man, and something about you makes me weak in the knees. But you don't have to worry about me coming on to you again," she added, getting to her feet. "You teach a pretty tough lesson yourself. Good night, Mr. Sutton. I appreciate your telling me about Elliot. You needn't worry that I'll say anything to him or to anybody else. I don't carry tales, and I don't gossip."

She turned toward the staircase, and Quinn's dark eyes followed her. She had an elegance of carriage that touched him, full of pride and grace. He was sorry now that he'd slapped her down so hard with cruel words. He really hadn't meant to. He'd been afraid that she was going to let him down, that she was playing. It hadn't occurred to him that she found him attractive or that she'd kissed him because she'd really wanted to.

He'd made a bad mistake with Amanda. He'd hurt her and sent her running, and now he wished he could take back the things he'd said. She wasn't like any woman he'd ever been exposed to. She actually seemed unaware of her beauty, as if she didn't think much of it. Maybe he'd gotten it all wrong and she wasn't much more experienced than he was. He wished he could ask her. She disturbed him very much, and now he wondered if it wasn't mutual.

Amanda was lying in bed, crying. The day had been horrible, and she hated Quinn for the way he'd treated her. It wasn't until she remembered what he'd told her that she stopped crying and started thinking. He'd said that he'd never slept with Elliot's mother, and that he hadn't been able to get dates in high school. Presumably that meant that his only experience with women had been after Elliot's mother died. She frowned.

There hadn't been many women, she was willing to
bet. He seemed to know relatively nothing about her
sex. She frowned. If he still hated women, how had he
gotten any experience? Finally her mind grew tired of
trying to work it out and she went to sleep.

Amanda was up helping Harry in the kitchen the
next morning when Quinn came downstairs after a
wild, erotic dream that left him sweating and swear-
ing when he woke up. Amanda had figured largely in
it, with her blond hair loose and down to her lower
spine, his hands twined in it while he made love to her
in the stillness of his own bedroom. The dream had
been so vivid that he could almost see the pink perfection of her breasts through the bulky, white-knit
sweater she was wearing, and he almost groaned as his
eyes fell to the rise and fall of her chest under it.

She glanced at Quinn and actually flushed before
she dragged her eyes back down to the pan of biscuits
she was putting into the oven.

"I didn't know you could make biscuits," Quinn
murmured.

"Harry taught me," she said evasively. Her eyes
went back to him again and flitted away.

He frowned at that shy look until he realized why he
was getting it. He usually kept his shirts buttoned up
to his throat, but this morning he'd left it open halfway down his chest because he was still sweating from
that dream. He pursed his lips and gave her a speculative stare. He wondered if it were possible that he
disturbed her as much as she disturbed him. He was
going to make it his business to find out before she left

here. If for no other reason than to salve his bruised ego.

He went out behind Elliot, pausing in the doorway. "How's the calf?" he asked Amanda.

"He wasn't doing very well yesterday," she said with a sigh. "Maybe he's better this morning."

"I'll have a look at him before I go out." He glanced out at the snow. "Don't try to get back to the cabin again, will you? You can't get through Mc-Naber's traps without knowing where they are."

He actually sounded worried. She studied his hard face quietly. That was nice. Unless, of course, he was only worried that she might get laid up and he'd have to put up with her for even longer.

"Is the snow ever going to stop?" she asked.

"Hard to say," he told her. "I've seen it worse than this even earlier in the year. But we'll manage, I suppose."

"I suppose." She glared at him.

He pulled on his coat and buttoned it, propping his hat over one eye. "In a temper this morning, are we?" he mused.

His eyes were actually twinkling. She shifted back against the counter, grateful that Harry had gone off to clean the bedrooms. "I'm not in a temper. Cheap little tarts don't have tempers."

One eyebrow went up. "I called you that, didn't I?" He let his eyes run slowly down her body. "You shouldn't have kissed me like that. I'm not used to aggressive women."

"Rest assured that I'll never attack you again, Goody Two Shoes."

He chuckled softly. "Won't you? Well, disappointment is a man's lot, I suppose."

Her eyes widened. She wasn't sure she'd even heard him. "You were horrible to me!"

"I guess I was." His dark eyes held hers, making little chills up and down her spine at the intensity of the gaze. "I thought you were playing games. You know, a little harmless fun at the hick's expense."

"I don't know how to play games with men," she said stiffly, "and nobody, anywhere, could call you a hick with a straight face. You're a very masculine man with a keen mind and an overworked sense of responsibility. I wouldn't make fun of you even if I could."

His dark eyes smiled into hers. "In that case, we might call a truce for the time being."

"Do you think you could stand being nice to me?" she asked sourly. "I mean, it would be a strain, I'm sure."

"I'm not a bad man," he pointed out. "I just don't know much about women, or hadn't that thought occurred?"

She searched his eyes. "No."

"We'll have to have a long talk about it one of these days." He pulled the hat down over his eyes. "I'll check on the calves for you."

"Thanks." She watched him go, her heart racing at the look in his eyes just before he closed the door. She was more nervous of him now than ever, but she didn't know what to do about it. She was hoping that the chinook would come before she had to start worrying too much. She was too confused to know what to do anymore.

# Chapter Five

Amanda finished the breakfast dishes before she went out to the barn. Quinn was still there, his dark eyes quiet on the smallest of the three calves. It didn't take a fortune teller to see that something was badly wrong. The small animal lay on its side, its dull, lackluster red-and-white coat showing its ribs, its eyes glazed and unseeing while it fought to breathe.

She knelt beside Quinn and he glanced at her with concern.

"You'd better go back in the house, honey," he said.

Her eyes slid over the small calf. She'd seen pets die over the years, and now she knew the signs. The calf was dying. Quinn knew it, too, and was trying to shield her.

That touched her, oddly, more than anything he'd said or done since she'd been on Ricochet. She looked up at him. "You're a nice man, Quinn Sutton," she said softly.

He drew in a slow breath. "When I'm not taking bites out of you, you mean?" he replied. "It hurts like hell when you back away from me. You'll never know how sorry I am for what happened yesterday."

One shock after another. At least it took her mind off the poor, laboring creature beside them. "I'm sorry, too," she said. "I shouldn't have been so..." She stopped, averting her eyes. "I don't know much about men, Quinn," she said finally. "I've spent my whole adult life backing away from involvement, emotional or physical. I know how to flirt, but not much more." She risked a glance at him, and relaxed when she saw his face. "My aunt is Mr. Durning's lover, you know. She's an artist. A little flighty, but nice. I've... never had a lover."

He nodded quietly. "I've been getting that idea since we wound up near McNaber's cabin yesterday. You reacted pretty violently for an experienced woman." He looked away from her. That vulnerability in her pretty face was working on him again. "Go inside now. I can deal with this."

"I'm not afraid of death," she returned. "I saw my mother die. It wasn't scary at all. She just closed her eyes."

His dark eyes met hers and locked. "My father went the same way." He looked back down at the calf. "It won't be long now."

She sat down in the hay beside him and slid her small hand into his big one. He held it for a long moment. Finally his voice broke the silence. "It's over. Go have a cup of coffee. I'll take care of him."

She hadn't meant to cry, but the calf had been so little and helpless. Quinn pulled her close, holding her with quiet comfort, while she cried. Then he wiped the tears away with his thumbs and smiled gently. "You'll do," he murmured, thinking that sensitivity and courage was a nice combination in a woman.

She was thinking the exact same thing about him. She managed a watery smile and with one last, pitying look at the calf, she went into the house.

Elliot would miss it, as she would, she thought. Even Quinn had seemed to care about it, because she saw him occasionally sitting by it, petting it, talking to it. He loved little things. It was evident in all the kittens and puppies around the place, and in the tender care he took of all his cattle and calves. And although Quinn cursed old man McNaber's traps, Elliot had told her that he stopped by every week to check on the dour old man and make sure he had enough chopped wood and supplies. For a taciturn iceman, he had a surprisingly warm center.

She told Harry what had happened and sniffed a little while she drank black coffee. "Is there anything I can do?" she asked.

He smiled. "You do enough," he murmured. "Nice to have some help around the place."

"Quinn hasn't exactly thought so," she said dryly.

"Oh, yes he has," he said firmly as he cleared away the dishes they'd eaten his homemade soup and corn bread in. "Quinn could have taken you to Mrs. Pearson down the mountain if he'd had a mind to. He doesn't have to let you stay here. Mrs. Pearson would be glad of the company." He glanced at her and grinned at her perplexed expression. "He's been watching you lately. Sees the way you sew up his shirts and make curtains and patch pillows. It's new to him, having a woman about. He has a hard time with change.''

''Don't we all?'' Amanda said softly, remembering how clear her own life had been until that tragic night. But it was nice to know that Quinn had been watching her. Certainly she'd been watching him. And this morning, everything seemed to have changed between them. ''When will it thaw?'' she asked, and now she was dreading it, not anticipating it. She didn't want to leave Ricochet. Or Quinn.

Harry shrugged. ''Hard to tell. Days. Weeks. This is raw mountain country. Can't predict a chinook. Plenty think they can, though,'' he added, and proceeded to tell her about a Blackfoot who predicted the weather with jars of bear grease.

She was much calmer, but still sad when Quinn finally came back inside.

He spared her a glance before he shucked his coat, washed his hands and brawny forearms and dried them on a towel.

He didn't say anything to her, and Harry, sensing the atmosphere, made himself scarce after he'd poured two cups of coffee for them.

''Are you all right?'' he asked her after a minute, staring down at her bent head.

''Sure.'' She forced a smile. ''He was so little, Quinn.'' She stopped when her voice broke and lowered her eyes to the table. ''I guess you think I'm a wimp.''

''Not really.'' Without taking time to think about the consequences, his lean hands pulled her up by the

arms, holding her in front of him so that her eyes were
on a level with his deep blue, plaid flannel shirt. The
sleeves were rolled up, and it was open at the throat,
where thick, dark hair curled out of it. He looked and
smelled fiercely masculine and Amanda's knees
weakened at the unexpected proximity. His big hands
bit into her soft flesh, and she wondered absently if he
realized just how strong he was.

The feel of him so close was new and terribly exciting, especially since he'd reached for her for the first
time. She didn't know what to expect, and her heart
was going wild. She lowered her eyes to his throat. His
pulse was jumping and she stared at it curiously, only
half aware of his hold and the sudden increase of his
breathing.

He was having hell just getting a breath. The scent
of her was in his nostrils, drowning him. Woman
smell. Sweet and warm. His teeth clenched. It was bad
enough having to look at her, but this close, she made
his blood run hot and wild as it hadn't since he was a
young man. He didn't know what he was doing, but
the need for her had haunted him for days. He wanted
so badly to kiss her, the way she'd kissed him the day
before, but in a different way. He wasn't quite sure
how to go about it.

"You smell of flowers," he said roughly.

That was an interesting comment from a nonpoetic
man. She smiled a little to herself. "It's my shampoo," she murmured.

He drew in a steadying breath. "You don't wear
your hair down at all, do you?"

"Just at night," she replied, aware that his face was
closer than it had been, because she could feel his

breath on her forehead. He was so tall and over-whelming this close. He made her feel tiny and very feminine.

"I'm sorry about the calf, Amanda," he said. "We lose a few every winter. It's part of ranching."

The shock of her name on his lips made her lift her head. She stared up at him curiously, searching his dark, quiet eyes. "I suppose so. I shouldn't have gotten so upset, though. I guess men don't react to things the way women do."

"You don't know what kind of man I am," he replied. His hands felt vaguely tremulous. He wondered if she knew the effect she had on him. "As it happens, I get attached to the damned things, too." He sighed heavily. "Little things don't have much choice in this world. They're at the mercy of every-thing and everybody."

Her eyes softened as they searched his. He sounded different when he spoke that way. Vulnerable. Al-most tender. And so alone.

"You aren't really afraid of me, are you?" he asked, as if the thought was actually painful.

She grimaced. "No. Of course not. I was ashamed of what I'd done, and a little nervous of the way you reacted to it, that's all. I know you wouldn't hurt me." She drew in a soft breath. "I know you resent having me here," she confessed. "I resented having to de-pend on you for shelter. But the snow will melt soon, and I'll leave."

"I thought you'd had lovers," he confessed quietly. "The way you acted...well, it just made all those suspicions worse. I took you at face value."

Amanda smiled. "It was all put-on. I don't even know why I did it. I guess I was trying to live down to your image of me."

He loved the sensation her sultry black eyes aroused in him. Unconsciously his hands tightened on her arms. "You haven't had a man, ever?" he asked huskily.

The odd shadow of dusky color along his cheekbones fascinated her. She wondered about the embarrassment asking the question had caused. "No. Not ever," she stammered.

"The way you look?" he asked, his eyes eloquent.

"What do you mean, the way I look?" she said, bristling.

"You know you're beautiful," he returned. His eyes darkened. "A woman who looks like you do could have her pick of men."

"Maybe," she agreed without conceit. "But I've never wanted a man in my life, to be dominated by a man. I've made my own way in the world. I'm a musician," she told him, because that didn't give away very much. "I support myself by playing a keyboard."

"Yes, Elliot told me. I've heard you play for him. You're good." He felt his heartbeat increasing as he looked at her. She smelled so good. He looked down at her mouth and remembered how it had felt for those few seconds when he'd given in to her playful kiss. Would she let him do it? He knew so little about those subtle messages women were supposed to send out when they wanted a man's lovemaking. He couldn't read Amanda's eyes. But her lips were parted and her breath was coming rather fast from between them. Her face was flushed, but that could have been from the cold.

She gazed up into his eyes and couldn't look away. He wasn't handsome. His face really seemed as if it had been chipped away from the side of the Rockies, all craggy angles and hard lines. His mouth was thin and faintly cruel looking. She wondered if it would feel as hard as it looked if he was in control, dominating her lips. It had been different when she'd kissed him....

"What are you thinking?" he asked huskily, because her eyes were quite frankly on his mouth.

"I...was wondering," she whispered hesitantly, "how hard your mouth would be if you kissed me."

His heart stopped and then began to slam against his chest. "Don't you know already?" he asked, his voice deeper, harsher. "You kissed me."

"Not...properly."

He wondered what she meant by properly. His wife had only kissed him when she had to, and only in the very beginning of their courtship. She always pushed him away and murmured something about mussing her makeup. He couldn't remember one time when he'd kissed anyone with passion, or when he'd ever been kissed by anyone else like that.

His warm, rough hands let go of her arms and came up to frame her soft oval face. His breath shuddered out of his chest when she didn't protest as he bent his dark head.

"Show me what you mean...by properly," he whispered.

He had to know, she thought dizzily. But his lips touched hers and she tasted the wind and the sun on them. Her hands clenched the thick flannel shirt and she resisted searching for buttons, because she wanted very much to touch that thicket of black, curling hair that covered his broad chest. She went on her tiptoes and pushed her mouth against his, the force of the action parting his lips as well as her own, and she felt him stiffen and heard him groan as their open mouths met.

She dropped back onto her feet, her wide, curious eyes meeting his stormy ones.

"Like that?" he whispered gruffly, bending to repeat the action with his own mouth. "I've never done it...with my mouth open," he said, biting off the words against her open lips.

She couldn't believe he'd said that. She couldn't believe, either, the sensations rippling down to her toes when she gave in to the force of his ardor and let him kiss her that way, his mouth rough and demanding as one big hand slid to the back of her head to press her even closer.

A soft sound passed her lips, a faint moan, because she couldn't get close enough to him. Her breasts were flattened against his hard chest, and she felt his heartbeat against them. But she wanted to be closer than that, enveloped, crushed to him.

"Did I hurt you?" he asked in a shaky whisper that touched her lips.

"What?" she whispered back dizzily.

"You made a sound."

Her eyes searched his, her own misty and half closed and rapt. "I moaned," she whispered. Her nails stroked him through the shirt and she liked the faint tautness of his body as he reacted to it. "I like being kissed like that." She rubbed her forehead against him, smelling soap and detergent and pure man. "Could we take your shirt off?" she whispered.

Her hands were driving him nuts, and he was wondering the same thing himself. But somewhere in the back of his mind he remembered that Harry was around, and that it might look compromising if he let her touch him that way. In fact, it might get compromising, because he felt his body harden in a way it hadn't since his marriage. And because it made him vulnerable and he didn't want her to feel it, he took her gently by the arms and moved her away from him with a muffled curse.

"Harry," he said, his breath coming deep and rough.

She colored. "Oh, yes." She moved back, her eyes a little wild.

"You don't have to look so threatened. I won't do it again," he said, misunderstanding her retreat. Had he frightened her again?

"Oh, it's not that. You didn't frighten me." She lowered her eyes to the floor. "I'm just wondering if you'll think I'm easy...."

He scowled. "Easy?"

"I don't usually come on to men," she said softly. "And I've never asked anybody to take his shirt off before." She glanced up at him, fascinated by the expression on his face. "Well, I haven't," she said belligerently. "And you don't have to worry; I won't throw myself at you anymore, either. I just got carried away in the heat of the moment...."

His eyebrows arched. None of what she was saying made sense. "Like you did yesterday?" he mused, liking the color that came and went in her face. "I did accuse you of throwing yourself at me," he said on a long sigh.

"Yes. You seem to think I'm some sort of liberated sex maniac."

His lips curled involuntarily. "Are you?" he asked, and sounded interested.

She stamped her foot. "Stop that. I don't want to stay here anymore!"

"I'm not sure it's a good idea myself," he mused, watching her eyes glitter with rage. God, she was pretty! "I mean, if you tried to seduce me, things could get sticky."

The red in her cheeks got darker. "I don't have any plans to seduce you."

"Well, if you get any, you'd better tell me in advance," he said, pulling a cigarette from his shirt pocket. "Just so I can be prepared to fight you off."

That dry drawl confused her. Suddenly he was a different man, full of male arrogance and amusement. Things had shifted between them during that long, hard kiss. The distance had shortened, and he was looking at her with an expression she couldn't quite understand.

"How did you get to the age you are without winding up in someone's bed?" Quinn asked then. He'd wondered at her shyness with him and then at the way she blushed all the time. He didn't know much about women, but he wanted to know everything about her.

Amanda wrapped her arms around herself and shrugged. When he lit his cigarette and still stood there waiting for an answer, she gave in and replied. "I couldn't give up control," she said simply. "All my life

I'd been dominated and pushed around by my father. Giving in to a man seemed like throwing away my rights as a person. Especially giving in to a man in bed," she stammered, averting her gaze. "I don't think there's anyplace in the world where a man is more the master than in a bedroom, despite all the liberation and freedom of modern life."

"And you think that women should dominate there."

She looked up. "Well, not dominate." She hesitated. "But a woman shouldn't be used just because she's a woman."

His thin mouth curled slightly. "Neither should a man."

"I wasn't using you," she shot back.

"Did I accuse you?" he returned innocently.

She swallowed. "No, I guess not." She folded her arms over her breasts, wincing because the tips were hard and unexpectedly tender.

"That hardness means you feel desire," he said, grinning when she gaped and then glared at him. She made him feel about ten feet tall. "I read this book about sex," he continued. "It didn't make much sense to me at the time, but it's beginning to."

"I am not available as a living model for sex education!"

He shrugged. "Suit yourself. But it's a hell of a loss to my education."

"You don't need educating," she muttered. "You were married."

He nodded. "Sure I was." He pursed his lips and let his eyes run lazily over her body. "Except that she never wanted me, before or after I married her."

Amanda's lips parted. "Oh, Quinn," she said softly. "I'm sorry."

"So was I, at the time." He shook his head. "I used to wonder at first why she pulled back every time I kissed her. I guess she was suffering it until she could get me to put the ring on her finger. Up until then, I thought it was her scruples that kept me at arm's length. But she never had many morals." He stared at Amanda curiously, surprised at how easy it was to tell her things he'd never shared with another human being. "After I found out what she really was, I couldn't have cared less about sharing her bed."

"No, I don't suppose so," she agreed.

He lifted the cigarette to his lips and his eyes narrowed as he studied her. "Elliot's almost thirteen," he said. "He's been my whole life. I've taken care of him and done for him. He knows there's no blood tie between us, but I love him and he loves me. In all the important ways, I'm his father and he's my son."

"He loves you very much," she said with a smile. "He talks about you all the time."

"He's a good boy." He moved a little closer, noticing how she tensed when he came close. He liked that reaction a lot. It told him that she was aware of him, but shy and reticent. "You don't have men," he said softly. "Well, I don't have women."

"Not for... a few months?" she stammered, because she couldn't imagine that he was telling the truth.

He shrugged his powerful shoulders. "Well, not for a bit longer than that. Not much opportunity up here. And I can't go off and leave Elliot while I tomcat around town. It's been a bit longer than thirteen years."

"A bit?"

He looked down at her with a curious, mocking smile. "When I was a boy, I didn't know how to get girls. I was big and clumsy and shy, so it was the other boys who scored." He took another draw, a slightly jerky one, from his cigarette. "I still have the same problem around most women. It's not so much hatred as a lack of ability, and shyness. I don't know how to come on to a woman," he confessed with a faint smile.

Amanda felt as if the sun had just come out. She smiled back. "Don't you, really?" she asked softly. "I thought it was just that you found me lacking, or that I wasn't woman enough to interest you."

He could have laughed out loud at that assumption. "Is that why you called me Goody Two Shoes?" he asked pleasantly.

She laughed softly. "Well, that was sort of sour grapes." She lowered her eyes to his chest. "It hurt my feelings that you thought I didn't have any morals, when I'd never made one single move toward any other man in my whole life."

He felt warm all over from that shy confession. It took down the final brick in his wall of reserve. She wasn't like any woman he'd ever known. "I'm glad to know that. But you and I have more in common than a lack of technique," he said, hesitating.

"We do?" she asked. Her soft eyes held his. "What do you mean?"

He turned and deliberately put out his cigarette in the ashtray on the table beside them. He straightened and looked down at her speculatively for a few seconds before he went for broke. "Well, what I mean, Amanda," he replied finally, "is that you aren't the only virgin on the place."

## Chapter Six

"I didn't hear that," Amanda said, because she knew she hadn't. Quinn Sutton couldn't have told her that he was a virgin.

"Yes, you did," he replied. "And it's not all that farfetched. Old McNaber down the hill's never had a woman, and he's in his seventies. There are all sorts of reasons why men don't get experience. Morals, scruples, isolation, or even plain shyness. Just like women," he added with a meaningful look at Amanda. "I couldn't go to bed with somebody just to say I'd had sex. I'd have to care about her, want her, and I'd want her to care about me. There are idealistic people all over the world who never find that particular combination, so they stay celibate. And really, I think that people who sleep around indiscriminately are in the minority even in these liberated times. Only a fool takes that sort of risk with the health dangers what they are."

"Yes, I know." She watched him with fascinated eyes. "Haven't you ever...wanted to?" she asked.

"Well, that's the problem, you see," he replied, his dark eyes steady on her face.

"What is?"

"I have...wanted to. With you."

She leaned back against the counter, just to make sure she didn't fall down. "With me?"

"That first night you came here, when I was so sick, and your hair drifted down over my naked chest. I shivered, and you thought it was with fever," he mused. "It was a fever, all right, but it didn't have anything to do with the virus."

Her fingers clenched the counter. She'd wondered about his violent reaction at the time, but it seemed so unlikely that a cold man like Quinn Sutton would feel that way about a woman. He was human, she thought absently, watching him.

"That's why I've given you such a hard time," he confessed with narrowed, quiet eyes. "I don't know how to handle desire. I can't throw you over my shoulder and carry you upstairs, not with Elliot and Harry around, even if you were the kind of woman I thought at first you were. The fact that you're as innocent as I am only makes it more complicated."

She looked at him with new understanding, as fascinated by him as he seemed to be by her. He wasn't that bad looking, she mused. And he was terribly strong, and sexy in an earthy kind of way. She especially liked his eyes. They were much more expressive than that poker face.

"Fortunately for you, I'm kind of shy, too," she murmured.

"Except when you're asking men to take their clothes off," Quinn said, nodding.

Harry froze in the doorway with one foot lifted while Amanda gaped at him and turned red.

"Put your foot down and get busy," Quinn muttered irritably. "Why were you standing there?"

"I was getting educated." Harry chuckled. "I didn't know Amanda asked people to take their clothes off!"

"Only me," Quinn said, defending her. "And just my shirt. She's not a bad girl."

"Will you stop!" Amanda buried her face in her hands. "Go away!"

"I can't. I live here," Quinn pointed out. "Did I smell brandy on your breath?" he asked suddenly.

Harry grimaced even as Amanda's eyes widened. "Well, yes you do," he confessed. "She was upset and crying and all..."

"How much did you give her?" Quinn persisted.

"Only a few drops," Harry promised. "In her coffee, to calm her."

"Harry, how could you!" Amanda laughed. The coffee had tasted funny, but she'd been too upset to wonder why.

"Sorry," Harry murmured dryly. "But it seemed the thing to do."

"It backfired," Quinn murmured and actually smiled.

"You stop that!" Amanda told him. She sat down at the table. "I'm not tipsy. Harry, I'll peel those apples for the pie if I can have a knife."

"Let me get out of the room first, if you please," Quinn said, glancing at her dryly. "I saw her measuring my back for a place to put it."

"I almost never stab men with knives," she promised impishly.

He chuckled. He reached for his hat and slanted it over his brow, buttoning his old shepherd's coat because it was snowing outside again.

Amanda looked past him, the reason for all the upset coming back now as she calmed down. Her expression became sad.

"If you stay busy, you won't think about it so much," Quinn said quietly. "It's part of life, you know."

"I know." She managed a smile. "I'm fine. Despite Harry," she added with a chuckle, watching Harry squirm before he grinned back.

Quinn's dark eyes met hers warmly for longer than he meant, so that she blushed. He tore his eyes away finally, and went outside.

Harry didn't say anything, but his smile was speculative.

Elliot came home from school and persuaded Amanda to get out the keyboard and give him some more pointers. He admitted that he'd been bragging about her to his classmates and that she was a professional musician.

"Where do you play, Amanda?" Elliot asked curiously, and he stared at her with open puzzlement. "You look so familiar somehow."

She sat very still on the sofa and tried to stay calm. Elliot had already told her that he liked rock music and she knew Quinn had hidden his tapes. If there was a tape in his collection by Desperado, it would have her picture on the cover along with that of her group.

"Do I really look familiar?" she asked with a smile. "Maybe I just have that kind of face."

"Have you played with orchestras?" he persisted.

"No. Just by myself, sort of. In nightclubs," she improvised. Well, she had once sang in a nightclub, to fill in for a friend. "Mostly I do backup. You know, I play with groups for people who make tapes and records."

"Wow!" he exclaimed. "I guess you know a lot of famous singers and musicians?"

"A few," she agreed.

"Where do you work?"

"In New York City, in Nashville," she told him. "All over. Wherever I can find work."

He ran his fingers up and down the keyboard. "How did you ever wind up here?"

"I needed a rest," she said. "My aunt is...a friend of Mr. Durning. She asked him if I could borrow the cabin, and he said it was all right. I had to get away from work for a while."

"This doesn't bother you, does it? Teaching me to play, I mean?" he asked and looked concerned.

"No, Elliot, it doesn't bother me. I'm enjoying it." She ran a scale and taught it to him, then showed him the cadences of the chords that went with it.

"It's so complicated," he moaned.

"Of course it is. Music is an art form, and it's complex. But once you learn these basics, you can do anything with a chord. For instance..."

She played a tonic chord, then made an impromptu song from its subdominant and seventh chords and the second inversion of them. Elliot watched, fascinated.

"I guess you've studied for years," he said with a sigh.

"Yes, I have, and I'm still learning," she said. "But I love it more than anything. Music has been my whole life."

"No wonder you're so good at it."

She smiled. "Thanks, Elliot."

"Well, I'd better get my chores done before supper," he said, sighing. He handed Amanda the keyboard. "See you later."

She nodded. He went out. Harry was feeding the two calves that were still alive, so presumably he'd tell Elliot about the one that had died. Amanda hadn't had the heart to talk about it.

Her fingers ran over the keyboard lovingly and she began to play a song that her group had recorded two years back, a sad, dreamy ballad about hopeless love that had won them a Grammy. She sang it softly, her pure, sweet voice haunting in the silence of the room as she tried to sing for the first time in weeks.

"Elliot, for Pete's sake, turn that radio down, I'm on the telephone!" came a pleading voice from the back of the house.

She stopped immediately, flushing. She hadn't realized that Harry had come back inside. Thank God he hadn't seen her, or he might have asked some pertinent questions. She put the keyboard down and went to the kitchen, relieved that her singing voice was back to normal again.

Elliot was morose at the supper table. He'd heard about the calf and he'd been as depressed as Amanda had. Quinn didn't look all that happy himself. They all picked at the delicious chili Harry had whipped up; nobody had much of an appetite.

After they finished, Elliot did his homework while Amanda put the last stitches into a chair cover she was making for the living room. Quinn had gone off to do his paperwork and Harry was making bread for the next day.

It was a long, lazy night. Elliot went to bed at eight-thirty and not much later Harry went to his room.

Amanda wanted to wait for Quinn to come back, but something in her was afraid of the new way he looked at her. He was much more a threat now than he had been before, because she was looking at him with new and interested eyes. She was drawn to him more than ever. But he didn't know who she really was, and she couldn't tell him. If she were persuaded into any kind of close relationship with him, it could lead to disaster.

So when Elliot went to bed, so did Amanda. She sat at the dresser and let down her long hair, brushing it with slow, lazy strokes, when there was a knock at the door.

She was afraid that it might be Quinn, and she hesitated. But surely he wouldn't make any advances toward her unless she showed that she wanted them. Of course he wouldn't.

She opened the door, but it wasn't Quinn. It was Elliot. And as he stared at her, wheels moved and gears clicked in his young mind. She was wearing a long granny gown in a deep beige, a shade that was too much like the color of the leather dress she wore on-stage. With her hair loose and the color of the gown, Elliot made the connection he hadn't made the first time he saw her hair down.

"Yes?" she prompted, puzzled by the way he was looking at her. "Is something wrong, Elliot?"

"Uh, no," he stammered. "Uh, I forgot to say good-night. Good night!" He grinned.

He turned, red faced, and beat a hasty retreat, but not to his own room. He went to his father's and searched quickly through the hidden tapes until he found the one he wanted. He held it up, staring blankly at the cover. There were four men who looked like vicious bikers surrounding a beautiful woman in buckskin with long, elegant, blond hair. The group was one of his favorites—Desperado. And the woman was Mandy. Amanda. His Amanda. He caught his breath. Boy, would she be in for it if his dad found out who she was! He put the tape into his pocket, feeling guilty for taking it when Quinn had told him not to. But these were desperate circumstances. He had to protect Amanda until he could figure out how to tell her that he knew the truth. Meanwhile, having her in the same house with him was sheer undiluted heaven! Imagine, a singing star that famous in his house. If only he could tell the guys! But that was too risky, because it might get back to Dad. He sighed. Just his luck, to find a rare jewel and have to hide it to keep someone from stealing it. He closed the door to Quinn's bedroom and went quickly back to his own.

Amanda slept soundly, almost missing breakfast. Outside, the sky looked blue for the first time in days, and she noticed that the snow had stopped.

"Chinook's coming," Harry said with a grin. "I knew it would."

Quinn's dark eyes studied Amanda's face. "Well, it will be a few days before they get the power lines back up again," he muttered. "So don't get in an uproar about it."

"I'm not in an uproar," Harry returned with a frown. "I just thought it was nice that we'll be able to get off the mountain and lay in some more supplies. I'm getting tired of beef. I want a chicken."

"So do I!" Elliot said fervently. "Or bear, or beaver or moose, anything but beef!"

Quinn glared at both of them. "Beef pays the bills around here," he reminded them.

They looked so guilty that Amanda almost laughed out loud.

"I'm sorry, Dad," Elliot sighed. "I'll tell my stomach to shut up about it."

Quinn's hard face relaxed. "It's all right. I wouldn't mind a chicken stew, myself."

"That's the spirit," Elliot said. "What are we going to do today? It's Saturday," he pointed out. "No school."

"You could go out with me and help me feed cattle," Quinn said.

"I'll stay here and help Harry," Amanda said, too quickly.

Quinn's dark eyes searched hers. "Harry can manage by himself. You can come with me and Elliot."

"You'll enjoy it," Elliot assured her. "It's a lot of fun. The cattle see us and come running. Well, as well as they can run in several feet of snow," he amended.

It was fun, too. Amanda sat on the back of the sled with Elliot and helped push the bales of hay off. Quinn cut the strings so the cattle could get to the hay. They did come running, reminding Amanda so vividly of women at a sale that she laughed helplessly until the others had to be told why she was laughing.

They came back from the outing in a new kind of harmony, and for the first time, Amanda understood what it felt like to be part of a family. She looked at Quinn and wondered how it would be if she never had to leave here, if she could stay with him and Elliot and Harry forever.

But she couldn't, she told herself firmly. She had to remember that this was a vacation, with the real world just outside the door.

Elliot was allowed to stay up later on Saturday night, so they watched a science-fiction movie together while Quinn grumbled over paperwork. The next morning they went to church on the sled, Amanda in the one skirt and blouse she'd packed, trying not to look too conspicuous as Quinn's few neighbors carefully scrutinized her.

When they got back home, she was all but shaking. She felt uncomfortable living with him, as if she really was a fallen woman now. He cornered her in the kitchen while she was washing dishes to find out why she was so quiet.

"I didn't think about the way people would react if you went with us this morning," he said quietly. "I wouldn't have subjected you to that if I'd just thought."

"It's okay," she said, touched by his concern. "Really. It was just a little uncomfortable."

He sighed, searching her face with narrowed eyes. "Most people around here know how I feel about women," he said bluntly. "That was why you attracted so much attention. People get funny ideas about woman haters who take in beautiful blondes."

"I'm not beautiful," she stammered shyly.

He stepped toward her, towering over her in his dress slacks and good white shirt and sedate gray tie. He looked handsome and strong and very masculine. She liked the spicy cologne he wore. "You're beautiful, all right," he murmured. His big hand touched her cheek, sliding down it slowly, his thumb brushing with soft abrasion over her full mouth.

Her breath caught as she looked up into his dark, soft eyes. "Quinn?" she whispered.

He drew her hands out of the warm, soapy water, still holding her gaze, and dried them on a dishcloth. Then he guided them, first one, then the other, up to his shoulders.

"Hold me," he whispered as his hands smoothed over her waist and brought her gently to him. "I want to kiss you."

She shivered from the sensuality in that soft whisper, lifting her face willingly.

He bent, brushing his mouth lazily over hers. "Isn't this how we did it before?" he breathed, parting his lips as they touched hers. "I like the way it feels to kiss you like this. My spine tingles."

"So...does mine." She slid her hands hesitantly into the thick, cool strands of hair at his nape and she went on tiptoe to give him better access to her mouth.

He accepted the invitation with quiet satisfaction, his mouth growing slowly rougher and hungrier as it

fed on hers. He made a sound under his breath and all
at once he bent, lifting her clear off the floor in a
bearish embrace. His mouth bit hers, parting her lips,
and she clung to him, moaning as the fever burned in
her, too.

He let her go at once when Elliot called, "What?"
from the living room. "Amanda, did you say something?"

"No... No, Elliot," she managed in a tone pitched
a little higher than normal. Her answer appeared to
satisfy him, because he didn't ask again. Harry was
outside, but he probably wouldn't stay there long.

She looked up at Quinn, surprised by the intent
stare he was giving her. He liked the way she looked,
her face flushed, her mouth swollen from his kisses,
her eyes wide and soft and faintly misty with emotion.

"I'd better get out of here," he said hesitantly.

"Yes." She touched her lips with her fingers and he
watched the movement closely.

"Did I hurt your mouth?" he asked quietly.

She shook her head. "No. Oh, no, not at all," she
said huskily.

Quinn nodded and sighed heavily. He smiled faintly
and then turned and went back into the living room
without another word.

It was a long afternoon, made longer by the strain
Amanda felt being close to him. She found her eyes
meeting his across the room and every time she flushed
from the intensity of the look. Her body was hungry
for him, and she imagined the reverse was equally
true. He watched her openly now, with smoldering
hunger in his eyes. They had a light supper and

watched a little more television. But when Harry went
to his room and Elliot called good-night and went up
to bed, Amanda weakly stayed behind.

Quinn finished his cigarette with the air of a man
who had all night, and then got up and reached for
Amanda, lifting her into his arms.

"There's nothing to be afraid of," he said quietly,
searching her wide, apprehensive eyes as he turned and
carried her into his study and closed the door behind
them.

It was a fiercely masculine room. The furniture was
dark wood with leather seats, the remnants of more
prosperous times. He sat down in a big leather armchair with Amanda in his lap.

"It's private here," he explained. His hand moved
one of hers to his shirt and pressed it there, over the
tie. "Even Elliot doesn't come in when the door's
shut. Do you still want to take my shirt off?" he asked
with a warm smile.

Amanda sighed. "Well, yes," she stammered. "I
haven't done this sort of thing before...."

"Neither have I, honey," he murmured dryly. "I
guess we'll learn it together, won't we?"

She smiled into his dark eyes. "That sounds nice."
She lowered her eyes to the tie and frowned when she
saw how it was knotted.

"Here, I'll do it." He whipped it off with the ease
of long practice and unlooped the collar button.
"Now. You do the rest," he said deeply, and looked
like a man anticipating heaven.

Her fingers, so adept on a keyboard, fumbled like
two left feet while she worried buttons out of buttonholes. He was heavily muscled, tanned skin under a

mass of thick, curling black hair. She remembered how it had looked that first night she'd been here, and how her hands had longed to touch it. Odd, because she'd never cared what was under a man's shirt before.

She pressed her hands flat against him, fascinated by the quick thunder of his heartbeat under them. She looked up into dark, quiet eyes.

"Shy?" he murmured dryly.

"A little. I always used to run a mile when men got this close."

The smile faded. His big hand covered hers, pressing them closer against him. "Wasn't there ever anyone you wanted?"

She shook her head. "The men I'm used to aren't like you. They're mostly rounders with a line a mile long. Everything is just casual to them, like eating mints." She flushed a little. "Intimacy isn't a casual thing to me."

"Or to me." His chest rose and fell heavily. He touched her bright head. "Now will you take your hair down, Amanda?" he asked gently. "I've dreamed about it for days."

Amanda smiled softly. "Have you, really? It's something of a nuisance to wash and dry, but I've gotten sort of used to it." She unbraided it and let it down, enchanted by Quinn's rapt fascination with it. His big hands tangled in it, as if he loved the feel of it. He brought his face down and kissed her neck through it, drawing her against his bare chest.

"It smells like flowers," he whispered.

"I washed it before church this morning," she replied. "Elliot loaned me his blow-dryer but it still took all of thirty minutes to get the dampness out.'' She relaxed with a sigh, nuzzling against his shoulder while her fingers tugged at the thick hair on his chest. "You feel furry. Like a bear," she murmured.

"You feel silky," he said against her hair. With his hand, Quinn tilted her face up to his and slid his mouth onto hers in the silent room. He groaned softly as her lips parted under his. His arms lifted and turned her, wrapped her up, so that her breasts were lying on his chest and her cheek was pressed against his shoulder by the force of the kiss.

He tasted of smoke and coffee, and if his mouth wasn't expert, it was certainly ardent. She loved kissing him. She curled her arms around his neck and turned a little more, hesitating when she felt the sudden stark arousal of his body.

Her eyes opened, looking straight into his, and she colored.

"I'm sorry," he murmured, starting to shift her, as if his physical reaction to her embarrassed him.

"No, Quinn," she said, resisting gently, holding his gaze as she relaxed into him, shivering a little. "There's nothing to apologize for. I . . . like knowing you want me," she whispered, lowering her eyes to his mouth. "It just takes a little getting used to. I've never let anyone hold me like this."

His chest swelled with that confession. His cheek rested on her hair as he settled into the chair and relaxed himself, taking her weight easily. "I'm glad about that," he said. "But it isn't just physical with me. I wanted you to know."

She smiled against his shoulder. "It isn't just physical with me, either." She touched his hard face, her fingers moving over his mouth, loving the feel of it, the smell of his body, the warmth and strength of it. "Isn't it incredible?" She laughed softly. "I mean, at our ages, to be so green . . ."

He laughed, too. It would have stung to have heard that from any other woman, but Amanda was different. "I've never minded less being inexperienced," he murmured.

"Oh, neither have I." She sighed contentedly.

His big hand smoothed over her shoulder and down her back to her waist and onto her rib cage. He wanted very much to run it over her soft breast, but that might be too much too soon, so he hesitated.

Amanda smiled to herself. She caught his fingers and, lifting her face to his eyes, deliberately pulled them onto her breast, her lips parting at the sensation that steely warmth imparted. The nipple hardened and she caught her breath as Quinn's thumb rubbed against it.

"Have you ever seen a woman . . . without her top on?" she whispered, her long hair gloriously tangled around her face and shoulders.

"No," he replied softly. "Only in pictures." His dark eyes watched the softness his fingers were tracing. "I want to see you that way. I want to touch your skin . . . like this."

She drew his hand to the buttons of her blouse and lay quietly against him, watching his hard face as he loosened the buttons and pulled the fabric aside. The bra seemed to fascinate him. He frowned, trying to decide how it opened.

"It's a front catch," she whispered. She shifted a little, and found the catch. Her fingers trembled as she loosened it. Then, watching him, she carefully peeled it away from the high, taut throb of her breasts and watched him catch his breath.

"My God," he breathed reverently. He touched her with trembling fingers, his eyes on the deep mauve of her nipples against the soft pink thrust of flesh, his body taut with sudden aching longing. "My God, I've never seen anything so beautiful."

He made her feel incredibly feminine. She closed her eyes and arched back against his encircling arm, moaning softly.

"Kiss me . . . there," she whispered huskily, aching for his mouth.

"Amanda . . ." He bent, delighting in her femininity, the obvious rapt fascination of the first time in her actions so that even if he hadn't suspected her innocence he would have now. His lips brushed over the silky flesh, and his hands lifted her to him, arched her even more. She tasted of flower petals, softly trembling under his warm, ardent mouth, her breath jerking past her parted lips as she lay with her eyes closed, lost in him.

"It's so sweet, Quinn," she whispered brokenly.

His lips brushed up her body to her throat, her chin, and then they locked against her mouth. He turned her slowly, so that her soft breasts lay against the muted thunder of his hair-roughened chest. He felt her shiver before her arms slid around his neck and she deliberately pressed closer, drawing herself against him and moaning.

"Am I hurting you?" he asked huskily, his mouth poised just above hers, a faint tremor in his arms. "Amanda, am I hurting you?"

"No." She opened her eyes and they were like black pools, soft and deep and quiet. With her blond hair waving at her temples, her cheeks, her shoulders, she was so beautiful that Quinn's breath caught.

He sat just looking at her, indulging his hunger for the sight of her soft breasts, her lovely face. She lay quietly in his arms without a protest, barely breathing as the spell worked on them.

"I'll live on this the rest of my life," he said roughly, his voice deep and soft in the room, with only an occasional crackle from the burning fire in the potbellied stove to break the silence.

"So will I," she whispered. She reached up to his face, touching it in silence, adoring its strength. "We shouldn't have done this," she said miserably. "It will make it ... so much more difficult, when I have to leave. The thaw ...!"

His fingers pressed against her lips. "One day at a time," he said. "Even if you leave, you aren't getting away from me completely. I won't let go. Not ever."

Tears stung her eyes. The surplus of emotion sent them streaming down her cheeks and Quinn caught his breath, brushing them away with his long fingers.

"Why?" he whispered.

"Nobody ever wanted to keep me before," she explained with a watery smile. "I've always felt like an extra person in the world."

He found that hard to imagine, as beautiful as she was. Perhaps her reticence made her of less value to sophisticated men, but not to him. He found her a pearl beyond price.

"You're not an extra person in my world," he replied. "You fit."

She sighed and nuzzled against him, closing her eyes as she drank in the exquisite pleasure of skin against skin, feeling his heart beat against her breasts. She shivered.

"Are you cold?" he asked.

"No. It's...so wonderful, feeling you like this," she whispered. "Quinn?"

He eased her back in his arm and watched her, understanding as she didn't seem to understand what was wrong.

His big, warm hand covered her breast, gently caressing it. "It's desire," he whispered softly. "You want me."

"Yes," she whispered.

"You can't have me. Not like this. Not in any honorable way." He sighed heavily and lifted her against him to hold her, very hard. "Now hold on, real tight. It will pass."

She shivered helplessly, drowning in the warmth of his body, in its heat against her breasts. But he was right. Slowly the ache began to ease away and her body stilled with a huge sigh.

"How do you know so much when you've... when you've never...?"

"I told you, I read a book. Several books." He chuckled, the laughter rippling over her sensitive breasts. "But, my God, reading was never like this!"

She laughed, too, and impishly bit his shoulder right through the cloth.

Then he shivered. "Don't," he said huskily.

She lifted her head, fascinated by the expression on his face. "Do you like it?" she asked hesitantly.

"Yes, I like it," he said with a rueful smile. "All too much." He gazed down at her bareness and his eyes darkened. "I like looking at your breasts, too, but I think we'd better stop this while we can."

He tugged the bra back around her with a grimace and hooked the complicated catch. He deftly buttoned her blouse up to her throat, his eyes twinkling as they met hers.

"Disappointed?" he murmured. "So am I. I have these dreams every night of pillowing you on your delicious hair while we make love until you cry out."

She could picture that, too, and her breath lodged in her throat as she searched his dark eyes. His body, bare and moving softly over hers on white sheets, his face above her...

She moaned.

"Oh, I want it, too," he whispered, touching his mouth with exquisite tenderness to hers. "You in my bed, your arms around me, the mattress moving under us." He lifted his head, breathing unsteadily. "I might have to hurt you a little at first," he said gruffly. "You understand?"

"Yes." She smoothed his shirt, absently drawing it back together and fastening the buttons with a sense of possession. "But only a little, and I could bear it for what would come afterward," she said, looking up. "Because you'd pleasure me then."

"My God, would I," he whispered. "Pleasure you until you were exhausted." He framed her face in his hands and kissed her gently. "Please go to bed, Amanda, before I double over and start screaming."

She smiled against his mouth and let him put her on her feet. She laughed when she swayed and he had to catch her.

"See what you do to me?" she mused. "Make me dizzy."

"Not half as dizzy as you make me." He smoothed down her long hair, his eyes adoring it. "Pretty little thing," he murmured.

"I'm glad you like me," she replied. "I'll do my best to stay this way for the next fifty years or so, with a few minor wrinkles."

"You'll be beautiful to me when you're an old lady. Good night."

She moved away from him with flattering reluctance, her dark eyes teasing his. "Are you sure you haven't done this before?" she asked with a narrow gaze. "You're awfully good at it for a beginner."

"That makes two of us," he returned dryly.

She liked the way he looked, with his hair mussed and his thin mouth swollen from her kisses, and his shirt disheveled. It made her feel a new kind of pride that she could disarrange him so nicely. After one long glance, she opened the door and went out.

"Lock your door," he whispered.

She laughed delightedly. "No, you lock yours the way you did the other night."

He shifted uncomfortably. "That was a low blow. I'm sorry."

"Oh, I was flattered," she corrected. "I've never felt so dangerous in all my life. I wish I had one of those long, black silk negligees . . ."

"Will you get out of here?" he asked pleasantly. "I think I did mention the urge to throw you on the floor and ravish you?"

"With Elliot right upstairs? Fie, sir, think of my reputation."

"I'm trying to, if you'll just go to bed!"

"Very well, if I must." She started up the staircase, her black eyes dancing as they met his. She tossed her hair back and smiled at him. "Good night, Quinn."

"Good night, Amanda. Sweet dreams."

"They'll be sweet from now on," she agreed. She turned reluctantly and went up the staircase. He watched her until she went into her room and closed the door.

It wasn't until she was in her own room that she realized just what she'd done.

She wasn't some nice domestic little thing who could fit into Quinn's world without any effort. She was Amanda Corrie Callaway, who belonged to a rock group with a worldwide reputation. On most streets in most cities, her face was instantly recognizable. How was Quinn going to take the knowledge of who she really was—and the fact that she'd deceived him by leading him to think she was just a vacationing keyboard player? She groaned as she put on her gown. It didn't bear thinking about. From sweet heaven to nightmare in one hour was too much.

## Chapter Seven

Amanda hardly slept from the combined shock of Quinn's ardor and her own guilt. How could she tell him the truth now? What could she say that would take away the sting of her deceit?

She dressed in jeans and the same button-up pink blouse she'd worn the night before and went down to breakfast.

Quinn looked up as she entered the room, his eyes warm and quiet.

"Good morning," she said brightly.

"Good morning yourself," Quinn murmured with a smile. "Sleep well?"

"Barely a wink," she said, sighing, her own eyes holding his.

He chuckled, averting his gaze before Elliot became suspicious. "Harry's out feeding your calves," he said, "and I'm on my way over to Eagle Pass to help one of my neighbors feed some stranded cattle. You'll have to stay with Elliot—it's teacher work-day."

"I forgot," Elliot wailed, head in hands. "Can you imagine that I actually forgot? I could have slept until noon!"

"There, there," Amanda said, patting his shoulder. "Don't you want to learn some more chords?"

"Is that what you do?" Quinn asked curiously, because now every scrap of information he learned about her was precious. "You said you played a keyboard for a living. Do you teach music?"

"Not really," she said gently. "I play backup for various groups," she explained. "That rock music you hate . . ." she began uneasily.

"That's all right," Quinn replied, his face open and kind. "I was just trying to get a rise out of you. I don't mind it all that much, I guess. And playing backup isn't the same thing as putting on those god-awful costumes and singing suggestive lyrics. Well, I'm gone. Stay out of trouble, you two," he said as he got to his feet in the middle of Amanda's instinctive move to speak, to correct his assumption that all she did was play backup. She wanted to tell him the truth, but he winked at her and Elliot and got into his outdoor clothes before she could find a way to break the news. By the time her mind was working again, he was gone.

She sat back down, sighing. "Oh, Elliot, what a mess," she murmured, her chin in her hands.

"Is that what you call it?" he asked with a wicked smile. "Dad's actually grinning, and when he looked at you, you blushed. I'm not blind, you know. Do you like him, even if he isn't Mr. America?"

"Yes, I like him," she said with a shy smile, lowering her eyes. "He's a pretty special guy."

"I think so, myself. Eat your breakfast. I want to ask you about some new chords."

"Okay."

They were working on the keyboard when the sound of an approaching vehicle caught Amanda's attention. Quinn hadn't driven anything motorized since the snow had gotten so high.

"That's odd," Elliot said, peering out the window curtain. "It's a four-wheel drive... Oh, boy." He glanced at Amanda. "You aren't gonna like this."

She lifted her eyebrows. "I'm not?" she asked, puzzled.

The knock at the back door had Harry moving toward it before Amanda and Elliot could. Harry opened it and looked up and up and up. He stood there staring while Elliot gaped at the grizzly-looking man who loomed over him in a black Western costume, complete with hat.

"I'm looking for Mandy Callaway," he boomed.

"Hank!"

Amanda ran to the big man without thinking, to be lifted high in the air while he chuckled and kissed her warmly on one cheek, his whiskers scratching.

"Hello, peanut!" he grinned. "What are you doing up here? The old trapper down the hill said you hadn't been in Durning's cabin since the heavy snow came."

"Mr. Sutton took me in and gave me a roof over my head. Put me down," she fussed, wiggling.

He put her back on her feet while Harry and Elliot still gaped.

"This is Hank," she said, holding his enormous hand as she turned to face the others. "He's a good friend, and a terrific musician, and I'd really appreciate it if you wouldn't tell Quinn he was here just yet. I'll tell him myself. Okay?"

"Sure," Harry murmured. He shook his head. "You for real, or do you have stilts in them boots?"

"I used to be a linebacker for the Dallas Cowboys." Hank grinned.

"That would explain it," Harry chuckled. "Your secret's safe with me, Amanda." He excused himself and went to do the washing.

"Me, too," Elliot said, grinning, "as long as I get Mr. Shoeman's autograph before he leaves."

Amanda let out a long breath, her eyes frightened as they met Elliot's.

"That's right," Elliot said. "I already knew you were Mandy Callaway. I've got a Desperado tape. I took it out of Dad's drawer and hid it as soon as I recognized you. You'll tell him when the time's right. Won't you?"

"Yes, I will, Elliot," she agreed. "I'd have done it already except that . . . well, things have gotten a little complicated."

"You can say that again." Elliot led the way into the living room, watching Hank sit gingerly on a sofa that he dwarfed. "I'll just go make sure that tape's hidden," he said, leaving them alone.

"Complicated, huh?" Hank said. "I hear this Sutton man's a real woman hater."

"He was until just recently." She folded her hands in her lap. "And he doesn't approve of rock music."

She sighed and changed the subject. "What's up, Hank?"

"We've got a gig at Larry's Lodge," he said. "I know, you don't want to. Listen for a minute. It's to benefit cystic fibrosis, and a lot of other stars are going to be in town for it, including a few pretty well-known singers." He named some of them and Amanda whistled. "See what I mean? It's strictly charity, or I wouldn't have come up here bothering you. The boys and I want to do it." His dark eyes narrowed. "Are you up to it?"

"I don't know. I tried to sing here a couple of times, and my voice seems to be good enough. No more lapses. But in front of a crowd..." She spread her hands. "I don't know, Hank."

"Here." He handed her three tickets to the benefit. "You think about it. If you can, come on up. Sutton might like the singers even if he doesn't care for our kind of music." He studied her. "You haven't told him, have you?"

She shook her head, smiling wistfully. "Haven't found the right way yet. If I leave it much longer, it may be too late."

"The girl's family sent you a letter," he said. "Thanking you for what you tried to do. They said you were her heroine... aw, now, Mandy, stop it!"

She collapsed in tears. He held her, rocking her, his face red with mingled embarrassment and guilt.

"Mandy, come on, stop that," he muttered. "It's all over and done with. You've got to get yourself together. You can't hide out here in the Tetons for the rest of your life."

"Can't I?" she wailed.

"No, you can't. Hiding isn't your style. You have to face the stage again, or you'll never get over it." He tilted her wet face. "Look, would you want somebody eating her guts out over you if you'd been Wendy that night? It wasn't your fault, damn it! It wasn't anybody's fault; it was an accident, pure and simple."

"If she hadn't been at the concert..."

"If, if, if," he said curtly. "You can't go back and change things to suit you. It was her time. At the concert, on a plane, in a car, however, it would still have been her time. Are you listening to me, Mandy?"

She dabbed her eyes with the hem of her blouse. "Yes, I'm listening."

"Come on, girl. Buck up. You can get over this if you set your mind to it. Me and the guys miss you, Mandy. It's not the same with just the four of us. People are scared of us when you aren't around."

That made her smile. "I guess they are. You do look scruffy, Hank," she murmured.

"You ought to see Johnson." He sighed. "He's let his beard go and he looks like a scrub brush. And Deke says he won't change clothes until you come back."

"Oh, my God," Amanda said, shuddering, "tell him I'll think hard about this concert, okay? You poor guys. Stay upwind of him."

"We're trying." He got up, smiling down at her. "Everything's okay. You can see the letter when you come to the lodge. It's real nice. Now stop beating yourself. Nobody else blames you. After all, babe, you risked your life trying to save her. Nobody's forgotten that, either."

She leaned against him for a minute, drawing on his strength. "Thanks, Hank."

"Anytime. Hey, kid, you still want that autograph?" he asked.

Elliot came back into the room with a pad and pen. "Do I!" he said, chuckling.

Hank scribbled his name and Desperado's curly-Q logo underneath. "There you go."

"He's a budding musician," Amanda said, putting an arm around Elliot. "I'm teaching him the keyboard. One of these days, if we can get around Quinn, we'll have him playing backup for me."

"You bet." Hank chuckled, and ruffled Elliot's red hair. "Keep at it. Mandy's the very best. If she teaches you, you're taught."

"Thanks, Mr. Shoeman."

"Just Hank. See you at the concert. So long, Mandy."

"So long, pal."

"What concert?" Elliot asked excitedly when Hank had driven away.

Amanda handed him the three tickets. "To a benefit in Jackson Hole. The group's going to play there. Maybe. If I can get up enough nerve to get back onstage again."

"What happened, Amanda?" he asked gently.

She searched his face, seeing compassion along with the curiosity, so she told him, fighting tears all the way.

"Gosh, no wonder you came up here to get away," Elliot said with more than his twelve years worth of wisdom. He shrugged. "But like he said, you have to go back someday. The longer you wait, the harder it's going to be."

"I know that," she groaned. "But Elliot, I..." She took a deep breath and looked down at the floor. "I love your father," she said, admitting it at last. "I love him very much, and the minute he finds out who I am, my life is over."

"Maybe not," he said. "You've got another week until the concert. Surely in all that time you can manage to tell him the truth. Can't you?"

"I hope so," she said with a sad smile. "You don't mind who I am, do you?" she asked worriedly.

"Don't be silly." He hugged her warmly. "I think you're super, keyboard or not."

She laughed and hugged him back. "Well, that's half the battle."

"Just out of curiosity," Harry asked from the doorway, "who was the bearded giant?"

"That was Hank Shoeman," Elliot told him. "He's the drummer for Desperado. It's a rock group. And Amanda—"

"—plays backup for him," she volunteered, afraid to give too much away to Harry.

"Well, I'll be. He's a musician?" Harry shook his head. "Would have took him for a bank robber," he mumbled.

"Most people do, and you should see the rest of the group." She grinned. "Don't give me away, Harry, okay? I promise I'll tell Quinn, but I've got to do it the right way."

"I can see that," he agreed easily. "Be something of a shock to him to meet your friend after dark, I imagine."

"I imagine so," she said, chuckling. "Thanks, Harry."

"My pleasure. Desperado, huh? Suits it, if the rest of the group looks like he does."

"Worse," she said, and shuddered.

"Strains the mind, don't it?" Harry went off into the kitchen and Amanda got up after a minute to help him get lunch.

Quinn wasn't back until late that afternoon. Nobody mentioned Hank's visit, but Amanda was nervous and her manner was strained as she tried not to show her fears.

"What's wrong with you?" he asked gently during a lull in the evening while Elliot did homework and Harry washed up. "You don't seem like yourself tonight."

She moved close to him, her fingers idly touching the sleeve of his red flannel shirt. "It's thawing outside," she said, watching her fingers move on the fabric. "It won't be long before I'll be gone."

He sighed heavily. His fingers captured hers and held them. "I've been thinking about that. Do you really have to get back?"

She felt her heart jump. Whatever he was offering, she wanted to say yes and let the future take care of itself. But she couldn't. She grimaced. "Yes, I have to get back," she said miserably. "I have commitments to people. Things I promised to do." Her fingers clenched his. "Quinn, I have to meet some people at Larry's Lodge in Jackson Hole next Friday night." She looked up. "It's at a concert and I have tickets. I know you don't like rock, but there's going to be all kinds of music." Her eyes searched his. "Would you go with me? Elliot can come, too. I...want you to see what I do for a living."

"You and your keyboard?" he mused gently.

"Sort of," she agreed, hoping she could find the nerve to tell him everything before next Friday night.

"Okay," he replied. "A friend of mine works there—I used to be with the Ski Patrol there, too. Sure, I'll go with you." The smile vanished, and his eyes glittered down at her. "I'll go damned near anywhere with you."

Amanda slid her arms around him and pressed close, shutting her eyes as she held on for dear life. "That goes double for me, mountain man," she said half under her breath.

He bent his head, searching for her soft mouth. She gave it to him without a protest, without a thought for the future, gave it to him with interest, with devotion, with ardor. Her lips opened invitingly, and she felt his hands on her hips with a sense of sweet inevitability, lifting her into intimate contact with the aroused contours of his body.

"Frightened?" he whispered unsteadily just over her mouth when he felt her stiffen involuntarily.

"Of you?" she whispered back. "Don't be absurd. Hold me any way you want. I adore you . . . !"

He actually groaned as his mouth pressed down hard on hers. His arms contracted hungrily and he gave in to the pleasure of possession for one long moment.

Her eyes opened and she watched him, feeding on the slight contortion of his features, his heavy brows drawn over his crooked nose, his long, thick lashes on his cheek as he kissed her. She did adore him, she thought dizzily. Adored him, loved him, worshiped him. If only she could stay with him forever like this.

Quinn lifted his head and paused as he saw her watching him. He frowned slightly, then bent again. This time his eyes stayed open, too, and she went under as he deepened the kiss. Her eyes closed in self-defense and she moaned, letting him see the same vulnerability she'd seen in him. It was breathlessly sweet.

"This is an education," he said, laughing huskily, when he drew slightly away from her.

"Isn't it, though?" she murmured, moving his hands from her hips up to her waist and moving back a step from the blatant urgency of his body. "Elliot and Harry might come in," she whispered.

"I wouldn't mind," he said unexpectedly, searching her flushed face. "I'm not ashamed of what I feel for you, or embarrassed by it."

"This from a confirmed woman hater?" she asked with twinkling eyes.

"Well, not exactly confirmed anymore," he confessed. He lifted her by the waist and searched her eyes at point-blank range until she trembled from the intensity of the look. "I couldn't hate you if I tried, Amanda," he said quietly.

"Oh, I hope not," she said fervently, thinking ahead to when she would have to tell him the truth about herself.

He brushed a lazy kiss across her lips. "I think I'm getting the hang of this," he murmured.

"I think you are, too," she whispered. She slid her arms around his neck and put her warm mouth hungrily against his, sighing when he caught fire and answered the kiss with feverish abandon.

A slight, deliberate cough brought them apart, both staring blankly at the small redheaded intruder.

"Not that I mind," Elliot said, grinning, "but you're blocking the pan of brownies Harry made."

"You can think of brownies at a time like this?" Amanda groaned. "Elliot!"

"Listen, he can think of brownies with a fever of a hundred and two," Quinn told her, still holding her on a level with his eyes. "I've seen him get out of a sickbed to pinch a brownie from the kitchen."

"I like brownies, too," Amanda confessed with a warm smile, delighted that Quinn didn't seem to mind at all that Elliot had seen them in a compromising position. That made her feel lighter than air.

"Do you?" Quinn smiled and brushed his mouth gently against hers, mindless of Elliot's blatant interest, before he put her back on her feet. "Harry makes his from scratch, with real baker's chocolate. They're something special."

"I'll bet they are. Here. I'll get the saucers," she volunteered, still catching her breath.

Elliot looked like the cat with the canary as she dished up brownies. It very obviously didn't bother him that Amanda and his dad were beginning to notice each other.

"Isn't this cozy?" he remarked as they went back into the living room and Amanda curled up on the sofa beside his dad, who never sat there.

"Cozy, indeed," Quinn murmured with a warm smile for Amanda.

She smiled back and laid her cheek against Quinn's broad chest while they watched television and ate brownies. She didn't move even when Harry joined them. And she knew she'd never been closer to heaven.

That night they were left discreetly alone, and she lay in Quinn's strong arms on the long leather couch in his office while wood burned with occasional hisses and sparks in the potbellied stove.

"I've had a raw deal with this place," he said eventually between kisses. "But it's good land, and I'm building a respectable herd of cattle. I can't offer you wealth or position, and we've got a ready-made family. But I can take care of you," he said solemnly, looking down into her soft eyes. "And you won't want for any of the essentials."

Her fingers touched his lean cheek hesitantly. "You don't know anything about me," she said. "When you know my background, you may not want me as much as you think you do." She put her fingers against his mouth. "You have to be sure."

"Damn it, I'm already sure," he muttered.

But was he? She was the first woman he'd ever been intimate with. Couldn't that blind him to her real suitability? What if it was just infatuation or desire? She was afraid to take a chance on his feelings, when she didn't really know what they were.

"Let's wait just a little while longer before we make any plans, Quinn. Okay?" she asked softly, turning in his hard arms so that her body was lying against his. "Make love to me," she whispered, moving her mouth up to his. "Please . . ."

He gave in with a rough groan, gathering her to him, crushing her against his aroused body. He wanted her beyond rational thought. Maybe she had cold feet, but he didn't. He knew what he wanted, and Amanda was it.

His hands smoothed the blouse and bra away with growing expertise and he fought out of his shirt so that he could feel her soft skin against his. But it wasn't enough. He felt her tremble and knew that it was reflected in his own arms and legs. He moved against her with a new kind of sensuousness, lifting his head to hold her eyes while he levered her onto her back and eased over her, his legs between both of hers in their first real intimacy.

She caught her breath, but she didn't push him to try to get away.

"It's just that new for you, isn't it?" he whispered huskily as his hips moved lazily over hers and he groaned. "God, it burns me to...feel you like this."

"I know." She arched her back, loving his weight, loving the fierce maleness of his body. Her arms slid closer around him and she felt his mouth open on hers, his tongue softly searching as it slid inside, into an intimacy that made her moan. She began to tremble.

His lean hand slid under her, getting a firm grip, and he brought her suddenly into a shocking, shattering position that made her mindless with sudden need. She clutched him desperately, shuddering, her nails digging into him as the contact racked her like a jolt of raw electricity.

He pulled away from her without a word, shuddering as he lay on his back, trying to get hold of himself.

"I'm sorry," he whispered. "I didn't mean to let it go so far with us."

She was trembling, too, trying to breathe while great hot tears rolled down her cheeks. "Gosh, I wanted you," she whispered tearfully. "Wanted you so badly, Quinn!"

"As badly as I wanted you, honey," he said heavily. "We can't let things get that hot again. It was a close call. Closer than you realize."

"Oh, Quinn, couldn't we make love?" she asked softly, rolling over to look down into his tormented face. "Just once...?"

He framed his face in his hands and brought her closed eyes to his lips. "No. I won't compromise you."

She hit his big, hair-roughened chest. "Goody Two Shoes...!"

"Thank your lucky stars that I am," he chuckled. His eyes dropped to her bare breasts and lingered there before he caught the edges of her blouse and tugged them together. "You sex-crazed female, haven't you ever heard about pregnancy?"

"That condition where I get to have little Quinns?"

"Stop it, you're making it impossible for me," he said huskily. "Here, get up before I lose my mind."

She sat up with a grimace. "Spoilsport."

"Listen to you," he muttered, putting her back into her clothes with a wry grin. "I'll give you ten to one that you'd be yelling your head off if I started taking off your jeans."

She went red. "My jeans...!"

His eyebrows arched. "Amanda, would you like me to explain that book I read to you? The part about how men and women..."

She cleared her throat. "No, thanks, I think I've got the hang of it now," she murmured evasively.

"We might as well add a word about birth control," he added with a chuckle when he was buttoning up his own shirt. "You don't take the pill, I assume?"

She shook her head. The whole thing was getting to be really embarrassing!

"Well, that leaves prevention up to me," he explained. "And that would mean a trip into town to the drugstore, since I never indulged, I never needed to worry about prevention. *Now* do you get the picture?"

"Boy, do I get the picture." She grimaced, avoiding his knowing gaze.

"Good girl. That's why we aren't lying down anymore."

She sighed loudly. "I guess you don't want children."

"Sure I do. Elliot would love brothers and sisters, and I'm crazy about kids." He took her slender hands in his and smoothed them over with his thumbs. "But kids should be born inside marriage, not outside it. Don't you think so?"

She took a deep breath, and her dark eyes met his. "Yes."

"Then we'll spend a lot of time together until you have to meet your friends at this concert," he said softly. "And afterward, you and I will come in here again and I'll ask you a question."

"Oh, Quinn," she whispered with aching softness.

"Oh, Amanda," he murmured, smiling as his lips softly touched hers. "But right now, we go to bed. Separately. Quick!"

"Yes, sir, Mr. Sutton." She got up and let him lead her to the staircase.

"I'll get the lights," he said. "You go on up. In the morning after we get Elliot off to school you can come out with me, if you want to."

"I want to," she said simply. She could hardly bear to be parted from him even overnight. It was like an addiction, she thought as she went up the staircase. Now if only she could make it last until she had the nerve to tell Quinn the truth....

The next few days went by in a haze. The snow began to melt and the skies cleared as the long-awaited chinook blew in. In no time at all it was Friday night and Amanda was getting into what Elliot would recognize as her stage costume. She'd brought it, with her other things, from the Durning cabin. She put it on, staring at herself in the mirror. Her hair hung long and loose, in soft waves below her waist, in the beige leather dress with the buckskin boots that matched, she was the very picture of a sensuous woman. She left off the headband. There would be time for that if she could summon enough courage to get onstage. She still hadn't told Quinn. She hadn't had the heart to destroy the dream she'd been living. But tonight he'd know. And she'd know if they had a future. She took a deep breath and went downstairs.

# Chapter Eight

Amanda sat in the audience with Quinn and Elliot at a far table while the crowded hall rang with excited whispers. Elliot was tense, like Amanda, his eyes darting around nervously. Quinn was frowning. He hadn't been quite himself since Amanda came down the staircase in her leather dress and boots, looking expensive and faintly alien. He hadn't asked any questions, but he seemed as uptight as she felt.

Her eyes slid over him lovingly, taking in his dark suit. He looked out of place in fancy clothes. She missed the sight of him in denim and his old shepherd's coat, and wondered fleetingly if she'd ever get to see him that way again after tonight—if she'd ever lie in his arms on the big sofa and warm to his kisses while the fire burned in the stove. She almost groaned. Oh, Quinn, she thought, I love you.

Elliot looked uncomfortable in his blue suit. He was watching for the rest of Desperado while a well-known Las Vegas entertainer warmed up the crowd and sang his own famous theme song.

"What are you looking for, son?" Quinn asked.

Elliot shifted. "Nothing. I'm just seeing who I know."

Quinn's eyebrows arched. "How would you know anybody in this crowd?" he muttered, glancing around. "My God, these are show people. Entertainers. Not people from our world."

That was a fact. But hearing it made Amanda heartsick. She reached out and put her hand over Quinn's.

"Your fingers are like ice," he said softly. He searched her worried eyes. "Are you okay, honey?"

The endearment made her warm all over. She smiled sadly and slid her fingers into his, looking down at the contrast between his callused, work-hardened hand and her soft, pale one. His was a strong hand, hers was artistic. But despite the differences, they fit together perfectly. She squeezed her fingers. "I'm fine," she said. "Quinn..."

"And now I want to introduce a familiar face," the Las Vegas performer's voice boomed. "Most of you know the genius of Desperado. The group has won countless awards for its topical, hard-hitting songs. Last year, Desperado was given a Grammy for 'Changes in the Wind,' and Hank Shoeman's song 'Outlaw Love' won him a country music award and a gold record. But their fame isn't the reason we're honoring them tonight."

To Amanda's surprise, he produced a gold plaque. "As some of you may remember, a little over a month ago, a teenage girl died at a Desperado concert. The group's lead singer leaped into the crowd, disregarding her own safety, and was very nearly trampled trying to protect the fan. Because of that tragedy, Desperado went into seclusion. We're proud to tell you tonight that they're back and they're in better form than ever. This plaque is a token of respect from the rest of us in the performing arts to a very special young woman whose compassion and selflessness have won the respect of all."

He looked out toward the audience where Amanda sat frozen. "This is for you—Amanda Corrie Callaway. Will you come up and join the group, please? Come on, Mandy!"

She bit her lower lip. The plaque was a shock. The boys seemed to know about it, too, because they went to their instruments grinning and began to play the downbeat that Desperado was known for, the deep throbbing counter rhythm that was their trademark.

"Come on, babe!" Hank called out in his booming voice, he and Johnson and Deke and Jack looking much more like backwoods robbers than musicians with their huge bulk and outlaw gear.

Amanda glanced at Elliot's rapt, adoring face, and then looked at Quinn. He was frowning, his dark eyes searching the crowd. She said a silent goodbye as she got to her feet. She reached into her pocket for her headband and put it on her head. She couldn't look at him, but she felt his shocked stare as she walked down the room toward the stage, her steps bouncing as the rhythm got into her feet and her blood.

"Thank you," she said huskily, kissing the entertainer's cheek as she accepted the plaque. She moved in between Johnson and Deke, taking the microphone. She looked past Elliot's proud, adoring face to Quinn's. He seemed to be in a state of dark shock. "Thank you all. I've had a hard few weeks. But I'm okay now, and I'm looking forward to better times. God bless, people. This one is for a special man and a special boy, with all my love." She turned to Hank, nodded, and he began the throbbing drumbeat of "Love Singer."

It was a song that touched the heart, for all its mad beat. The words, in her soft, sultry, clear voice caught every ear in the room. She sang from the heart, with the heart, the words fierce with meaning as she sang them to Quinn. "Love you, never loved anybody but you, never leave me lonely, love . . . singer."

But Quinn didn't seem to be listening to the words. He got to his feet and jerked Elliot to his. He walked out in the middle of the song and never looked back once.

Amanda managed to finish, with every ounce of willpower she had keeping her onstage. She let the last few notes hang in the air and then she bowed to a standing ovation. By the time she and the band did an encore and she got out of the hall, the truck they'd come in was long gone. There was no note, no message. Quinn had said it all with his eloquent back when he walked out of the hall. He knew who she was now, and he wanted no part of her. He couldn't have said it more clearly if he'd written it in blood.

She kept hoping that he might reconsider. Even after she went backstage with the boys, she kept hoping for a phone call or a glimpse of Quinn. But nothing happened.

"I guess I'm going to need a place to stay," Amanda said with a rueful smile, her expression telling her group all they needed to know.

"He couldn't handle it, huh?" Hank asked quietly. "I'm sorry, babe. We've got a suite, there's plenty of room for one more. I'll go up and get your gear tomorrow."

"Thanks, Hank." She took a deep breath and clutched the plaque to her chest. "Where's the next gig?"

"That's my girl," he said gently, sliding a protective arm around her. "San Francisco's our next stop. The boys and I are taking a late bus tomorrow." He grimaced at her knowing smile. "Well, you know how I feel about airplanes."

"Chicken Little," she accused. "Well, I'm not going to sit on a bus all day. I'll take the first charter out and meet you guys at the hotel."

"Whatever turns you on," Hank chuckled. "Come on. Let's get out of here and get some rest."

"You did good, Amanda," Johnson said from behind her. "We were proud."

"You bet," Deke and Jack seconded.

She smiled at them all. "Thanks, group. I shocked myself, but at least I didn't go dry the way I did last time." Her heart was breaking in two, but she managed to hide it. Quinn, she moaned inwardly. Oh, Quinn, was I just an interlude, an infatuation?

She didn't sleep very much. The next morning Amanda watched Hank start out for Ricochet then

went down to a breakfast that she didn't even eat while
she waited for him to return.

He came back three hours later, looking ruffled.

"Did you get my things?" she asked when he came
into the suite.

"I got them." He put her suitcase down on the
floor. "Part at Sutton's place, part at the Durning
cabin. Elliot sent you a note." He produced it.

"And . . . Quinn?"

"I never saw him," he replied tersely. "The boy and
the old man were there. They didn't mention Sutton
and I didn't ask. I wasn't feeling too keen on him at
the time."

"Thanks, Hank."

He shrugged. "That's the breaks, kid. It would have
been a rough combination at best. You're a bright-
lights girl."

"Am I?" she asked, thinking how easily she'd fit
into Quinn's world. But she didn't push it. She sat
down on the couch and opened Elliot's scribbled note.

Amanda,
I thought you were great. Dad didn't say anything all the way home and last night he went into
his study and didn't come out until this morning.
He went hunting, he said, but he didn't take any
bullets. I hope you are okay. Write me when you
can. I love you.
                              Your friend, Elliot.

She bit her lip to keep from crying. Dear Elliot. At
least he still cared about her. But her fall from grace
in Quinn's eyes had been final, she thought bitterly.

He'd never forgive her for deceiving him. Or maybe it was just that he'd gotten over his brief infatuation with her when he found out who she really was. She didn't know what to do. She couldn't remember ever feeling so miserable. To have discovered something that precious, only to lose it forever. She folded Elliot's letter and put it into her purse. At least it would be something to remember from her brief taste of heaven.

For the rest of the day, the band and Jerry, the road manager, got the arrangements made for the San Francisco concert, and final travel plans were laid. The boys were to board the San Francisco bus the next morning. Amanda was to fly out on a special air charter that specialized in flights for business executives. They'd managed to fit her in at the last minute when a computer-company executive had canceled his flight.

"I wish you'd come with us," Hank said hesitantly. "I guess I'm overreacting and all, but I hate airplanes."

"I'll be fine," she told him firmly. "You and the boys have a nice trip and stop worrying about me. I'll be fine."

"If you say so," Hank mumbled.

"I do say so." She patted him on the shoulder. "Trust me."

He shrugged and left, but he didn't look any less worried. Amanda, who'd gotten used to his morose predictions, didn't pay them any mind.

She went to the suite and into her bedroom early that night. Her fingers dialed the number at Ricochet. She had to try one last time, she told herself.

There was at least the hope that Quinn might care enough to listen to her explanation. She had to try.

The phone rang once, twice, and she held her breath, but on the third ring the receiver was lifted.

"Sutton," came a deep weary-sounding voice.

Her heart lifted. "Oh, Quinn," she burst out. "Quinn, please let me try to explain—"

"You don't have to explain anything to me, Amanda," he said stiffly. "I saw it all on the stage."

"I know it looks bad," she began.

"You lied to me," he said. "You let me think you were just a shy little innocent who played a keyboard, when you were some fancy big-time entertainer with a countrywide following."

"I knew you wouldn't want me if you knew who I was," she said miserably.

"You knew I'd see right through you if I knew," he corrected, his voice growing angrier. "You played me for a fool."

"I didn't!"

"All of it was a lie. Nothing but a lie! Well, you can go back to your public, Miss Callaway, and your outlaw buddies, and make some more records or tapes or whatever the hell they are. I never wanted you in the first place except in bed, so it's no great loss to me." He was grimacing, and she couldn't see the agony in his eyes as he forced the words out. Now that he knew who and what she was, he didn't dare let himself weaken. He had to make her go back to her own life, and stay out of his. He had nothing to give her, nothing that could take the place of fame and fortune and the world at her feet. He'd never been more aware of his own inadequacies as he had been when he'd seen

Amanda on that stage and heard the applause of the audience. It ranked as the worst waking nightmare of his life, putting her forever out of his reach.

"Quinn!" she moaned. "Quinn, you don't mean that!"

"I mean it," he said through his teeth. He closed his eyes. "Every word. Don't call here again, don't come by, don't write. You're a bad influence on Elliot now that he knows who you are. I don't want you. You've worn out your welcome at Ricochet." He hung up without another word.

Amanda stared at the telephone receiver as if it had sprouted wings. Slowly she put it back in the cradle just as the room splintered into wet crystal around her.

She put on her gown mechanically and got into bed, turning out the bedside light. She lay in the dark and Quinn's words echoed in her head with merciless coolness. *Bad influence. Don't want you. Worn out your welcome. Never wanted you anyway except in bed.*

She moaned and buried her face in her pillow. She didn't know how she was going to go on, with Quinn's cold contempt dogging her footsteps. He hated her now. He thought she'd been playing a game, enjoying herself while she made a fool out of him. The tears burned her eyes. How quickly it had all ended, how finally. She'd hoped to keep in touch with Elliot, but that wouldn't be possible anymore. She was a bad influence on Elliot, so he wouldn't be allowed to contact her. She sobbed her hurt into the cool linen. Somehow, being denied contact with Elliot was the last straw. She'd grown so fond of the boy during those days she'd spent at Ricochet, and he cared about her, too. Quinn was being unnecessarily harsh. But perhaps he was right, and it was for the best. Maybe she could learn to think that way eventually. Right now she had a concert to get to, a sold-out one from what the boys and Jerry had said. She couldn't let the fans down.

Amanda got up the next morning, looking and feeling as if it were the end of the world. The boys took her suitcase downstairs, not looking too closely at her face without makeup, her long hair arranged in a thick, haphazard bun. She was wearing a dark pantsuit with a cream-colored blouse, and she looked miserable.

"We'll see you in San Francisco," Jerry told her with a smile. "I have to go nursemaid these big, tough guys, so you make sure the pilot of your plane has all his marbles, okay?"

"I'll check him out myself," she promised. "Take care of yourselves, guys. I'll see you in California."

"Okay. Be good, babe," Hank called. He and the others filed into the bus Jerry had chartered and Jerry hugged her impulsively and went in behind them.

She watched the bus pull away, feeling lost and alone, not for the first time. It was cold and snowy, but she hadn't wanted her coat. It was packed in her suitcase, and had already been put on the light aircraft. With a long sigh, she went back to the cab and sat disinterestedly in it as it wound over the snowy roads to the airport.

Fortunately the chinook had thawed the runways so that the planes were coming and going easily. She got out at the air charter service hangar and shook hands with the pilot.

"Don't worry, we're in great shape," he promised Amanda with a grin. "In fact, the mechanics just gave us another once-over to be sure. Nothing to worry about."

"Oh, I wasn't worried," she said absently and allowed herself to be shepherded inside. She slid into an empty aisle seat on the right side and buckled up. Usually she preferred to sit by the window, but today she wasn't in the mood for sight-seeing. One snow-covered mountain looked pretty much like another to her, and her heart wasn't in this flight or the gig that would follow it. She leaned back and closed her eyes.

It seemed to take forever for all the businessmen to get aboard. Fortunately there had been one more cancellation, so she had her seat and the window seat as well. She didn't feel like talking to anyone, and was hoping she wouldn't have to sit by some chatterbox all the way to California.

She listened to the engines rev up and made sure that her seat belt was properly fastened. They would be off as soon as the tower cleared them, the pilot announced. Amanda sighed. She called a silent good-bye to Quinn Sutton, and Elliot and Harry, knowing that once this plane lifted off, she'd never see any of them again. She winced at the thought. Oh, Quinn, she moaned inwardly, why wouldn't you *listen*?

The plane got clearance and a minute later, it shot down the runway and lifted off. But it seemed oddly sluggish. Amanda was used to air travel, even to charter flights, and she opened her eyes and peered forward worriedly as she listened to the whine become a roar.

She was strapped in, but a groan from behind took her mind off the engine. The elderly man behind her was clutching his chest and groaning.

"What's wrong?" she asked the worried businessman in the seat beside the older man.

"Heart attack, I think." He grimaced. "What can we do?"

"I know a little CPR," she said. She unfastened her seat belt; so did the groaning man's seat companion. But just as they started to lay him on the floor, someone shouted something. Smoke began to pour out of the cockpit, and the pilot called for everyone to assume crash positions. Amanda turned, almost in slow motion. She could feel the force of gravity increase as the plane started down. The floor went out from under her and her last conscious thought was that she'd never see Quinn again....

Elliot was watching television without much interest, wishing that his father had listened when Amanda had phoned the night before. He couldn't believe that he was going to be forbidden to even speak to her again, but Quinn had insisted, his cold voice giving nothing away as he'd made Elliot promise to make no attempt to contact her.

It seemed so unfair, he thought. Amanda was no wild party girl, surely his father knew that? He sighed heavily and munched on another potato chip.

The movie he was watching was suddenly interrupted as the local station broke in with a news bulle-

tin. Elliot listened for a minute, gasped and jumped up
to get his father.

Quinn was in the office, not really concentrating on
what he was doing, when Elliot burst in. The boy
looked odd, his freckles standing out in an unnaturally pale face.

"Dad, you'd better come here," he said uneasily.
"Quick!"

Quinn's first thought was that something had happened to Harry, but Elliot stopped in front of the television. Quinn frowned as his dark eyes watched the
screen. They were showing the airport.

"What's this all—" he began, then stopped to listen.

"...plane went down about ten minutes ago, according to our best information," the man, probably
the airport manager, was saying. "We've got helicop-
ters flying in to look for the wreckage, but the wind is
up, and the area the plane went down in is almost in-
accessible by road."

"What plane?" Quinn asked absently.

"To repeat our earlier bulletin," the man on television seemed to oblige, "a private charter plane has
been reported lost somewhere in the Grand Teton
Mountains just out of Jackson Hole. One eyewitness
interviewed by KWJC-TV newsman Bill Donovan
stated that he saw flames shooting out of the cockpit
of the twin-engine aircraft and that he watched it
plummet into the mountains and vanish. Aboard the
craft were prominent San Francisco businessmen Bob
Doyle and Harry Brown, and the lead singer of the
rock group Desperado, Mandy Callaway."

Quinn sat down in his chair hard enough to shake
it. He knew his face was as white as Elliot's. In his
mind, he could hear his own voice telling Mandy he
didn't want her anymore, daring her to ever contact
him again. Now she was dead, and he felt her loss as
surely as if one of his arms had been severed from his
body.

That was when he realized how desperately he loved
her. When it was too late to take back the harsh words,
to go after her and bring her home where she belonged. He thought of her soft body lying in the cold
snow, and a sound broke from his throat. He'd sent
her away because he loved her, not because he'd
wanted to hurt her, but she wouldn't have known that.
Her last memory of him would have been a painful,
hateful one. She'd have died thinking he didn't care.

"I don't believe it," Elliot said huskily. He was
shaking his head. "I just don't believe it. She was onstage Friday night, singing again—" His voice broke
and he put his face in his hands.

Quinn couldn't bear it. He got up and went past a
startled Harry and out the back door in his shirt-
sleeves, so upset that he didn't even feel the cold. His
eyes went to the barn, where he'd watched Amanda
feed the calves, and around the back where she'd run
from him that snowy afternoon and he'd had to save
her from McNaber's bear traps. His big fists clenched
by his sides and he shuddered with the force of the
grief he felt, his face contorting.

"Amanda!" He bit off the name.

A long time later, he was aware of someone standing nearby. He didn't turn because his face would have
said too much.

"Elliot told me," Harry said hesitantly. He stuck his hands into his pockets. "They say where she is, they may not be able to get her out."

Quinn's teeth clenched. "I'll get her out," he said huskily. "I won't leave her out there in the cold." He swallowed. "Get my skis and my boots out of the storeroom, and my insulated ski suit out of the closet. I'm going to call the lodge and talk to Terry Meade."

"He manages Larry's Lodge, doesn't he?" Harry recalled.

"Yes. He can get a chopper to take me up."

"Good thing you've kept up your practice," Harry muttered. "Never thought you'd need the skis for something this awful, though."

"Neither did I." He turned and went back inside. He might have to give up Amanda forever, but he wasn't giving her up to that damned mountain. He'd get her out somehow.

He grabbed the phone, ignoring Elliot's questions, and called the lodge, asking for Terry Meade in a tone that got instant action.

"Quinn!" Terry exclaimed. "Just the man I need. Look, we've got a crash—"

"I know," Quinn said tightly. "I know the singer. Can you get me a topo map of the area and a chopper? I'll need a first-aid kit, too, and some flares—"

"No sooner said than done," Terry replied tersely. "Although I don't think that first-aid kit will be needed, Quinn, I'm sorry."

"Well, pack it anyway, will you?" He fought down nausea. "I'll be up there in less than thirty minutes."

"We'll be waiting."

Quinn got into the ski suit under Elliot's fascinated gaze.

"You don't usually wear that suit when we ski together," he told his father.

"We don't stay out that long," Quinn explained. "This suit is a relatively new innovation. It's such a tight weave that it keeps out moisture, but it's made in such a way that it allows sweat to get out. It's like having your own heater along."

"I like the boots, too," Elliot remarked. They were blue, and they had a knob on the heel that allowed them to be tightened to fit the skier's foot exactly. Boots had to fit tight to work properly. And the skis themselves were equally fascinating. They had special brakes that unlocked when the skier fell, which stopped the ski from sliding down the hill.

"Those sure are long skis," Elliot remarked as his father took precious time to apply hot wax to them.

"Longer than yours, for sure. They fit my height," Quinn said tersely. "And they're short compared to jumping skis."

"Did you ever jump, Dad, or did you just do downhill?"

"Giant slalom," he replied. "Strictly Alpine skiing. That's going to come in handy today."

Elliot sighed. "I don't guess you'll let me come along?"

"No chance. This is no place for you." His eyes darkened. "God knows what I'll find when I get to the plane."

Elliot bit his lower lip. "She's dead, isn't she, Dad?" he asked in a choked tone.

Quinn's expression closed. "You stay here with Harry, and don't tie up the telephone. I'll call home as soon as I know anything."

"Take care of yourself up there, okay?" Elliot murmured as Quinn picked up the skis and the rest of his equipment, including gloves and ski cap. "I don't say it a lot, but I love you, Dad."

"I love you, too, son." Quinn pulled him close and gave him a quick, rough hug. "I know what I'm doing. I'll be okay."

"Good luck," Harry said as Quinn went out the back door to get into his pickup truck.

"I'll need it," Quinn muttered. He waved, started the truck, and pulled out into the driveway.

Terry Meade was waiting with the Ski Patrol, the helicopter pilot, assorted law enforcement officials and the civil defense director and trying to field the news media gathered at Larry's Lodge.

"This is the area where we think they are," Terry said grimly, showing Quinn the map. "What you call Ironside peak, right? It's not in our patrol area, so we don't have anything to do with it officially. The helicopter tried and failed to get into the valley below it because of the wind. The trees are dense down there and visibility is limited by blowing snow. Our teams are going to start here," he pointed at various places on the map. "But this hill is a killer." He grinned at Quinn. "You cut your teeth on it when you were practicing for the Olympics all those years ago, and you've kept up your practice there. If anyone can ski it, you can."

"I'll get in. What then?"

"Send up a flare. I'm packing a cellular phone in with the other stuff you asked for. It's got a better range than our walkie-talkies. Everybody know what to do? Right. Let's go."

He led them out of the lodge. Quinn put on his goggles, tugged his ski cap over his head and thrust his hands into his gloves. He didn't even want to think about what he might have to look at if he was lucky enough to find the downed plane. He was having enough trouble living with what he'd said to Amanda the last time he'd talked to her.

He could still hear her voice, hear the hurt in it when he'd told her he didn't want her. Remembering that was like cutting open his heart. For her sake, he'd sent her away. He was a poor man. He had so little to offer such a famous, beautiful woman. At first, at the lodge, his pride had been cut to ribbons when he discovered who she was, and how she'd fooled him, how she'd deceived him. But her adoration had been real, and when his mind was functioning again, he realized that. He'd almost phoned her back, he'd even dialed the number. But her world was so different from his. He couldn't let her give up everything she'd worked all her life for, just to live in the middle of nowhere. She deserved so much more. He sighed wearily. If she died, the last conversation would haunt him until the day he died. He didn't think he could live with it. He didn't want to have to try. She had to be alive. Oh, dear God, she had to be!

## Chapter Nine

The sun was bright, and Quinn felt its warmth on his face as the helicopter set him down at the top of the mountain peak where the plane had last been sighted.

He was alone in the world when the chopper lifted off again. He checked his bindings one last time, adjusted the lightweight backpack and stared down the long mountainside with his ski poles restless in his hands. This particular slope wasn't skied as a rule. It wasn't even connected with the resort, which meant that the Ski Patrol didn't come here, and that the usual rescue toboggan posted on most slopes wouldn't be in evidence. He was totally on his own until he could find the downed plane. And he knew that while he was searching this untamed area, the Ski Patrol would be out in force on the regular slopes looking for the aircraft.

He sighed heavily as he stared down at the rugged, untouched terrain, which would be a beginning skier's nightmare. Well, it was now or never. Amanda was down there somewhere. He had to find her. He couldn't leave her there in the cold snow for all eternity.

He pulled down his goggles, suppressed his feelings and shoved the ski poles deep as he propelled himself down the slope. The first couple of minutes were tricky as he had to allow for the slight added weight of the backpack. But it took scant time to adjust, to balance his weight on the skis to compensate.

The wind bit his face, the snow flew over his dark ski suit as he wound down the slopes, his skis throwing up powdered snow in his wake. It brought back memories of the days when he'd maneuvered through the giant slalom in Alpine skiing competition. He'd been in the top one percent of his class, a daredevil skier with cold nerve and expert control on the slopes. This mountain was a killer, but it was one he knew like the back of his hand. He'd trained on this peak back in his early days of competition, loving the danger of skiing a slope where no one else came. Even for the past ten years or so, he'd honed his skill here every chance he got.

Quinn smiled to himself, his body leaning into the turns, not too far, the cutting edge of his skis breaking his speed as he maneuvered over boulders, down the fall line, around trees and broken branches or over them, whichever seemed more expedient.

His dark eyes narrowed as he defeated the obstacles. At least, thank God, he was able to do something instead of going through hell sitting at home waiting for word. That in itself was a blessing, even if it ended in the tragedy everyone seemed to think it would. He couldn't bear to imagine Amanda dead. He had to think positively. There were people who walked away from airplane crashes. He had to believe that she could be one of them. He had to keep thinking that or go mad.

He'd hoped against hope that when he got near the bottom of the hill, under those tall pines and the deadly updrafts and downdrafts that had defeated the helicopter's reconnoitering, that he'd find the airplane. But it wasn't there. He turned his skis sideways and skidded to a stop, looking around him. Maybe the observer had gotten his sighting wrong. Maybe it was another peak, maybe it was miles away. He bit his lower lip raw, tasting the lip balm he'd applied before he came onto the slope. If anyone on that plane was alive, time was going to make the difference. He had to find it quickly, or Amanda wouldn't have a prayer if she'd managed to survive the initial impact.

He started downhill again, his heartbeat increasing as the worry began to eat at him. On an impulse, he shot across the fall line, parallel to it for a little while before he maneuvered back and went down again in lazy S patterns. Something caught his attention. A sound. Voices!

He stopped to listen, turning his head. There was wind, and the sound of pines touching. But beyond it was a voice, carrying in the silence of nature. Snow blanketed most sound, making graveyard peace out of the mountain's spring noises.

Quinn adjusted his weight on the skis and lifted his hands to his mouth, the ski poles dangling from his wrists. "Hello! Where are you?" he shouted, taking a chance that the vibration of his voice wouldn't dislodge snow above him and bring a sheet of it down on him.

"Help!" voices called back. "We're here! We're here!"

He followed the sound, praying that he wasn't following an echo. But no, there, below the trees, he saw a glint of metal in the lowering sun. The plane! Thank God, there were survivors! Now if only Amanda was one of them . . .

He went the rest of the way down. As he drew closer, he saw men standing near the almost intact wreckage of the aircraft. One had a bandage around his head, another was nursing what looked like a broken arm. He saw one woman, but she wasn't blond. On the ground were two still forms, covered with coats. Covered up.

Please, God, no, he thought blindly. He drew to a stop.

"I'm Sutton. How many dead?" he asked the man who'd called to him, a burly man in a gray suit and white shirt and tie.

"Two," the man replied. "I'm Jeff Coleman, and I sure am glad to see you." He shook hands with Quinn. "I'm the pilot. We had a fire in the cockpit and it was all I could do to set her down at all. God, I feel bad! For some reason, three of the passengers had their seat belts off when we hit." He shook his head. "No hope for two of them. The third's concussed and looks comatose."

Quinn felt himself shaking inside as he asked the question he had to ask. "There was a singer aboard," he said. "Amanda Callaway."

"Yeah." The pilot shook his head and Quinn wanted to die, he wanted to stop breathing right there... "She's the concussion."

Quinn knew his hand shook as he pushed his goggles up over the black ski cap. "Where is she?" he asked huskily.

The pilot didn't ask questions or argue. He led Quinn past the two bodies and the dazed businessmen who were standing or sitting on fabric they'd taken from the plane, trying to keep warm.

"She's here," the pilot told him, indicating a makeshift stretcher constructed of branches and pillows from the cabin, and coats that covered the still body.

"Amanda," Quinn managed unsteadily. He knelt beside her. Her hair was in a coiled bun on her head. Her face was alabaster white, her eyes closed, long black lashes lying still on her cheekbones. Her mouth was as pale as the rest of her face, and there was a bruise high on her forehead at the right temple. He stripped off his glove and felt the artery at her neck. Her heart was still beating, but slowly and not very firmly. Unconscious. Dying, perhaps. "Oh, God," he breathed.

He got to his feet and unloaded the backpack as the pilot and two of the other men gathered around him.

"I've got a modular phone," Quinn said, "which I hope to God will work." He punched buttons and waited, his dark eyes narrowed, holding his breath.

It seemed to take forever. Then a voice, a recognizable voice, came over the wire. "Hello."

"Terry!" Quinn called. "It's Sutton. I've found them."

"Thank God!" Terry replied. "Okay, give me your position."

Quinn did, spreading out his laminated map to verify it, and then gave the report on casualties.

"Only one unconscious?" Terry asked again.

"Only one," Quinn replied heavily.

"We'll have to airlift you out, but we can't do it until the wind dies down. You understand, Quinn, the same downdrafts and updrafts that kept the chopper out this morning are going to keep it out now."

"Yes, I know, damn it," Quinn yelled. "But I've got to get her to a hospital. She's failing already."

Terry sighed. "And there you are without a rescue toboggan. Listen, what if I get Larry Hale down there?" he asked excitedly. "You know Larry; he was national champ in downhill a few years back, and he's a senior member of the Ski Patrol now. We could airdrop you the toboggan and some supplies for the rest of the survivors by plane. The two of you could tow her to a point accessible by chopper. Do you want to risk it, Quinn?"

"I don't know if she'll be alive in the morning, Terry," Quinn said somberly. "I'm more afraid to risk doing nothing than I am of towing her out. It's fairly level, if I remember right, all the way to the pass that leads from Caraway Ridge into Jackson Hole. The chopper might be able to fly down Jackson Hole and come in that way, without having to navigate the peaks. What do you think?"

"I think it's a good idea," Terry said. "If I remember right, they cleared that pass from the Ridge into Jackson Hole in the fall. It should still be accessible."

"No problem," Quinn said, his jaw grim. "If it isn't cleared, I'll clear it, by hand if necessary."

Terry chuckled softly. "Hale says he's already on the way. We'll get the plane up—hell of a pity he can't land where you are, but it's just too tricky. How about the other survivors?"

Quinn told him their conditions, along with the two bodies that would have to be airlifted out.

"Too bad," he replied. He paused for a minute to talk to somebody. "Listen, Quinn, if you can get the woman to Caraway Ridge, the chopper pilot thinks he can safely put down there. About the others, can they manage until morning if we drop the supplies?"

Quinn looked at the pilot. "Can you?"

"I ate snakes in Nam and Bill over there served in Antarctica." He grinned. "Between us, we can keep these pilgrims warm and even feed them. Sure, we'll be okay. Get that little lady out if you can."

"Amen," the man named Bill added, glancing at Amanda's still form. "I've heard her sing. It would be a crime against art to let her die."

Quinn lifted the cellular phone to his ear. "They say they can manage, Terry. Are you sure you can get them out in the morning?"

"If we have to send the snowplow in through the valley or send in a squad of snowmobiles and a horse-drawn sled, you'd better believe we'll get them out. The Ski Patrol is already working out the details."

"Okay."

Quinn unloaded his backpack. He had flares and matches, packets of high protein dehydrated food, the first-aid kit and some cans of sterno.

"Paradise," the pilot said, looking at the stores. "With that, I can prepare a seven-course meal, build a bonfire and make a house. But those supplies they're going to drop will come in handy, just the same."

Quinn smiled in spite of himself. "Okay."

"We can sure use this first-aid kit, but I've already set a broken arm and patched a few cuts. Before I became a pilot, I worked in the medical corps."

"I had rescue training when I was in the Ski Patrol," Quinn replied. He grinned at the pilot. "But if I ever come down in a plane, I hope you're on it."

"Thanks. I hope none of us ever come down again." He glanced at the two bodies. "God, I'm sorry about them." He glanced at Amanda. "I hope she makes it."

Quinn's jaw hardened. "She's a fighter," he said. "Let's hope she cares enough to try." He alone knew how defeated she'd probably felt when she left the lodge. He'd inflicted some terrible damage with his coldness. Pride had forced him to send her away, to deny his own happiness. Once he knew how famous and wealthy she was in her own right, he hadn't felt that he had the right to ask her to give it all up to live with him and Elliot in the wilds of Wyoming. He'd been doing what he thought was best for her. Now he only wanted her to live.

He took a deep breath. "Watch for the plane and Hale, will you? I'm going to sit with her."

"Sure." The pilot gave him a long look that he didn't see before he went back to talk to the other survivors.

Quinn sat down beside Amanda, reaching for one cold little hand under the coats that covered her. It was going to be a rough ride for her, and she didn't need any more jarring. But if they waited until morning, without medical help, she could die. It was much riskier to do nothing than it was to risk moving her. And down here in the valley, the snow was deep and fairly level. It would be like Nordic skiing; cross-country skiing. With luck, it would feel like a nice lazy sleigh ride to her.

"Listen to me, honey," he said softly. "We've got a long way to go before we get you out of here and to a hospital. You're going to have to hold on for a long time." His hand tightened around hers, warming it. "I'll be right with you every step of the way. I won't leave you for a second. But you have to do your part, Amanda. You have to fight to stay alive. I hope that you still want to live. If you don't, there's something I need to tell you. I sent you away not because I hated you, Amanda, but because I loved you so much. I loved you enough to let you go back to the life you needed. You've got to stay alive so that I can tell you that," he added, stopping because his voice broke.

He looked away, getting control back breath by breath. He thought he felt her fingers move, but he couldn't be sure. "I'm going to get you out of here, honey, one way or the other, even if I have to walk out with you in my arms. Try to hold on, for me." He brought her hand to his mouth and kissed the palm hungrily. "Try to hold on, because if you die, so do I.

I can't keep going unless you're somewhere in the world, even if I never see you again. Even if you hate me forever."

He swallowed hard and put down her hand. The sound of an airplane in the distance indicated that supplies were on the way. Quinn put Amanda's hand back under the cover and bent to brush his mouth against her cold, still one.

"I love you," he whispered roughly. "You've got to hold on until I can get you out of here."

He stood, his face like the stony crags above them, his eyes glittering as he joined the others.

The plane circled and seconds later, a white parachute appeared. Quinn held his breath as it descended, hoping against hope that the chute wouldn't hang up in the tall trees and that the toboggan would soft-land so that it was usable. A drop in this kind of wind was risky at best.

But luck was with them. The supplies and the sled made it in one piece. Quinn and the pilot and a couple of the sturdier survivors unfastened the chute and brought the contents back to the wreckage of the commuter plane. The sled was even equipped with blankets and a pillow and straps to keep Amanda secured.

Minutes later, the drone of a helicopter whispered on the wind, and not long after that, Hale started down the mountainside.

It took several minutes. Quinn saw the flash of rust that denoted the distinctive jacket and white waist pack of the Ski Patrol above, and when Hale came closer, he could see the gold cross on the right pocket of the jacket—a duplicate of the big one stenciled on the jacket's back. He smiled, remembering when he'd worn that same type of jacket during a brief stint as a ski patrolman. It was a special kind of occupation, and countless skiers owed their lives to those brave men and women. The National Ski Patrol had only existed since 1938. It was created by Charles Dole of Connecticut, after a skiing accident that took the life of one of his friends. Today, the Ski Patrol had over 10,000 members nationally, of whom ninety-eight percent were volunteers. They were the first on the slopes and the last off, patroling for dangerous areas and rescuing injured people. Quinn had once been part of that elite group and he still had the greatest respect for them.

Hale was the only color against the whiteness of the snow. The sun was out, and thank God it hadn't snowed all day. It had done enough of that last night.

Quinn's nerves were stretched. He hadn't had a cigarette since he'd arrived at the lodge, and he didn't dare have one now. Nicotine and caffeine tended to constrict blood vessels, and the cold was dangerous enough without giving it any help. Experienced skiers knew better than to stack the odds against themselves.

"Well, I made it." Hale grinned, getting his breath. "How are you, Quinn?" He extended a hand and Quinn shook it.

The man in the Ski Patrol jacket nodded to the others, accepted their thanks for the supplies he'd brought with him, which included a makeshift shelter and plenty of food and water and even a bottle of cognac. But he didn't waste time. "We'd better get

moving if we hope to get Miss Callaway out of here by
dark."

"She's over here," Quinn said. "God, I hate doing
this," he added heavily when he and Hale were standing over the unconscious woman. "If there was any
hope, any at all, that the chopper could get in here..."

"You can feel the wind for yourself," Hale replied,
his eyes solemn. "We're the only chance she has. We'll
get her to the chopper. Piece of cake," he added with
a reassuring smile.

"I hope so," Quinn said somberly. He bent and
nodded to Hale. They lifted her very gently onto the
long sled containing the litter. It had handles on both
ends, because it was designed to be towed. They attached the towlines, covered Amanda carefully and set
out, with reassurances from the stranded survivors.

There was no time to talk. The track was fairly
straightforward, but it worried Quinn, all the same,
because there were crusts that jarred the woman on the
litter. He towed, Hale guided, their rhythms matching perfectly as they made their way down the snow-
covered valley. Around them, the wind sang through
the tall firs and lodgepole pines, and Quinn thought
about the old trappers and mountain men who must
have come through this valley a hundred, two hundred years before. In those days of poor sanitation and
even poorer medicine, Amanda wouldn't have stood
a chance.

He forced himself not to look back. He had to concentrate on getting her to the Ridge. All that was important now, was that she get medical help while it
could still do her some good. He hadn't come all this
way to find her alive, only to lose her.

It seemed to take forever. Once Quinn was certain that they'd lost their way as they navigated through the narrow pass that led to the fifty-mile valley between the Grand Tetons and the Wind River Range, an area known as Jackson Hole. But he recognized landmarks as they went along, and eventually they wound their way around the trees and along the sparkling river until they reached the flats below Caraway Ridge.

Quinn and Hale were both breathing hard by now. They'd changed places several times, so that neither got too tired of towing the toboggan, and they were both in peak condition. But it was still a difficult thing to do.

They rested, and Quinn reached down to check Amanda's pulse. It was still there, and even seemed to be, incredibly, a little stronger than it had been. But she was pale and still and Quinn felt his spirits sink as he looked down at her.

"There it is," Hale called, sweeping his arm over the ridge. "The chopper."

"Now if only it can land," Quinn said quietly, and he began to pray.

The chopper came lower and lower, then it seemed to shoot up again and Quinn bit off a hard word. But the pilot corrected for the wind, which was dying down, and eased the helicopter toward the ground. It seemed to settle inch by inch until it landed safe. The pilot was out of it before the blades stopped.

"Let's get out of here," he called to the men. "If that wind catches up again, I wouldn't give us a chance in hell of getting out. It was a miracle that I even got in!"

Quinn released his bindings in a flash, leaving his skis and poles for Hale to carry, along with his own. He got one side of the stretcher while the pilot, fortunately no lightweight himself, got the other. They put the stretcher in the back of the broad helicopter, on the floor, and Quinn and Hale piled in—Hale in the passenger seat up front, Quinn behind with Amanda, carefully laying ski equipment beside her.

"Let's go!" the pilot called as he revved up the engine.

It was touch and go. The wind decided to play tag with them, and they almost went into a lodgepole pine on the way up. But the pilot was a tenacious man with good nerves. He eased down and then up, down and up until he caught the wind off guard and shot up out of the valley and over the mountain.

Quinn reached down and clasped Amanda's cold hand in his. Only a little longer, honey, he thought, watching her with his heart in his eyes. Only a little longer, for God's sake, hold on!

It was the longest ride of his entire life. He spared one thought for the people who'd stayed behind to give Amanda her chance and he prayed that they'd be rescued without any further injuries. Then his eyes settled on her pale face and stayed there until the helicopter landed on the hospital lawn.

The reporters, local, state and national, had gotten word of the rescue mission. They were waiting. Police kept them back just long enough for Amanda to be carried into the hospital, but Quinn and Hale were caught. Quinn volunteered Hale to give an account of the rescue and then he ducked out, leaving the other man to field the enthusiastic audience while he trailed quickly behind the men who'd taken Amanda into the emergency room.

He drank coffee and smoked cigarettes and glared at walls for over an hour until someone came out to talk to him. Hale had to go back to the lodge, to help plan the rescue of the rest of the survivors, but he promised to keep in touch. After he'd gone, Quinn felt even more alone. But at last a doctor came into the waiting room, and approached him.

"Are you related to Miss Callaway?" the doctor asked with narrowed eyes.

Quinn knew that if he said no, he'd have to wait for news of her condition until he could find somebody who was related to her, and he had no idea how to find her aunt.

"I'm her fiancé," he said without moving a muscle in his face. "How is she?"

"Not good," the doctor, a small wiry man, said bluntly. "But I believe in miracles. We have her in intensive care, where she'll stay until she regains consciousness. She's badly concussed. I gather she hasn't regained consciousness since the crash?" Quinn shook his head. "That sleigh ride and helicopter lift didn't do any good, either," he added firmly, adding when he saw the expression on Quinn's tormented face, "but I can understand the necessity for it. Go get some sleep. Come back in the morning. We won't know anything until then. Maybe not until much later. Concussion is tricky. We can't predict the outcome, as much as we'd like to."

"I can't rest," Quinn said quietly. "I'll sit out here and drink coffee, if you don't mind. If this is as close to her as I can get, it'll have to do."

The doctor took a slow breath. "We keep spare beds in cases like this," he said. "I'll have one made up for you when you can't stay awake any longer." He smiled faintly. "Try to think positively. It isn't medical, exactly, but sometimes it works wonders. Prayer doesn't hurt, either."

"Thank you," Quinn said.

The doctor shrugged. "Wait until she wakes up. Good night."

Quinn watched him go and sighed. He didn't know what to do next. He phoned Terry at the lodge to see if Amanda's band had called. Someone named Jerry and a man called Hank had been phoning every few minutes, he was told. Quinn asked for a phone number and Terry gave it to him.

He dialed the area code. California, he figured as he waited for it to ring.

"Hello?"

"This is Quinn Sutton," he began.

"Yes, I recognize your voice. It's Hank here. How is she?"

"Concussion. Coma, I guess. She's in intensive care and she's still alive. That's about all I know."

There was a long pause. "I'd hoped for a little more than that."

"So had I," Quinn replied. He hesitated. "I'll phone you in the morning. The minute I know anything. Is there anybody we should notify...her aunt?"

"Her aunt is a scatterbrain and no help at all. Anyway, she's off with Blalock Durning in the Bahamas on one of those incommunicado islands. We couldn't reach her if we tried."

"Is there anybody else?" Quinn asked.

"Not that I know of." There was a brief pause. "I feel bad about the way things happened. I hate planes, you know. That's why the rest of us went by bus. We stopped here in some hick town to make sure Amanda got her plane, and Terry told us what happened. We got a motel room and we're waiting for a bus back to Jackson. It will probably be late tomorrow before we get there. We've already canceled the gig. We can't do it without Amanda.

"I'll book a room for you," Quinn said.

"Make it a suite," Hank replied, "and if you need anything, you know, anything, you just tell us."

"I've got plenty of cigarettes and the coffee machine's working. I'm fine."

"We'll see you when we get there. And Sutton— thanks. She really cares about you, you know?"

"I care about her," he said stiffly. "That's why I sent her away. My God, how could she give all that up to live on a mountain in Wyoming?"

"Amanda's not a city girl, though," Hank said slowly. "And she changed after those days she spent with you. Her heart wasn't with us anymore. She cried all last night..."

"Oh, God, don't," Quinn said.

"Sorry, man," Hank said quietly. "I'm really sorry, that's the last thing I should have said. Look, go smoke a cigarette. I think I'll tie one on royally and have the boys put me to bed. Tomorrow we'll talk. Take care."

"You, too."

Quinn hung up. He couldn't bear to think of Amanda crying because of what he'd done to her. He might lose her even yet, and he didn't know how he was going to go on living. He felt so alone.

He was out of change after he called the lodge and booked the suite for Hank and the others, but he still had to talk to Elliot and Harry. He dialed the operator and called collect. Elliot answered the phone immediately.

"How is she?" he asked quickly.

Quinn went over it again, feeling numb. "I wish I knew more," he concluded. "But that's all there is."

"She can't die," Elliot said miserably. "Dad, she just can't!"

"Say a prayer, son," he replied. "And don't let Harry teach you any bad habits while I'm gone."

"No, sir, I won't," Elliot said with a feeble attempt at humor. "You're going to stay, I guess?"

"I have to," Quinn said huskily. He hesitated. "I love her."

"So do I," Elliot said softly. "Bring her back when you come."

"If I can. If she'll even speak to me when she wakes up," Quinn said with a total lack of confidence.

"She will," Elliot told him. "You should have listened to some of those songs you thought were so horrible. One of hers won a Grammy. It was all about having to give up things we love to keep from hurting them. She always seemed to feel it when somebody was sad or hurt, you know. And she risked her own life trying to save that girl at the concert. She's not someone who thinks about getting even with people. She's got too much heart."

Quinn drew deeply from his cigarette. "I hope so, son," he said. "You get to bed. I'll call you tomorrow."

"Okay. Take care of yourself. Love you, Dad."

"Me, too, son," Quinn replied. He hung up. The waiting area was deserted now, and the hospital seemed to have gone to sleep. He sat down with his Styrofoam cup of black coffee and finished his cigarette. The room looked like he felt—empty.

# Chapter Ten

It was late morning when the nurse came to shake Quinn gently awake. Apparently around dawn he'd gone to sleep sitting up, with an empty coffee cup in his hand. He thought he'd never sleep at all.

He sat up, drowsy and disheveled. "How is Amanda?" he asked immediately.

The nurse, a young blonde, smiled at him. "She's awake and asking for you."

"Oh, thank God," he said heavily. He got quickly to his feet, still a little groggy, and followed her down to the intensive-care unit, where patients in tiny rooms were monitored from a central nurses' station and the hum and click and whir of life-supporting machinery filled the air. If she was asking for him, she must not hate him too much. That thought sustained him as he followed the nurse into one of the small cubicles where Amanda lay.

Amanda looked thinner than ever in the light, her face pinched, her eyes hollow, her lips chapped. They'd taken her hair down somewhere along the way and tied it back with a pink ribbon. She was propped up in bed, still with the IV in position, but she'd been taken off all the other machines.

She looked up and saw Quinn and all the weariness and pain went out of her face. She brightened, became beautiful despite her injuries, her eyes sparkling. Her last thought when she'd realized in the plane what was going to happen had been of Quinn. Her first thought when she'd regained consciousness had been of him. The pain, the grief of having him turn away from her was forgotten. He was here, now, and that meant he had to care about her.

"Oh, Quinn!" she whispered tearfully, and held out her arms.

He went to her without hesitation, ignoring the nurses, the aides, the whole world. His arms folded gently around her, careful of the tubes attached to her hand, and his head bent over hers, his cheek on her soft hair, his eyes closed as he shivered with reaction. She was alive. She was going to live. He felt as if he were going to choke to death on his own rush of feeling.

"My God," he whispered shakily. "I thought I'd lost you."

That was worth it all, she thought, dazed from the emotion in his voice, at the tremor in his powerful body as he held her. She clung to him, her slender arms around his neck, drowning in pleasure. She'd wondered if he hadn't sent her away in a misguided belief that it was for her own good. Now she was sure of it. He couldn't have looked that haggard, that terrible, unless she mattered very much to him. Her aching heart soared. "They said you brought me out."

"Hale and I did," he said huskily. He lifted his head, searching her bright eyes slowly. "It's been the longest night of my life. They said you might die."

"Oh, we Callaways are tough birds," she said, wiping away a tear. She was still weak and sore and her headache hadn't completely gone away. "You look terrible, my darling," she whispered on a choked laugh.

The endearment fired his blood. He had to take a deep breath before he could even speak. His fingers linked with hers. "I felt pretty terrible when we listened to the news report, especially when I remembered the things I said to you." He took a deep breath. "I didn't know if you'd hate me for the rest of your life, but even if you did, I couldn't just sit on my mountain and let other people look for you." His thumb gently stroked the back of her pale hand. "How do you feel, honey?"

"Pretty bad. But considering it all, I'll do. I'm sorry about the men who died. One of them was having a heart attack," she explained. "The other gentleman who was sitting with him alerted me. We both unfastened our seat belts to try and give CPR. Just after I got up, the plane started down," she said. "Quinn, do you believe in predestination?"

"You mean, that things happen the way they're meant to in spite of us?" He smiled. "I guess I do." His dark eyes slid over her face hungrily. "I'm so glad it wasn't your time, Amanda."

"So am I." She reached up and touched his thin mouth with just the tips of her fingers. "Where is it?" she asked with an impish smile as a sudden delicious thought occurred to her.

He frowned. "Where's what?"

"My engagement ring," she said. "And don't try to back out of it," she added firmly when he stood there looking shocked. "You told the doctor and the whole medical staff that I was your fiancée, and you're not ducking out of it now. You're going to marry me."

His eyebrows shot up. "I'm what?" he said blankly.

"You're going to marry me. Where's Hank? Has anybody phoned him?"

"I did. I was supposed to call him back." He checked his watch and grimaced. "I guess it's too late now. He and the band are on the way back here."

"Good. They're twice your size and at least as mean." Her eyes narrowed. "I'll tell them you seduced me. I could be pregnant." She nodded, thinking up lies fast while Quinn's face mirrored his stark astonishment. "That's right, I could."

"You could not," he said shortly. "I never ...!"

"But you're going to," she said with a husky laugh. "Just wait until I get out of here and get you alone. I'll wrestle you down and start kissing you, and you'll never get away in time."

"Oh, God," he groaned, because he knew she was right. He couldn't resist her that way, it was part of the problem.

"So you'll have to marry me first," she continued. "Because I'm not that kind of girl. Not to mention that you aren't that kind of guy. Harry likes me and Elliot and I are already friends, and I could even get used to McNaber if he'll move those traps.'' She pursed her lips, thinking. ''The concert tour is going to be a real drag, but once it's over, I'll retire from the stage and just make records and tapes and CDs with the guys. Maybe a video now and again. They'll like that, too. We're all basically shy and we don't like live shows. I'll compose songs. I can do that at the house, in between helping Harry with the cooking and looking after sick calves, and having babies,'' she added with a shy smile.

He wanted to sit down. He hadn't counted on this. All that had mattered at the time was getting her away from the wreckage and into a hospital where she could be cared for. He hadn't let himself think ahead. But she obviously had. His head spun with her plans.

''Listen, you're an entertainer,'' he began. His fingers curled around hers and he looked down at them with a hard, grim sigh. ''Amanda, I'm a poor man. All I've got is a broken-down ranch in the middle of nowhere. You'd have a lot of hardships, because I won't live on your money. I've got a son, even if he isn't mine, and...''

She brought his hand to her cheek and held it there, nuzzling her cheek against it as she looked up at him with dark, soft, adoring eyes. ''I love you,'' she whispered.

He faltered. His cheeks went ruddy as the words penetrated, touched him, excited him. Except for his mother and Elliot, nobody had ever said that to him before Amanda had. ''Do you?'' he asked huskily. ''Still? Even after the way I walked off and left you there at the lodge that night? After what I said to you on the phone?'' he added, because he'd had too much time to agonize over his behavior, even if it had been for what he thought was her own good.

"Even after that," she said gently. "With all my heart. I just want to live with you, Quinn. In the wilds of Wyoming, in a grass shack on some island, in a mansion in Beverly Hills—it would all be the same to me—as long as you loved me back and we could be together for the rest of our lives."

He felt a ripple of pure delight go through him. "Is that what you really want?" he asked, searching her dark eyes with his own.

"More than anything else in the world," she confessed. "That's why I couldn't tell you who and what I really was. I loved you so much, and I knew you wouldn't want me..." Her voice trailed off.

"I want you, all right," he said curtly. "I never stopped. Damn it, woman, I was trying to do what was best for you!"

"By turning me out in the cold and leaving me to starve to death for love?" she asked icily. "Thanks a bunch!"

He looked away uncomfortably. "It wasn't that way and you know it. I thought maybe it was the novelty. You know, a lonely man in the backwoods," he began.

"You thought I was having the time of my life playing you for a fool," she said. Her head was beginning to hurt, but she had to wrap it all up before she gave in and asked for some more medication. "Well, you listen to me, Quinn Sutton, I'm not the type to go around deliberately trying to hurt people. All I ever wanted was somebody to care about me—just me, not the pretty girl on the stage."

"Yes, I know that now," he replied. He brought her hand to his mouth and softly kissed the palm. The look on his face weakened her. "So you want a ring, do you? It will have to be something sensible. No flashy diamonds, even if I could give you something you'd need sunglasses to look at."

"I'll settle for the paper band on a King Edward cigar if you'll just marry me," she replied.

"I think I can do a little better than that," he murmured dryly. He bent over her, his lips hovering just above hers. "And no long engagement," he whispered.

"It takes three days, doesn't it?" she whispered back. "That *is* a long engagement. Get busy!"

He stifled a laugh as he brushed his hard mouth gently over her dry one. "Get well," he whispered. "I'll read some books real fast."

She colored when she realized what kind of books he was referring to, and then smiled under his tender kiss. "You do that," she breathed. "Oh, Quinn, get me out of here!"

"At the earliest possible minute," he promised.

The band showed up later in the day while Quinn was out buying an engagement ring for Amanda. He'd already called and laughingly told Elliot and Harry what she'd done to him, and was delighted with Elliot's pleasure in the news and Harry's teasing. He did buy her a diamond, even if it was a moderate one, and a gold band for each of them. It gave him the greatest kind of thrill to know that he was finally marrying for all the right reasons.

When he got back to the hospital, the rest of the survivors had been airlifted out and all but one of them had been treated and released. The news media had tried to get to Amanda, but the band arrived shortly after Quinn left and ran interference. Hank gave out a statement and stopped them. The road manager, as Quinn found out, had gone on to San Francisco to make arrangements for canceling the concert.

The boys were gathered around Amanda, who'd been moved into a nice private room. She was sitting up in bed, looking much better, and her laughing dark eyes met Quinn's the minute he came in the door.

"Hank brought a shotgun," she informed him. "And Deke and Johnson and Jack are going to help you down the aisle. Jerry's found a minister, and Hank's already arranged a blood test for you right down the hall. The license—"

"Is already applied for," Quinn said with a chuckle. "I did that myself. Hello, boys," he greeted them, shaking hands as he was introduced to the rest of the band. "And you can unload the shotgun. I'd planned to hold it on Amanda, if she tried to back out."

"Me, back out? Heaven forbid!" she exclaimed, smiling as Quinn bent to kiss her. "Where's my ring?" she whispered against his hard mouth. "I want it on, so these nurses won't make eyes at you. There's this gorgeous redhead . . ."

"I can't see past you, pretty thing," he murmured, his eyes soft and quiet in a still-gaunt face. "Here it is." Quinn produced it and slid it on her finger. He'd measured the size with a small piece of paper he'd wrapped around her finger, and he hoped that the method worked. He needn't have worried, because the ring was a perfect fit, and she acted as if it were the three-carat monster he'd wanted to get her. Her face lit up, like her pretty eyes, and she beamed as she showed it to the band.

"Did you sleep at all?" Hank asked him while the others gathered around Amanda.

"About an hour, I think," Quinn murmured dryly. "You?"

"I couldn't even get properly drunk," Hank said, sighing, "so the boys and I played cards until we caught the bus. We slept most of the way in. It was a long ride. From what I hear," he added with a level look, "you and that Hale fellow had an even longer one, bringing Amanda out of the mountains."

"You'll never know." Quinn looked past him to Amanda, his dark eyes full of remembered pain. "I had to decide whether or not to move her. I thought it was riskier to leave her there until the next morning. If we'd waited, we had no guarantee that the helicopter would have been able to land even then. She could have died. It's a miracle she didn't."

"Miracles come in all shapes and sizes," Hank mused, staring at her. "She's been ours. Without her, we'd never have gotten anywhere. But being on the road has worn her out. The boys and I were talking on the way back about cutting out personal appearances and concentrating on videos and albums. I think Amanda might like that. She'll have enough to do from now on, I imagine, taking care of you and your boy," he added with a grin. "Not to mention all those new brothers and sisters you'll be adding. I grew up on a ranch," he said surprisingly. "I have five brothers."

Quinn's eyebrows lifted. "Are they all runts like you?" he asked with a smile.

"I'm the runt," Hank corrected.

Quinn just shook his head.

Amanda was released from the hospital two days later. Every conceivable test had been done, and fortunately there were no complications. The doctor had been cautiously optimistic at first, but her recovery was rapid—probably due, the doctor said with a smile, to her incentive. He gave Amanda away at the brief ceremony, held in the hospital's chapel just before she was discharged, and one of the nurses was her matron of honor. There were a record four best men; the band. But for all its brevity and informality, it was a ceremony that Amanda would never forget. The Methodist minister who performed it had a way with words, and Amanda and Quinn felt just as married as if they'd had the service performed in a huge church with a large crowd present.

The only mishap was that the press found out about the wedding, and Amanda and Quinn and the band were mobbed as they made their way out of the hospital afterward. The size of the band members made them keep well back. Hank gave them his best wildman glare while Jack whispered something about the bandleader becoming homicidal if he was pushed too far. They escaped in two separate cars. The driver of the one taking Quinn and Amanda to the lodge managed to get them there over back roads, so that nobody knew where they were.

Terry had given them the bridal suite, on the top floor of the lodge, and the view of the snowcapped mountains was exquisite. Amanda, still a little shaky and very nervous, stared out at them with mixed feelings.

"I don't know if I'll ever think of them as postcards again," she remarked to Quinn, who was trying to find places to put everything from their suitcase. He'd had to go to Ricochet for his suit and a change of clothing.

"What, the mountains?" he asked, smiling at her. "Well, it's not a bad thing to respect them. But airplanes don't crash that often, and when you're well enough, I'm going to teach you to ski."

She turned and looked at him for a long time. Her wedding outfit was an off-white, a very simple shirtwaist dress with a soft collar and no frills. But with her long hair around her shoulders and down to her waist, framed in the light coming through the window, she looked the picture of a bride. Quinn watched her back and sighed, his eyes lingering on the small sprig of lily of the valley she was wearing in her hair—a present from a member of the hospital staff.

"One of the nurses brought me a newspaper," Amanda said. "It told all about how you and Mr. Hale got me out." She hesitated. "They said that only a few men could ski that particular mountain without killing themselves."

"I've been skiing it for years," he said simply. He took off the dark jacket of his suit and loosened his tie with a long sigh. "I knew that the Ski Patrol would get you out, but they usually only work the lodge slopes—you know, the ones with normal ski runs. The peak the plane landed on was off the lodge property and out-of-the-way. It hadn't even been inspected. There are all sorts of dangers on slopes like that—fallen trees, boulders, stumps, debris, not to mention the threat of avalanche. The Ski Patrol marks dangerous runs where they work. They're the first out in the morning and the last off the slopes in the afternoon."

"You seem to know a lot about it," Amanda said.

"I used to be one of them," he replied with a grin. "In my younger days. It's pretty rewarding."

"There was a jacket Harry showed me," she frowned. "A rust-colored one with a big gold cross on the back..."

"My old patrol jacket." He chuckled. "I wouldn't part with it for the world. If I'd thought of it, I'd have worn it that day." His eyes darkened as he looked at her. "Thank God I knew that slope," he said huskily. "Because I'd bet money that you wouldn't have lasted on that mountain overnight."

"I was thinking about you when the plane went down," she confessed. "I wasn't sure that I'd ever see you again."

"Neither was I when I finally got to you." He took off his tie and threw it aside. His hand absently unfastened the top buttons of his white shirt as he moved toward her. "I was trying so hard to do the right thing," he murmured. "I didn't think I could give you what you needed, what you were used to."

"I'm used to you, Mr. Sutton," she murmured with a smile. Amanda slid her arms under his and around him, looking up at him with her whole heart in her dark eyes. "Bad temper, irritable scowl and all. Anything you can't give me, I don't want. Will that do?"

His broad chest rose and fell slowly. "I can't give you much. I've lost damned near everything."

"You have Elliot and Harry and me," she pointed out. "And some fat, healthy calves, and in a few years, Elliot will have a lot of little brothers and sisters to help him on the ranch."

A faint dusky color stained his high cheekbones. "Yes."

"Why, Mr. Sutton, honey, you aren't shy, are you?" she whispered dryly as she moved her hands back around to his shirt and finished unbuttoning it down his tanned, hair-roughened chest.

"Of course I'm shy," he muttered, heating up at the feel of her slender hands on his skin. He caught his breath and shuddered when she kissed him there. His big hands slid into her long, silky hair and brought her even closer. "I like that," he breathed roughly. "Oh, God, I love it!"

She drew back after a minute, her eyes sultry, drowsy. "Wouldn't you like to do that to me?" she whispered. "I like it, too."

He fumbled with buttons until he had the dress out of the way and she was standing in nothing except a satin teddy. He'd never seen one before, except in movies, and he stared at her with his breath stuck somewhere in his chest. It was such a sexy garment low on her lace-covered breasts, nipped at her slender waist, hugging her full hips. Below it were her elegant silk-clad legs, although he didn't see anything holding up her hose.

"It's a teddy," she whispered. "If you want to slide it down," she added shyly, lowering her eyes to his pulsating chest, "I could step out of it."

He didn't know if he could do that and stay on his feet. The thought of Amanda unclothed made his knees weak. But he slid the straps down her arms and slowly, slowly, peeled it away from her firm, hard-tipped breasts, over her flat stomach, and then over the panty hose she was wearing. He caught them as well and eased the whole silky mass down to the floor.

She stepped out of it, so much in love with him that all her earlier shyness was evaporating. It was as new for him as it was for her, and that made it beautiful. A true act of love.

She let him look at her, fascinated by the awe in his hard face, in the eyes that went over her like an artist's brush, capturing every line, every soft curve before he even touched her.

"Amanda, you're the most beautiful creature I've ever seen," he said finally. "You look like a drawing of a fairy I saw in an old-time storybook...all gold and ivory."

She reached up and leaned close against him, shivering a little when her breasts touched his bare chest. The hair was faintly abrasive and very arousing. She moved involuntarily and gasped at the sensation.

"Do you want to help me?" he whispered as he stripped off his shirt and his hands went to his belt.

"I . . ." She hesitated, her nerve retreating suddenly at the intimacy of it. She grimaced. "Oh, Quinn, I'm such a coward!" She hid her face against his chest and felt his laughter.

"Well, you're not alone," he murmured. "I'm not exactly an exhibitionist myself. Look, why don't you get under the covers and close your eyes, and we'll pretend it's dark."

She looked up at him and laughed. "This is silly."

"Yes, I know." He sighed. "Well, honey, we're married. I guess it's time to face all the implications of sharing a bed."

He sat down, took off his boots and socks, stood to unbuckle his belt, holding her eyes, and slid the zip down. Everything came off, and seconds later, she saw for herself all the differences between men and women.

"You've gone scarlet, Mrs. Sutton," he observed.

"You aren't much whiter yourself, Mr. Sutton," she replied.

He laughed and reached for her and she felt him press against her. It was incredible, the feel of skin against skin, hair-rough flesh against silky softness. He bent and found her mouth and began to kiss her lazily, while his big, rough hands slid down her back and around to her hips. His mouth opened at the same time that his fingers pulled her thighs against his, and she felt for the first time the stark reality of arousal.

He felt her gasp and lifted his head, searching her flushed face. "That has to happen before anything else can," he whispered. "Don't be afraid. I think I know enough to make it easy for you."

"I love you, Quinn," she whispered back, forcing her taut muscles to relax, to give in to him. She leaned her body into his with a tiny shiver and lifted her mouth. "However it happens between us, it will be all right."

He searched her eyes and nodded. His mouth lowered to hers. He kissed her with exquisite tenderness while his hands found the softness of her breasts. Minutes later, his mouth traced them, covered the hard tips in a warm, moist suction that drew new sounds from her. He liked that, so he lifted her and put her on the big bed, and found other places to kiss her that made the sounds louder and more tormented.

The book had been very thorough and quite explicit, so he knew what to do in theory. Practice was very different. He hadn't known that women could lose control, too. That their bodies were so soft, or so strong. That their eyes grew wild and their faces contorted as the pleasure built in them, that they wept with it. Her pleasure became his only goal in the long, exquisite oblivion that followed.

By the time he moved over her, she was more than ready for him, she was desperate for him. He whispered to her, gently guided her body to his as he fought for control of his own raging need so that he could satisfy hers first.

There was one instant when she stiffened and tried to pull away, but he stopped then and looked down into her frightened eyes.

"It will only hurt for a few seconds," he whispered huskily. "Link your hands in mine and hold on. I'll do it quickly."

"All . . . all right." She felt the strength in his hands and her eyes met his. She swallowed.

He pushed, hard. She moaned a little, but her body accepted him instantly and without any further difficulty.

Her eyes brightened. Her lips parted and she breathed quickly and began to smile. "It's gone," she whispered. "Quinn, I'm a woman now. . . ."

"My woman," he whispered back. The darkness grew in his eyes. He bent to her mouth and captured it, held it as he began to move, his body dancing above

hers, teaching it the rhythm. She followed where he
led, gasping as the cadence increased, as the music
began to grow in her mind and filtered through her
arms and legs. She held on to him with the last of her
strength, proud of his stamina, of the power in his
body that was taking hers from reality and into a place
she'd never dreamed existed.

She felt the first tremors begin, and work into her
like fiery pins, holding her body in a painful arch as
she felt the tension build. It grew to unbearable lev-
els. Her head thrashed on the pillow and she wanted
to push him away, to make him stop, because she
didn't think she could live through what was happening to her. But just as she began to push him the tension broke and she fell, crying out, into a hot, wild
satisfaction that convulsed her. Above her, Quinn saw
it happen and finally gave in to the desperate fever of
his own need. He drove for his own satisfaction and
felt it take him, his voice breaking on Amanda's name
as he went into the fiery depths with her.

Afterward, he started to draw away, but her arms
went around him and refused to let go. He felt her
tears against his hot throat.

"Are you all right?" he asked huskily.

"I died," she whispered brokenly. Her arms contracted. "Don't go away, please don't. I don't want to
let you go," she moaned.

He let his body relax, giving her his full weight. "I'll
crush you, honey," he whispered in her ear.

"No, you won't." She sighed, feeling his body pulse
with every heartbeat, feeling the dampness of his skin
on her own, the glory of his flesh touching hers. "This
is nice."

He laughed despite his exhaustion. "There's a new word for it," he murmured. He growled and bit her shoulder gently. "Wildcat," he whispered proudly. "You bit me. Do you remember? You bit me and dug your nails into my hips and screamed."

"So did you," she accused, flushing. "I'll have bruises on my thighs..."

"Little ones," he agreed. He lifted his head and searched her dark, quiet eyes. "I couldn't help that, at the last. I lost it. Really lost it. Are you as sated as I am?" he mused. "I feel like I've been walking around like half a person all my life, and I've just become whole."

"So do I." Her eyes searched his, and she lifted a lazy hand to trace his hard, thin lips. After a few seconds, she lifted her hips where they were still joined to his and watched his eyes kindle. She drew in a shaky breath and did it again, delighting in the sudden helpless response of his body.

"That's impossible," he joked. "The book said so."

Amanda pulled his mouth down to hers. "Damn the book," she said and held on as he answered her hunger with his own.

They slept and finally woke just in time to go down to dinner. But since neither of them wanted to face having to get dressed, they had room service send up a tray. They drank champagne and ate thick steaks and went back to bed. Eventually they even slept.

The next morning, they set out for Ricochet, holding hands all the way home.

## Chapter Eleven

Elliot and Harry were waiting at the door when Quinn brought Amanda home. There was a big wedding cake on the table that Harry had made, and a special present that Elliot had made Harry drive him to town in the sleigh to get—a new Desperado album with a picture of Amanda on the cover.

"What a present," Quinn murmured, smiling at Amanda over the beautiful photograph. "I guess I'll have to listen to it now, won't I?"

"I even got Hank Shoeman's autograph," Elliot enthused. "Finally I can tell the guys at school! I've been going nuts ever since I realized who Amanda was...."

"You knew?" Quinn burst out. "And you didn't tell me? So that's why that tape disappeared."

"You were looking for it?" Elliot echoed.

"Sure, just after we got home from the lodge that night I deserted Amanda," Quinn said with a rueful glance at her. "I was feeling pretty low. I just wanted to hear her voice, but the tape was missing."

"Sorry, Dad," Elliot said gently. "I'll never do it again, but I was afraid you'd toss her out if you knew she was a rock singer. She's really terrific, you know, and that song that won a Grammy was one of hers."

"Stop, you'll make me blush," Amanda groaned.

"I can do that," Quinn murmured dryly and the look he gave Amanda brought scarlet color into her hot cheeks.

"You were in the paper, Dad," Elliot continued excitedly. "And on the six o'clock news, too! They told all about your skiing days and the Olympic team. Dad, why didn't you keep going? They said you were one of the best giant slalom skiers this country ever produced, but that you quit with a place on the Olympic team in your pocket."

"It's a long story, Elliot," he replied.

"It was because of my mother, wasn't it?" the boy asked gravely.

"Well, you were on the way and I didn't feel right about deserting her at such a time."

"Even though she'd been so terrible to you?" he probed.

Quinn put his hands on his son's shoulders. "I'll tell you for a fact, Elliot, you were mine from the day I knew about your existence. I waited for you like a kid waiting for a Christmas present. I bought stuff and read books about babies and learned all the things I'd need to know to help your mother raise you. I'd figured, you see, that she might eventually decide that having you was pretty special. I'm sorry that she didn't.'

"That's okay," Elliot said with a smile. "You did."

"You bet I did. And do."

"Since you like kids so much, you and Amanda might have a few of your own," Elliot decided. "I can help. Me and Harry can wash diapers and make formula..."

Amanda laughed delightedly. "Oh, you doll, you!" She hugged Elliot. "Would you really not mind other kids around?"

"Heck, no," Elliot said with genuine feeling. "All the other guys have little brothers and sisters. It gets sort of lonely, being the only one." He looked up at her admiringly. "And they'd be awful pretty, if some of them were girls."

She grinned. "Maybe we'll get lucky and have another redhead, too. My mother was redheaded. So was my grandmother. It runs in the family."

Elliot liked that, and said so.

"Hank Shoeman has a present for you, by the way," she told Elliot. "No, there's no use looking in the truck, he ordered it."

Elliot's eyes lit up. "What is it? An autographed photo of the group?"

"It's a keyboard," Amanda corrected gently, smiling at his awe. "A real one, a moog like I play when we do instrumentals."

"Oh, my gosh!" Elliot sat down. "I've died and gone to heaven. First I get a great new mother and now I get a moog. Maybe I'm real sick and have a high fever," he frowned, feeling his forehead.

"No, you're perfectly well," Quinn told him. "And I guess it's all right if you play some rock songs," he added with a grimace. "I got used to turnips, after all, that time when Harry refused to cook any more greens. I guess I can get used to loud music."

"I refused to cook greens because we had a blizzard and canned turnips was all I had," Harry reminded him, glowering. "Now that Amanda's here, we won't run out of beans and peas and such, because she'll remember to tell me we're out so I can get some more."

"I didn't forget to remind you," Quinn muttered.

"You did so," Elliot began. "I remember—"

"That's it, gang up on me," Quinn glowered at them.

"Don't you worry, sweet man, I'll protect you from ghastly turnips and peas and beans," she said with a quick glance at Harry and Elliot. "I like asparagus, so I'll make sure that's all we keep here. Don't you guys like asparagus?"

"Yes!" they chorused, having been the culprits who told Amanda once that Quinn hated asparagus above all food in the world.

Quinn groaned.

"And I'll make liver and onions every night," Amanda added. "We love that, don't we, gang?"

"We sure do!" they chorused again, because they knew it was the only meat Quinn wouldn't eat.

"I'll go live with McNaber," he threatened.

Amanda laughed and slid her arms around him. "Only if we get to come, too." She looked up at him. "It's all right. We all really hate asparagus and liver and onions."

"That's a fact, we do," Elliot replied. "Amanda, are you going to go on tour with the band?"

"No," she said quietly. "We'd all gotten tired of the pace. We're going to take a well-earned rest and concentrate on videos and albums."

"I've got this great idea for a video," Elliot volunteered.

She grinned. "Okay, tiger, you can share it with us when Hank and the others come for a visit."

His eyes lit up. "They're all coming? The whole group?"

"My aunt is marrying Mr. Durning," she told him, having found out that tidbit from Hank. "They're going to live in Hawaii, and the band has permission to use the cabin whenever they like. They've decided that if I like the mountains so much, there must be something special about them. Our next album is going to be built around a mountain theme."

"Wow." Elliot sighed. "Wait'll I tell the guys."

"You and the guys can be in the video," Amanda promised. "We'll find some way to fit you into a scene or two." She studied Harry. "We'll put Harry in, too."

"Oh, no, you won't!" he said. "I'll run away from home first."

"If you do, we'll starve to death." Amanda sighed. "I can't do cakes and roasts. We'll have to live on potatoes and fried eggs."

"Then you just make a movie star out of old Elliot and I'll stick around," he promised.

"Okay," Amanda said, "but what a loss to women everywhere. You'd have been super, Harry."

He grinned and went back to the kitchen to cook. Elliot eventually wandered off, too, and Quinn took Amanda into the study and closed the door.

They sat together in his big leather armchair, listening to the crackling of the fire in the potbellied stove.

"Remember the last time we were in here together?" he asked lazily between kisses.

"Indeed, I do," she murmured with a smile against his throat. "We almost didn't stop in time."

"I'm glad we did." He linked her fingers with his. "We had a very special first time. A real wedding night. That's marriage the way it was meant to be; a feast of first times."

She touched his cheek lightly and searched his dark eyes. "I'm glad we waited, too. I wanted so much to go to my husband untouched. I just want you to know that it was worth the wait. I love you, really love you, you know?" She sighed shakily. "That made it much more than my first intimate experience."

He brought his mouth down gently on hers. "I felt just that way about it," he breathed against her lips. "I never asked if you wanted me to use anything...?"

"So I wouldn't get pregnant?" She smiled gently. "I love kids."

"So do I." He eased back and pulled her cheek onto his chest, smoothing her long, soft hair as he smiled down into her eyes. "I never dreamed I'd find anyone like you. I'd given up on women. On life, too, I guess. I've been bitter and alone for such a long time, Amanda. I feel like I was just feverish and dreaming it all."

"You aren't dreaming." She pulled him closer to her and kissed him with warm, slow passion. "We're married and I'm going to love you for the rest of my life, body and soul. So don't get any ideas about trying to get away, I've caught you fair and square and you're all mine."

He chuckled. "Really? If you've caught me, what are you going to do with me?"

"Have I got an answer for that," she whispered with a sultry smile. "You did lock the door, didn't you?" she murmured, her voice husky as she lifted and turned so that she was facing him, her knees beside him on the chair. His heart began to race violently.

"Yes, I locked the door. What are you...Amanda!"

She smiled against his mouth while her hands worked at fastenings. "That's my name, all right," she whispered. She nipped his lower lip gently and laughed delightedly when she felt him helping her. "Life is short. We'd better start living it right now."

"I couldn't possibly agree more," he whispered back, and his husky laugh mingled with hers in the tense silence of the room.

Beside them, the burning wood crackled and popped in the stove while the snow began to fall again outside the window. Amanda had started it, but almost immediately Quinn took control and she gave in with a warm laugh. She knew already that things were done Sutton's way around Ricochet. And this time, she didn't really mind at all.

\* \* \* \* \*

# ETHAN

## Diana Palmer

# Chapter One

Arabella was drifting. She seemed to be floating along on a particularly fast cloud, high above the world. She murmured contentedly and sank into the fluffy nothingness, aware somewhere of a fleeting pain that began to grow with every passing second until it was a white-hot throb in one of her hands.

"No!" she exclaimed, and her eyes flew open.

She was lying on a cold table. Her dress, her beautiful gray dress, was covered with blood and she felt bruised and cut all over. A man in a white jacket was examining her eyes. She groaned.

"Concussion," the man murmured. "Abrasions, contusions. Compound fracture of the wrist, one ligament almost severed. Type and cross-match her blood, prep her for surgery, and get me an operating room."

"Yes, Doctor."

"Well?" The other voice was harsh, demanding. Very male and familiar, but not her father's.

"She'll be all right," the doctor said with resignation. "Now will you please go outside and sit down, Mr. Hardeman? While I can appreciate your concern—" and that was an understatement, the physician thought "—you can do her more good by letting us work."

*Ethan!* The voice was Ethan's! She managed to turn her head, and yes, it was Ethan Hardeman. He looked as if they'd dragged him out of bed. His black hair was rumpled, apparently by his own fingers. His hard, lean face was drawn, his gray eyes so dark with worry that they looked black. His white shirt was half-unbuttoned, as if he'd thrown it on, and his dark jacket was open. He'd all but crushed the brim of the creamy Stetson in his hand.

"Bella," he breathed, when he saw her pale, damaged face.

"Ethan," she managed in a hoarse whisper. "Oh, Ethan, my hand!"

His expression tautened as he moved closer to her, despite the doctor's protests. He reached down and touched her poor, bruised cheek. "Baby, what a scare you gave me!" he whispered. His hand actually seemed to be trembling as he brushed back her disheveled long brown hair. Her green eyes were bright with pain and welcome, all mixed up together.

"My father?" she asked with apprehension, because he'd been driving the car.

"They flew him to Dallas. He had an ocular injury, and they've got some of the top men in the field there. He's all right, otherwise. He couldn't take care of you, so he had the hospital call me." Ethan smiled coldly. "God knows, that was a gut-wrenching decision on his part."

She was in too much pain to pick up on the meaning behind the words. "But . . . my hand?" she asked.

He stood up straight. "They'll talk to you about that later. Mary and the rest will be here in the morning. I'll stay until you're out of surgery."

She caught at his arm with her good hand, feeling the hard muscle tighten. "Make them understand . . . how important my hand is, please," she pleaded.

"They understand. They'll do what can be done." He touched her cracked lips gently with his forefinger. "I won't leave you," he said quietly. "I'll be here."

She grabbed his hand, holding it, feeling his strength, drawing on his strength for the first time in recent memory. "Ethan," she whispered as the pain built, "remember the swimming hole . . . ?"

His expression closed up. He actually flinched as her face contorted. "My God, can't you give her something?" he asked the doctor, as if the pain were his own.

The doctor seemed to understand at last that it was more than bad temper driving the tall, angry man who'd stormed into the emergency room barely ten minutes ago. The look on those hard features as he'd held the woman's hand had said everything.

"I'll give her something," the doctor promised. "Are you a relative? Her husband, perhaps?"

Ethan's silver eyes cut at him. "No, I'm not a relative. She's a concert pianist, very commercial these days. She lives with her father and she's never been allowed to marry."

The doctor didn't have time for discussion. He settled Ethan with a nurse and vanished gratefully into the emergency room.

Hours later, Arabella drifted in and out of the anesthesia in a private room. Ethan was there again, staring angrily out the window at the pastel colors of the sky at dawn, still in the same clothes he'd been wearing the night before. Arabella was in a floral hospital gown and she felt as she probably looked— weak and wrung out.

"Ethan," she called.

He turned immediately, going to the bedside. He did look terrible, all right. His face was white with strain and bridled anger.

"How are you?" he asked.

"Tired and sore and groggy," she murmured, trying to smile at him. He looked so fierce, just as he had when they were younger. She was almost twenty-three now, and Ethan was thirty, but he'd always been worlds ahead of her in maturity. With Ethan standing over her, it was hard to remember the anguish of the past four years. So many memories, she thought drowsily, watching that dear face. Ethan had been her heart four years ago, but he'd married Miriam. Ethan had forced Miriam into a separation only a little while after they married, but she'd fought Ethan's divorce action tooth and nail for almost four years. Miriam had given up, at last, this year. Their divorce had only become final three months ago.

Ethan was a past master at hiding his feelings, but the deep lines in his face spoke for themselves. Miriam had hurt him dreadfully. Arabella had tried to warn him, in her own shy way. They'd argued over Miriam and because of it, Ethan had shut Arabella out of his life with cold cruelty. She'd seen him in passing since then because she and his sister-in-law were best friends, and visits were inevitable. But Ethan had been remote and unapproachable. Until last night.

"You should have listened to me about Miriam," she said groggily.

"We won't talk about my ex-wife," he said coldly. "You're coming home with me when you're able to get around again. Mother and Mary will look after you and keep you company."

"How's my father?" she asked.

"I haven't found out anything new. I'll check later. Right now, I need breakfast and a change of clothes. I'll come back as soon as I've got my men started at home. We're in the middle of roundup."

"What a time to be landed with me," she said with a deep sigh. "I'm sorry, Ethan. Dad could have spared you this."

He ignored the comment. "Did you have any clothes in the car with you?"

She shook her head. The slight movement hurt, so she stopped. She reached up with her free hand to smooth back the mass of waving dark brown hair from her bruised face. "My clothes are back in the apartment in Houston."

"Where's the key?"

"In my purse. They should have brought it in with me," she murmured drowsily.

He searched in the locker on the other side of the room and found her expensive leather purse. He carried it to the bed with the air of a man holding a poisonous snake. "Where is it?" he muttered.

She stared at him, amused despite the sedatives and the growing pain. "The key is in the zipper compartment," she managed.

He took out a set of keys and she showed him the right one. He put the purse away with obvious relief. "Beats me why women can't use pockets, the way men do."

"The stuff we carry wouldn't fit into pockets," she said reasonably. She laid back on the pillows, her eyes open and curious. "You look terrible."

He didn't smile. He hardly ever had, except for a few magical days when she was eighteen. Before Miriam got her beautiful hands on him. "I haven't had much sleep," he said, his voice sharp and cutting.

She smiled drowsily. "Don't growl at me. Coreen wrote to me last month in Los Angeles. She said you're impossible to live with these days."

"My mother always thought I was impossible to live with," he reminded her.

"She said you'd been that way for three months, since the divorce was final," she replied. "Why did Miriam finally give in? She was the one who insisted on staying married to you, despite the fact that she stopped living with you ages ago."

"How should I know?" he asked abruptly, and turned away.

She saw the way he closed up at the mention of his ex-wife's name, and her heart felt heavy and cold. His marriage had hurt her more than anything in her life.

It had been unexpected, and she'd almost gone off the deep end when she'd heard. Somehow she'd always thought that Ethan cared for her. She'd been too young for him at eighteen, but that day by the swimming hole, she'd been sure that he felt more than just a physical attraction for her. Or maybe that had been one more hopeless illusion. Whatever he'd felt, he'd started going around with Miriam immediately after that sweet interlude, and within two months he'd married the woman.

Arabella had mourned him bitterly. He'd been the first man in her life in all the important ways, except for the most intimate one. She was still waiting for that first intimacy, just as she'd waited most of her adult life for Ethan to love her. She almost laughed out loud. Ethan had never loved her. He'd loved Miriam, who'd come to the ranch to film a commercial. She'd watched it happen, watched Ethan falling under the spell of the green-eyed, redheaded model with her sophisticated beauty.

Arabella had never had the measure of self-confidence and teasing sophistication that Miriam had. And Miriam had walked off with Ethan, only to leave him. They said that Ethan had become a woman-hater because of his marriage. Arabella didn't doubt it. He'd never been a playboy in the first place. He was much too serious and stoical. There was nothing happy-go-lucky or carefree about Ethan. He'd had the responsibility for his family for a long time now, and even Arabella's earliest memories of him were of a quiet, hard man who threw out orders like a commanding general, intimidating men twice his age when he was only just out of his teens.

Ethan was watching her, but his scrutiny ceased when she noticed him standing beside the bed. "I'll send someone to your apartment in Houston for your things."

"Thank you." He wouldn't talk to her about Miriam. Somehow, she'd expected that reaction. She took a deep breath and started to lift her hand. It felt heavy. She looked down and realized that it was in a small cast. Red antiseptic peeked out from under it, stark against her pale skin. She felt the threat of reality and withdrew from it, closing her eyes.

"They had to set the bones," Ethan said. "The cast comes off in six weeks, and you'll have the use of your hand again."

Use of it, yes. But would she be able to play again as she had? How long would it take, and how would she manage to support herself and her father if she couldn't? She felt panic seeping in. Her father had a heart condition. She knew, because he'd used it against her in the early days when she hadn't wanted the years of study, the eternal practice that made it impossible for her to go places with her friends Mary and Jan, Ethan's sister, and Matt, his brother whom Mary had later married.

It was astonishing that her father had called Ethan after the wreck. Ever since Arabella had blossomed into a young woman, her father had made sure that Ethan didn't get too close to her. He'd never liked Ethan. The reverse was also true. Arabella hadn't understood the friction, because Ethan had never made any serious advances toward her, until that day she and Ethan had gone swimming at the creek, and things had almost gone too far. Arabella had told no one, so her father hadn't known about that. It was her own private, special secret. Hers and Ethan's.

She forced her mind back to the present. She couldn't let herself become maudlin now. She had enough complications in her life without asking for more. She vaguely remembered mentioning to Ethan that day she and he had gone swimming together, when she was eighteen. She hoped against hope that he'd been too worried to pay attention to the remark, that she hadn't given away how precious the memory was to her.

"You said I'd stay with you," she began falteringly, trying to make her mind work. "But, my father...?"

"Your uncle lives in Dallas, remember?" he asked curtly. "Your father will probably stay there."

"He won't like having me this far away," she said doggedly.

"No, he won't, will he?" He pulled the sheet up to her chin. "Try to sleep. Let the medicine work."

Her wide green eyes opened, holding his. "You don't want me at your house," she said huskily. "You never did. We quarreled over Miriam and you said I was a pain in the neck and you never wanted to have to see me again!"

He actually winced. "Try to sleep," he said tersely.

She was drifting in and out of consciousness, blissfully unaware of the tortured look on the dark face above her. She closed her eyes. "Yes. Sleep..."

The world seemed very far away as the drugs took hold at last and she slept. Her dreams were full of the old days, of growing up with Mary and Matt, of Ethan always nearby, beloved and taciturn and completely unattainable. No matter how hard she tried to act her age, Ethan had never looked at her as a woman in those early days.

Arabella had always loved him. Her music had been her escape. She could play the exquisite classical pieces and put all the love Ethan didn't want into her fingers as she played. It was that fever and need that had given her a start in the musical world. At the age of twenty-one, she'd won an international competition with a huge financial prize, and the recognition had given her a shot at a recording contract.

Classical music was notoriously low-paying for pianists, but Arabella's style had caught on quickly when she tried some pop pieces. The albums had sold well, and she was asked to do more. The royalties began to grow, along with her fame.

Her father had pushed her into personal appearances and tours, and, basically shy in front of people she didn't know, she'd hated the whole idea of it. She'd tried to protest, but her father had dominated her all her life, and she hadn't had the will to fight him. Incredible, that, she told herself, when she could stand up to Ethan and most other people without a qualm. Her father was different. She loved him and he'd been her mainstay when her mother had died so long ago. She couldn't bear to hurt her father by refusing his guidance in her career. Ethan had hated the hold her father had on her, but he'd never asked her to try to break it.

Over the years, while she was growing up in Jacobsville, Ethan had been a kind of protective but distant big brother. Until that day he'd taken her swimming down at the creek and everything had changed. Miriam had been at the ranch even then, starting on a layout with a Western theme for a fashion magazine. Ethan had paid her very little notice until he'd almost lost control with Arabella when they started kissing, but after that day he'd begun pursuing Miriam. It hadn't taken long.

Arabella had heard Miriam bragging to another model that she had the Hardeman fortune in the palm of her hand and that she was going to trade Ethan her body for a life of luxury. It had sickened Arabella to think of the man she loved being treated as a meal ticket and nothing more, so she'd gone to him and tried to tell him what she'd heard.

He hadn't believed her. He'd accused her of being jealous of Miriam. He'd hurt her with his cold remarks about her age and inexperience and naïveté, then he'd ordered her off the ranch. She'd run away, all the way out of the state and back to music school.

How strange that Ethan should be the one to look after her. It was the first time she'd ever been in a hospital, the first time she'd been anything except healthy. She wouldn't have expected Ethan to bother with her, despite her father's request. Ethan had studiously ignored Arabella since his marriage, right down to deliberately disappearing every time she came to visit Mary and Coreen.

Mary and Matt lived with Matt and Ethan's mother, Coreen, at the big rambling Hardeman house. Coreen always welcomed Arabella as if she were family when she came to spend an occasional afternoon with her friend Mary. But Ethan was cold and unapproachable and barely spoke to her.

Arabella hadn't expected more from Ethan, though. He'd made his opinion of her crystal clear when he'd announced his engagement to Miriam shortly after he'd started dating the model. The engagement had shocked everyone, even his mother, and the rushed wedding had been a source of gossip for months. But Miriam wasn't pregnant, so obviously he'd married her for love. If that was the case, it was a brief love. Miriam had gone, bag and baggage, six months later, leaving Ethan alone but not unattached. Arabella had never learned why Miriam had refused the divorce or why Miriam had started running around on a man she'd only just married. It was one of many things about his marriage that Ethan never discussed with anyone.

Arabella felt oblivion stealing her away. She gave in to it at last, sighing as she fell asleep, leaving all her worries and heartaches behind.

## Chapter Two

When Arabella woke up again, it was daylight. Her hand throbbed in its white cast. She ground her teeth together, recalling the accident all too vividly—the impact, the sound of broken glass, her own cry, and then oblivion rushing over her. She couldn't blame the accident on her father; it had been unavoidable. Slick roads, a car that pulled out in front of them, and they'd gone off the pavement and into a telephone pole. She was relieved to be alive, despite the damage to her hand. But she was afraid her father wasn't going to react well to the knowledge that her performing days might be over. She refused to think about that possibility. She had to be optimistic.

Belatedly she wondered what had become of the car they'd been driving. They'd been on their way to Jacobsville from Corpus Christi, where she'd been performing in a charity concert. Her father hadn't told her why they were going to Jacobsville, so she'd assumed that they were taking a brief vacation in their old home town. She'd thought then about seeing Ethan again, and her heart had bounced in her chest. But she hadn't expected to see him under these circumstances.

They'd been very close to Jacobsville, so naturally they'd been taken to the hospital there. Her father had been transferred to Dallas and had called Ethan, but why? She couldn't imagine the reason he should have asked a man he obviously disliked to look after his daughter. She was no closer to solving the mystery when the door opened.

Ethan came in with a cup of black coffee, looking out of sorts as if he'd never smiled in his life. He had a faint arrogance of carriage that had intrigued her from the first time she'd seen him. He was as individual as his name. She even knew how he'd come by the name. His mother Coreen, a John Wayne fan, had loved the movie *The Searchers*, which came out before Ethan was born. When Coreen became pregnant, she couldn't think of a better name for her firstborn son than the first name John Wayne had been given in the movie. So he became Ethan Hardeman. His middle name was John, but few people outside the family knew it.

Arabella loved looking at him. He had a rodeo rider's physique, powerful shoulders and chest that wedged down to narrow hips, a flat belly and long, muscular legs. His face wasn't bad, either. He was tanned and his eyes were deep-set and very gray, although sometimes they looked silver and other times they had the faintest hint of blue. His hair was dark and conventionally cut. His nose was straight, his mouth sensuous, his cheekbones high and his chin faintly jutting with a slight cleft. He had lean hands with long fingers and neatly trimmed flat nails.

She was staring at him again, helplessly she supposed. From his blue-checked Western shirt to his gray denims and black boots, he was impeccably dressed, elegant for a cowboy, even if he was the boss.

"You look like hell," he said, and all her romantic dreams were pushed aside at once.

"Thank you," she replied with a little of her old spirit. "That kind of flattery is just what I needed."

"You'll mend." He sounded unruffled; he always did. He sat down in the armchair next to the bed and leaned back with one long leg crossed over the other, sipping his coffee. "Mother and Mary will be in to see you later. How's the hand?"

"It hurts," she said simply. She used the good one to brush back her hair. She could hear Bach preludes and Clementi sonatinas in the back of her mind. Always the music. It gave her life, made her breathe. She couldn't bear to think that she might lose it.

"Have they given you anything?"

"Yes, just a few minutes ago. I'm a little groggy, but I don't hurt as much as I did," she assured him. She'd already seen one orderly run for cover when he walked in. All she needed was to have Ethan bulldoze any more of the staff on her behalf.

He smiled faintly. "I won't cause too much trouble," he assured her. "I just want to make sure you're being treated properly."

"So does the staff," she murmured dryly, "and I hear at least two doctors are thinking of resigning if I'm not released soon."

He looked the least bit uncomfortable. "I wanted to make sure you got the best care possible."

"I did, never fear." She averted her eyes. "From one enemy to another, thanks for the T.L.C."

He stiffened. "I'm not your enemy."

"No? We didn't part as friends all those years ago." She leaned back, sighing. "I'm sorry things didn't work out for you and Miriam, Ethan," she said quietly. "I hope it wasn't because of anything I said..."

"It's past history," he said curtly. "Let it drop."

"Okay." He intimidated her with those black stares.

He sipped his coffee, allowing his eyes to wander. down the length of her slender body. "You've lost weight. You need a rest."

"I haven't been able to afford that luxury," she told him. "We've only begun to break even this year."

"Your father could get a job and help out," he said coldly.

"You don't have the right to interfere in my life, Ethan," she said, staring back at him. "You gave that up years ago."

The muscles in his face contracted, although his gaze didn't waver. "I know better than you do what I gave up." He stared her down and drank some more coffee. "Mother and Mary are fixing up the guest room for you," he told her. "Matt's off at a sale in Montana, so Mary will be glad of the company."

"Doesn't your mother mind having me landed on her?"

"My mother loves you," he said. "She always has, and you've always known it, so there's no need to pretend."

"Your mother is a nice person."

"And I'm not?" He studied her face. "I've never tried to win any popularity contests, if that's what you mean."

She shifted against the pillows. "You're very touchy these days, Ethan. I wasn't looking for ways to insult you. I'm very grateful for what you've done."

He finished his coffee. His gray eyes met hers and for an instant, they were held against their will. He averted his gaze instantly. "I don't want gratitude from you."

That was the truth; not gratitude or anything else—least of all love.

She let her eyes fall to her hand in its cast. "Did you call the hospital at Dallas to ask about my father?"

"I phoned your uncle early this morning. The eye specialist is supposed to see your father today; they're more optimistic than they were last night."

"Did he ask about me?"

"Of course he asked about you," Ethan replied. "He was told about your hand."

She stiffened. "And?"

"He didn't say another word, according to your uncle." Ethan smiled without humor. "Well, what did you expect? Yours hands are his livelihood. He's just seen a future that's going to require him to work for a living again. I expect he's drowning in self-pity."

"Shame on you," she snapped.

He stared at her, unblinking. "I know your father. You do, too, despite the fact that you've spent your life protecting him. You might try living your own way for a change.''

''I'm content with my life,'' she muttered.

His pale eyes caught and held hers, and he was very still. The room was so quiet that they could hear the sound of cars outside the hospital, in the nearby streets of Jacobsville.

''Do you remember what you asked me when they brought you in?''

She shook her head. ''No. I was hurting pretty badly just then,'' she lied, averting her eyes.

''You asked if I remembered the swimming hole.''

Her cheeks went hot. She pleated the material of the hospital gown they'd put her in, grimacing. ''I can't imagine why I'd ask such a question. That's ancient history.''

''Four years isn't ancient history. And to answer the question belatedly, yes, I remember. I wish I could forget.''

Well, that was plain enough, wasn't it, she thought, hurt. She couldn't bring herself to meet his gaze. She could imagine the mockery in his eyes. ''Why can't you?'' she asked, trying to sound as unconcerned as he did. ''After all, you told me yourself that I'd asked for it, that you'd been thinking about Miriam.''

''Damn Miriam!'' He got up, upsetting the coffee cup in the process, splattering a few drops of scalding coffee onto his hand. He ignored the sting, turning away to stare out the window at Jacobsville, his body rigid. He lifted the cup to his lips and sipped the hot liquid again to steady himself. Even the mention of his ex-wife made him tense, wounded him. Arabella had no idea of the hell Miriam had made of his life, or why he'd let her trap him into marriage. It was four years too late for explanations or apologies. His memories of the day he'd made love to Arabella were permanent, unchanged, a part of him, but he couldn't even tell her that. He was so locked up inside that he'd almost forgotten how to feel, until Arabella's father had telephoned him to tell him that Arabella had been injured. Even now, he could taste the sick fear he'd felt, face all over again the possibility that she might have died. The world had gone black until he'd gotten to the hospital and found her relatively unhurt.

"Do you hear from Miriam anymore?" she asked.

He didn't turn around. "I hadn't since the divorce was final, until last week." He finished the coffee and laughed coldly. "She wants to talk about a reconciliation."

Arabella felt her heart sink. So much for faint hope, she thought. "Do you want her back?"

Ethan came back to the bedside, and his eyes were blazing with anger. "No, I don't want her back," he said. He stared down at her icily. "It took me years to talk her into a divorce. Do you really think I have any plans to put my neck in that noose again?" he asked.

"I don't know you, Ethan," she replied quietly. "I don't think I ever did, really. But you loved Miriam once," she added with downcast eyes. "It's not inconceivable that you could miss her, or want her back."

He didn't answer her. He turned and dropped back down into the armchair by the bed, crossing his legs. Absently he played with the empty coffee cup. Loved Miriam? He'd wanted her. But love? No. He wished he could tell Arabella that, but he'd become too adept at keeping his deepest feelings hidden.

He put the cup down on the floor beside his chair. "A cracked mirror is better replaced than mended," he said, lifting his eyes back to Arabella's. "I don't want a reconciliation. So, that being the case," he continued, improvising as he began to see a way out of his approaching predicament, "we might be able to help each other."

Arabella's heart jumped. "What?"

He stared at her, his eyes probing, assessing. "Your father raised you in an emotional prison. You never tried to break out. Well, here's your chance."

"I don't understand."

"That's obvious. You used to be better at reading between the lines." He took a cigarette from the pack in his pocket and dangled it from his fingers. "Don't worry, I won't light it," he added when he saw the look she gave him. "I need something to do with my hands. What I meant was that you and I can pretend to be involved."

She couldn't prevent the astonished fear from distorting her features. He'd pushed her out of his life once, and now he had the audacity to want her to pretend to be involved with him? It was cruel.

"I thought you'd be bothered by the suggestion," he said after a minute of watching her expression. "But think about it. Miriam won't be here for another week or two. There's time to map out some strategy."

"Why can't you just tell her not to come?" she faltered.

He studied his boot. "I could, but it wouldn't solve the problem. She'd be dancing in and out of my life from now on. The best way, the only way," he corrected, "is to give her a good reason to stay away. You're the best one I can think of."

"Miriam would laugh herself sick if anyone told her you were involved with me," she said shortly. "I was only eighteen when you married her. She didn't consider me any kind of competition then, and she was right. I wasn't, and I'm not." She lifted her chin with mangled pride. "I'm talented, but I'm not pretty. She'll never believe you see anything interesting about me."

He had to control his expression not to betray the sting of those words. It hurt him to hear Arabella talk so cynically. He didn't like remembering how badly he'd had to hurt her. At the time, it didn't seem that he'd had a choice. But explaining his reasoning to Arabella four years too late would accomplish nothing.

His eyes darkened as he watched Arabella with the old longing. He didn't know how he was going to bear having to let her walk out of his life a second time. But at least he might have a few weeks with her under the pretext of a mutual-aid pact. Better that than nothing. At least he might have one or two sweet memories to last him through the barren years ahead.

"Miriam isn't stupid," he said finally. "You're a young woman now, well-known in your field and no longer a country mouse. She won't know how sheltered you've been, unless you tell her." His eyes slid gently over her face. "Even without your father's interference, I don't imagine you've had much time for men, have you?"

"Men are treacherous," she said without thinking. "I offered you my heart and you threw it in my teeth. I haven't offered it again, to anyone, and I don't intend to. I've got my music, Ethan. That's all I need."

He didn't believe her. Women didn't go that sour over a youthful infatuation, especially when it was mostly physical to begin with. Probably the drugs they'd given her had upset her reasoning, even if he'd give an arm to believe she'd cared that much. "What if you don't have music again?" he asked suddenly.

"Then I'll jump off the roof," she replied with conviction. "I can't live without it. I don't want to try."

"What a cowardly approach." He said the words coldly to disguise a ripple of real fear at the way she'd looked when she said that.

"Not at all," she contradicted him. "At first it was my father's idea to push me into a life of concert tours. But I love what I do. Most of what I do," she corrected. "I don't care for crowds, but I'm very happy with my life."

"How about a husband? Kids?" he probed.

"I don't want or need either," she said, averting her face. "I have my life planned."

"Your damned father has your life planned," he shot back angrily. "He'd tell you when to breathe if you'd let him!"

"What I do is none of your concern," she replied. Her green eyes met his levelly. "You have no right whatsoever to talk about my father trying to dominate me, when you're trying to manipulate me yourself to help you get Miriam out of your hair."

One silvery eye narrowed. "It amazes me."

"What does?" she asked.

"That you hit back at me with such disgusting ease and you won't say boo to your father."

"I'm not afraid of you," she said. She laced her fingers together. "I've always been a little in awe of my father. The only thing he cares about is my talent. I thought if I got famous, he might love me." She laughed bitterly. "But it didn't work, did it? Now he thinks I may not be able to play again and he doesn't want anything to do with me." She looked up with tear-bright eyes. "Neither would you, if it wasn't for Miriam hotfooting it down here. I've never been anything but a pawn where men were concerned, and you think my *father* is trying to run my life?"

He stuck the hand that wasn't holding the cigarette into his pocket. "That's one miserable self-image you've got," he remarked quietly.

She looked away. "I know my failings," she told him. She closed her eyes. "I'll help you keep Miriam at bay, but you won't need to protect me from my father. I very much doubt if I'll ever see him again after what's happened."

"If that hand heals properly, you'll see him again." Ethan tossed the unlit cigarette into an ashtray. "I have to get Mother and Mary and drive them in to see you. The man I sent for your clothes should be back by then. I'll bring your things with us."

"Thank you," she said stiffly.

He paused by the bedside, his eyes attentive. "I don't like having to depend on other people, either," he said. "But you can carry independence too far. Right now, I'm all you've got. I'll take care of you until you're back on your feet. If that includes keeping your father away, I can do that, too.''

She looked up. "What do you have in mind to keep Miriam from thinking our relationship is a sham?''

"You look nervous," he remarked. "Do you think I might want to make love to you in front of her?''

Her cheeks went hot. "Of course not!''

"Well, you can relax. I won't ask you for the ultimate sacrifice. A few smiles and some hand-holding ought to get the message across." He laughed bitterly as he looked down at her. "If that doesn't do it, I'll announce our engagement. Don't panic," he added icily when he saw the expression on her face. "We can break it off when she leaves, if we have to go that far.''

Her heart was going mad. He didn't know what the thought of being engaged to him did to her. She loved him almost desperately, but it was obvious that he had no such feeling for her.

Why did he need someone to help him get Miriam to leave him alone? she wondered. Maybe he still loved Miriam and was afraid of letting her get to him. Arabella closed her eyes. Whatever his reason, she couldn't let him know how she felt. "I'll go along, then," she said. "I'm so tired, Ethan.''

"Get some rest. I'll see you later.''

She opened her eyes. "Thank you for coming to see me. I don't imagine it was something you'd have chosen to do, except that Dad asked you.''

"And you think I care enough for your father's opinion to make any sacrifices on his behalf?" he asked curiously.

"Well, I don't expect you to make any on mine," she said coolly. "God knows, you disliked me enough in the old days. And still do, I imagine. I shouldn't have said anything to you about Miriam—''

She was suddenly talking to thin air. He was gone before the words were out of her mouth.

Ethan was back with Coreen and Mary later that day, but he didn't come into the room.

Coreen, small and delicate, was everything Arabella would have ordered in a custom-made mother. The little woman was spirited and kind, and her battles with Ethan were legendary. But she loved Arabella and Mary, and they were as much her daughters as Jan, her own married daughter who lived out of state.

"It was a blessing that Ethan was home," Coreen told Arabella while Mary, Arabella's best friend in public school, sat nearby and listened to the conversation with twinkling brown eyes. "He's been away from home every few days since his divorce was final, mostly business trips. He's been moody and brooding and restless. I found it amazing that he sent Matt on his last one."

"Maybe he was out making up for lost time after the divorce was final," Arabella said quietly. "After all, he was much too honorable himself to indulge in anything indecent while he was technically married."

"Unlike Miriam, who was sleeping with anything in pants just weeks after they married," Coreen said bluntly. "God knows why she held on to him for so long, when everyone knew she never loved him."

"There's no alimony in Texas," Mary grinned. "Maybe that's why."

"I offered her a settlement," Coreen said, surprising the other two women. "She refused. But I hear that she met someone else down in the Caribbean and there are rumors that she may marry her new man friend. That's more than likely why she agreed to the divorce."

"Then why does she want to come back?" Arabella asked.

"To make as much trouble as she can for Ethan, probably," Coreen said darkly. "She used to say things to him that cut my heart out. He fought back, God knows, but even a strong man can be wounded by ceaseless ridicule and humiliation. My dear, Miriam actually seduced a man at a dinner party we gave for Ethan's business associates. He walked in on them in his own study."

Arabella closed her eyes and groaned. "It must have been terrible for him."

"More terrible than you know," Coreen replied. "He never really loved her and she knew it. She wanted him to worship at her feet, but he wouldn't. Her extramarital activities turned him off completely. He told me that he found her repulsive, and probably he told her, too. That was about the time she started trying to create as many scandals as possible, to embarrass him. And they did. Ethan's a very conventional man. It crushed him that Miriam thought nothing of seducing his business associates." Coreen actually shuddered. "A man's ego is his sensitive spot. She knew it, and used it, with deadly effect. Ethan's changed. He was always quiet and introverted, but I hate what this marriage has done to him."

"He's a hard man to get close to," Arabella said quietly. "Nobody gets near him at all now, I imagine."

"Maybe you can change that," Coreen said, smiling. "You could make him smile when no one else could. You taught him how to play. He was happier that summer four years ago than he ever was before or since."

"Was he?" Arabella smiled painfully. "We had a terrible quarrel over Miriam. I don't think he's ever forgiven me for the things I said."

"Anger can camouflage so many emotions, Bella," Coreen said quietly. "It isn't always as cut-and-dried as it seems."

"No, it isn't," Mary agreed. "Matt and I hated each other once, and we wound up married."

"I doubt if Ethan will ever marry anyone again," Arabella said, glancing at Coreen. "A bad burn leaves scars."

"Yes," Coreen said sadly. "By the way, dear," she said then, changing the subject, "we're looking forward to having you with us while you recuperate. Mary and I will enjoy your company so much."

Arabella thought about what Coreen had said long after they left. She couldn't imagine a man as masculine as Ethan being so wounded by any woman, but perhaps Miriam had some kind of hold on him that no one knew about. Probably a sensual one, she thought miserably, because everyone who'd seen them together knew how attracted he'd been to Miriam physically. Miriam had been worldly and sophisticated. It was understandable that he'd fallen so completely un-

der her spell. Arabella had been much too innocent to
even begin to compete for him.

A nurse came in, bearing a huge bouquet of flowers, and Arabella's eyes glistened with faint tears at
their beauty. There was no card, but she knew by the
size and extravagance of the gift that it had to be Coreen. She'd have to remember to thank the older
woman the next day.

It was a long night, and she didn't sleep well. Her
dreams were troubled, full of Ethan and pain. She lay
looking up at the ceiling after one of the more potent
dreams, and her mind drifted back to a late-sum-
mer's day, with the sound of bees buzzing around the
wildflowers that circled the spot where the creek widened into a big hole, deep enough to swim in. She and
Ethan had gone there to swim one lazy afternoon . . .

She could still see the butterflies and hear the crick-
ets and July flies that populated the deserted area.
Ethan had driven them to the creek in the truck, because it was a long and tiring walk in the devastating
heat of a south Texas summer. He'd been wearing
white trunks that showed off his powerful body in an
all-too-sensuous way, his broad shoulders and chest
tapering to his narrow hips and long legs. He was
deeply tanned, and his chest and flat belly were thick
with curling dark hair. Seeing him in trunks had never
bothered Arabella overmuch until that day, and then
just looking at him made her blush and scamper into
the water.

She'd been wearing a yellow one-piece bathing suit,
very respectable and equally inexpensive. Her father's job had supported them frugally, and she was
working part-time to help pay her tuition at the music

school in New York. She was on fire with the promise of being a superb pianist, and things were going well for her. She'd come over to spend the afternoon with his sister Jan, but she and her latest boyfriend had gone to a barbecue, so Ethan had offered to take her swimming.

The offer had shocked and flattered Arabella, because Ethan was in his mid-twenties and she was sure his taste didn't run to schoolgirls. He was remote and unapproachable most of the time, but in the weeks before they went swimming together, he'd always seemed to be around when she visited his sister. His eyes had followed Arabella with an intensity that had disturbed and excited her. She'd loved him for so long, ached for him. And then, that day, all her dreams had come true when he'd issued his casual invitation to come swimming with him.

Once he'd rescued her from an overamorous would-be suitor, and another time he'd driven her to a school party along with Jan and Matt and Mary. To everyone's surprise, he'd stayed long enough to dance one slow, lazy dance with Arabella. Jan and Mary had teased her about it mercilessly. That had started the fantasies, that one dance. Afterwards, Arabella had watched Ethan and worshipped him from afar.

Once they were at the swimming hole, the atmosphere had suddenly changed. Arabella hadn't understood the way Ethan kept looking at her body, his silver eyes openly covetous, thrilling, seductive. She'd colored delicately every time he glanced her way.

"How do you like music school?" he'd asked while they sat in the grass at the creek's edge, and Ethan quietly smoked a cigarette.

She'd had to drag her eyes away from his broad chest. "I like it," she said. "I miss home, though." She'd played with a blade of grass. "I guess things have been busy for you and Matt."

"Not busy enough," he'd said enigmatically. He'd turned his head and his silver eyes had cut at her. "You didn't even write. Jan worried."

"I haven't had time. I had so much to catch up on."

"Boys?" he questioned, his eyes flickering as he lifted the cigarette to his thin lips.

"No!" She averted her face from that suddenly mocking gaze. "I mean, there hasn't been time."

"That's something." He'd crushed out the cigarette in the grass. "We've had visitors. A film crew, doing a commercial of all things, using the ranch as a backdrop. The models are fascinated by cattle. One of them actually asked me if you really pumped a cow's tail to get milk."

She laughed delightedly. "What did you tell her?"

"That she was welcome to try one, if she wanted to."

"Shame on you, Ethan!" Her face lit up as she stared at him. Then, very suddenly, the smile died and she was looking almost straight into his soul. She shivered with the feverish reaction of her body to that long, intimate look, and Ethan abruptly got to his feet and moved toward her with a stride that was lazy, graceful, almost stalking.

"Trying to seduce me, Bella?" he'd taunted softly, all too aware of how her soft eyes were smoothing over his body as he stopped just above her.

She'd really colored then. "Of course not!" she'd blurted out. "I was ... just looking at you."

"You've been doing that all day." He'd moved then, straddling her prone body so that he was kneeling with her hips between his strong thighs. He'd looked at her, his eyes lingering on her breasts for so long that they began to feel tight and swollen. She followed his gaze and found the nipples hard and visible under the silky fabric. She'd caught her breath and lifted her hands to cover them, but his steely fingers had snapped around her wrists and pushed them down beside her head. He'd leaned forward to accomplish that, and now his hips were squarely over hers and she could feel the contours of his body beginning to change.

Her shocked eyes met his. "Ethan, what are you..." she began huskily.

"Don't move your hips," he said, his voice deep and soft as he eased his chest down over hers and began to drag it slowly, tenderly, against her taut nipples. "Lock your fingers into mine," he whispered, and still that aching, arousing pressure went on and on. He bent, so that his hard, thin mouth was poised just above hers. He bit softly at her lower lip, drawing it into his lips, teasing it, while his tongue traced the moist inner softness.

She moaned sharply at the intimacy of his mouth and his body, her eyes wide open, astonished.

"Yes," he said, lifting his face enough to see her eyes, to hold them with his glittering ones. "You and me. Hadn't you even considered the possibility while you were being thrown at one eligible man after another by Jan's ceaseless matchmaking a few months ago?"

"No," she confessed unsteadily. "I thought you wouldn't be interested in somebody my age."

"A virgin has her own special appeal," he replied. "And you are still a virgin, aren't you?"

"Yes," she managed, wondering at her inability to produce anything except monosyllables while Ethan's body made hers ache all over.

"I'll stop before we do anything risky," he said quietly. "But we're going to enjoy each other for a long, long time before it gets to that point. Open your mouth when I kiss it, little one. Let me feel your tongue touching mine..."

She did moan then, letting his tongue penetrate the soft recesses of her mouth. The intimacy of it lifted her body against his and he made a deep, rough sound in his throat as he let his hips down over hers completely.

He felt her faint panic and subdued it with soft words and the gentle caress of his lean, strong hands on her back. Under her, the soft grass made a tickly cushion while she looked up into Ethan's quiet eyes.

"Afraid?" he asked gently. "I know you can feel how aroused I am, but I'm not going to hurt you. Just relax. We can lie together like this. I won't lose control, even if you let me do what comes next."

She felt the faint tenderness of her lips as she spoke, tasted him on them with awe. "What...comes next?" she asked.

"This." He lifted up on one elbow and traced his fingers over her shoulder and her collarbone, down onto the faint swell of her breast. He stroked her with the lightest kind of touch, going close to but never actually touching the taut nipple. She couldn't help her own reaction to the intimate feel of his lean fingers on her untouched body. She shuddered with pure pleasure, and the silver eyes above her watched with their own pleasure in her swift response.

"I know what you want," he whispered softly, and holding her gaze, he began to tease the nipple with a light, repetitive stroke that made her arch with each exquisite movement. "Have you ever done this with a man?"

"Never," she confessed jerkily. She shivered all over and her fingers bit into his muscular arms.

His face changed at her admission. It grew harder and his eyes began to glow. He lifted himself away a few inches. "Pull your bathing suit down to your hips," he said with rough tenderness.

"I couldn't!" she gasped, flushing.

"I want to look at you while I touch you," he said. "I want to show you how intimate it is to lie against a man's body with no fabric in the way to blunt the sweetness of touching."

"But, I've never . . ." she protested weakly.

His voice, when he spoke, was slow and soft and solemn. "Bella, is there another man you want this first time to be with?"

That put it all in perspective. "No," she said finally. "I couldn't let anyone else look at me. Only you."

His chest rose and fell heavily. "Only me," he breathed. "Do it."

She did, amazed at her own abandon. She pulled the straps gingerly down her arms and loosened the fabric from her breasts. His eyes slid down with the progress of the bathing suit and when she was nude from the waist up, he hung there above her, just looking at the delicate rise of her hard-tipped breasts, drinking in their beauty.

She gasped and his eyes lifted to hers, as they shared the impact of the first intimate thing they'd ever done together.

"I didn't think it would be you, the first time," she whispered shakily.

"That makes us even," he replied. His hand moved, tracing around her breast. His hips shifted, and she felt his pulsating need with awe as she registered his blatant masculinity.

His hand abruptly covered her breast, his palm taking in the hard nipple, and she moaned as his mouth ground down into hers.

Her body was alive. It wanted him, needed him. She felt her hips twist instinctively upward, seeking an even closer contact. He groaned, and one long, powerful leg insinuated itself between hers, giving her the contact she wanted. But it wasn't enough. It was fever, burning, blistering, and she felt her hands go to his hips, digging in, her voice breaking under the furious crush of his mouth. His hands slid under her, his hair-roughened chest dragged over her soft breasts while his hips thrust down rhythmically against hers and she felt him in a contact that made her cry out.

The cry was what stopped him. He had to drag his mouth away. She saw the effort it took, and he stared down at her with eyes that were frankly frightening. He was barely able to breathe. He groaned out loud. Then he'd arched away from her and gotten jerkily to his feet, to dive headfirst into the swimming hole, leaving a dazed, shocked Arabella on the bank with her bathing suit down around her hips.

She'd only just managed to pull it up when he finally climbed out of the water and stood over her. She was at a definite disadvantage, but she let him pull her to her feet.

He didn't let go of her hand. His fingers lifted it to his mouth, and he put his lips to its soft palm. "I envy the man who gets you, Bella," he said solemnly. "You're very special."

"Why did you do that?" she asked hesitantly.

He averted his eyes. "Maybe I wanted a taste of you," he said with a cynical smile before he turned away from her to get his towel. "I've never had a virgin."

"Oh."

He watched her gather up her own things and slip into her shoes as they went back to the pickup truck. "You didn't take that little interlude seriously, I hope?" he asked abruptly as he held the door open for her.

She had, but the look on his face was warning her not to. She cleared her throat. "No, I didn't take it seriously," she said.

"I'm glad. I don't mind furthering your education, but I love my freedom."

That stung. Probably it was meant to. He'd come very close to losing control, and he didn't like it. His anger had been written all over his face.

"I didn't ask you to further my education," she'd snapped.

And he'd smiled, mockingly. "No? It seemed to me that you'd done everything but wear a sign. Or maybe I just read you too well. You wanted me, honey, and I was glad to oblige. But only to a certain point. Virgins are exciting to kiss, but I like an experienced woman under me in bed.''

She'd slapped him. It hadn't been something she meant to do, but the remark had stung viciously. He hadn't tried to slap her back. He hadn't said anything. He'd smiled that cold, mocking, arrogant smile that meant he'd scored and nothing else mattered. Then he'd put her in the truck and driven her home.

The next week he'd been seen everywhere with Miriam, and Arabella overheard Miriam telling the other model about her plans for Ethan. Arabella had gone straight to Ethan, despite their strained relationship, to tell him what Miriam had said before it was too late. But he'd laughed at her, accused her of being jealous. And then he'd sent her out of his life with a scorching account of her inadequacies.

Four years ago, and she could still hear every word. She closed her eyes. She wondered if his memories were as bitter and as painful as her own. She doubted it. Surely Miriam had left him with some happy ones.

Finally, worn out and with her wounds reopened, she slept.

## Chapter Three

The house Ethan and his family called home was a huge two-story Victorian. Set against the softly rolling land of south Texas, with cattle grazing in pastures that seemed to stretch forever, it was the very picture of an old-time Western movie set. Except that the cattle in their fenced pastures were very real, and the fences were sturdy and purposeful, not picture-perfect and overly neat. Jacobsville was within an easy drive of Houston, and Victoria was even closer. It had a small-town atmosphere that Arabella had always loved, and she'd known the people who lived there most of her life. Like the Ballenger brothers, who ran the biggest feedlot in the territory, and the Jacobs—Tyler and Shelby Jacobs Ballenger—whose ancestor the town was named for.

The elegant old mansion with its bone-white walls and turret and gingerbread latticework was beautiful enough to have been featured in life-style magazines from time to time. It contained some priceless antiques both from early Texas and from England, because the first Hardeman had come over from London. The Hardemans were old money. Their fortune dated to an early cattle baron who made his fortune in the latter part of the nineteenth century during a blizzard that wiped out half the cattle ranches in the West. Actually, in the beginning, the family name had been Hartmond, but owing to the lack of formal education of their ancestor, the name was hopelessly misspelled on various documents until it became Hardeman.

Ethan looked like the portrait of that earlier Hardeman that graced the living-room mantel. They were probably much the same personality type, too, Arabella thought as she studied Ethan over the coffee he'd brought to the guest room for her. He was a forbidding-looking man with a cool, very formal manner that kept most people at arms' length.

"Thank you for letting me come here," she said.

He shrugged. "We've got plenty of room." He looked around the high ceiling of the room she'd been given. "This was my grandmother's bedroom," he mused. "Remember hearing Mother talk about her? She lived to be eighty and was something of a hell-raiser. She was a vamp or some such thing back during the twenties, and *her* mother was a died-in-the-wool suffragette. One of the bloomer girls, out campaigning for the vote for women."

"Good for her," Arabella laughed.

"She'd have liked you," he said, glancing down at her. "She had spirit, too."

She sipped her coffee. "Do I have spirit?" she mused. "I let my father lead me around by the nose my whole life, and I guess I'd still be doing it if it hadn't been for the accident." She glanced at the cast on her wrist, sighing as she juggled the coffee mug in one hand. "Ethan, what am I going to do? I won't even have a job, and Daddy always took care of the money."

"This is no time to start worrying about the future," he said firmly. "Concentrate on getting well."

"But—"

"I'll take care of everything," he interrupted. "Your father included."

She put the coffee mug down and lay back against the pillows. Her wrist was still uncomfortable and she was taking pain capsules fairly regularly. She felt slightly out of focus, and it was so nice to just lie there and let Ethan make all the decisions.

"Thank you, Ethan," she said and smiled up at him.

He didn't smile back. His eyes slid over her face in an exploration that set all her nerves tingling. "How long has it been since you've had any real rest?" he asked after a minute.

She shifted on the pillows. "I don't know. It seems like forever." She sighed. "There was never any time." Her stomach muscles clenched as she remembered the constant pressure, the practice that never stopped, the planes and motel rooms and concert halls and recording dates and expectant audiences. She felt her body going rigid with remembered stress as she recalled how she'd had to force herself more and more to go out on the stage, to keep her nerve from shattering at the sight of all those people.

"I suppose you'll miss the glamour," Ethan murmured.

"I suppose," she said absently and closed her eyes, missing the odd look that passed over his dark face.

"You'd better get some sleep. I'll check on you later."

The bed rose as he got up and left the room. She didn't even open her eyes. She was safe here. Safe from the specter of failure, safe from her father's long, disapproving face, safe from the cold whip of his eyes. She wondered if he was ever going to forgive her for failing him, and decided that he probably wouldn't. Tears slid down her cheeks. If only he could have loved her, just a bit, for what she was underneath her talent. He'd never seemed to love her.

Coreen sat with her for most of the day. Ethan's little mother was a holy terror when she was upset, but everyone loved her. She was the first person in the door when someone was sick or needed help, and the last to leave. She gave generously of her time and money, and none of her children had a bad word to say about her, even in adulthood. Well, except Ethan, and sometimes Arabella thought he did that just for amusement because he loved to watch his mother throw things in a temper.

Arabella had seen the result of one memorable fight between mother and son, back during her teenage years when she was visiting Ethan's brother and sister with Mary. Arabella, Mary, Jan and Matt had been playing Monopoly on the living-room floor when

Ethan and his mother got into it in the kitchen. The voices were loud and angry, and unfortunately for Ethan, his mother had been baking a cake when he provoked her. She threw a whole five-pound bag of flour at him, followed by an open jar of chocolate syrup. Arabella and Mary and Jan and Matt had seen Ethan walk by, covered from Stetson hat to booted feet in white flour and chocolate syrup, leaving a trail of both behind him on the wooden floor as he strode toward the staircase.

Arabella and the others had gaped at him, but one cold-eyed look in their direction dared them to open their mouths. Arabella had hidden behind the sofa and collapsed in silent laughter while the others struggled valiantly to keep straight faces. Ethan hadn't said a word, but Coreen had continued to fling angry insults after him from the kitchen doorway as he stomped upstairs to shower and change. For a long time afterward, Arabella had called him, "the chocolate ghost." But not to his face.

Coreen was just a little over five foot three, with the dark hair all her children had inherited, but hers was streaked with silver now. Only Ethan shared her gray eyes. Jan and Matt had dark blue eyes, like their late father.

"Do you remember when you threw the flour at Ethan?" Arabella asked, thinking aloud as she watched Coreen's deft fingers working a crochet hook through a growing black-and-red afghan.

Coreen looked up, her plump face brightening. "Oh, yes, I do," she said with a sigh. "He'd refused to sell that bay gelding you always liked to ride. One of my best friends wanted him, you see, and I knew you'd be away at music school in New York. He wasn't a working horse." She chuckled. "Ethan dug in his heels and then he gave me that smile. You know the one, when he knows he's won and he's daring you to do anything about it. I remember looking at the open flour sack." She cleared her throat and went back to work on the afghan. "The next thing I knew, Ethan was stomping down the hall leaving a trail of flour and chocolate syrup in his wake, and I had to clean it up." She shook her head. "I don't throw things very often these days. Only paper or baskets— and nothing messy."

Arabella smiled at the gentle countenance, wishing deep in her heart that she'd had a mother like Coreen. Her own mother had been a quiet, gentle woman whom she barely remembered. She'd died in a wreck when Arabella was only six. Arabella didn't remember ever hearing her father talk about it, but she recalled that he'd become a different man after the funeral.

She twisted her fingers in the blue quilted coverlet. Her father had discovered by accident that Arabella had a natural talent for the piano, and he'd become obsessed with making her use it. He'd given up his job as a clerk in a law office, and he'd become a one-man public relations firm with his daughter as his only client.

"Don't brood, dear," Coreen said gently when she saw the growing anguish on Arabella's lovely face. "Life is easier when you accept things that happen to you and just deal with them as they crop up. Don't go searching for trouble."

Arabella looked up, shifting the cast with a wince because the break was still tender. They'd taken out the clamps that had held the surgical wound together before they put on the cast, but it still felt as if her arm had been through a meat grinder.

"I'm trying not to," she told Ethan's mother. "I thought my father might have called, at least, since they put me back together. Even if it was just to see if I had a chance of getting my career back."

"Being cynical suits my son. It doesn't suit you," Coreen said, glancing at her over the small reading glasses that she wore for close work. "Betty Ann is making a cherry cobbler for dessert."

"My favorite," Arabella groaned.

"Yes, I know, Ethan told us. He's trying to fatten you up."

She frowned at the older woman. "Is Miriam really trying to come back to him?"

With a long-suffering sigh, Coreen laid the afghan and crochet hook over her knees. "I'm afraid so. It's the last thing in the world he needs, of course, after the way she cut up his pride."

"Maybe she still loves him," Arabella suggested.

Coreen cocked her head. "Do you know what I think? I think she's just lost her latest lover and he's left her pregnant. She'll try to lure Ethan into bed and convince him it's his child, so that he'll take her back."

"You really should write books," Arabella said dryly. "That's a great plot."

Coreen made a face at her. "Don't laugh. I wouldn't put it past her. She isn't as pretty as she used to be. All that hard living and hard drinking have left their mark on her. One of my friends saw her on a cruise recently, and Miriam was pumping her for all sorts of information about Ethan—if he'd remarried or was keeping company with anyone."

"He wants me to keep company with him," Arabella mentioned, "to keep Miriam at bay."

"Is that what he told you?" Coreen smiled gently. "I suppose it's as good an excuse as any."

"What do you mean?" Arabella asked curiously.

Coreen shook her head. "That's for Ethan to tell you. Are you going to keep company with him?"

"It seems little enough to do for him, when he's kind enough to give me a roof over my head and turn the whole household upside down on my account," she said miserably. "I feel like an intruder."

"Nonsense," Coreen said easily. "We all enjoy having you here, and none of us wants Miriam to come back. Do play up to Ethan. It will turn Miriam green with envy and send her running."

"Is she going to stay here?" Arabella asked worriedly.

"Over my dead body," Ethan drawled from the doorway, staring across the room at Arabella.

"Hello, dear. Been rolling in the mud with the horses again?" Coreen asked pleasantly.

He did look that way, Arabella had to admit. He was wearing working gear—chambray shirt, thick denims, weathered old leather chaps, boots that no self-respecting street cowboy would have touched with a stick, and a hat that some horse had stepped on several times. His dark skin had a thin layer of dust on it, and his work gloves were grasped in one lean hand that didn't look much cleaner.

"I've been doctoring calves," he replied. "It's March," he reminded her. "Roundup is in full swing, and we're on the tail end of calving. Guess who's going to be nighthawking the prospective mamas this week?"

"Not Matt," Coreen groaned. "He'll leave home!"

"He needs to," Ethan said imperturbably. "He and Mary can't cuss each other without an audience around here. It's going to affect their marriage sooner or later."

"I know," Coreen said sadly. "I've done my best to persuade Matt that he can make it on his own. God knows, he can afford to build a house and furnish it on his income from those shares Bob left him."

"We're too good to him," Ethan pointed out. "We need to start refusing to speak to him and putting salt in his coffee."

"If you put salt in my coffee, I'd stuff the cup up your..." Coreen began hotly.

"Go ahead," Ethan said when she hesitated, his pale eyes sparkling. "Say it. You won't embarrass me."

"Oh, I'll drink to that," Coreen murmured. "You're too much my son to be embarrassed."

Arabella looked from one to the other. "You do favor each other," she said. "Your eyes are almost exactly the same shade."

"He's taller," Coreen remarked.

"Much taller, shrimp," he agreed, but he smiled when he said it.

Coreen glared at him. "Did you come up here for any particular reason, or do you just enjoy annoying me?"

"I came to ask Arabella if she wanted a cat."

Arabella gaped at him. "A what?"

"A cat," he repeated. "Bill Daniels is out front with a mother cat and four kittens that he's taking to the vet to be put down."

"Yes, I want a cat," Arabella said at once. "Five cats." She gnawed her lower lip. "God knows what my father will say when he finds out, though. He hates cats."

"Why not think about what *you* want for a change, instead of what your father wants?" Ethan asked curtly. "Or have you ever had your own way?"

"Once, he let me have chocolate ice cream when he told me to get vanilla," she replied.

"That isn't funny," Ethan said darkly.

"Sorry." She leaned back against the pillows. "I guess I've never tried to stand up to him." It was the truth. Even though she'd rebelled from time to time, her father's long-standing domination had made it difficult for her to assert herself. Incredible, when she thought nothing of standing up to Ethan . . .

"No time like the present. I'll tell Bill we'll keep the cats." He moved away from the doorjamb. "I've got to get back to work."

"Like that?" Coreen asked. "You'll embarrass your men. They won't want to admit they work for someone as filthy as you are."

"My men are even filthier than I am," he replied proudly. "Jealous because you're clean?"

Coreen moved her hand toward the trash basket, but Ethan just smiled and left the room.

"You wouldn't have thrown it at him, would you?" Arabella asked.

"Why not?" Coreen asked. "It doesn't do to let men get the upper hand, Bella. Especially not Ethan," she added, looking at Arabella thoughtfully. "You've learned that much, I see. Ethan is a good man, a strong man. But that's all the more reason to stand up to him. He wants his own way, and he won't give an inch."

"Maybe that was one reason he and Miriam couldn't make a go of it."

"That, and her wild ways. One man just wasn't enough for her," Coreen replied.

"I can't imagine anyone going from Ethan to someone else," Arabella said. "He's unique."

"I think so, even if he is my son." Coreen picked up her afghan and her crochet hook. "How do you feel about him, Bella?"

"I'm very grateful to him for what he's done for me," she said evasively. "He's always been like a big brother...."

"You don't have to pretend," Coreen said gently. "I'm perceptive, even if I don't look it." She lowered her eyes to her crocheting. "He made the mistake of his life by letting you get away. I'm sorry for both of you that it didn't work out."

Arabella studied the coverlet under her nervous hands. "It's just as well that it didn't," she replied. "I have a career that I hope to go back to. Ethan...well, maybe he and Miriam will patch things up."

"God forbid," Coreen muttered. She sighed wearily. "Life goes on. But I'm glad Ethan brought you home with him, Bella." She looked up. "He isn't a carefree man, and he takes on too much responsibility sometimes. He's forgotten how to play. But he changes when he's with you. It makes me happy to see how different he is when you're around. You always could make him smile.''

Arabella thought about that long after Coreen had gone downstairs to help Betty Ann in the kitchen. Ethan did smile more with her than he did with other people. He always had. She'd noticed it, but it surprised her that his mother had.

For two days, Arabella was confined to bed against her will. Doctor's orders, they told her, because she'd been concussed and badly bruised in the wreck. But on the third day, the sun came out and the temperature was unnaturally high that afternoon for early March. She got downstairs by herself, a little wobbly from her enforced leisure, and sat down in the porch swing.

Coreen had gone to a ladies' circle meeting and Mary was shopping, so there was no one to tell her she couldn't go outside. Mary had helped her dress that morning in a snap-front, full denim skirt and a long-sleeved blue sweatshirt. She'd tied her hair back with a blue velvet ribbon. She looked elegant even in such casual attire, and the touch of makeup she'd used made her look more alive. Not that anyone would be around to notice.

And that was where she was mistaken. The pickup truck pulled into the yard and Ethan got out of it, pausing on the steps when he saw her sitting in the swing.

"Who the hell told you to get out of bed?" he demanded.

"I'm tired of staying in bed," she replied. Her heart went wild just at the sight of him. He was wearing faded jeans and a chambray shirt with a beat-up, tan Stetson, and his boots were muddy as he joined her on the porch. "I only had a little concussion, and my hand isn't hurting. It's such a beautiful day," she added hopefully.

"So it is." He lit a cigarette and leaned against the post, his pale eyes lancing over her. "I checked with your uncle this morning."

"Did you?" She watched him curiously.

"Your father left Dallas for New York this morning." His eyes narrowed. "Do you know why?"

She grimaced. "The bank account, I guess. If there's anything in it."

"There's something in it," he said pleasantly enough. "But he won't get to it. I had my attorney slap an injunction on your father, and the bank has orders not to release a penny to him. That's where I've been."

"Ethan!"

"It was that or have him get you by the purse strings," he said quietly. "When you're back on your feet again, you can play twenty questions with him. Right now, you're here to get well, not to have yourself left penniless by your mercenary father."

"Do I have much?" she asked, dreading the answer, because her father had enjoyed a luxurious lifestyle.

"You have twenty-five thousand," he replied. "Not a fortune, but it will keep you if it's invested properly."

She stared at his muscular arms, remembering the strength of them. "I didn't think ahead," she said. "I let him put the money in a joint account because he said it was the best way. I guess I owe you my liveli-hood, don't I?" she added with a smile.

"You're earning it," he replied quietly.

"By helping you get rid of Miriam," she agreed.

"We'll have to do a little work on you first," he re-turned. He studied her for a long moment. "You washed your hair."

"Actually, Mary and I washed my hair. I have to get Mary to help me dress with this thing on," she mut-tered, holding up the arm with the cast and then grimacing at the twinge of pain it caused. "I can't even fasten my bra—" She bit off the rest of the word.

His eyes narrowed. "Embarrassed to talk about undergarments with me?" he asked. "I know what women wear under their clothes." He grew suddenly distant and cold. "I know all too well."

"Miriam hurt you very badly, didn't she, Ethan?" she asked without meeting his eyes. "I suppose hav-ing her come back here makes all the scars open up again." She looked up then, catching the bitterness in his expression before he could erase it.

He sighed heavily and lifted the cigarette to his lips with a vicious movement of his fingers. He stared out over the horizon blankly. "Yes, she hurt me. But it was my pride, not my heart, that took a beating. When I threw her out, I vowed that no woman was going to get a second shot at me. So far, no one has."

Was he warning her off? Surely he knew that she'd never have the courage to set her cap for him again. He'd knocked her back hard enough over Miriam.

"Well, don't look at me," she said with a forced smile. "I'm definitely not Mata Hari material."

Some of the tenseness left him. He stubbed out the finished cigarette in an ashtray nearby. "All the same, little one, I can't see you sleeping around. Before or after marriage."

"We go to church," she said simply.

"I go to church myself."

She clasped her hands in her lap. "I read about this poll they took. It said that only four percent of the people in the country didn't believe in God."

"The four percent that produce motion pictures and television programs, no doubt," he muttered dryly.

She burst out laughing. "That was unkind," she said. "They aren't atheists, they're just afraid of offending somebody. Religion and politics are dangerous subjects."

"I've never worried about offending people," Ethan replied. "In fact, I seem to have a knack for it."

She smiled at him. He made her feel alive and free, as if she could do anything. Her green eyes sparkled as they met and held his silver ones, and the same electricity ran between them that had bound them together, years ago, one lazy day in late summer. The look had been translated into physical reality that one time, but now it only made Arabella sad for something she'd never have again. Even so, Ethan didn't look away. Perhaps he couldn't, she thought dazedly, feeling her heart shake her with its beat, her body tingle all over with sweet, remembered pleasure.

He said something rough under his breath and abruptly turned away. "I've got to get down to the holding pens. If you need anything, sing out. Betty Ann's in the kitchen."

He left without a backward glance.

Arabella stared after him with open longing. It seemed that she couldn't breathe without setting him off. And even if he could have felt something for her, he wasn't going to let his guard down again. He'd already said so. Miriam had really done a job on his pride.

She leaned back in the swing and started it swinging. Odd that he hadn't found someone to replace Miriam as soon as his marriage was over. He could have had his pick on looks alone, never mind the fortune behind his name. But he'd been a loner ever since, from what Mary had said. Surely Miriam couldn't have hurt him that much—unless he was still in love with her.

She sighed. She was a little afraid of Ethan. She was much too vulnerable and he was close at hand and alone. Ironically, Miriam's arrival might be her only hope of keeping her heart from being broken by him all over again.

# *Chapter Four*

Arabella had supper with the family for the first time that night, and Matt announced that he was taking Mary to the Bahamas for a much-needed vacation.

"Vacation?" Ethan glared at him. "What's that?"

Matt grinned. He looked a lot like his brother, except that he had deep blue eyes and Ethan's were silver. Matt was shorter, less formidable, but a hard worker in spite of his easygoing nature.

"A vacation is a thing I haven't had since I got married. I'm leaving and Mary is going with me."

"It's March," Ethan pointed out. "Calving? Roundup...?"

"I never asked for a honeymoon," Matt replied with an eloquent glance.

Ethan and Coreen exchanged wry looks. "All right. Go ahead," Ethan told him dryly. "I'll just have an extra set of arms put on and manage without you."

"Thanks, Ethan," Mary said gently. Her eyes glanced shyly off his and she smiled at her husband with pure delight.

"Where in the Bahamas did you plan to go?" Ethan asked.

Matt grinned. "That's a secret. If you don't know where I am, you can't look for me."

Ethan glared at him. "I tried that four years ago. You found me."

"That was different," Matt said. "A note came due at the bank and they wouldn't let me arrange the renewal."

"Excuses, excuses," Ethan replied.

"You might look at houses before you come back," Coreen murmured.

Matt shook his finger at her. "Not nice."

"Just a thought," she replied.

"If we leave, who'll save you from Ethan?" Matt asked smugly.

Arabella glanced at Ethan, who looked more approachable tonight than he had since she'd come home from the hospital. She felt suddenly mischievous. She raised her hand. "I volunteer."

Ethan's silvery eyes lanced her way with faint surprise and a little delight in them as he studied her face. "It'll take more than you, cupcake," Ethan said, and he smiled.

The smile reminded her of what Coreen had said, about how easily Ethan had once smiled for Arabella. The knowledge went to her head. She wrinkled her nose at him. "I'll recruit help. At least one of the cowboys was offering to spray you with malathion late this afternoon. I heard him."

"He was offering to spray *me* with insecticide?" Ethan glowered. "Which cowboy?" he demanded, with a look that meant trouble for the man.

"I won't tell. He might come in handy later," Arabella returned.

"Feeling better, are we?" Ethan murmured. He lifted an eyebrow. "Watch out. We'll get in trouble."

Arabella looked around. "I thought there was only one of me."

Ethan felt frankly exhilarated, and that disturbed him. He had to drag his eyes away from Arabella's soft face. He stared at his brother instead. "Why don't you want a house of your own?" Ethan asked him.

"I can't afford one."

"Horsefeathers," Ethan muttered. "You've got a great credit rating."

"I don't like the idea of going that deep in debt."

Ethan sat back in his chair and chuckled. "You don't know what debt is until you spend ninety thousand dollars for a combine."

"If you think that's high for a harvesting machine, just consider the total cost of tractors, hay balers and cattle trailers," Coreen added.

"I know, I know," Matt conceded. "But you're used to it. I'm not. Mary's applied for a job at the new textile plant that just opened. They're looking for secretarial help. If she gets it, we might take the plunge. But first we take a vacation. Right, honey?"

"Right," Mary said eagerly.

"Suit yourself," Ethan said. He finished his coffee and stood up. "I've got to make a couple of phone calls." Involuntarily, his eyes were drawn to Arabella. She looked up in time to meet that searching gaze, and a long, static moment passed during which Ethan's jaw clenched and Arabella flushed.

Arabella managed to look away first, embarrassed even though Coreen and the others were engaged in conversation and hadn't noticed.

Ethan paused by her chair and his lean hand went to her dark hair, lightly brushing it. He was gone before she could question whether it had been accidental or deliberate. Either way, her heart went wild.

She spent the evening listening to Matt and Mary talk about their planned trip, and when bedtime came, she was the first to go up. She was on the bottom·step of the staircase when Ethan came out of his study and joined her there.

"Come here, little one, I'll carry you up." He bent, swinging her gently into his arms, careful of the hand that was in the cast.

"It's my arm, not my leg," she stammered.

He started up the stairs, easily taking her weight. He glanced down at her. "I don't want you to overdo it."

She was silent, and he drank in the feel of her in his arms. He'd never managed to forget how she felt close against him, and he'd tried, for years. Of course she didn't need to be carried. But he needed to carry her, to feel her body against him, to bring back the bittersweet memories of the one time he'd made love to her. It had haunted him ever since, especially now that she was here, in his house. He hardly slept at all these days, and when he did, his dreams were full of her. She didn't know that, and he wasn't going to admit it. It was much too soon.

She felt her breath whispering out at the concern in his deep voice. She couldn't think of anything to say.

She curled her arms hesitantly around his neck and nuzzled her face into his shoulder. His breath caught and his step faltered for an instant, as if her soft movement had startled and disturbed him.

"Sorry," she whispered.

He didn't answer. He'd felt something when she moved that way. Something that he hadn't felt in a long time. His arms tightened as he savored the warm weight of Arabella's body, the faint scent of flowers that clung to her dark hair.

"You've lost weight," he said as he reached the landing.

"I know." Her breasts rose and fell in a gentle sigh, bringing them into a closer, exciting contact with his chest. "Aren't you glad? I mean, if I weighed twice as much as I do, you might pitch headfirst down the stairs and we'd both wind up with broken necks."

He smiled faintly. "That's one way of looking at it." He shifted her as he reached her bedroom, edging through the doorway. "Hold tight while I close the door."

She did, shivering a little at his closeness. He felt that betraying tremble and stopped dead, lifting his head to look into her wide, bright eyes with a heart-stopping intensity.

"You like being close to me, don't you?" he asked. His senses stirred with a sensuality that he hadn't felt in years.

Arabella went scarlet. She dropped her eyes and went rigid in his arms, struggling for something to say.

Amazingly, her embarrassment intensified the excitement he was feeling. It was like coming to life after being dead. His body rippled with desire and he felt like a man for the first time in four years. He kicked the door shut and carried her to the bed. He tossed her onto it gently and stood over her, his eyes lingering on the soft thrust of her breasts. His eyes darted back up to catch hers, his heart feeding on the helpless desire he found on her face.

So she hadn't forgotten, any more than he had. For one wild minute, he thought about going down beside her, arching his body over her own and kissing her until she gasped. But he moved away from the bed before his body could urge him on. Arabella might want him, but her virginal state was enough of a brake for both of them. She was still bitter about the past, and what he was feeling might not last. He had to be sure. . . .

He lit a cigarette, repocketing his lighter roughly.

"I thought you'd quit, until this afternoon," Arabella said sitting up. She was uncomfortable with the silence and his sudden withdrawal. Why had he taunted her with that intimate remark and then looked as if she'd asked him to do it? Shades of the past, she thought.

"I had quit until you got yourself banged up in that wreck," he agreed with a cold glance. "That started me back."

"So did having a flat tire in the truck." She began to count off the reasons on one hand. "There was the time the men got drunk the night before roundup started. Then there was the day your horse went lame. And once, a horse bit you. . . ."

"I don't have to have excuses to smoke," he reminded her. "I've always done it and you've always known it." His eyes narrowed as he studied her soft face. "I was smoking that day by the creek. You didn't complain about the taste of it when I kissed you."

She felt the sadness that must have been reflected in her eyes. "I was eighteen," she said. "A couple of boys had kissed me, but you were older and more worldly." She lowered her eyes. "I was trying so hard to behave like a sophisticated woman, but the minute you touched me, I went to pieces." She sighed heavily. "It seems like a hundred years ago. I guess you were right, too; I did throw myself at you. I was besotted with you."

He had to struggle not to go to her, to pull her into his arms and kiss the breath out of her. She felt guilty, when he was the one who'd been wrong. He'd hurt her. He'd wounded her pride, just as Miriam had wounded his, and sent her running. Perhaps her father would never have gotten such a hold on her if he'd told Miriam to go to hell and asked Arabella to marry him.

"What tangled webs we weave," he said quietly. "Even when we aren't trying to deceive people."

"You couldn't help loving Miriam," she replied.

His face froze. Amazing how just the sound of his ex-wife's name could turn him off completely. He lifted the cigarette to his mouth, the hardness in him almost brittle as he stared down at Arabella.

Arabella watched him. "Do you realize how you look when someone mentions her, Ethan?" she asked gently.

"I realize it," he said curtly.

"And you don't want to talk about it. All right, I won't ask," she replied. "I can imagine she dealt your pride a horrible blow. But sometimes all it takes to repair the damage is having your ego built back up again.''

His pale eyes pierced hers, and the look they exchanged was even more electric and intimate than the one downstairs.

''Are you offering to give me back my self-esteem?'' he asked.

Years seemed to pass while she tried to decide if he meant that question. He couldn't have, she decided finally. He'd made it clear four years ago just how he felt. She shivered. ''No, I'm not offering anything, except to give a good performance when Miriam gets here,'' she told him. ''I owe you that much for taking me in while I get well.''

His eyes blazed. ''You owe me nothing,'' he said coldly.

''Then I'll do it for old times' sake,'' she returned with icy pride. ''You were like the big brother I never had. I'll do it to pay you back for looking out for me.''

He felt as if she'd hit him. The only thing that gave him any confidence was the way she'd reacted to being in his arms. He blew out a cloud of smoke, staring at her with total absorption. ''Any reason will do,'' he said. ''I'll see you in the morning.''

He turned and started toward the door.

''Well, what do you want me to say?'' she burst out. ''That I'd do anything you asked me to do short of murder? Are you looking for miracles?''

He stopped with his hand on the doorknob and looked at her. ''No, I'm not looking for miracles.'' He searched her face. Somewhere inside, he felt dead. ''I put the cat and kittens in the barn,'' he said after a minute. "If you'd like to see them, I'll take you down there in the morning."

She hesitated. It was an olive branch of sorts. And if they were going to convince Miriam, they couldn't do it in a state of war. She moved restlessly on the bed. "Yes, I'd like that. Thank you."

*"De nada,"* he said in careless Spanish, a habit because of the Mexican vaqueros who worked for him, who still understood their own language best. Ethan spoke three or four languages fluently, which often surprised visitors who felt his Texas drawl indicated a deprived education.

She watched him leave with pure exasperation. He kept her so confused and upset that she didn't know if she was coming or going.

Mary and Matt left the next morning. Arabella hugged Mary goodbye, feeling a little lost without her best friend. Ethan's new outlook and the specter of Miriam's approach seemed daunting, to say the least.

"Don't look so worried," Mary said gently. "Ethan and Coreen will take good care of you. And Miriam won't be staying here. Ethan wouldn't have it."

"I hope you're right. I have a feeling Miriam could take skin off with words."

"I wouldn't doubt that," Mary replied, grimacing. "She can be nasty, all right. But I think you might be equal to her, once you got going. You used to be eloquent when you lost your temper. Even Ethan listened." She laughed.

"I haven't had much practice at losing my temper, except with Ethan," Arabella replied. "Wish me luck."

"I will, but you won't need it, I'm sure," Mary said.

Ethan drove them to the airport in Houston so they wouldn't have to take the shuttle flight out of Jacobsville airport. But he was back before Arabella expected him, and he hadn't forgotten about the kittens.

"Come on, if you're still interested." He took her good hand, tugging her along with him, not a trace of emotion showing on his face.

"Shouldn't we tell your mother where we're going?" she protested.

"I haven't told my mother where I was going since I was eight," he said shortly. "I don't need her permission to walk around the ranch."

"I didn't mean it that way," she muttered.

It did no good at all. He ignored her. He was still wearing what he called his city clothes, charcoal slacks with a pale blue shirt and a Western-cut gray-and-black sport jacket.

"You'll get dirty," she said as they entered the wide-aisled barn.

He glanced down at her. "How?"

She could have made a joke about it with a less intimidating man, but not with Ethan. This unapproachable man would have cut her to pieces.

"Never mind." She moved ahead of him, neatly dressed herself in a pair of designer jeans and a pale yellow pullover that would show the least hint of dirt.

She walked down the aisle and went where he gestured, feeling his presence with fear and delight. It was sobering to think that but for the accident that had damaged her hand, she might never have seen Ethan again.

Her hand. She glanced down at it, seeing the help-lessness of it emphasized by the cast. Threads of music drew through her mind. She could hear the keys, feel the chords, the melody, the minors, the subdominants....

She closed her eyes and heard Clementi's *Sonatina*, its three movements one of the first pieces she'd mastered when she began as an intermediary student. She smiled as it was replaced in her thoughts by the exquisite *English Suite* by Bach, and *Finlandia* by Grieg.

"I said, here are the kittens. Where were you?" Ethan asked quietly.

She opened her eyes, and realized as she did that her fingers might never feel those notes again. She might never be able to play a melody in more than a parody of her former ability. Even the pop tunes would be beyond her. She'd have no way to support herself. And she certainly couldn't expect her father to do it, not when he wouldn't even phone or come near her. At least Ethan had managed to save some of her earnings, but they wouldn't last long if her father hadn't paid off the debts.

There was panic in her eyes, in her pale face.

Ethan saw it. He tapped her gently on the nose, the antagonism dying out of him all at once when he saw her tormented expression. He had to stop baiting her. It wasn't her fault that Miriam had crippled him as a man. "Stop trying to live your life all at one time. There's nothing to panic about."

Her eyes met his. "That's what you think."

"Let tomorrow take care of itself." He went down on one knee. "Now this is worth seeing."

He gestured for her to kneel down beside him, and all her cares were lost in the magic of five snow-white, newborn kittens. Their mother, too, was a snow-white shorthair with deep blue eyes.

"Why, I've never seen a cat like this!" she exclaimed. "A white cat with blue eyes!"

"They're pretty rare, I'm told. Bill found them in his barn, and he's not a cat fancier."

"And they were going to be put to sleep." She groaned. "I'll rent them an apartment if my father gives me any trouble," she said firmly. She smiled at the mother cat and then looked longingly at the kittens. "Will she let me hold one?"

"Of course. Here." He lifted a tiny white kitten and placed it gently in Arabella's hand, which she held close to her body to make sure it didn't fall. She nuzzled its tiny head with her cheek, lost in the magic of the new life.

Ethan watched her, his eyes indulgent and without mockery. "You love little things, don't you?"

"I always have." She handed back the kitten with obvious reluctance, taking the opportunity to stroke it gently. "I always thought that one day I'd get married and have children, but there seemed to be one more concert, one more recording date." She smiled wistfully. "My father was determined to make sure that I never had the chance to get serious about anyone."

"He couldn't risk losing you." Ethan put the kitten back down, stroking the mother's head gently before he rose, bringing Arabella up with him. He brushed back her long, loose dark hair with both hands. Then, in the silence of the barn, which was only broken by an occasional movement or sound from the horses nearby, his hands moved to frame her face. "I used to take you riding. Remember?"

"Yes. I haven't been on a horse since. Ethan, why wouldn't you let your mother sell the horse I used to ride here?" she asked suddenly, remembering what Coreen had said about it.

He shifted restlessly. "I had my reasons."

"And you won't tell me what they were?"

"No." He searched her eyes slowly, hungrily. He felt his heartbeat increasing as the nearness of her began to affect him, just as it had the night before. "It's been a hell of a long time since you and I have been alone together," he said quietly.

She lowered her eyes to his broad chest, watching its heavy rise and fall. "Years," she agreed nervously.

He touched her hair gently, trailing it through his fingers, feeling the silkiness of it. "Your hair was long, then, too," he recalled, catching her soft eyes. "I pillowed you on it in the grass when we made love by the old swimming hole."

Her heart went wild. It was all she could do to hold on to her self-control. "We didn't make love," she said through her teeth. "You kissed me a few times and made sure I didn't take it seriously. It was to 'further my education,' didn't you say?"

"You were grass-green and stupid about men," he said curtly. "You felt my body against yours. You may have been a kid then, but you sure as hell ought to know by now how dangerous the situation was getting when I called a halt."

"It doesn't make any difference now," she said miserably. "As I said, you made sure I didn't take it seriously. I was just being my usual stupid self. Now can we go back to the house?''

He slid his hands roughly into her hair and held her face up to his pale, glittering eyes. "You were eighteen," he said shortly. "A virginal eighteen with a father who hated my guts and had complete control of your life. Only a heartless fool would have seduced you under those circumstances!''

She stared at him, shocked by the fury in his eyes, his voice. "And you were nobody's fool," she agreed, almost shaking with mingled fear and hurt. "But you don't have to pretend that you cared about my feelings, not after the things you said to me . . . !''

His hands contracted and he drew in a sharp breath. "God in heaven, how can you be so blind?" he groaned. His gaze fell to her mouth and he drew her face up toward his, his lips parting. "I wanted you!''

The words went into her mouth. He was fitting his lips with exquisite slowness to her own in a silence thick with tense emotion. But even as his mouth brushed against hers, even as she felt the sharp intake of his breath and felt the pressure of his hands on her face, a sound broke the spell and froze him in place.

It was the loud roar of a car driving up outside. Ethan's head lifted abruptly and the look in his eyes was almost feverish. His hands had a faint tremor as he drew them away from her face, and he was breathing roughly. So was she. She felt as if her legs wouldn't even support her.

Her eyes asked the question she didn't dare.

"I've been alone a long time," he said curtly, and he gave her a mocking smile. "Isn't that what you'd like to believe?''

Before she could answer, he let go of her and turned toward the front of the barn.

"I'm expecting a buyer this morning," he said gruffly. "That must be him."

He went down the wide aisle ahead of her, almost grateful for the diversion. He'd lost his head just then, gotten drunk on the exquisite promise of Arabella's mouth under his. He hadn't realized how vulnerable he'd become since she'd been here. He was going to have to be more careful. Rushing her would accomplish nothing; he should be thankful that his buyer had interrupted.

But when he reached the yard, the visitor wasn't his buyer at all. It was a taxi, and getting out of the back seat, all leggy glamour and red lipstick, was Miriam Hardeman. If she wasn't going to be a houseguest, obviously nobody had thought to inform her of it, because the cabdriver was slowly getting six expensive suitcases out of the trunk of the car.

Ethan's face went stiff as Arabella joined him and he felt as if he were breaking out in a cold sweat. Miriam. Just the sight of his ex-wife was enough to shake his self-confidence to its foundations. He schooled his face to show nothing as he turned toward Arabella and held out his hand, silently commanding her cooperation, as she'd promised it.

Beside him, Arabella stared at the newcomer as if she were a particularly vicious disease. Which, in fact, was a fair analogy. She let Ethan's hand envelop hers and she held on for dear life. They were in it together now, for better or worse.

# Chapter Five

**M**iriam raised a delicately etched eyebrow as Ethan and Arabella joined her. She stared hard at Arabella, almost incredulously, her eyes sharp and immediately hostile. She noticed that Ethan and the younger woman were holding hands, and for a minute, she seemed to lose a little of her poise. Then she smiled, almost as if by force of will, because there was no joy in her dark green eyes.

"Hello, Ethan." She tossed back her long auburn hair nervously. "I hope you got my telegram?"

He stared back at her, refusing to be taunted. "I got it."

"Pay the cab driver, would you?" she persisted. "I'm flat broke. I hope you don't mind my staying here, Ethan, because I blew my last dollar on this outfit and I just can't afford a hotel."

Ethan didn't say a word, but his expression grew even more remote.

Arabella watched Ethan pay the driver, then her eyes darted to Miriam. The woman was perfection itself. Flaming red highlights in her long auburn hair, dark green, witchy eyes, an exquisite face and figure. But she was showing her age a bit, and she was heavier than she had been. What Coreen had said about pregnancy came home with full force. Yes, Miriam could be pregnant, all right. That would explain that slight weight gain, mostly in her waist.

"Hello, Arabella," Miriam said as she studied the younger woman coldly. "I've heard enough about you over the years. I remember you, of course. You were only a child when Ethan and I married."

"I've grown up," Arabella said quietly. She stared after Ethan with soft longing. "At least, Ethan thinks so."

Miriam laughed haughtily. "Does he, really?" she asked. "I suppose a very young woman would appeal to him, since she wouldn't know what she was missing."

That was an unexpected taunt. Arabella didn't understand it, or the way Ethan looked when he came back, after gesturing for one of his passing cowboys to carry Miriam's luggage up to the house.

"Tell her why you won't get involved with experienced women, Ethan, dear," Miriam murmured sarcastically.

Ethan stared at her with the intimidating look that Arabella hated. It even seemed to work on Miriam.

"Arabella and I go back a long way. We were involved before you and I were, Miriam," he added, staring levelly at his ex-wife.

Miriam's eyes blazed. "Yes, I remember your mother saying that," she replied.

The expression on Miriam's face did Ethan more good than anything had in years. He drew Arabella close against his side, giving her a quick, pleased glance when she let her body go lax against him. "You weren't expected until next week," he told Miriam.

"I just finished a modeling assignment down in the Caribbean and I thought I'd stop by on my way back to New York," Miriam replied. She fidgeted with her purse, nervously it seemed.

Arabella stared at Miriam from the shelter of Ethan's hard arm. It was almost rigid around her, which told her plenty about how he was reacting to the woman's presence. She didn't understand the undercurrents. If he still loved Miriam, she didn't see why he couldn't just say it. Why this pretense, when Miriam was obviously still jealous of him?

"How long do you want to stay?" Ethan asked. "We're pretty busy right now and I hope you understand that Arabella and I consider our time together precious."

Miriam lifted an eyebrow. "How convenient that you should turn up just now, Arabella. You've been pursuing your career for several years, I believe?"

"Bella was injured in a wreck. Naturally I want her where I am," Ethan replied with a cool smile. "I hope you'll enjoy spending your evenings talking to Mother."

"I'll manage," Miriam said irritably. "Well, let's go up to the house. I'm tired and I want a drink."

"You won't drink here," Ethan said firmly. "We don't keep liquor in the house."

"Don't keep . . . !" Miriam gasped. "But we always had a full liquor cabinet!"

"You did," Ethan corrected. "When you left, I had the bottles thrown out. I don't drink."

"You don't do anything," Miriam said with a nasty inflection. "Especially in bed!" she lashed out.

Ethan's arm tightened around her. Arabella was beginning to catch on, or she thought she was. She felt her hair bristling as she stared at the older woman with pure fury. Ethan didn't need defending, and he'd probably be furious that she dared say anything, but this was too much! Miriam had run around on him; what did she expect when he was repulsed by it? Even love would have a hard time excusing that kind of hurt.

Ethan himself was having to bite his tongue. He knew how Miriam would love to provoke him into losing his temper, to give her an excuse to tell Arabella all their dark secrets. He didn't want that, not until he'd had time to tell her himself. His pride demanded that much.

But Arabella got in the first words, her face lifted proudly as she faced the older woman without flinching. "You may have had problems in bed," Arabella said quietly, clinging to Ethan's hand. "Ethan and I don't." Which was the gospel truth, but not the way Miriam took it. Ethan smothered a shocked gasp. He hadn't expected her to sacrifice her reputation for him, certainly not with such surprising courage.

Miriam shuddered with fury. "You little...!"

The word she'd used was dying on the air even as Ethan broke into it, his face fiercely angry at the way Arabella was trembling despite her brave front. "The road is that direction," Ethan indicated. "I'll send a cab after you. No way are you going to exercise your vicious tongue on my future wife!"

Miriam backed down immediately. Arabella didn't do anything; she was too shocked at being referred to as Ethan's future wife.

"I'm sorry," Miriam said on a swallowed breath. "I suppose I did lay it on with a trowel." She glanced at Ethan, curious and nervous now, unusually so. "I...I guess it shocked me to think you'd gotten over me."

"I meant what I said," he replied, his voice cutting. "If you stay here, it's on my terms. If I hear so much as one sharp word to Bella, off you go. Is that clear?"

"It had better be, isn't that what you mean, Ethan?" Miriam forced a smile. "All right, I'll be the perfect houseguest. I thought we were going to talk about a reconciliation."

"Perhaps you did," Ethan said calmly. "Bella and I are going to be married. There's no room in my life for you now or ever."

Miriam seemed to go pale. She straightened, elegant in her pale gray suit, and smiled again. "That's pretty blunt."

"Blunt is the only way to be with you," Ethan said. "After you," he said, standing aside to let her enter the house.

Arabella was still stunned, although she had the presence of mind to wonder if Miriam's outburst hadn't been prompted by fear rather than anger. Which made her wonder why Miriam was so afraid of having Ethan involved with another woman. Ethan took her hand in his, feeling its soft coldness.

"You're doing fine," he said quietly, so that Miriam couldn't hear. "Don't worry, I won't let her savage you."

"I didn't mean to say that...."

He smiled gently, despite his drawn features. "I'll explain it to you later."

"You don't have to explain anything to me," she said, her eyes level and unblinking. "I don't care what Miriam says."

He drew in a deep breath. "You're full of surprises."

"So are you. I thought you were going to save the engagement threat as a last resort," she murmured.

"Sorry. This seemed the best time. Come on. Chin up."

She managed a smile and, holding tight to his lean hand, followed him into the house.

Coreen was unwelcoming, but she was too much a lady to show her antagonism for Miriam outright. She camouflaged it behind impeccable manners and cold courtesy. The only time a smile touched her lips was when Ethan sat down close beside Arabella on the sofa and drew her against him with a possessive arm.

It had thrilled Arabella earlier when Ethan had defended her so fiercely. Perhaps it had just been his distaste for Miriam's manners, but it was nice to think that he cared enough to stand up for her. She curled up on the sofa against him, drinking in his nearness, loving the scent and feel of him so close. This was the one nice thing that had come out of Miriam's visit. Arabella could indulge her longing for Ethan without giving herself away. What a pity that he was only pretending, to keep Miriam from seeing how vulnerable he was.

She glanced up at him, watching his lean face as he listened with coolly polite interest to Miriam's monologue about her travels. He was so tense, and she felt that what Miriam had said about him in bed had hurt him. She remembered what Coreen had said about his finding Miriam repulsive and she wondered if that was what Miriam had been referring to. Odd that he'd gone so white at the reference. Well, a woman like that could do plenty of damage even to a strong man's pride. She had a vicious tongue and no tolerance for other people. It wasn't the kind of attitude that kept a marriage together, especially when she'd never given Ethan any kind of fidelity. That must have cut his heart to pieces, loving her as he had.

"What are you doing down here, Arabella?" Miriam asked eventually. "I thought you were in New York."

"I was touring," Arabella replied. "I was on my way back from a charity performance when the car was wrecked."

"She was coming back here," Ethan inserted smoothly with a warning glance at Arabella. "She'd gone with her father. I should have driven her myself."

Arabella let out an inaudible sigh at the way she'd almost slipped up. Miriam would hardly believe that she and Ethan were engaged if Arabella was living in New York and they never saw each other.

"Will you be able to use your hand again, or is your career up the creek?" Miriam asked with a pointed smile. "I guess Ethan wouldn't want you to do anything except have babies anyway."

"As I recall," Ethan said coldly, "you were quite emphatic about not wanting any. That was after I married you, of course," he added meaningfully.

Miriam shifted restlessly. "So I was. Is there anything to do around here? I hate television," she said, quickly changing the subject.

"Ethan and Arabella and I like to watch the nature specials," Coreen said. "In fact, there's a fascinating program about polar bears on tonight, isn't there, dear?" she asked Ethan.

Ethan exchanged a glance with his mother. "There is, indeed."

Miriam groaned.

It was the longest day Arabella could remember. She managed to dodge Miriam by staying with Ethan, even when he went out to check on the roundup. He usually took a horse, but in deference to Arabella's injured wrist, he was driving the ranch pickup.

He glanced at her. "Doing okay?" he asked.

She smiled. "I'm fine, thanks." He'd changed out of his traveling clothes into his worn jeans and boots and a blue plaid Western-cut shirt. His wide-brimmed hat was tilted at a rakish angle over his forehead. He looked very cowboyish, and Arabella grinned at the thought.

"Something funny?" he asked with a narrow, suspicious gaze.

"I was just thinking how much like a cowboy you look," she replied. "Not bad, for the boss."

"I don't have to wear suits around the men to get their attention."

"I remember." She shuddered.

"Stop that." He took a draw from the smoking cigarette in his hand. "You were a surprise this morning," he said unexpectedly. "You handled Miriam very well."

"Did you expect me to break into tears and run for cover?" she asked. "I've had a lot of practice with bad-tempered people. I lived with my father, remember."

"I remember. Miriam's the one who ran for cover this time."

"You had a few bites of her, yourself. My gosh, what a venomous woman!" she said huskily. "I don't remember her being that bad before."

"You didn't know her before. Or maybe you did," he added quietly. "You saw through her from the beginning."

She studied his averted face for a long moment, wanting to ask him something more, but uncertain of the way to go about it.

He sensed her curiosity and glanced toward her. "Go ahead. Ask me."

She started. "Ask you what?"

He laughed coldly as he drove the truck along the rough track beside the fence, bouncing them both in the seats even with the superior shocks under the truck body. "Don't you want to know why she was surprised when you gave her the impression we were lovers?"

"I thought she was just being sarcastic," she began.

He turned the truck and headed it toward another rutted path. Then abruptly he stopped it and cut off the engine. He had the windows down, and the sounds of birds and the distant bawling of cattle filtered in through it.

He sat with one hand on the steering wheel, the other holding the cigarette. He shifted in the seat and stared at Arabella fully, his silver eyes touching her face while he struggled with an explanation he didn't want to make. But Miriam was bound to say something to Arabella, and he wanted it to come from him, not from his venomous houseguest.

"Miriam took a lover two weeks after we were married," he said quietly. "There was a procession of them until I divorced her. She said that I couldn't satisfy her in bed."

He said it with icy bluntness, his eyes dark with pain, as if it were a reflection on his manhood. Perhaps it was. Arabella had read that a man's ego was the most vulnerable part of him.

She searched his face quietly. "It seems to me that nobody could satisfy her, Ethan. She certainly had a lot of lovers."

He didn't realize that he'd been holding his breath until then. Arabella's attitude took the sting out of the admission. He relaxed a little. "They say everything goes if both partners want it, but I was too old-fashioned to suit Miriam." He smoked his cigarette quietly.

She glanced at him. "Coreen thinks Miriam's pregnant and that's why she came back to try for a reconciliation. She wants to get you into bed and pretend it's yours."

"I told you at the outset, I don't want her," he said bluntly. "In bed or otherwise. She'd have to do a hell of a lot of pretending to get me to go along."

"She could tell people you were the father," she countered.

He sighed. "Yes, she probably could. That may be what she has in mind."

"What are we going to do?" she asked.

"I'll think of something," he said without looking at her. Locking his bedroom door might be the best answer, but wouldn't Miriam enjoy that, he thought bitterly.

"I could help if you'd tell me what to do," she replied. "All I know about sex is what you taught me that day," she added without looking at him.

That got his full attention. His breath was expelled in an audible rush. "My God," he said roughly. "You're kidding."

"I'm afraid not."

"Surely there were other men?"

"Not in the way you mean."

"You had to go out on dates in the past four years," he persisted. "You could be a virgin and still have some experience."

She'd backed herself into a corner now, she thought worriedly. How could she tell him that the thought of any other man's hands and eyes on her body had nauseated her? She looked for a way to change the subject.

"Answer me, Arabella," he said firmly.

She glared at him. "I won't."

He began to smile. "Was it so good with me that you didn't want it with anyone else?" he asked slowly.

She blushed and averted her eyes, and he felt as if he were floating.

He reached out unexpectedly and caught a strand of her hair, savoring its silky softness. "I don't know how I managed to stop. You were extraordinarily responsive."

"I was infatuated with you," she replied. "I wanted so desperately to show you that I was grown up." She stared at his broad chest. "I suppose I did, but it didn't help. We'd at least been on relatively friendly terms until then."

He closed the ashtray and sat up straight again to study her through narrowed eyes. "I suppose you're right. If we're going to pull this off, you and I are going to have to give the appearance of intimacy when we're around Miriam," he said abruptly, changing the subject.

She was glad to return to the present. Discussion about the past was still unpleasant. "You mean, I need to wear low-cut dresses and slink when I walk and sit on your lap and curl your hair around my fingers? Especially in front of Miriam?"

"You're catching on, cupcake," he replied.

"It wouldn't embarrass you?" she asked with a faint grin.

"Well, as long as you don't try to take my clothes off in public," he said. It was the first trace of humor she'd noticed in him since Miriam came. "We wouldn't want to embarrass my mother."

"You'll have to settle for partial seduction right now, I'm afraid," she sighed, indicating her wrist in the cast. "It's hard enough undressing myself without having to undress you, too."

"That reminds me," he murmured with a pointed look at the straps under her blouse, "how do you manage to get undressed?"

She lifted her shoulders. "I can manage most everything. Except what's underneath."

"You might consider going without what's underneath for the duration of Miriam's stay," he suggested somberly. "I'll try not to stare, but it might give her food for thought if you walk around in front of me that way."

"Your mother will have a heart attack," she replied.

"Not my mother. She's been in your corner since you were eighteen." His eyes darkened as they searched hers. "She never could understand why I preferred Miriam to you."

"I could," she said with a harsh laugh. "Miriam was everything I wasn't. Especially sophisticated and experienced." She stared down at her lap with returning bitterness. "All I had going for me was a little talent. And now I may not even have that."

"None of that," he said curtly. His hand tightened around hers. "We won't think ahead. We won't think about when that cast comes off or your father's reaction. We'll think about Miriam and how to get her out of here. That's our first priority. You give me a hand and I'll do the same for you when your father shows up."

"Will he show up, Ethan?" she asked miserably.

The soft green eyes looking so trustingly into his made his pulse hammer in his throat. She was as pretty as she'd been at eighteen, and just as shyly innocent. He wouldn't have traded her tenderness for all of

Miriam's glittery sophistication, but he no longer had that choice. Arabella was only playing a part in this mutual-protection pact. He couldn't lose sight of that fact. Arabella wasn't his. With the bitterness of the past between them, she probably never would be.

"It doesn't matter whether or not he does," he replied. He studied her long, elegant fingers. "I'll take care of you."

She felt little thrills down her spine. If only he meant it! She closed her eyes, drinking in the scent of his cologne, the warmth of his lean, powerful body so close to her.

There had been so little affection in her life. She'd been alone and unloved. Her father had only wanted her talent, not her company. No one had ever loved her, but she wanted Ethan to. She wanted him to care as much as she did. But that would never happen now. Miriam had killed what love there was in him.

"You're so quiet, little one," Ethan said. He tilted her chin up and searched her sad eyes. "What's wrong?"

The softness of his voice brought tears. They stung her eyelids and when she tried to hide them, he held her face firmly in both lean hands and made her look at him.

"Why?" he asked roughly.

Her lower lip trembled and she caught it in her teeth to still it. "It's nothing," she managed. Her eyes closed. She was a hopeless coward, she thought. She wanted to say why can't you love me, but she was afraid to.

"Stop trying to live your whole life in one day," he said sharply. "It won't work."

"I guess I worry too much," she confessed, brushing away a shiny tear from her cheek. "But everything's turned upside down. I had a promising career and a nice apartment in New York. I traveled ... and now I may be a has-been. My father won't even talk to me," she faltered.

"He'll be in touch," he said. "Your hand will mend. Right now you don't need a job; you've already got one."

"Yes," she said with a weak smile. "Helping you stay single."

He gave her an odd look. "I wouldn't put it that way," he corrected. "The idea is to get Miriam to leave without bloodshed."

She lifted her face. "She's very beautiful," she said, searching his pale silver eyes. "Are you sure you don't want her back, Ethan? You loved her once."

"I loved an illusion," he said. His fingers brushed at a long strand of dark brown hair, moving it behind her ear. "Outward beauty isn't any indication of what's inside, Arabella. Miriam thought that beauty was enough, but a kind spirit and a warm heart mean a lot more to most people than a pretty face."

"She's not quite as cold as she was," she said.

He smiled faintly, searching her eyes. "Are you trying to push me into her arms?"

"No." She lowered her eyes to his hard mouth. "I just wondered if you were sure that getting rid of her is what you really want."

He drew her forehead against his chest, smoothing down her ruffled hair as he stared over her head and out the window. "I'm sure," he replied. "It wasn't much of a marriage to begin with." He drew back and looked at Arabella's soft face, drinking in its delicate beauty, its strength of character. "I wanted her," he said absently. "But wanting isn't enough."

Perhaps wanting was all he was capable of, though, Arabella thought miserably. He'd wanted her years ago, but he hadn't loved her. He said he hadn't loved Miriam, but since he married her, he must have felt something pretty powerful for her.

"What are you thinking about now?" he asked at her forehead.

"Just long thoughts," she confessed. She drew in a steadying breath and lifted a smile to show him. "I'm all—"

His mouth settled unexpectedly on hers, covering the word even as she spoke it.

She stiffened at the feel of his firm lips on hers. All the years since he'd touched her, and it was as if they'd never been apart. She remembered the scent of him, the way his mouth bit at hers to make it open just as it had the first time he'd ever kissed her. She remembered the sound he made in his throat when he dragged her face under his with rough, warm hands and the feverish intensity of the mouth that grew instantly more demanding and intimate on her lips.

"Kiss me," he whispered, his breath making little chills on her moist lips. "Don't hold back."

"I don't want this—" she protested with her last whisper of will.

"You want me. You always have and I've always known it," he said roughly.

His fingers speared into her long hair, tangling in its dark softness while his mouth crushed down on hers again, pressing her lips firmly apart as he began to build the intensity of the kiss from a slow possession to a devastating intimacy.

She stiffened and he hesitated, his mouth poised just above her own.

"Don't fight me," he said huskily. His hands moved, faintly tremulous where they held her face captive. He was burning. On fire for her. The old need was back, in full force, and she was his, if only for a space of seconds. He wanted her so desperately. She was his heart. Miriam and all the pain were forgotten in his driving hunger to hold Arabella's soft body in his arms, to feel again the aching sweetness of her mouth under his. "Oh, God, let me love you," he ground out.

"You don't," she said miserably. "You don't, you never did . . . !"

He took the words into his open mouth. He groaned heavily and his hands slid over her back, bringing her gently against him, so that her breasts flattened against his hard chest while he kissed her. Her hands pressed against his warm shirtfront, but she didn't kiss him back or put her arms around him. She was too afraid that he'd been stirred up by his ex-wife and now he needed an outlet. It was . . . demeaning.

He felt her lack of response and lifted his head. He could hardly breathe. His chest actually throbbed with the fierce thunder of his heart, and the sight of Arabella's flushed, lovely face under his made it go even faster. She looked frightened, although there was something under the fear, a leashed hunger that she was refusing to satisfy.

And that wasn't the only thing he noticed. Despite the blow Miriam had dealt his pride, he discovered that he was suddenly very much a man. He felt desire as he held Arabella; a raging desire he'd thought for four years he'd never be able to feel again for a woman. The impact of it brought a muffled curse from his lips. Of all the times for it to happen, and with Arabella, of all people!

## Chapter Six

Arabella couldn't meet Ethan's searching gaze, and the faint tremor in his arms frightened her. He looked and felt out of control, and she knew the strength in that lean body. She tried to pull away, but he drew her even closer, his hard, dark face poised just above her own.

"What's wrong?" he asked roughly.

"You want Miriam," she said through numb lips. "You want her, and I'm substituting, all over again."

He was utterly shocked. His arms loosened and she took advantage of the momentary slackening to pull away from him. She couldn't bear the confinement of the cab a minute longer. She opened the door and climbed down, locking her arms around her breasts as she stared at the flat horizon and listened to the buzzing noise of insects in the heat of the day.

Ethan got out, too, lighting a cigarette. He walked along beside her with apparent carelessness, steering her toward a grove of mesquite trees by the small stream that led eventually to the swimming hole. He leaned against the rough trunk of a huge mesquite tree, smoking quietly while Arabella leaned against a nearby tree and watched butterflies fluttering around a handful of straggly wildflowers on the creek bank.

The silence became unnerving. Ethan's eyes narrowed as he studied Arabella's slender body. "You weren't substituting for Miriam in the truck."

She colored, avoiding his level gaze. "Wasn't I?"

He took a draw from the cigarette and stared at the ripples in the water. "My marriage is over."

"Maybe she's changed," she said, rubbing salt in her own wounds. "It could be a second chance for you."

"Miriam's the one with the second chance," he returned, his cold eyes biting into her face. "To bring me to my knees. The only thing she ever saw in me was the size of my wallet."

And that was the most hurtful part of it, she imagined. He'd loved Miriam and all she'd wanted was his money. She rubbed her cast with a light finger, tracing patterns on it. "I'm sorry. I guess that was rough."

"No man likes being a walking meal ticket," he said shortly. He finished the cigarette and tossed it onto the ground, putting it out with a vicious movement of his boot.

"Then maybe she'll give up and go away," she said.

"Not if you don't help me give her the right impression about our relationship," he said curtly. He pushed away from the tree and walked toward her with somber intent in his pale eyes. "You said you'd need a little cooperation. All right. You'll get it."

"No, Ethan," she choked. Even in her innocence, she recognized the purposeful stride, the glitter in his enveloping gaze. It was the same look he'd had on his face that day at the swimming hole. "Oh, Ethan, don't! It's just a game to you. It's Miriam you want. It's always been Miriam, never me!"

He moved in front of her and his lean hands shot past her to the broad tree trunk, imprisoning her. He held her eyes relentlessly. "No," he said huskily. He searched her face and his heart went wild. Even his body, frozen though it had been for four long years, was alive as never before.

"Don't," she pleaded as her breath caught in her throat. The scent and feel of him was making her weak. She didn't want to be vulnerable again, she didn't want to be hurt. "Please don't."

"Look at me."

She shook her head.

"I said, look at me!"

The sheer force of will in the deep drawl brought her rebellious eyes up, and he trapped them.

Still holding her eyes with his, he lowered his body against hers, letting her feel the raging arousal she'd kindled.

Her eyes dilated. She could barely breathe. After one shocked minute, she tried to struggle, but he groaned and his eyes closed. He shuddered. She stood very still, her lips parted.

He looked down at her for a long time, his eyes dark with desire, his body rigid with it. "My God," he whispered almost reverently. "It's been so long...."

His mouth ground into hers with fierce delight. He was a man again, whole again. He could hardly believe what he was feeling.

Arabella was drowning in him. His warm masculine body was making her ache terribly, but she couldn't afford to give in.

"I won't love you, Ethan," she whispered, her expression tormented as memories of the past wounded her. "I won't, I won't!"

His heart began to swell in his chest. So that was it. The secret fear. He smiled faintly, letting his gaze fall to her soft bow of a mouth as he began to realize how vulnerable she was, and why. "We'll take it one day at a time," he breathed as his head bent. "Do you remember how I taught you to kiss—with your teeth and your tongue as well as your lips?"

She did, but it wouldn't have mattered, because he was teaching her all over again. She felt the brush of his warm, hard lips over her own, felt them tug on her lower lip and then her upper lip, felt the soft tracing of his tongue between them and the gentle bite of his teeth as he coaxed her mouth to open and admit the slow, deliberate penetration of his tongue.

A sound escaped her tight throat. Her body stiffened under his. The fingers of her uninjured hand began to open and close, her nails making tiny scraping sensations even through his shirt to his throbbing chest.

"Open my shirt," he said into her mouth.

She hesitated and he kissed her roughly.

"Do it," he bit off against her lips. "You've never touched me that way. I want you to."

She knew it was emotional suicide to obey him, but her fingers itched to touch his warm, dark skin. She felt his lips playing gently against her mouth while she fumbled the buttons out of the buttonholes until, finally, her fingers could tangle in the thick dark growth of hair over his chest to find the warm, taut skin beneath it.

Unthinking, she drew back to look at where her fingers were touching, fascinated concentration in her soft green eyes as she registered the paleness of her long fingers against the darkness of his hair-matted skin.

"Put your mouth against me," he said unsteadily. "Here. Like this." He caught the back of her head and coaxed her face against him. She breathed in soap and cologne and pure, sweet man as her lips pressed softly where he guided them.

"Ethan?" she whispered uncertainly. This was unfamiliar territory, and she could feel that his body was rigid with desire. He was shuddering with it.

"There's nothing to be afraid of, Arabella," he said at her lips. "Let me lift you...God, baby!" he ground out, shuddering. His hips pinned hers to the tree, but she never felt the rough bark at her spine. Her arms went around him, both of them trembling as the intimate contact locked them together as forcefully as a blazing electric current.

She was crying with the sheer impact of it, her arms holding him even as his full weight came down against her.

"You can't get close enough to me, can you?" he groaned. "I know. I feel the same way! Move your legs, sweet...yes!"

His leg insinuated its powerful length between hers, intensifying the intimacy of the embrace.

"I want you." His hands caught her hips, moving them with slow, deliberate intent into his while his mouth probed hers. "I want you, Arabella. God, I want you so!"

She was incapable of answering him. She felt him pick her up, but her eyes were closed. She was his. Whatever he wanted, whatever he did, she had no desire to stop him.

She felt the wind in her hair and Ethan's mouth on hers. The strength of his arms absorbed the shock of his footsteps as he carried her back to the truck.

He opened the door and put her in the passenger seat, sliding her to the middle of the cab so that he could fit facing her, his eyes intent on her flushed face.

Arabella could hardly breathe for the enormity of what had just happened. She'd never expected Ethan to make such a heavy pass at her with Miriam in residence. But it was because of Miriam, she was sure of it. He just didn't want to admit that his heart was still in bondage to the woman he couldn't satisfy. Her eyes fell to his opened shirt, to the expanse of his muscular chest, and lingered there.

"Nothing to say?" he asked quietly.

She shook her head slowly.

"I won't let you pretend that it didn't happen." He tilted her face up to his. "We made love."

Her cheeks went scarlet. "Not... not quite."

"You wouldn't have stopped me." He traced her lower lip with a long, teasing forefinger. "Four years, and the intensity hasn't lessened. We touch each other and catch fire."

"It's just physical, Ethan," she protested weakly.

He caught her long hair in his hands and drew it around her throat. "No."

"Miriam's here and you're frustrated because she didn't want you...."

He lifted an eyebrow. "Really?"

She folded the arm in the cast and stared at it. "Shouldn't we go back?"

"You were the one asking for cooperation," he reminded her.

"Was that why you kissed me?" she ventured.

"Not really." He brushed his lips over her eyes, closing her eyelids gently. "You make me feel like a man," he whispered huskily. "I'm whole again, with you."

She didn't understand that. He'd said that he couldn't satisfy Miriam, but he was certainly no novice. She was shaking from the intensity of his lovemaking.

"What are you going to do about tonight?" She tried to change the subject. "Miriam will surely make a beeline for your bedroom."

"Let me handle Miriam," he said. "Are you sure you want to go home?"

She wasn't, but she nodded.

He framed her face in his lean hands and made her look at him. "If your body was all I wanted, I could have had it four years ago," he reminded her gently. "You would have given yourself to me that day at the swimming hole."

Her lips parted on a rush of breath. "I don't understand."

"That's obvious." He kissed her roughly and let her go, climbing down out of the cab. He shut the door, went around to get in himself, and started the truck with a jerky motion of his fingers.

"You said it was just to get rid of Miriam, that we'd pretend to be involved," she began dazedly.

He glanced at her, his pale eyes approving the swell of her mouth, the faint flush of her cheeks. "But we weren't pretending just now, were we?" he asked quietly. "I said we'd take it one day at a time, and that's how it's going to be. Just let it happen."

"I don't want to have an affair," she whispered.

"Neither do I." He put the truck in gear and pulled back into the ruts, bouncing them over the pasture. "Light this for me, honey."

He handed her a cigarette and his lighter, but it took her three tries before her trembling fingers would manage the simple action. She handed him the cigarette and then the lighter, her eyes lingering on his hard mouth.

"You've thought about sleeping with me, haven't you?" he asked unexpectedly.

Why lie? she asked herself. She sighed. "Yes."

"There's no reason to be embarrassed. It's a perfectly natural curiosity between two people who've known each other as long as we have." He took a draw from the cigarette. "But you don't want sex outside marriage."

She stared out the windshield. "No," she said honestly.

He glanced at her and then nodded absently. "Okay."

She felt as if she were struggling out of a web of vagueness. Nothing made sense anymore, least of all Ethan's suddenly changed attitude toward her. He wanted her, that was patently obvious. But wasn't it because he couldn't have Miriam? Or was there some reason that she'd missed entirely?

Well, there was going to be plenty of time to figure it out, she supposed. Ethan sat beside her quietly smoking his cigarette while she shot covert glances his way and tried to understand what he wanted from her. Life was suddenly growing very complicated.

Supper that night was a stilted affair, with Miriam complaining delicately about every dish and eating hardly anything. She glared at Arabella as if she wished her on Mars. Probably, Arabella mused, because she'd seen the two of them when they came in from their ride in the truck. Arabella's hair had been mussed, her makeup missing, her lips obviously swollen. It didn't take a mind reader to know that she and Ethan had been making love.

And in that supposition, Arabella was right. Miriam did recognize the signs and they made her furious. The way Ethan was looking at the younger woman under his thick dark eyelashes was painful to her. Ethan had looked at her that way once, in the early days of their courtship. But now he had eyes only for Arabella, and Miriam's hope for a reconciliation was going up in smoke. Not that she loved Ethan; she didn't. But it hurt her pride that he could love someone else, especially when that someone was Arabella. It had been because of Arabella that Ethan had never fallen completely under Miriam's spell. He'd wanted her, but his heart had always belonged to that young woman sitting beside him. Arabella would have known that, of course, even in the old days. That was why Miriam had fought the divorce. She'd known that Arabella and Ethan would wind up together, and she hadn't wanted it to happen. But all her efforts hadn't stopped it.

Ethan didn't see Miriam's pointed glare. He was too busy watching the expression on Arabella's face. Her mouth had a soft swell where his had pressed against it, and it made him burn with pride to know how easily she'd given in to him at the last. He was a man again, a whole, capable man again, and for the first time, Miriam's presence didn't unsettle him. She'd wounded his ego to the quick with her taunts and ridicule about his prowess in the bedroom. But now he was beginning to understand that it wasn't strictly a physical problem. Not the way his body had reacted to Arabella earlier.

Miriam saw his smug expression and shifted uncomfortably.

"Thinking long thoughts, darling?" she taunted with a cold smile. "Or are you just reminiscing about the way we used to be together?"

Ethan pursed his thin lips and studied her. The anguish he felt from her taunts was suddenly gone. He knew now that the only failure was hers. She was conceited and cold and cruel, a sexless woman who basically hated men and used her beauty to punish them.

"I was thinking that you must have had a hell of a childhood," he replied.

Miriam went stark white. She dropped her fork and fumbled to pick it up again. "What in the world made you say such a thing?" she faltered.

He went from contempt to pity in seconds. Everything suddenly became crystal clear, and he understood her better now than he ever had before. Not that it changed his feelings. He couldn't want her, or love her. But he hated her less.

"No reason," he replied, but not unkindly. "Eat your beef. To hell with what they say about it, red meat's been sustaining human beings for hundreds of years in this country."

"I do seem to have a rather large appetite these days," Miriam replied. She glanced at Ethan suspiciously and then dropped her eyes.

Arabella had been watching the byplay with cold misery. Ethan was warming to the older woman, she could feel it. So what did she do now? Should she play up to him or not? She only wanted him to be happy. If that meant helping him get Miriam back, then she supposed she could be strong enough to do it.

As if he sensed her regard, he turned his head and smiled at her. He laid his hand on the table, inviting hers. After a second's hesitation, she slid her fingers across the palm and had them warmly, softly enfolded. He brought them to his mouth and kissed them hungrily, oblivious to his mother's shocked delight and Miriam's bridled anger.

Arabella colored and caught her breath. There had been a breathless tenderness in that caress, and the way he was looking at her made her body ripple with the memory of that afternoon.

"Are we really going to sit through a nature special?" Miriam asked, breaking into the tense silence.

Ethan lifted an eyebrow at her. "Why not? I like polar bears."

"Well, I don't," Miriam muttered. "I hate polar bears, in fact. I hate living out in the country, I hate the sound of animals in the distance, I hate this house, and I even hate you!"

"I thought you wanted to talk about a reconciliation," Ethan pointed out.

"How can I, when you've obviously been out in the fields making love with Miss Concert Pianist!"

Arabella flushed, but Ethan just laughed. The sound was unfamiliar, especially to Miriam.

"As it happens, it was in the truck, not in the fields," Ethan said with outrageous honesty. "And engaged people do make love."

"Yes, I remember," Miriam said icily. She threw her napkin down and stood up. "I think I'll lie down. I'll see you all in the morning. Good night."

She left, and Coreen sat back with a loud sigh. "Thank God! Now I can enjoy what's left of my meal." She picked up a homemade roll and buttered it. "What's this about making love in the pickup?" she asked Ethan with a grin.

"We need to keep Miriam guessing," he replied. He leaned back in his chair and watched his mother. "You tell me what we were doing."

"Arabella's a virgin," Coreen pointed out, noting Arabella's discomfort.

"I know that," Ethan said gently and smiled in her direction. "That won't change. Not even to run Miriam off."

"I didn't think it would." Coreen patted Arabella's hand. "Don't look so embarrassed, dear. Sex is part of life. But you aren't the kind of woman Miriam is. Your conscience would beat you to death. And to be perfectly blunt, so would Ethan's. He's a puritan."

"I'm not alone," Ethan said imperturbably. "What would you call a twenty-two-year-old virgin?"

"Sensible," Coreen replied. "It's dangerous to play around these days, and it's stupid to give a man the benefits of marriage without making him assume responsibility for his pleasure. That isn't just old-fashioned morality, it's common sense. I'm a dyed-in-the-wool women's libber, but I'll be damned if I'd give my body to any man without love and commitment."

Ethan stood up calmly, and pushed his chair toward his mother. "Stand on that," he invited. "If you're going to give a sermon, you need to be seen as well as heard, shrimp."

Coreen drew back the hand holding the roll and Ethan chuckled. He bent and picked his little mother up in his arms and kissed her resoundingly on the cheek.

"I love you," he said as he put her down again, flustered and breathless. "Don't ever change."

"Ethan, you just exasperate me," she muttered.

He kissed her forehead. "That's mutual." He glanced at Arabella, whose eyes were adoring him. "I have to make some phone calls. If she comes back downstairs, come into the office and we'll give her something else to fuss about."

Arabella colored again, but she smiled at him. "All right."

He winked and left the two women at the table.

"You still love him, don't you?" Coreen asked as she sipped her coffee.

Arabella shrugged. "It seems to be an illness without a cure," she agreed. "Despite Miriam and the arguments and all the years apart, I've never wanted anyone else."

"It seems to be mutual."

"Seems to be, yes, but that's just the game we're playing to keep Miriam from getting to him again."

"Isn't it odd how he's changed in one day," Coreen said suddenly, watching the younger woman with narrowed eyes. "This morning he was all starch and bristle when Miriam came, and now he's so relaxed and careless of her pointed remarks that he seems like another man." She narrowed one eye. "Just what did you do to him while the two of you were out alone?"

"I just kissed him, honest," Arabella replied. "But he is different, isn't he?" She frowned. "He said something odd, about being whole again. And he did say that Miriam told him he couldn't satisfy her. Maybe he just needed an ego boost."

His mother smiled secretively and stared down into her coffee. "Maybe he did." She leaned back. "She'll make another play for him, you know. Probably tonight."

"I told him I thought she would, too," Arabella said. "But I couldn't get up enough nerve to offer to sleep with him." She cleared her throat. "He really is a puritan. I thought he'd be outraged if I mentioned it. I could sleep on a chair or something. I didn't mean..." she added, horrified at what his mother might think.

"I know, dear. You don't have to worry about that. But I do think it might be a good idea if you spend some time in his room tonight. Miriam would think twice before she invaded his bedroom if she thought you were in it with him." She grinned. "It would damage her pride."

"Ethan may damage my ears," Arabella said ruefully. "He won't like it. And what if Miriam tells you about it? You're a puritan, too, about having unmarried people sleeping together under your roof."

"I'll pretend to be horrified and surprised and I'll insist that Ethan set a wedding date," Coreen promised.

"Oh, no, you can't!" Arabella gasped.

Coreen got up and began removing crockery. She darted an amused glance at her houseguest. "Don't worry about a thing. I know something you don't. Help me get these things into the kitchen, would you, dear? Betty Ann went home an hour ago, so you can help me do dishes. Then, you can start making plans for later. Do you have a slinky negligee?"

The whole thing was taking on the dimensions of a dream, Arabella thought as she waited in Ethan's room dressed in the risqué white negligee and peignoir that Coreen had given her. How was she ever going to tell him that this was his mother's idea?

She'd brushed her long hair until it shone. She was still wearing her bra under the low-cut gown because she couldn't unfasten the catch and Coreen had already gone to bed. But it did make her breasts look sexier, and the way the satin clung to her body she felt like a femme fatale.

She draped herself across the foot of Ethan's antique four-poster bed, the white satin contrasting violently with the brown-and-black-and white plaid of his coverlet. The room was so starkly masculine that she felt a little out of place in it.

There were a couple of heavy leather armchairs by the fireplace, and a few Indian rugs on the floor. The beige draperies at the windows were old and heavy, blocking out the crescent moon and the expanse of open land. The ceiling light fixture was bold and masculine, shaped like a wagon wheel. There was a tallboy against one wall and a dresser and mirror against another, next to the remodeled walk-in closet. It was a big room, but it suited Ethan. He liked a lot of space.

The door began to open and she struck a pose. Perhaps this was Miriam getting a peek in. She tugged the gown off one shoulder, hating the ugly cast that ruined the whole effect. She put it behind her and pushed her breasts forward, staring toward the door with what she hoped was a seductive smile.

But it wasn't Miriam. It was Ethan, and he stopped dead in the doorway, his fingers in the act of unbuttoning his shirt frozen in place.

## Chapter Seven

"Oh!" Arabella gasped. She scrambled into a sitting position, painfully aware of how much cleavage she was showing, not to mention the liquid way the satin adhered to her slender curves.

Ethan slammed the door behind him, his face unreadable. He was bareheaded and he looked very tired and worn, but the light in his eyes was fascinating. He stared at her as if he'd never seen a woman's body before, lingering on the thrust of her breasts under the satin with its exquisite, lacy trim.

"My God," he breathed finally. "You could bring a man to his knees."

It wasn't what she'd expected him to say, but it made her efforts with her appearance worthwhile. "I could?" she echoed blankly as delight made her face radiant.

He moved toward her. His shirt was halfway unbuttoned, and he looked rough and dangerous and very sexy with his hair disheveled and that faint growth of beard on his deeply tanned face.

"Is the bra really necessary, or couldn't you get it off?" he asked as he sat down beside her on the coverlet.

She smiled shyly. "I couldn't get it off," she admitted, lifting the cast. "I still can't use these fingers."

He smiled gently. "Come here." He tugged her forward and reached around her, his lean, rough-skinned hands pushing the straps down over her arms to give him access to the fastening. But the bodice was loose and it fell to her waist, giving him a total view of her breasts in their brief, lacy covering.

He caught his breath. His body made a quick, emphatic statement about what her curves did to it and he laughed even through the discomfort. "My God," he said, chuckling deeply.

"What is it?" she asked breathlessly.

"Don't ask." He reached behind her and unfastened the bra, amused at her efforts to catch the front as it fell. She held it against her, but one of his hands went to her smooth, bare back and began to caress it gently.

"Let it fall," he whispered against her lips as he took them.

It was the most erotic experience of her life, even more than the interlude by the swimming hole, because she was a woman now and her love for him had grown. She released the fabric and her good arm went up around his neck, lifting her breasts.

He drew back to look down at them with pure male appreciation. His fingers touched her, and he looked into her eyes, watching the pupils dilate as he teased the soft contour of her breast and brushed his forefinger tenderly over the taut nipple. She bit back a moan and his free hand lanced into the thick hair at her nape and contracted. He held her prisoner with delicious sensuality while his other hand snaked to her waist and around her, lifting her body in a delicate arch.

"I've dreamed of this," he said, lowering his eyes and then his hard, warm mouth to the swollen softness of her breast.

She watched his mouth open as it settled on her, felt the soft, warm suction, felt the rough drag of his tongue, the faint threat of his teeth and a sound she'd never made pushed out of her throat.

He heard it. His arousal grew by the second, until he was shaking with the force of it. She was everything he'd ever wanted. Young, virginal, achingly receptive to his advances, glorying in his need of her, giving of herself without reservation. He could barely believe what was happening.

His dark eyebrows drew together in harsh pleasure as he increased the pressure of his mouth, feeling her shiver as the intensity of the caress grew. He felt her nails digging into his back and he groaned, his lean hand sweeping down her waist to her hip, edging the fabric up until he could touch her soft, bare thigh.

"Ethan, no...!" she whispered frantically, but his head lifted from her breast and he eased her back onto the coverlet, knowing she was helpless now, totally at his mercy in a sensual limbo.

"I'm not going to hurt you," he said gently, bending over her. "Unbutton my shirt." His fingers slid between her legs, tenderly separating them, and he watched her face waver between acceptance and fear of the unknown. He bent to her lips, brushing them with soft reassurance. "I want to make love to you," he whispered. "We don't have to go all the way."

"I don't understand," she choked.

He kissed her accusing eyes shut. "I'll teach you. One way or another, I'm going to be your lover. It might as well begin now. Get my shirt out of the way, sweet," he breathed into her open mouth. "And then lift your body against mine and let me feel your breasts against my skin."

She'd never dreamed that men said things like that to women, but it had an incredible effect on her emotions. She cried out, her hands fumbling buttons out of buttonholes, and then she arched up, pulling him down on her with the one good arm she had. The experience was staggering. She shuddered as his hair-roughened skin dragged against hers in a terribly arousing caress, weeping helplessly in his arms.

He groaned. All his dreams were coming true. This was his Arabella, and she wanted him. She wanted him!

He eased one powerful leg between hers, and he caught her hand without lifting his mouth and pulled it up against his taut stomach.

"I can't!" she protested wildly.

"You can, sweetheart," he said against her mouth. "Touch me like this," he whispered, opening her clenched fingers and splaying them against his body. "Arabella. Arabella, I need you so!" he ground out.

His fingers trembled as they guided hers. "Don't stop," he groaned harshly, dragging in an audible breath as his teeth clenched.

She watched his face with astonished awe. He let her watch, glorying in the forbidden pleasure of her touch, aching to tell her how incredible this was for him, but he couldn't get words out.

The sudden opening of the door was a cruel, vicious shock.

"Oh, for God's sake!" Miriam exclaimed, horrified. She went out again, slamming the door, her furious voice echoing down the hall along with her running feet.

Ethan shuddered helplessly above Arabella. He rolled over onto his back, groaning.

She sat up, her breasts still bare, her eyes apprehensive. "Are you all right?" she asked hesitantly.

"Not really," he managed with a rueful smile. He laughed in spite of the throbbing ache in his body. "But, oh, God, what a beautiful ache it is, little one."

She tugged the gown up over her breasts, frowning slightly. "I don't understand, Ethan," she said.

He laughed, keeping his secret to himself. "It's just as well that you don't. Not yet, anyway." He lay breathing deeply until he could control it, until the ache began to subside, and all the while his silver eyes lanced over her face and her body with tender delight.

"Miriam saw us," she said uncomfortably.

"Wasn't that the whole idea?" he asked.

"Well, yes. But..." She colored and averted her eyes.

He sat up, stretching lazily before he brought her face up to his and began to press soft, undemanding kisses over it. "Women have been touching men like that since the beginning of time," he whispered at her closed eyelids. "I'll bet most of your girlfriends at school indulged, including Mary."

"But she wouldn't . . . !"

"If she was in love, why not?" He lifted his head and searched her worried face. "Arabella, it's not a sin to want someone. Especially not when you care deeply for them. It's a physical expression of something intangible."

"I have a lot of hang-ups . . ." she began.

He brushed back her damp, disheveled hair. "You have principles. I can understand that. I'm not going to seduce you in my own bed, in case you were wondering." His pale eyes twinkled with humor. He felt alive as never before, masculine, capable of anything. He brushed his mouth lazily over her nose. "We'll save sex for our wedding night."

She stared at him. "I beg your pardon?"

"Marriage is inevitable," he said. "Miriam isn't going to go away, not if you spend every night in here to keep her out. She's the kind of woman who doesn't understand rejection. She's got her mind made up that she's back to stay, and she thinks she can bulldoze me into it."

"She should know better."

"Oh, but she thinks she has an edge," he murmured. He looked down at her hand, clutching the gown to her body. "Let go of that," he murmured. "I love looking at you."

"Ethan!"

He chuckled. "You love letting me, so you can stop pretending. I've spent a lot of years being convinced that I wasn't a man anymore, so you'll have to for-give me for sounding a little arrogant right now. I've just learned something shocking about myself."

"What?" she asked breathlessly.

"That I'm not impotent," he said simply.

She frowned. Didn't that mean that a man couldn't...? Her eyes widened. "That was what Miriam meant when she taunted you!"

"You've got it," he agreed. "She couldn't arouse me with all her tricks. It was why I was able to get her to leave. But she wouldn't give me a divorce. She was sure she could get me back under her spell. What she didn't realize was that I was never really under it in the first place. I was briefly infatuated in a purely physi-cal sense. But a craving, once indulged, is usually sat-isfied. Mine was."

"I guessed she'd know what to do in bed," she sighed. "I'm such a coward...."

He drew her face into his warm, damp throat and smoothed her dark hair gently. "Intimacy is hard, even for men, the first time, Arabella," he said at her ear. "You'll get used to it. I'll never hurt you."

"I know that." And she did. But would he ever be able to love her? That was what she wanted most in the world. She clung to him with a long sigh. "You really don't feel that with Miriam?" she asked lazily. "She's so beautiful and experienced."

His hands hardened on her bare back. "She isn't a patch on you," he said huskily. "She never was."

But you married her, she wanted to say. You loved her, and tonight at supper, you were so gentle with her. But she never got the words out. His hands had tugged the fabric away from her breasts while she was busy thinking, and he wrapped her up against his bare chest with slow expertise, his fingers warm on her rib cage as he traced it.

She moaned and he smiled against her forehead.

"I'd had women by the time you were eighteen," he whispered. "But I felt more with you that day by the swimming hole than I'd ever felt with any of the others, and we did less than I'd ever done with a woman. I've dreamed about that day ever since."

"But you married Miriam," she said quietly. She closed her eyes, unaware of Ethan's expression. "And that says it all, doesn't it? You never loved me. You just wanted me. That's all it's ever going to be. Oh, let me go, Ethan!" She wept, pushing at his shoulders.

But he tightened his hold, easing her down on the bed with him. "It isn't just wanting," he said gently. "Don't fight me," he breathed, settling his mouth on hers. "Don't fight me, honey."

Tears rolled down her face into his hard mouth, but he didn't stop until she was pliant and moaning under the crush of his long, powerful body. Only then did he lift his head and look down at her soft, enraptured face.

His silver eyes searched hers. "If desire was all I felt, do you think I'd spare your chastity?"

She swallowed. "I don't guess you would."

"A man in the throes of passion doesn't usually give a damn what he says or does to get a woman's cooperation," he replied. "I could have had you this afternoon. I could have had you just now. But I stopped."

That could also mean that he didn't want her enough to press his advantage, but she didn't say it.

He sat up, his eyes skimming with warm appreciation over her breasts before he covered them himself, pulling the straps of her gown back up her arms. "You don't have much self-confidence, do you?" he asked when she was standing again. He got to his own feet, towering over her, deliciously sensuous with his chest bare and his mouth faintly swollen from her kisses. "I'll have to work on that."

"It's just to keep Miriam at bay, or so you said," she reminded him shakily.

"Yes, I did say that." He ran his forefinger down her nose. "But in order to do this properly, you're going to have to marry me." He grinned. "It won't be that bad. You can sleep with me and we'll make babies. We'll have a good life together, even if that hand won't let you do anything except give piano lessons."

"And you think that would be enough to satisfy me?" she asked sadly.

The smile left his face. He thought she loved him. She'd acted as if she had. Was she telling him that marriage wouldn't be enough, that she wanted her career instead?" He scowled.

"Don't you think you could be happy here?" he asked.

She shifted restlessly. "I'm tired, Ethan. I don't want to talk about marriage tonight. All right?"

He drew a cigarette from his pocket and lit it, still frowning down at her. "All right. But sooner or later you and I are going to have a showdown."

"Meanwhile, I'll do everything I can to help you send Miriam off. If you're sure you want to," she added hesitantly.

"You can't think I want her back?" he demanded.

"Can't you?" she asked sadly, her heart in her soft green eyes.

"Didn't you hear what I told you earlier? Do you know what impotent means?" he added angrily, and gave her the slang for it, watching her face color.

"I—I—know what it means!" she stammered. She moved away from him. "I don't know that I like being a catalyst in that way. Maybe you really want Miriam but you're too afraid of losing her again to... to be capable with her. She betrayed you once...."

"Oh, hell." He took a draw from his cigarette and sighed angrily. He couldn't get through to her what he felt, and he was too tired to try tonight, anyway. There was time. He hoped there was enough. "You'd better get back to your own room before Miriam drags my mother up here and gives her the shock of her life."

"She wouldn't be shocked," she said absently.

"What makes you think so?"

She lifted her eyes. "Because this was her idea. She even gave me the negligee."

"My God! Women!" he burst out.

"We were saving you from Miriam."

"Fair enough. Who's going to save you from me?" he asked, his hands catching her waist and holding fast as he bent toward her mouth. "I want you. Take off your gown and get into bed. I'll love you up to the ceiling."

She tingled all over. "It isn't me you want, it's Miriam!" she sputtered, pulling away from him.

"You blind little bat," he said, shaking his head. "All right, run. But I'll be two steps behind you from now on. I let you get away once. Never again."

She didn't understand that, either. He was saying a lot of strange things. She colored, wondering at his response to her when he said it didn't happen with Miriam. But she was still certain that it had some psychological basis, that inability, and probably it had been triggered by the fear that Miriam would take his heart and betray him again. She didn't want to think about it. It hurt too much. Ethan's ardor had uplifted and upset her, all at once. She'd have the memory of it, but it would be a bittersweet one. She'd always feel that she was nothing more than a physical substitute for the woman he loved.

"I'll lead my own life, thank you," she said, moving toward the door. "I haven't forgotten what you said to me when you told me not to come back to the ranch all those years ago, Ethan."

"You will," he replied, opening the door for her. "You don't know why I said it."

She looked up at him. "But I do. You wanted me out of the way."

"So that I could marry Miriam," he suggested.

"Yes."

He sighed, letting the cigarette dangle in his hand while he searched Arabella's soft eyes. "There are none so blind as those who will not see," he murmured. "You were eighteen," he said quietly. "You were your father's emotional slave, a talented novice with an incredible career potential and infatuated for the first time in your innocent life. You're almost the age I was then. Think about how it would be for you, if our positions were reversed. Think about what you'd feel, and what you'd think, and what you might do about it."

She stared up at him helplessly. "What did my age have to do with it?" she faltered.

"Everything." His face hardened. "My God, don't you see? Arabella, what if I'd made you pregnant that day by the swimming hole?"

Her face went white. She could imagine the horror her father would have felt. She knew what he'd have done, too. She'd never have been allowed to have a child out of wedlock. Ethan might have insisted on marrying her, if he'd known, but he'd have been forced into it.

"I might not have gotten pregnant," she said hesitantly. "Some women never do."

"A few can't, that's so," he replied. "But the majority of women can and do. I wasn't prepared that day, and I can't for one minute imagine holding back long enough to protect you. There's every chance that we'd have created a child together." His eyes grew darker, warmer. "I'd like that," he said huskily. "Oh, God, I'd like making you pregnant, Arabella."

She felt hot all over. She managed to get her fingers on the doorknob. "I'd better...go to bed, Ethan," she managed unsteadily.

"You'd like it, too, wouldn't you?" he asked knowingly, smiling in a way that made her toes curl.

"We aren't married," she said, trying to hold on to her sanity.

"We will be." He leaned against the door facing her, his eyes possessive on her satin-and-lace-clad body. "I won't mind changing diapers and giving bottles, just for the record. I'm not one of those Neanderthal men who think anything short of football and beer is woman's work."

She stared up at him with a soft glow in her face, giving in despite her misgivings. "What if I couldn't give you a baby?" she whispered softly.

He smiled tenderly and touched her mouth with his fingertips. "Then you and I would become closer than most couples do, I suppose," he said, his voice deep and gentle. "We'd be inseparable. We could adopt a child, or maybe several of them, or we could do volunteer work that involved children." He bent and kissed her eyes closed. "Don't ever think that you're only of value to me because of your potential as a mother. Children are, and should be, a precious fringe benefit of marriage. They shouldn't be the only reason for it."

She'd never dreamed of hearing Ethan say such a thing to her. Tears ran down her cheeks and she began to sob.

"Oh, for God's sake . . . !" He bent and picked her up in his arms, shaken by her reaction. "Arabella, don't," he whispered. His mouth covered hers, faintly tremulous as he savored the tear-wet softness of it, the kiss absolutely beyond his experience as he held her, rocking her in his arms. His head began to spin. Her good arm was around his neck, and she was kissing him back, moaning softly under the crush of his lips, trembling in his protective embrace.

"Now, now, I'm all for the spirit of the thing, but let's not carry it to extremes," Coreen Hardeman murmured dryly.

Ethan lifted his head and stared blankly at his mother. She was leaning against the wall, her gray eyes so smugly pleased that Ethan actually flushed.

# Chapter Eight

Arabella was much more embarrassed than Ethan or his indomitable parent. She colored delicately and stiffened in Ethan's arms.

"Uh, shouldn't you put me down?" Arabella asked.

"Why?" Ethan murmured dryly. "It was just getting to the good part."

"I thought it already had, from what Miriam said," Coreen replied, and then spoiled her disapproving-mother stance by bursting into laughter. "You two are heading straight for a fiery end, or so I'm told. Shameful behavior, and Arabella such an innocent." She raised an eyebrow at Ethan. "How could you, and other platitudes."

Ethan grinned. "I had a lot of cooperation," he returned, with a wicked glance at Arabella.

"Miriam said that, too," Coreen nodded.

"You put me down, you corrupting influence!" Arabella muttered, struggling. "I knew you'd lead me astray if I wasn't careful."

He set her gently on her feet. "Would you like to try again? I seem to remember finding you lying in exquisite repose on my bed...?" He glanced at Coreen. "She said it was your idea, too."

"Actually, it was," Coreen confessed. "I didn't know what else to do. I was absolutely certain that Miriam would make a play for you, and I had a fairly good idea why. I think she's pregnant."

"So Arabella told me." He rubbed a hand over his broad chest, staring appreciatively at the younger of the two women. "We're getting married. Arabella doesn't know it yet, but you might go ahead and start making the arrangements and we'll get her to the altar before she has time to work it out."

"Good idea," Coreen laughed delightedly. "Oh, Arabella, I couldn't be more pleased. You'll be the most wonderful daughter-in-law."

"But..." Arabella began, looking from mother to son with dazed eyes.

"She will at that," Ethan agreed. "I'll take her downtown tomorrow to buy a ring. What do you think about having the wedding at the Methodist church? Reverend Boland could perform the service."

"Yes, he'll do nicely. And we can have the reception at the Jacobsville Inn. It's big enough. I'll ask Shelby Ballenger if she'll help with the arrangements. She did the most beautiful job with our charity fashion show last month—amazing how well she manages her volunteer work and their two sons at the same time."

"Do that," Ethan replied. "Now, how about the invitations?"

"I don't think—" Arabella tried again.

"That's a good idea. Don't," Ethan said approvingly. He folded his arms across his chest and turned back to his mother. "Can you handle the invitations?"

"It's my wedding!" Arabella burst out. "Surely I can do something to help!"

"Of course you can," Ethan agreed. "You can try on the wedding gown. Take her to the best store in Houston," he told his mother, "and find the most expensive gown they have. Don't let her get away with something ordinary."

"I won't," Coreen promised. "A white wedding," she sighed. "I never thought I'd live to see you happily married, Ethan."

He was watching Arabella with an odd kind of tenderness. "Neither did I. Not like this," he said huskily, and his eyes blazed.

But it's only to get Miriam out of his life for good, Arabella wanted to wail. He doesn't love me, he wants me. I make him whole again physically. But that's no reason to get married!

She started to tell him that, but he was already going back into his room.

"I think I'll lock the door, just in case," he chuckled. "Good night, Mother." He stared at Arabella. "Good night, little one."

"Good night, Ethan," Arabella said softly. "But, there's just one thing—"

He closed the door before he could tell him what it was.

"I hate to look smug, but I can't help it," Coreen said with a smile as she walked down the hall with Arabella. "Miriam was so certain she could get under Ethan's skin again. I couldn't bear to see her hurt him so badly twice."

"He was different with her at supper," Arabella said, voicing her biggest fear, that Ethan was once again falling under his ex-wife's spell.

Coreen glanced at her. "Ethan is deep. Don't worry. He wouldn't marry you just to chase Miriam away. I can guarantee it," she added, looking as if she wanted to say something more. But she shrugged and smiled faintly. "I'd better get to bed. Sleep tight, darling, and congratulations."

"Nothing happened," Arabella blurted out. "I don't know what Miriam said—"

Coreen patted her cheek gently. "I know you, and I know my son. You don't have to tell me anything. Besides," she added with a grin, "men who aren't frustrated don't look like Ethan looked when he went back into his room. I'm old, but I'm not blind. 'Night!"

Arabella stared after her, nervous and uncertain. She went on down the hall, hoping against hope that she wouldn't encounter Miriam on the way to her room.

She should have known the woman would be lying in wait for her. Miriam opened her door just as Arabella drew even with it. Her face was flushed and her eyes were red. She'd obviously been crying.

"You snake," Miriam accused furiously. She threw back her auburn hair contemptuously. "He's mine! I'm not going to give him up without a fight!"

"Then you can have one," Arabella said quietly. "We're getting married. Ethan told you so."

"He won't marry you," the other woman replied. "He loves me! He always has! He only wants you." She let her eyes punctuate that coldly sarcastic remark. "You're quite a novelty, but you'll wear thin pretty quickly. You'll never get him to the altar."

"He's making the wedding arrangements already."

"He won't marry you, I tell you!" Miriam flashed. "He only divorced me because I ran around on him."

"That seems like a good reason to me," Arabella returned. She was shaking inside, but she wouldn't back down. "You hurt his pride."

"What do you think it did to mine, having you thrown in my face from the day we married?" she burst out. "It was always Arabella this, Arabella that, from the whole damned family! Nobody could have lived up to you, nobody! I hated you from the start, because Ethan wanted you!" Her eyes were wet with tears and she was sobbing as she tried to speak. "Imagine that!" she laughed brokenly. "I had twice your experience and sophistication, I was more beautiful and sought-after than you could ever hope to be. But it was you he wanted, your name he whispered when he made love to me." She leaned against the wall, crying helplessly while Arabella gaped at her.

"Wha...what?" Arabella gasped.

"It was only when I accused him of using me as a substitute for you that he stopped being capable of making love to me," Miriam said, slumping. "He was obsessed with your body. He still is. Probably," she added, rallying a little, "because he's never had it. Now he'll get his fill of you, and then maybe I can have him back. Maybe I can make him want me. He did love me," she whispered achingly. "He loved me, but I couldn't make him want me, too. Damn you, Arabella! He would have wanted me if it hadn't been for you!"

She went back into her room and slammed the door, leaving a shocked, staggered Arabella in the hall.

She managed to get into her room without really seeing where she was going. She fumbled the light switch on and locked the door before she collapsed on the bed.

Was Miriam telling the truth? Had Ethan been so obsessed by her body that it even affected his marriage? Was it possible for a man to love one woman but lust after another? She knew so little, had such a faint experience of men that she didn't know.

The one thing she was certain of was that Ethan still wanted her. It might not be enough to base a marriage on, but she loved him more than her own life. If desire was all he had to give her, perhaps she could build on that and teach him, someday, to love her. She wasn't as beautiful as Miriam, but he'd said once that inner qualities were just as important.

His ardor that afternoon and that night were proof that his so-called impotence with Miriam was just a fluke. Surely if he could want one woman, he could want another? Miriam had hurt his pride and his body had rebelled. But at supper he'd warmed to Miriam, so might that not affect his ability to want the other woman? Miriam had declared war in the hall and Arabella was afraid that she might not be able to compete. Especially when compared to the more beautiful older woman.

Her mind gave her no peace at all. It was much later when she closed her eyes and went to sleep, leaving all the worries behind.

Things looked a little brighter when she awoke the next morning. She had to be more confident. She could work at her appearance, at her personality. Perhaps she could become like Miriam, and then Ethan might be able to love her. She might still get Miriam to acknowledge defeat, using her own tactics against her.

She put on her prettiest pale green cotton sundress with its dropped square neck and cinched waist and full skirt. It was a flirty kind of dress and it matched her eyes. She put her hair into a neatly coiled chignon on top of her head and deliberately used more make-up than normal. She had a pair of huge earrings she'd never liked, but she wore those, too. The result was a much more sophisticated version of herself. She smiled seductively and nodded. Yes. If a sophisticated woman was what Ethan wanted, she could be that. Certainly she could!

She went downstairs with a bounce in her stride. If only it wasn't for the stupid cast, she might really look seductive, she thought, glaring at the bulky thing. Well, only a little while longer and it would be off, then she could really do some important shopping for the right clothes.

When she got to the breakfast table, Ethan and Miriam were already there, with Coreen and the housekeeper, Betty Ann, busy alternating between kitchen and dining room with platters of food.

Miriam and Ethan appeared to be in intense conversation, and not a hostile one, because he was smiling gently and Miriam was hanging on his every word. Miriam even looked different this morning. Her long hair was plaited and hanging down her back. She was wearing a T-shirt and jeans and no makeup at all. What a change, Arabella thought almost hysterically. She and the other woman looked their own opposites.

Ethan turned and saw Arabella and his jaw clenched. His eyes narrowed with something she couldn't quite define.

"Well, good morning," she called gaily, bluffing it out. She bent over Ethan's tall figure and brushed her mouth teasingly over his nose. "How are you? And how are you, Miriam? Isn't it a beautiful morning?"

Miriam murmured something appropriate and concentrated on her coffee, giving Arabella a glare before she lifted her cup to her lips.

Arabella sat down, still with a bounce, and poured herself a cup of coffee. "I guess Coreen and I will go to Houston today to find my wedding gown, if you don't mind, Ethan," she said breezily. "I do want something exquisite."

Ethan stared down into his coffee cup. Images of the past were dancing before his eyes. Miriam had said something similar when they became engaged. She'd even looked as Arabella did now, oh, so sophisticated and lighthearted. Had he been completely and totally wrong about Arabella? Did money matter to her now that she was apparently without a career, now that she couldn't earn her own way? Or was she trying to compete with Miriam by becoming the same kind of woman? Mentally he dismissed the latter. Arabella knew he didn't want another Miriam. She wouldn't make the mistake of trying to emulate a woman he despised. He couldn't bear the thought of another marriage like his first one. Why had he committed himself? He'd wanted to get rid of Miriam, but now it seemed he might be walking back into the same trap.

Coreen came in with a plate of biscuits, took a look at Arabella and did a double take. "Arabella? How... different you look, dear."

"Do you like it?" Arabella asked with a smile. "I thought I'd try something new. Do you feel like going to Houston with me today?"

Coreen put the plate of biscuits down. "Certainly. If you'd like to...."

"By all means, go ahead," Miriam said huskily. "I'll keep Ethan company," she added with a rather shy smile at her ex-husband.

Ethan didn't answer. He was still trying to absorb the change in Arabella.

He didn't say anything to her all through breakfast and Arabella began to feel nervous. He and Miriam had been talking earnestly, and now he looked uncomfortable when she'd mentioned the wedding gown. Was he having second thoughts? Didn't he want to marry her after all?

Suddenly, he got up from the table and started out of the room.

"Just a minute, Ethan," Miriam called quickly, seeing her chance. "I need to ask you something."

She ran to join him, clutching seductively at his arm as they went outside together.

* * *

"What a nice way to start the morning," Arabella said over her second cup of coffee about half an hour later.

Coreen patted her hand. "Don't worry so. Let's get going. I'll just run into the kitchen and tell Betty Ann where we'll be."

While Arabella continued to think about the scene at breakfast, the phone rang and she got up to answer it, since Coreen and Betty Ann were occupied.

Considering the sour note the day had started on, she should have expected it to be her father, she thought when his curt voice came over the line.

"How are you?" he asked stiffly.

She curled the cord around her fingers. "I'm much better, thank you," she replied, her tone just as stilted.

"And your hand?"

"I won't know until the cast comes off," she said.

"I hope you had the sense to let an orthopedic surgeon look at it," he said after a minute.

"A specialist was called in, yes," she replied. Her father made her feel ten years old again. "There's a good chance that I may be able to play normally again."

"Your host filed an injunction against me, so that I can't touch the joint account," he told her. "That wasn't kind of you, Arabella. I have to live, too."

She bit her lip. "I . . . I know, but . . ."

"You'll have to send me a check," he continued. "I can't live off my brother. I'll need at least five hundred to get me through. Thank God we had good insurance. And I'll want to hear from you as soon as your cast is off and you've seen the specialist."

She hesitated. She wanted to tell him that she was marrying Ethan, but she couldn't get the words out. It was amazing how he intimidated her, and she a grown woman! It was habit, she supposed. He'd always controlled her. He still did. She was just a wimp, she thought angrily.

"I'll...call you," she promised.

"Don't forget the check. You know Frank's address."

That was all. No words of affection, no comfort. He hung up. She stood staring blankly at the receiver. Before she had time to show her concern, Coreen was back and they were off to Houston in Coreen's black Mercedes-Benz.

They browsed through the exclusive bridal department at an exclusive store in Houston for an hour before Arabella was able to choose between three exquisite designer gowns. The one she settled on was traditional with Alençon lace over white *peau de soie*, a delicate, modified V neckline that plunged to the waist but in such a way as to be discreet. It was unique and incredibly sensuous all at once. She chose a traditional veil as well, one with yards and yards of fabric which Ethan would be required to lift during the ceremony. Arabella felt the sense of tradition to her toes, because she was going to her wedding bed a virgin.

The pleasure of the day had been faintly spoiled by Ethan's attitude and Miriam's changed image. Arabella still didn't understand what had gone wrong so suddenly, and even as she was choosing the gown she wondered if she'd really get to wear it. Ethan could change his mind. She wouldn't even blame him. Probably he was finding it hard going to give up Miriam, and the divorce had only been final for three months. Coreen had said that he'd been moody during those three months, too. She frowned at the gown as the saleswoman wrapped it with care in its distinctive box.

"What a blessing you're a perfect size," Coreen smiled. "No alterations. That's a good omen."

Arabella managed a wan smile. "I could use one."

The older woman gave her a curious look as she gave the saleswoman her credit card. But it wasn't until they'd completed their shopping, right down to delicate silk-and-lace undergarments and nylon hose, and were on their way back to Jacobsville that she finally asked Arabella what was wrong.

"I wish I knew why Ethan was so distant this morning," she told the other woman.

"Miriam's doing, no doubt," Coreen said curtly. "Don't underestimate her. Ethan's treating her too nicely and she likes it."

"I won't underestimate her." She hesitated. "That phone call I got this morning was from my father. He called and asked me to send him a check...." She cleared her throat. "Well, he's still my father," she said defensively.

"Of course he is."

"I should have paid for the gown," she said suddenly. "Then, if the wedding is called off, it won't put any strain on your budget."

"Listen, dear, our budget doesn't get strained and you know it." She frowned at Arabella. "This was

Ethan's idea. He wanted you to have a designer gown."

"I think he's changed his mind. He and Miriam were getting thick before breakfast," Arabella said miserably.

Coreen sighed gently. "Oh, Arabella, I wish I knew what was in my eldest's mind. Surely he isn't letting that woman get under his skin again!"

"Miriam said that he wanted me when he married her," Arabella blurted out. Her lower lip trembled. "She accused me of ruining her marriage."

"Ethan's always wanted you," the older woman said surprisingly. "He should have married you instead of letting your father spirit you away. He was never happy with Miriam. I've always felt that she was just a stopgap for him, a poor substitute for you. Perhaps Miriam realized it, and that was what went wrong."

"Wanting isn't loving." Arabella twisted her purse in her lap. "I may not be sophisticated, but I know that."

"You look pretty uptown to me today," Coreen comforted with a smile. "That sundress is very attractive, and I like the way you're wearing your hair. Ethan certainly noticed," she added wickedly.

"I thought Miriam was getting his undivided attention this morning and he wasn't snarling at her."

"Men get funny when they start thinking about marriage," Coreen assured her. "Now, stop worrying. Ethan knows what he's doing."

But did he? Arabella wondered. She might be helping him to make an even bigger mistake than he had before.

And when they got back to the ranch, she found
more cause than ever to be concerned. Betty Ann was
coming down the staircase with a tray when Coreen
and Arabella walked in with the huge dress box.

"What are you doing carrying a tray upstairs at this
hour?" Coreen asked the housekeeper, and frowned.

Arabella had a faint premonition even as Betty Ann
spoke.

"Ethan fell," Betty Ann said tersely. "Had to be
took to the hospital and X-rayed, with herself—" she
jerked her head toward the staircase "—hanging on
him for dear life."

"Is he all right?" Coreen asked the question for
both of them.

"Mild concussion, nothing really serious. They
wanted to keep him overnight, but he insisted on
coming home." The housekeeper sighed. "He's been
up in his room ever since, with herself hovering, and
when he wasn't demanding things, he was cussing."
She glanced warily at Arabella. "I don't know what
Miriam told him, but he's been anxious to see Arabella. Too anxious and too angry."

Arabella felt her knees going weak. Could her father have called back and told Ethan about the check
he'd demanded? She knew Ethan would be furious.
She just hadn't counted on him finding out so quickly.
How had he found out?

"I guess I'd better go up and see him," she murmured.

"We both will," Coreen said shortly.

They marched upstairs. Ethan was lying on top of
his bed with a faint gash on his forehead that had been
stitched, making a red-and-black pattern on the dark

skin. He was fully clothed, and Miriam was sitting with an angelic look by his bedside. The ministering angel.

"So you finally came back," Ethan began, glaring at Arabella. "I hope you enjoyed your shopping trip."

"You knew we were going to get my wedding gown," she said, mildly defensive.

"It's lovely, too, one of their most expensive," Coreen seconded. "A designer gown..."

"Yes, I had one of theirs when I was married," Miriam said with a demure flirting glance at Ethan. "Didn't I, darling?"

"What happened to you?" Coreen asked.

"I got tossed," Ethan said shortly. "Every rider comes off now and again. I was helping Randy with that new mustang in the string we bought from Luke Harper. I got pitched into the fence on my way down. It's nothing."

"Except concussion," Coreen muttered.

"Obviously that didn't bother anybody except Miriam," he said enigmatically, glaring at his mother and Arabella.

Coreen glared back at him. "You're in a sweet mood, I see. Well, I'll help Betty Ann. Are you coming, Miriam?" she added pointedly.

"Oh, no. I'll sit with Ethan. He shouldn't be alone, since he has a concussion," Miriam said, smiling as she laid a protective hand on Ethan's big, lean one.

Coreen went out. Arabella didn't know what to do. Ethan didn't look as if he needed protecting from his ex-wife, and the way he was looking at Arabella made her want to hide.

"Did you hear from my father?" she asked him hesitantly.

"No, I didn't hear from your father," he said coldly. "Get me a beer, will you, Miriam?"

Miriam looked as if leaving was the last thing she wanted to do, but Ethan glared at her and she left, reluctantly, her eyes darting nervously from Ethan to Arabella.

That nervous glance made better sense when she closed the door and Ethan let Arabella have it with both barrels.

"Thank you for your loving concern," he said coldly. "How kind of you to give a damn if I killed myself on a horse!"

She felt her knees going weak. "What do you mean?" she asked.

"You might have told Mother, at least," he persisted. He tried to sit up, grimaced and grabbed his head, but he scowled furiously when she made an automatic move toward him. "Just keep your distance, honey," he said harshly. "I don't want your belated attention. Miriam was here, thank God. She looked after me."

"I don't understand what you're talking about," she said, exasperated.

"You had a phone call before you left the ranch, didn't you?" he demanded.

"Why, yes, of course..." she began.

"Miriam told you I'd been hurt and I needed Mother to drive me in to the hospital, but you didn't say anything," he accused. "Not one word to her. Were you getting even, because I didn't pay you enough attention at breakfast? Or was it a way to get back at me for what happened last night? Did I go too far and scare you out of your virginal wits?"

Her head was swimming. Surely he wasn't quite rational after that knock on the head, with all these wild statements. "Ethan, Miriam didn't call me," she protested. "I didn't know you were hurt!"

"You just admitted that you got the phone call, so don't bother denying it," he added furiously when she started to do just that, to explain that it was her father who called, not Miriam. "I should never have divorced Miriam. When the chips were down, she cared and you didn't. I hope that damned dress you brought is returnable, honey, because I wouldn't marry you on a bet! Now get out of my room!"

"Ethan!" she burst out, horrified that he could actually believe her capable of such hard-boiled behavior.

"I only took you in because I felt sorry for you," he said, giving her a cold appraisal with silver eyes. "I wanted you like hell, but marriage is too high a price to pay for a mercenary virgin with eyes like cash registers. It's all too plain now that I was right, that all you were interested in was financial security for you, and probably for your damned father!" Before she could answer that unfounded charge, he sat straight up in bed, glaring. "I said get out! I don't want to see you again!"

"If you believe I'm that mercenary, then I'll go," she replied, shaking with mingled hurt and fury. "I'm glad to know how you really feel about me, that it was only desire and pity all along."

His eyes flashed silver fire. "The same goes for me. You're no different than Miriam was—out for all you can get. You even look like she used to!"

So that was it. Too late, she realized how her sudden change of appearance and her interest in an expensive wedding gown must have seemed to a man who'd already been used for his wealth once.

"You don't understand," she began.

"Oh, yes, I do," he returned hotly. His head was throbbing. Somewhere inside, he knew he was being unreasonable, but he could hardly think at all for pain and outrage. "Will you get out!"

She went. She could barely see through her tears, almost bumping into a satisfied-looking Miriam as she went down the hall toward her own room. Her temper flared at the smug expression on the older woman's face.

"Congratulations," she flashed at Miriam. "You've got what you wanted. I hope your conscience lets you enjoy it—if you have one."

Miriam shifted uncomfortably. "I told you he's mine," she said defensively.

"He was never yours," Arabella said, brushing angrily at her tears. "He was never mine, either, but at least I loved him! You only wanted what he had, I heard you say so before you married him. It isn't your heart that he broke, it was your ego. He was the one who got away, and you couldn't take it! So now you're going to get him back, but you'll be cheating him. You don't love him, even now. And if you're not pregnant, I'm a brain surgeon!"

Miriam went white. "What did you say?" she gasped.

"You heard me," Arabella said. "What are you going to do, get Ethan to the altar and pretend it's his? That's just what he needs now, to have you come back and finish what you started. You almost destroyed him once. Are you going to finish the job?"

"I need someone!" Miriam protested.

"Try the father of the child you're carrying," Arabella replied.

Miriam wrapped her arms around her chest. "My child is none of your business. And neither is Ethan. If he loved you, he'd never have believed you could ignore him when he was hurt."

Arabella nodded quietly. "Yes, I know that," she said, pain deepening her tone. "And that's the only reason I'm leaving. If I thought he cared, even a little, I'd stay and fight you to the death. But if it's you he wants, then I can bow out gracefully." She laughed bitterly. "I should be used to it. I did it four years ago, and look how happy you made him."

Miriam grimaced "It could be different this time."

"It could. But it won't. You don't love him," Arabella said. "That's what makes it so terrible, even if he loves you." She turned away and went into her room sickened by the thought. It was like history repeating itself.

The wedding gown, in its box, was lying on her bed. She tossed it into a chair and threw herself across the bed, crying her heart out. It didn't matter that Miriam was the snake who'd betrayed her, it was the fact that Ethan didn't believe she was innocent. That was what hurt the most. If he didn't trust her, he certainly didn't love her. She'd been living in a fool's paradise, thinking his ardor might lead to love. Now she knew that it wouldn't. Desire was never enough to compensate for a lack of real feeling.

She pleaded a headache and spent the rest of the night in her room, even refusing supper. Having to watch Miriam gloat would be the last straw, and she had no stomach for any more arguments with Ethan. She knew from painful experience that once his mind was made up, nothing was going to change it. She'd have to leave in the morning. At least she did still have a little money and her credit cards. She could manage on that. She could go to a hotel.

Her eyes were red with tears. Damn Miriam! The other woman had found the perfect way to foul up everything. Now she'd have Ethan again, just as she'd planned. Well, Arabella thought viciously, they deserved each other. So much for all the pretense. Ethan had admitted that it had only been desire that he felt, that he'd pitied her and that's why he'd invited her here. Probably the excuse of keeping Miriam at bay had been fictitious—like his so-called impotence. She'd never believe another word he said, she told herself firmly. If they were quits, it was just fine with her. If Miriam was what he wanted, he could have her. She put on her gown, turned out the light, and lay down. Amazingly, she slept.

Coreen finally found five minutes alone with her son, Miriam having given in to drowsiness and gone to bed.

"Can I bring you anything?" Coreen asked him. "We didn't have a proper supper. Arabella went to bed hours ago with a headache."

"Too bad," Ethan said coldly.

Coreen scowled at him. "What's eating you? Come on, out with it!"

"Miriam phoned the house before you and Arabella left for Houston to tell you I needed a ride to the hospital," he said curtly. "Arabella didn't even bother to tell you. Apparently the shopping trip meant more than any little injury of mine."

Coreen gaped at him. "What are you talking about? There was only one phone call and it was from Arabella's father!"

"Is that what she told you?" he asked with a hard laugh. "Did you talk to him, or hear him? Did Betty Ann?"

Coreen moved close to the bed, her eyes full of disapproval and concern. "I had hoped that you cared about Arabella," she said. "I hoped that you'd be able to see through Miriam's glitter this time to the cold, selfish woman underneath. Perhaps that kind of woman really appeals to you because you're as incapable of real love as she is."

Ethan's eyebrows went straight up. "I beg your pardon?"

"You heard me. I don't need proof that Arabella didn't lie. She wouldn't walk away and leave an injured animal, much less an injured person. I believe that because I know her, because I care about her." She stared down at him. "Love and trust are two sides of one coin, Ethan. If you can believe Arabella capable of such a cold-blooded act, then I'd suggest that you forget marriage and put Miriam's ring back through your nose. God knows, right now I think the two of you deserve each other."

She turned and left him there. He picked up a cup from the table and slammed it furiously at the closed door. He knew he was fuddled, but his mother had no right to say things like that to him. Why would Miriam lie about a phone call that he could certainly check? All he had to do was get the record of where the call originated from the phone company to prove a lie. Anyway, Miriam had been different lately, very caring and warm, and he'd actually enjoyed her company. He knew all about the man she was in love with, and he'd done his best to encourage her to go back to the Caribbean and try again. So that meant she wasn't interested in him as a man anymore, and it gave her no reason to try and break up his apparent romance with Arabella.

Or was it all a ruse on Miriam's part to get him back? Could Arabella be innocent of what he'd accused her of? He didn't want to think about that, because if she was, he'd just ruined everything. Again. He groaned. It was the way Arabella had dressed, the things she'd said about getting an expensive wedding gown, and then the way it had hurt when Miriam said Arabella was going to Houston anyway, despite his condition.

He was concussed and his mind wasn't working properly. He'd been sure that Arabella loved him, but when Miriam said she wouldn't come to see about him, he thought he'd been mistaken. Then he'd worked himself into a lather thinking that she'd only wanted to use him, as Miriam once had. Miriam had been so different lately that he'd been sure she'd changed, that she wasn't the same self-seeking woman she had been. But was she different? Or was he just susceptible because his head was throbbing and Arabella had hurt him?

He lay down and closed his eyes. He wouldn't—he couldn't—think about that right now. He'd think about it in the morning, instead, when his throbbing head was a little clearer. Then he'd face the future, if he still had one with Arabella.

# Chapter Nine

Arabella woke to the sound of voices the next morning. She sat up in bed, her pale blue gown twisted around her slender body, her long brown hair a tangle around her shoulders, just as Mary knocked briefly then opened the door, rushing inside.

"Hello!" she said, laughing, as she hugged Arabella and placed a bag of souvenir items on the bed. Mary was tan and relaxed and looked lovely. "These are all for you," she said. "T-shirts, shell things, necklaces, skirts, and even a few postcards. Did you miss me?"

"Oh, Mary, yes, I did," Arabella said with a long sigh, hugging her back. Mary was the best, and the only, real friend she'd ever had. "Things are getting so complicated."

"I heard you and Ethan are going to be married," Mary continued, all eyes.

Arabella's face fell. "Yes. Well, that was just what we told Miriam. The wedding is off."

"But your gown!" Mary protested, nodding toward the box in the armchair. "Coreen told us all about it."

"It's going back today," Arabella said firmly. "Ethan broke off the engagement last night. He wants Miriam back."

Mary sat very still. "He what?"

"Wants Miriam back," Arabella said quietly. "She's changed, or so he says. They've gotten real thick in the past couple of days." Which was odd, she told herself, because she herself had gotten real thick with Ethan in the past couple of days. She felt sick all over. "And I'm leaving," she added, giving in to a decision she'd made the night before. "I hate to ask when you're just off the plane, but could you drive me into Jacobsville later?"

Mary almost refused, but the look in her friend's eyes killed all her hopeful words. Whatever had happened, Arabella had been terribly hurt by it. "All right," she said with a forced smile. "I'll be glad to. Does Ethan know you're going?"

"Not yet," Arabella said. "He doesn't need to. He fell yesterday and got concussed." She had to bite back all her concern for him. She couldn't afford to let it show. "He's all right. Miriam's taking care of him, and that's the way he wants it. He said so."

Mary knew there had to be more to it than that, but she kept her silence. "I'll let you dress and pack. I gather that I'm not to tell anyone you're going?"

"Please."

"All right. Come downstairs when you're ready."

"I'll do that. Could you...take that with you?" she asked, nodding toward the box.

Mary picked it up, thinking privately that it was a pity Ethan had waited until she bought the dress to call off the wedding. He didn't seem to care very much for Arabella's feelings, either, because she was obviously crushed.

"I'll see you directly," Arabella said as Mary went out and closed the door.

She got dressed, minus the bra that she still couldn't fasten, in a suit with a thick jacket that she buttoned up. She packed her few things with her good hand and tied a scarf around her neck to hold the cast at her waist. It got heavy when she moved around very much. She picked up her suitcase, then, after a final glance in the mirror at her pale face without makeup, left the room where she'd been so happy and so sad.

There was one last thing she wanted to do. She had to say goodbye to Ethan. She wouldn't admit, even to herself, how much she hoped he'd changed his mind.

Actually, at that moment, Ethan was having a long talk with a quiet and dejected Miriam. He'd asked for the truth, and she'd reluctantly given it to him, her conscience pricked by the conversation that Ethan didn't know she'd had with Arabella the night before.

"I shouldn't have done it," she told him, smiling mistily. "You've been so different, and I saw the way things could have been if you'd loved me when we first married. I knew I didn't stand a chance against Arabella, so I had other men to get even," she confessed for the first time. She met his eyes apologetically. "You should have married her. I'm sorry I made things difficult for you. And I'm very sorry about the lie I told yesterday."

Ethan was having trouble breathing properly. All he could think of was what he'd said to Arabella the night before. He'd been out of his muddled head with anger.

"I called off the wedding," he said absently, and winced.

"She'll forgive you," Miriam said sadly. "I'm sure she feels the same way about you." She reached out and touched his face. "I do love my Jared, you know." She sighed. "I ran because of the baby. I thought he wouldn't want it, but now I'm not so sure. I could at least give him the benefit of the doubt, I suppose. I didn't sleep last night thinking about it. I'll phone him this morning and see what develops."

"You may find he wants the baby as much as you do," he replied. He smiled at her. "I'm glad we can part as friends."

"So am I," she said fervently. "Not that I deserve it. I know I've been a royal pain in the neck."

"Not so much anymore," he assured her.

"I'll go and make that call. Thank you, Ethan, for everything. I'm so sorry about what I did. You deserve more than I ever gave you." She bent and kissed him with warm tenderness.

He reached up, giving her back the kiss, for old times' sake. A kiss of parting, between friends, with no sexual overtones.

That was what Arabella saw when she stopped in the open door. A kiss that wasn't sexual and held such exquisite tenderness that it made her feel like a voyeur. She knew she'd gone white. So it was that way.

They'd reconciled. Miriam loved him and now they were going to remarry and live happily ever after. Miriam had won.

She smiled bitterly and retraced her steps so that they didn't even know she'd been in the room.

She ran into Coreen going down the staircase.

"I'm just on my way to see Ethan...." She stopped dead, staring at Arabella's suitcase.

"Mary's driving me to town," Arabella said, her voice a little wobbly. "And I wouldn't disturb Ethan just now, if I were you. He's rather involved with Miriam."

"Oh, this is getting completely out of hand!" Coreen said harshly. "Why won't he listen?"

"He's in love with her, Coreen," the younger woman said. "He can't help that, you know. He said last night that it was really only out of pity that he asked me here. He wanted me, but he loves Miriam. It would never have worked. It's best that I leave now, so that I won't be an embarrassment to him."

"My dear," Coreen said miserably. She hugged Arabella warmly. "You know the door is always open. I'll miss you."

"I'll miss you, too. Mary was going to take the dress back to the store for me, but...but Miriam might like it," she said bravely. "All it would need is a little alteration."

"I'll take care of the dress," Coreen said. "Will you be all right? Where will you go?"

"I'll go to a motel for the time being. I'll phone my father when I've settled in. Don't worry, I've got money, thanks to Ethan's intervention. I won't go hungry, and I can take care of myself. But thank you for all you've done for me. I'll never forget you."

"I'll never forget you either, darling," Coreen said quietly. "Keep in touch, won't you?"

"Of course," Arabella lied with a smile. That was the very last thing she intended doing now, for Ethan's sake.

She followed Mary out to the car after exchanging farewells with Betty Ann and a puzzled Matt. She didn't even look back as the car wound down the driveway to the road.

Just as Arabella was going out to the car, Miriam was lifting her head and smiling at Ethan. "Not bad. I'm sorry we didn't make it. Shall I go downstairs and explain it all to Arabella and your mother?" she asked with a grimace. "I guess they'll pitch me out the back door on my head when I get through."

"It's my head that's going to be in danger, I'm afraid," he said ruefully. "No, I'll handle it. You'd better go and call your Caribbean connection."

"I'll do that. Thanks."

He watched her go, and lay back against the pillows. He'd heard Matt and Mary come in and he was waiting for them to come and say hello. Maybe he could get Arabella up here and try to sort things out before it was too late. He heard a car door slam twice and an engine rev up, and he frowned. Surely Mary and Matt weren't leaving already.

Minutes later, a coldly furious Coreen walked into his room and glared at him.

"Well, I hope you're happy," she told him. "You've got what you wanted. She just left."

He sat up, scowling at her. "Who just left?" he asked with a chilling sense of loss.

"Arabella," Coreen informed him. "She said you'd called off the wedding. She left her dress for Miriam and said to congratulate you on your forthcoming re-marriage."

"Oh, for God's sake!" he burst out. He threw his legs off the bed and tried to get up, but his head was still spinning with the aftereffects of the day before. He sat down again and rubbed his forehead. "I'm not marrying Miriam! Where in hell did she get that idea?"

"From you, I suppose, after the bite you apparently took out of her last night. And something must have been going on in here when she left, because she said you and Miriam were involved when she came downstairs."

She'd seen Miriam kiss him. He remembered the kiss, realized how it would look to an outsider, and he groaned out loud. "My God, I've got a knack for ruining my life," he said with a rough sigh. "I must have a deep-buried death wish. Where did she go?"

"To a motel, she said. Mary will know which one."

He lifted his head, and his eyes were anguished. "She'll call her father," he said. "He'll be here like a shot to take her over again."

"Do remember who pushed her out of the door, won't you, dear boy?" his mother asked with smiling venom.

"I thought she'd deserted me!" he burst out.

"As if Arabella would do any such thing," she scoffed. "How could you have believed it?"

"Because I had a concussion and I was half out of my head," he returned angrily.

"And what did she see on her way out that convinced her Miriam needed the wedding gown?" Coreen added.

"I kissed her. She kissed me," he corrected. He threw up his hands. "Miriam's going back to the Caribbean to marry the father of her child, if everything works out all right," he said. "It was a goodbye kiss."

"You fool," Coreen said evenly. "Four years ago, you put Arabella's welfare above your own. You married the wrong woman and cheated her as well as yourself, and now you've thrown away the second chance you might have had. Why didn't you tell Arabella how you feel about her!"

He lowered his eyes. Some things he couldn't share, even with his mother. "She's career-minded. She always was. She came here because she was hurt and needed some security. She was reluctant from the first when I tried to get her to marry me. I think she was afraid that she'd be able to play again and be stuck here with me."

"More likely she was afraid you were just using her as a blind for the feelings you had for Miriam," Coreen replied. "She said you only wanted her, but you loved Miriam. She believed it."

Ethan sighed heavily and lay back down. "I'll go after her, when I get my head together."

"Never mind," Coreen said. "She won't come back. She's let you cut up her heart twice already. She won't risk it again."

His eyes opened. "What do you mean, cut up her heart?"

"Ethan," she said patiently, "she was in love with you four years ago. Desperately in love. She thought Miriam just wanted what you had, not you. She was trying to protect you, but you accused her of interfering and God knows what else. She ran then, too, and kept running. Didn't you ever wonder why she arranged to come here to see Jan, and later Mary, only when she knew you wouldn't be here?"

"No, because I was too busy making sure I didn't have to see her," he said doggedly. He averted his eyes. "It hurt too much. I was married, Miriam wouldn't divorce me. . . ." His broad shoulders rose and fell. "I couldn't bear the torment of seeing her and not being able to touch her honorably." He looked up at his mother. "How do you know how she felt about me?" he asked.

"It's obvious," she said simply. "She chose music as a substitute, just as you chose Miriam. You're both fools. What a horrible waste of time."

Ethan was inclined to agree. So Arabella had loved him. He lay back down and closed his eyes, trying to imagine how it would have been if he'd given up his plans to save her from what he thought would have been a mistake, if he'd married her instead. They'd have children by now, they'd be a family. Arabella would sleep in his arms every night and love him. He couldn't bear the images that haunted him. He'd driven her away a second time with his idiotic accusations, and now he'd probably never be able to get her back. He heard his mother leave, but he didn't bother to open his eyes.

* * *

Arabella got a room in a downtown Jacobsville motel. There were several to choose from, but her favorite was an adobe-style one with a Spanish flavor. She settled into her room, trying not to think how bare and austere and impersonal it was compared to the one she'd had at the Hardeman ranch.

Mary hadn't wanted to leave her there, but she'd insisted. She couldn't stay in the house now that she knew how it was between Ethan and Miriam. It was too painful. A clean break was best. She picked up the phone when she'd unpacked and phoned her father in Dallas. The cast came off in nine days. Her father would meet her here then and they'd go back to Houston. He'd sublet their apartment there while he was in Dallas, but they could get another temporarily. Odd that it didn't even bother her to think about being back with her parent again. She didn't feel intimidated any more.

Time went by slowly. Mary came to visit, but Arabella was reluctant to listen to any news from the ranch, especially about Ethan. She didn't want to hear what was going on at the house, it would be too painful. The only reality was that Ethan hadn't bothered to call or come by or even drop her a postcard, even though he knew by now—or so Mary had said before Arabella protested listening to news of Ethan—that Miriam had lied about the phone call. He knew, but he wouldn't apologize for the things he'd said. He never apologized, she reflected. Since Miriam was still with him, why should he bother? He and Arabella were now past history.

Meanwhile, Ethan was trying to come to grips with his own idiocy. He was certain that Arabella wouldn't listen to him. He couldn't blame her; he'd certainly been eloquent in his condemnation. He thought it would be better if he let things cool down for a few days before they had a showdown. In the meantime, Miriam's man was on his way up to Texas. They'd reconciled and Miriam had been on a cloud ever since, barely coherent except when she was talking about the planter she was going to marry. Ethan enjoyed her company, especially now that he was well and truly off the hook, now that he was able to understand the past and why things had happened the way they had. Miriam had suffered an unfortunate experience with a family friend as a child. As a result, she'd become brittle in her dealings with men, and very hostile toward them. Only now, secure in her pregnancy and the love of her planter, was she able to come to grips with the past that had made her what she was when she'd married Ethan.

Ethan's only regret was that he'd married her in the first place. It had been unfair to her, to Arabella and even to himself. He should have followed his instincts, which were to marry Arabella and let the chips fall where they may. He'd never been able to give Miriam anything except the dregs of his desires for another woman and, eventually, not even that. He hadn't understood that Miriam's childhood had made it impossible for her to give herself wholly to any man. She'd been looking for love in a series of impossible physical liaisons that were only briefly satisfying. She'd wanted Ethan's love, but he'd withheld it, and she'd tried to punish him. Arabella, though, had suffered as well, trapped in a career that her father controlled, with no hope of escape.

It had thrilled him when Coreen had told him Arabella had once loved him. But he didn't know what she felt now. She probably hated him. He'd started for town three times in the past several days, but he'd stopped. She needed time. So did he.

Mary came up the steps as he was going down them, and he stopped her, trying not to look as unhappy as he felt.

"How is she?" he asked bluntly, because he was certain she'd been to see her friend.

"Lonely," Mary said, her voice gentle. "The cast comes off Tuesday."

"Yes." He stared off over the tree-lined horizon. "Is her father here yet?"

"He'll be here Tuesday." Mary was nervous of Ethan, but she hesitated. "She won't talk about you," she said. "She doesn't look well."

He glanced down at her with flashing silver eyes. "Nobody told her to leave," he said cuttingly, stung by the remark.

"How could she stay, knowing that you're going to marry Miriam all over again?" she asked. "I guess you two do deserve each other," she added with the first show of spirit Ethan had ever seen in her, and she was gone before he could correct her impression of the situation.

What made everyone think Miriam was marrying him? He sighed angrily as he went down the steps. Probably because neither of them had told the rest of the family what was going on. Well, when her planter arrived they'd get the picture. For now, he couldn't let himself dwell on how bad Arabella looked. If he thought about it long enough, he was sure he'd go stark, raving mad.

Mary and Matt had studiously ignored Miriam since Arabella's departure, and Coreen had been so coldly polite to the woman that she might as well have had icicles dripping off her. Ethan tried to make up for his family, which only reinforced their speculation about Miriam's status in his life.

Miriam's intended and Arabella's father arrived in town at the same time. While Jared was being introduced to the Hardemans, Arabella was having the cast off and being told that her hand and wrist had healed almost to perfection. Her father had beamed at the specialist. But only at first.

"Almost to perfection," Dr. Wagner repeated, frowning at Arabella's father. "Translated, that means that Miss Craig will play the piano again. Unfortunately it also means that she will never regain her former mastery. Severed tendons are never the same when they heal, for the primary reason that they're shortened by the process of reattaching them. I'm sorry."

Arabella didn't realize how much she'd been counting on favorable prognosis. She collapsed into tears.

Her father forgot his own disappointment when he saw hers. Clumsily, he took her in his arms and held her, patting her ineffectually on the back while he murmured words of comfort.

He took her out to dinner that night. She dressed in her one good cocktail dress, black with a scattering of sequins, and knotted her long hair at her nape. She looked elegant, but even with the unwieldy cast off, she felt dowdy. The skin that had been under the cast was unnaturally pale and there were scars. But she kept her hand in her lap and in the dark atmosphere of the restaurant and lounge, she was certain that nobody noticed.

"What will we do?" Arabella asked quietly.

Her father sighed. "Well, for now, I'll see about releasing some of the new recordings and re-releasing the older ones." He looked across the table at her. "I haven't been much of a father, have I? Deserting you after the wreck...I guess you thought I didn't want you without a career to keep us up."

"Yes, I did," she confessed.

"The wreck brought back your mother's accident," he said. It was a subject he'd never discussed before, but she sensed that he was getting something off his chest. "Arabella, she died because I had one drink too many at a party. I was driving, and my reaction time was down. Oh, there were no charges," he said with a cold laugh when he saw her expression. "I wasn't even legally drunk. But the police knew, and I knew, that I could have reacted quicker and avoided the other car. She died instantly. I've lived with that guilt for so long." He leaned back in his chair, making patterns in the condensation on his water glass. "I couldn't admit my mistake. I buried the past in my mind and concentrated on you. I was going to be noble, I was going to dedicate my life to your talent, to your glorious career." He studied her wan face. "But you didn't want a career, did you? You wanted Ethan Hardeman."

"And he wanted Miriam, so what difference does it make now? In fact," she added without looking at him, "Miriam is back and they're reconciling."

"I'm sorry," he said. He studied her. "You know, the wreck brought it all back," he continued. "Your mother's death, trying to cope without her, trying to live with my guilt." He studied his locked-together fingers on the table. "You needed me and I couldn't bear to face you. I came so close to losing you the way I lost her...."

His voice broke and Arabella suddenly saw her father as a man. Just a man, with all the fears and failings of any other human. It shocked her to realize that he wasn't omnipotent. Parents always seemed to be, somehow.

"I didn't remember how Mama died," she said, searching for words. "And I certainly didn't blame you for our wreck. There was nothing you could have done. Really," she emphasized when he lifted tormented eyes to hers. "Dad, I don't blame you."

He bit his lower lip hard and looked away. "Well, I blamed me," he said. "I called Ethan because there was no one else, but I thought in a way, it might make up to you what I'd cheated you out of. I figured with your hand in that shape, Ethan might decide to stop being noble and give you a chance."

"Thank you," she said gently. "But all Ethan wants is his ex-wife. Maybe that's just as well. Four years ago, I worshipped the ground he walked on, but I'm older now...."

"And still in love with him," he finished for her. He shook his head. "All my efforts backfired, didn't they? All right, Arabella. What do you want to do now?''

She was amazed that he was asking her opinion. It was a first—like realizing that he was human and fallible. She liked him much better this way. It was a whole new relationship, because he was treating her like an adult for the first time. "Well, I don't want to stay in Jacobsville," she said firmly. "The sooner we can leave here, the better."

"I guess I'll have to go to Houston and find a place, first," he said. "Then I'll see what I can do about finding myself a job." He waved aside her objections. "I've spent altogether too much time in the past. You have a right to your own life. I'm only sorry that it took another near-fatal wreck to bring me to my senses."

Arabella slid her hand into his and clasped it warmly. "You've been very good to me, Dad," she said gently. "I don't have any complaints."

"Are you sure about Miriam?" he asked with a frown. "Because I don't believe Ethan really wanted to marry her in the first place. And I know he was damned near crazy when I phoned him about you being hurt in the wreck."

"I'm sure," she said, closing the book on that subject forever.

He relented. "All right. We'll start again. And don't worry about that hand," he added. "You can always teach, if everything else fails." He smiled at her gently. "There's a great deal of satisfaction in seeing someone you've coached become famous. Take my word for it."

She smiled at him. "I can live with that," she said. Inwardly, she was almost relieved. She loved to play the piano, but she'd never wanted the tours, the endless road trips, the concerts. Now they were gone forever, and she wasn't really sorry.

Her father left the next morning for Houston in the car he'd rented for the trip to Jacobsville. Arabella was lazy, not rising until late morning. She decided to have lunch in the restaurant and went early.

Their seafood was delicious, so she ordered that and settled back to wait for it.

Incredible how her life had changed, she thought as she came to grips finally with what the surgeon had told her about her hand. What could have been traumatic wasn't that at all. She accepted it with relative ease. Of course, her father's new attitude had helped.

She felt a shadow fall over her and turned with an automatic smile to face the waiter. But it wasn't a waiter. It was Ethan Hardeman.

# Chapter Ten

Arabella schooled her features not to show any of the emotions she was feeling. She stared up at him with a blank expression, while her poor heart ran wild and fed on the sight of him.

"Hello, Ethan," she said. "Nice to see you. Is Miriam with you?" she added with a pointed glance behind him.

He put his hat on an empty seat and lowered himself into the chair beside hers. "Miriam is getting married."

"Yes, I know," she began.

So Mary had already told her, he thought. That wasn't surprising, Mary came to see her almost every day. He caught her eyes, but she quickly lowered her gaze to the beige sport coat he was wearing with dark slacks, a white silk shirt and striped tie.

He toyed with the utensils at his place. "I wanted to come sooner, but I thought you needed a little time to yourself. What did the doctor say about your hand?" he added.

She managed to disguise her broken heart very well. To save her pride, she was going to have to lay it on thick. She couldn't let him know her predicament. Besides, he was getting married, and she wished the best for him. He didn't need her problems to mar his happiness. "It's fine," she said. "I have to have a little physical therapy and then I'm back to New York, by way of Houston, to take up where I left off."

His face hardened. He couldn't help it. He'd thought for certain that she'd never use that hand again, knowing how much damage had been done to it. Of course, these days they had all sorts of methods of repairing damaged tendons, so maybe there was a new technique. But it didn't help his pride. He'd left things too late. If he'd told her how he felt at the beginning, if he'd revealed his feelings, things might have been different. His whole life seemed to be falling apart, and all because of his lousy timing.

He stared at her across the table. "Then you've got what you want," he said.

"Yes. But so have you," she reminded him with a forced smile. "I hope you and Miriam will be very happy. I really do, Ethan."

He gaped at her. Meanwhile, the waiter appeared with her salad and paused to ask Ethan if he was ready to order. Absently, he ordered a steak and salad and coffee and sat back heavily in the chair when the man left.

"Arabella, I'm not getting married."

She blinked. "You said you were."

"I said Miriam was."

"What's the difference?" she asked.

He sighed heavily. "She's marrying a man she met down in the Caribbean," he said. "He's the father of her child."

"Oh." She watched the way he twirled his water glass, his eyes downcast, his face heavily lined. "Ethan, I'm so sorry," she said gently. She reached out hesitantly and touched one of his hands.

Electric current shot through him. He lifted his eyes to catch hers while his fingers linked around and through her own. He'd missed her more than he even wanted to admit. The house, and his life, had been empty without her. "Care to console me?" he asked half-seriously. "She and her fiancé are staying for a few days." He lowered his eyes to their linked hands so that she wouldn't see the hunger in them. "You could come back with me and help me bluff it out until they leave."

She closed her eyes briefly. "I can't."

"Why not? It's only for a couple of days. You could have your old room. Coreen and Mary would enjoy your company."

She weakened, but her pride was still smarting from the beating it had taken. "I shouldn't, Ethan."

His fingers tightened. "Will it help if I apologize?" he asked quietly. "I never meant to be so rough on you. I should have known better, but I was half out of my mind and I swallowed everything Miriam said."

"I thought you knew me better than that," she said sadly. "I suppose you have to love people to trust them, though."

He flinched. He felt as if he'd had a stake put through his heart. Yes, he should have trusted her. He hadn't, and now she was running away because he'd hurt her. He couldn't let her get away from him now. No matter what it took.

"Listen, honey," he said softly, coaxing her eyes up to his, "it's been hard on all of us, having Miriam around. But she'll be gone soon."

Taking his heart with her, Arabella thought. She wished, oh how she wished, that he could love her. "My father and I are going to Houston as soon as he finds a place for us," she said.

His jaw clenched. He hadn't counted on that complication, although he should have expected it. She had her career to think of, and that was her father's grubstake. "You could stay with us until he finds one," he said curtly.

"I'm happy here in the motel," she protested.

"Well, I'm not happy with you here," he said, his own voice arctic. His eyes began to kindle with feeling. "It's my fault you left. We were off to a good start, until I started jumping to conclusions."

"That's just as well." She searched his face. "I guess it's pretty painful for you. Losing her again."

"If you only knew," he replied, his voice deep and slow, but he wasn't thinking of Miriam. He brought her fingers to his lips and nibbled at them, watching the reaction color her face and bring a soft, helpless light to her green eyes. "Come home with me," he said. "You can sprawl across my bed in that satin gown and we'll make love again."

"Hush!" she exclaimed, looking around to make sure they weren't overheard.

"You're blushing."

"Of course I'm blushing. I want to forget that it ever happened!" she muttered. She tried to draw her fingers away, but he held them tightly.

"We could give Miriam and her intended a grand send-off," he coaxed. "By the time she left, she'd be convinced that I didn't have a broken heart."

"And why should I want to do you another favor?" she demanded.

He looked her right in the eye. "I can't think of a single reason," he confessed with a warm, quiet smile. "But I hope you'll come, all the same. Maybe I can make up for the way I treated you."

Her fingers jerked in his and she went scarlet. "By making love to me again? Do you think I care so much that I'll be grateful for any crumbs left over from your relationship with Miriam?" she asked bluntly.

"No. I don't think that at all." He held her gaze, trying to find any sign that she still cared, that he hadn't quite ruined everything. That he might have one last chance before she resumed her career to make her understand how deeply involved his feelings were, how much he cared.

"I've heard you play." He lowered his eyes to her hands, caressing them gently. "You have genius in your hands. I'm glad you haven't lost that talent, Arabella, even if it means that I have to let you go again." And he might, but now he had the hope that it might not be a permanent loss this time. If he could convince her that he cared, she might yet come back to him one day.

She wanted to tell him. She started to tell him, to draw him out, to try to make him tell her if wanting was all he felt. But the waiter arrived with their order, and the moment was lost. She couldn't find the nerve to reopen the subject, especially when he started talking about Miriam's husband-to-be and the way he'd come dashing across the sea to get her.

After lunch, Ethan waited while she packed and left a message at the desk for her father to call her at the Hardeman ranch. Going back was against her better judgment, but she couldn't resist the temptation. In the long years ahead, at least she'd have a few bittersweet memories.

He drove her out to the ranch, his eyes thoughtful, his face quiet and brooding.

"Roundup's over," he announced as they sped down the road out of Jacobsville. "It feels good to have a little free time."

"I imagine so." She glanced off the highway at the massive feedlot that seemed to stretch forever toward the horizon. "Do the Ballenger brothers still own that feedlot?"

"They certainly do," he mused, following her glance. "Calhoun and Justin are making a mint on it. Good thing, too, the way they're procreating. Calhoun and Abby have a son and a daughter and Justin and Shelby have two sons."

"What ever happened to Shelby's brother, Tyler?" she asked absently.

"Tyler married an Arizona girl. They don't have any kids yet, but their dude ranch just made headlines—Tyler and his wife have expanded it to include a whole authentic Old-West adobe village as a tourist attraction, and they've enlarged their tourist facilities. It looks as if they're going to make a mint too."

"Good for them," Arabella said. She stared down at the floorboard of the car. "It's nice to hear about local people making good."

"That's what we thought about you," he said, "when you started making headlines. We all knew you had the talent."

"But not the ambition," she confessed. "My father had that, for both of us. I only loved music. I still do."

"Well, you'll be on your way again when you get the physical therapy out of the way, I guess," he said, his voice hardening.

"Of course," she mumbled numbly and moved her damaged hand to stare down at its whiteness. She flexed the muscles, knowing she'd never be the same again.

Ethan caught a glimpse of the expression on her face. It kept him puzzled and quiet all the way home.

Miriam and her fiancé were beaming like newlyweds. Even Coreen seemed to have warmed toward her, and Miriam went out of her way to make Arabella feel comfortable.

"I'm really sorry for messing things up between you and Ethan," the older woman said when she and Arabella were briefly alone during the long afternoon. In her newfound happiness, she could afford to be generous, and she'd seen the misery she'd caused Ethan already. "I was evening up old scores, but it wasn't Ethan's fault, or yours, that he couldn't love me." She glanced toward Jared, a tall, pleasant man with elegance and obvious breeding, and her face softened with emotion. "Jared is everything I dreamed of in a husband. I ran because I didn't think he'd want our child, as I did. My emotions were all over the place. I guess I had some wild idea of getting Ethan to marry me again to get even with Jared." She looked at Arabella with quiet apology. "I'm sorry. I hope this time you and Ethan will make a go of it."

That wasn't possible now, but it was kind of Miriam to think, even belatedly, of Ethan's happiness. She managed a smile. "Thank you. I hope you'll be happy, too."

"I don't deserve it, but so do I," Miriam murmured. She smiled self-consciously and went back to her fiancé.

Mary was giving Arabella curious looks. Later on, she dragged her friend to one side.

"What's going on? You could have knocked me over with a feather when I saw Ethan walk in with you," she whispered. "Have you made up?"

"Not really. He wants me to help him put on a good front so Miriam won't think she's broken his heart," Arabella said, her eyes going to Ethan like homing pigeons.

Mary watched the look and smiled secretly. "I don't think she could get that impression, not considering the way he's been sneaking looks at you ever since he brought you in."

Arabella laughed halfheartedly. "He's just putting on an act," she said.

"Is that what it's called?" Mary murmured dryly. "Well, ignore it while you can."

"I thought I was...." Her voice trailed off as she encountered a long, simmering gaze from Ethan's silver eyes and got lost in the fierce hunger in them. The rest of the people seemed to vanish. She didn't look away and neither did he, and electricity sizzled between them for one long, achingly sweet minute. Then Coreen diverted his attention and Arabella was able to breathe again.

For the remainder of the day, he didn't leave the house. After supper, while the rest of the family watched a movie in the living room on the VCR, Arabella excused herself and changed into comfortable jeans and a white tank top before she sneaked back downstairs and went into the library to try the piano for the first time since the wreck.

She closed the door quietly, so that no one would hear her. She positioned the piano bench carefully and sat down, easing up the cover over the keyboard. It was a grand piano, because Coreen played herself, and it was in perfect tune. She touched middle C and ran a scale one octave lower with her left hand.

Very nice, she thought, smiling. Then she put her right hand on the keyboard. It trembled and the thumb protested when she tried to turn it under on F. She grimaced. All right, she thought after a minute. Perhaps scales would be just too difficult right now. Perhaps a simple piece would be easier.

She chose a Chopin nocturne, a beginner's piece she'd played in her early days at the piano. She began very slowly, but it made no difference. Her hand was lax and trembly and totally uncooperative. She groaned and her hands crashed down despairingly on the keyboard, seeing months of work ahead before she could even do a scale, perhaps years before she could play again normally, if at all.

She didn't hear Ethan come in. She didn't hear him close the door behind him and stand staring at her downbent head for a long time. He'd heard the crash of her hands on the piano and it had made him curious. He knew she was probably feeling frustrated, that it would take a long time for her hand to be able to stand the torment of long practice.

It was only when he came up to her and straddled the piano bench facing her that she looked up.

"You can't play," he said. He'd heard her from outside the door. He knew the truth, now. She gritted her teeth, waiting for the blow to fall. "It will take time," he said. "Don't be impatient."

She let out a slow breath. So he didn't know. At least her pride was safe.

"That's right." She met his eyes and felt her heart drop. "So you don't have to feel sorry for me. I can still play, Ethan. I'll just need a little more time to heal, and then a lot of practice."

"Of course." He looked down at the keyboard. "Hurt, didn't it? What I said about feeling sorry for you."

"The truth is always the best way," she said numbly.

He shifted, his eyes pinning hers. "What are you and your father going to do until you're proficient again?"

"He's going to see about releasing some of my new recordings and re-releasing some of the older ones," she replied. Her left hand touched the keyboard reverently and she mourned fiercely the loss of her abilities. She couldn't even show it, couldn't cry her eyes out on Ethan's broad chest, because she didn't dare admit it to him. "So, you see, I won't have any financial worries right away. Dad and I will look after each other."

He drew in a short, angry breath. "Is he going to win again?" he asked coldly.

She drew away, puzzled by the fury in his tone. "Again?"

"I let him take you away from here once," he said, his jaw taut, his silver eyes flashing. "I let you walk away, because he convinced me that you needed him and music more than you needed me. But I can't do that again, Arabella."

She hesitated. "You . . . you loved Miriam."

His face hardened. "No."

"You only want me," she began again, searching his eyes while her heart threatened to run away with her. "And not enough to marry me."

"No."

He was confusing her. She pushed back her long, dark hair nervously. "Can't you say something besides just 'no'?" she asked slowly.

"Put your leg over here." He readjusted her so that she was facing him on the long, narrow piano bench. Then he pulled her jean-clad legs gently over his so that they were in the most intimate position they'd ever shared. His lean hands held her hips, pulling them hard into his, and then he looked down into her eyes and deliberately moved her so that she felt, with shocking emphasis, the slow arousal of his body.

Her nails dug into his shoulders. "Ethan, for heaven's sake!" she protested in shocked outrage.

But he held her there despite her struggles. His jaw was taut and his breathing unsteady. "I'll be damned if I'll let you go," he said huskily. "You're going to marry me."

She couldn't believe what she was hearing. The feel of him against her was making reason almost impossible, anyway.

"Say yes," he said, bending to her mouth. "Say it now, or so help me God, I'll have you where you sit!" His hands pulled her closer and she felt the physical reality of the threat.

"Yes, Ethan," she could manage that, barely. Not because she was afraid of him, but because she loved him too much to refuse him a second time. Then his lips were against hers and she was clinging to him like ivy, only living through his mouth and his hands and his body.

Somehow he managed to get his shirt and hers out of the way, and she felt him from the waist up, bare and hair-roughened muscles warm and hard against her sensitive breasts while he kissed her until her mouth ached. His strong hands slid up and down her back, moving her in a new and shameless rhythm against his thighs, making her moan with the intimacy of their position.

"It will be like this in bed," he whispered, his deep voice shaken as it made tiny chills against her moist, swollen lips. "Except that we'll join in the most intimate way of all first. Then I'll rock you against me...like this...and we'll have each other on crisp, white sheets in my bed...!"

His tongue penetrated her mouth. She arched against him, moaning, her hands trembling as they caught in his hair and held his mouth against her own. She could see them—Ethan's lean, dark-skinned body over hers, the light glistening on his damp skin, the movement of it against her own pale flesh in a rhythm as deep, as slow, as waves against the beach. His strained face above hers, his breath shaking, as hers would be, his mouth moving to her breasts...

She caught her breath. Sensations of pleasure made her shudder as his hands clenched on her hips and forced her even closer.

"I want you," he groaned against her mouth. His fingers trembled as they slid under the waistband of her jeans.

"I know," she whispered feverishly. Her hands slid to his thighs, trembling too. "I want... you, too."

He shuddered with the fierce need to give in to what he was feeling, what she was feeling. But it couldn't happen like this. No, he told himself. No! He eased back a breath and looked down into her soft, misty eyes. "Not like this," he bit off. "Our first time shouldn't be on a piano bench in an unlocked room. Should it?"

She stared up at him, shivering. It had only then occurred to her where they were. "I saw us," she whispered unsteadily. "In bed."

His face clenched. "My God, so did I, twisting against each other in a fever so hot it burned." He buried his face in her throat, and it was burning hot. His arms contracted.

His hands smoothed against her bare back and he touched her soft breasts. He lifted his head, looking down at the rose-tipped softness in his hands. "Did you ever dream that we'd be like this together one day?" he asked, almost in awe, and lifted his eyes to hold hers. "Sitting alone in a quiet room with your body open to my eyes and my hands, and so natural that we both accepted it without embarrassment?"

"I dreamed of it," she confessed in a soft whisper. She looked down at the darkness of his hands against the creamy beauty of her breasts. She trembled, and didn't mind letting him see. She belonged to him now. If wanting was all he felt, she could live with it. She'd have to.

"So did I," he whispered huskily. "Every long, lonely night." And he bent to take one small, perfect breast into his mouth.

She arched to him, clinging to his hair, gasping at the delicious sensations that washed over her, loving the warm moist suction of his mouth on her.

"It will be like this in bed, too," he whispered against her flushed skin. "Except that I'll kiss more than your breasts this way, and I won't stop until you're as satisfied as I am."

She drew her mouth over his eyes, his cheekbones, his nose, his mouth. "I hope you won't be sorry," she said quietly.

He lifted his head and looked down at her. If she'd ever loved him, he'd killed it. He was bulldozing her into this wedding, but it seemed the only way out. Perhaps love could be taught. "We'll have a white wedding, with all the trimmings," he added. "Complete with a wedding night. There won't be any anticipating our vows, and to hell with modern attitudes." He kissed her gently. "This is what marriage should be. A good marriage, with respect on both sides and honor to make it all perfect."

Respect. Honor. No mention of love, but perhaps she was being greedy. "Your mother was right. You are a puritan," she teased.

"So are you." He lifted her away from him with rueful reluctance and fastened her clothes again, then his. "I like the idea of a blushing, shy bride," he murmured, watching her face color. "Do you mind?"

"No," she assured him. "Not at all. I've waited so long to be one."

"As long as I've waited for you," he replied, his face almost a stranger's with its hard restraint. He moved away from her. "We'll make it together this time," he said. "Despite your father and Miriam and all the other obstacles, this time we'll make it."

She looked up at him with hope and quiet adoration. "Yes. This time we'll make it," she whispered.

They had to. She knew that she'd never survive having to leave him again. Later, she'd explain about her father and the peace they'd made. For now, it was enough that they were facing a future with each other. Love might come later, if she could be the kind of wife he wanted, and needed. In the meantime, she'd live one day at a time.

Her only worry was what he was going to think if he found out that her career was over. He might think again that she was marrying him for security.

She phoned her father that night and explained the situation to him. Oddly enough, he wasn't disappointed, and he even congratulated her. He'd make do, he promised, and she'd get the lion's share of the deals he was working on her behalf.

That reassured her. She'd have her little nest egg. Then, in the future, when Ethan finally tired of her body, she'd have something to fall back on. She could have a kind of life, even though it wouldn't include him.

She slept fitfully, wondering if she'd made the right decision. Was it right for Ethan, who was losing the woman he really loved? Or should she have let him go for good? By morning, she was no closer to a decision.

# Chapter Eleven

"So it's back on again," Coreen said with a nod, eyeing her son warily as he and a somber Arabella broke the news to her. "Uh-huh. For how long this time?"

"For good." He lifted his chin. "You took the gown back, I suppose," he added.

"No, I didn't take the gown back," Coreen replied. "I stuck it in the closet because I was reasonably sure that you inherited enough of my common sense not to duplicate the worst mistake of your life."

He stared at her. "You kept it?"

"Yes." She smiled at Arabella. "I hoped he'd come to his senses. I just wasn't sure that he could get past his old doubts. Especially," she added, with a grim glance in Miriam's direction, "when the past started to interfere with the present."

"I'll tell you all about that, someday," Ethan promised his mother. "In the meantime, how about those plans for the wedding?"

"I'll call Shelby tonight. Is that all right with you, Arabella?"

"I'd like that," Arabella said with downcast eyes. "Are you sure Shelby will have time to help us?"

"She'll make it. Her mother and I were best friends, many years ago. This time, don't let Arabella get away," Coreen cautioned her son.

He looked down at Arabella with open hunger. "Not on your life. Not this time."

Arabella was trying not to look as nervous as she felt. That hunger in Ethan's eyes was real, even if he didn't love her, and she was suddenly uncertain about being able to satisfy it. If it hadn't dimmed in four years, how was she, a virgin, going to be woman enough to quench it?

He saw that fear in her eyes and misinterpreted it. He drew her to one side, scowling. "You aren't getting cold feet?"

"It's a big step, marriage," she said, hedging. "I'll get my nerve back."

"I'll give you anything you want," he said curtly. "You can have the moon, if you like."

She averted her gaze to Miriam and her fiancé. They looked the picture of coming nuptial bliss. Nothing like Arabella and Ethan, so tense and nervous with each other, stepping gingerly around the big issues they still had to face.

"I don't want the moon," she said. "I'll settle for a good marriage."

"We come from similar backgrounds and we have a lot in common," he said stubbornly. "We'll make it."

Shelby Jacobs Ballenger came by the next morning to talk to Arabella while Coreen and Mary listened in. She was a beautiful woman, much prettier than Miriam, and there had been a lot of gossip about the rocky romance she and her husband, Justin, had weathered. If it was true, none of it showed on her supremely happy face, and even the birth of two sons hadn't ruined her slender figure.

"I can't tell you how much we appreciate your help," Arabella said, smiling at Shelby. "I've never had to worry about arrangements of this sort before."

"It's my pleasure," Shelby replied, beaming. "I have a special place in my heart for weddings. My own was something to remember—unfortunately, for all the wrong reasons. But even with a bad start, it's been a miracle of togetherness. Justin is all I ever wanted, he and my boys."

"How do you manage any free time?" Arabella asked.

"It's not easy, with preschoolers," Shelby laughed, "but my sister-in-law is a jewel. Abby's keeping them while she's confined to the house. It's their third child on the way, you know. Justin said he was going to have a long talk with Calhoun and see if he knew what was causing them!"

Everyone laughed. It was well known around Jacobsville that Calhoun and Abby would have loved an even dozen.

"Now." Shelby got out a notebook. "Let me run you through the possibilities and then we'll sort out the particulars."

It took the better part of the morning. Shelby left just before lunch and Arabella's head was swimming with it all.

"I don't want a wedding," she moaned to Coreen. "It's too complicated."

"We could elope," Ethan suggested.

Coreen glared at him. "Mary and Matt already did that. I won't let you. It's a church wedding or you'll live in sin!"

"Mother!" Ethan gave a theatrical expression of shock.

"It won't be that difficult. We already have the bride and the dress; all we have to worry about are invitations and food."

"Well, we could phone the guests and have a barbecue," he replied.

"Go away, Ethan," Coreen invited.

"Only if Arabella comes with me. I thought she might like to see the kittens. They've grown since she's been away," he added offhandedly.

She was tempted, but she wasn't sure she wanted to be alone with him. She'd successfully avoided him the night before, because of that look in his eyes that made her skin tingle.

"Come on, chicken," he taunted, so handsome in his jeans and chambray shirt that he looked the epitome of the movie cowboy.

"All right." She capitulated, following him out the door, to Coreen and Mary's amusement.

He caught her hand in his as they walked, linking her fingers sensuously through his own. He glanced down, his silver eyes approving of her gray slacks and gray-and-yellow patterned sweater. "You look good with your hair down like that."

She smiled. "It gets in my eyes."

He tilted his hat low over his eyes as they went out into the sunlight. "It's going to get hot today. We might go swimming."

"No, thanks," she said. Too quickly. She felt his eyes probing.

"Afraid history might repeat itself?" he asked softly. He stopped at the barn door and turned her, his hands gentle, his eyes questioning. "We're engaged. I might not draw back this time. I might take you."

She dropped her eyes to his chest. "I want a white wedding."

His own eyes were looking for telltale signs, for anything that would give him a hint of what she really was feeling. "So do I. Will it be any less white if we express what we feel for each other with our bodies?"

Her gaze shot up, her face flaming with bad temper. "That's all you feel for me, though. You said so. Wanting. You want me. I'm something you'd like to use...!"

He let her go abruptly, literally pushing her away from him. "My God, I can't get through to you, can I?" he asked bitterly.

She wrapped her arms across her breasts. "I wouldn't put it like that," she replied. "You wanted me four years ago, but you married Miriam. You loved her, not me."

"Four years ago, Miriam told me she was pregnant," he said, his face hardening at the memory. "By the time I realized she wasn't, we were married."

Her face tightened. She knew what he was saying. He and Miriam had anticipated their wedding vows. Probably by the time he'd made love to her at the swimming hole, he'd already been intimate with Miriam. She felt sick.

She started past him, but he caught her arms and held her. "No!" he said roughly. "It wasn't like that! It was you from the very beginning. Miriam was the substitute, Arabella, not you." He pulled her back against him, his teeth grinding together in anguish. "I knew that afternoon that if I didn't do something, I'd have you in spite of all my noble intentions. Miriam was handy and willing." He bent his head over hers. "I used her, and she knew it, and hated me for it. I cheated all three of us. She came to me and told me she thought she was pregnant, so I married her. You had your career and I didn't think you were old enough to cope with marriage, so I let you go. My God, don't you think I paid for that decision? I paid for it for four long years. I'm still paying!"

Time slowed to a standstill as what he was saying penetrated her mind. "You made love to Miriam because you wanted me?" she asked wanly. That was just what Miriam had said. That it had been a physical obsession on his part.

"Yes," he said with a heavy sigh. His fingers smoothed over the fabric of her sweater, caressing her shoulders. "And couldn't have you." His mouth pressed her hair away from her neck and sought it, warm and hard and fiercely passionate. "I wouldn't have been able to stop, Arabella," he whispered huskily. "Once I had you, I couldn't have stopped." His mouth opened, warm and moist against the tender flesh, arousing and slow. "You'd never have been able to leave, don't you see, baby? You'd have been mine. Totally mine."

Her eyes closed as the arousing movement of his lips made her knees go weak. He was seducing her with words. She shouldn't let him do this to her. She was weak.

He edged her into the deserted barn, against the inside of the closed door, so that the weight of his lean body pinned her there from breast to thighs. He shuddered with his need.

"I'm going to make you marry me," he said into her mouth. "If it takes seduction, that's all right, too. I'll get you to the altar anyway I have to."

"Blackmailer," she protested shakenly.

"Kiss me back." He moved against her and felt her begin to tremble. Her mouth lifted and he took it with slow, aching movements that made her moan under the crush of the kiss, that made her give it back in a feverish surge of passion.

A long time later, he dragged her arms from around his neck and stepped away from her, a reddish burn along his cheeks, a tremor in the lean, sure hands that held her wrists.

"You can have a month," he said with savage hunger just barely held in check. "If the ring isn't on your finger by then, look out. I won't wait a night longer."

He turned and left her there, still shaking, with her back to the wall.

* * *

Exactly one month later, she spoke her vows in the small Jacobsville Methodist church with her father there to give her away and half of Jacobsville in attendance. Ethan hadn't touched her since that day in the barn, but his eyes threatened her every time he looked at her. He might not love her, but his passion for her was as alive and hot as the weather.

Miriam had long since gone back to the Caribbean with Jared, and she'd sent them a wedding invitation. She'd beaten Ethan to the altar by two weeks, but Ethan hadn't seemed to mind. He'd been busy, and away a good bit recently on ranch business. Coreen remarked dryly that it was probably just as well, because his moods were making everyone nervous.

Only Arabella understood exactly what those moods were about, and tonight she was going to have to cope with the cause of them. He'd reserved a hotel room for them at a resort on the Gulf of Mexico, and she was more nervous than she'd ever been in her life. All the walls were going to come down and she'd be alone with Ethan and his fierce desire for her. She didn't know how she was going to survive a possession that was purely physical.

"You made a beautiful bride," Coreen said, kissing her just before she went upstairs to change. She wiped away tears. "I just know you and Ethan are going to make it this time."

"I hope so," Arabella confessed, radiant despite her fears as she paused to kiss Mary and Matt and to thank Shelby.

"It was my pleasure," Shelby assured her, and tightened her grip on her tall husband's hand. Justin

Ballenger was altogether too much man for the average woman, but Shelby had moved in under his heart, and he looked as if he didn't mind one bit. He smiled down at her, his lean face briefly radiant as his dark eyes swept over her with possession and pride.

"I won't forget all you've done for me," Arabella murmured, a little shy of Justin. She leaned forward and kissed Shelby's cheek. "Thank you."

"I hope you'll be very happy," Shelby said gently.

"You get out of marriage what you put into it," Justin added and smiled at her. "Give a little and take a little. You'll do fine."

"Thanks," Arabella replied.

He and Shelby moved off, hand in hand, and Arabella watched them with pure envy.

Ethan caught her hand, pulling her around. He searched her eyes with a light in his that puzzled her. It was the first time he'd come near her since he'd said, "I do," and he hadn't kissed her at the altar, to everyone's surprise and puzzlement.

"The luggage is in the car. Let's go," he said quietly, his eyes narrowing as they smoothed over her body. "I want you to myself."

"But... aren't we going to change?" she faltered.

"No." He framed her face in his lean hands and pulled it up to the descent of his. "I want to take that dress off you myself," he whispered, and his lips touched hers in a promise of a kiss that made her knees go weak. "Come along, Mrs. Hardeman."

He made the name sound new and sweet. She took his hand and let him lead her out, coping somehow with the shock and amusement of all the people who'd gathered around them here. The reception was supposed to be held in the fellowship hall, but Ethan had apparently decided that they were going to forego the traditional celebration. He grinned, whispered something to his delighted mother, and they left in a hail of rice and confetti and good wishes.

They drove to Galveston in his mother's Mercedes-Benz, since his own car had been left as a decoy for well-wishers with their soap and tin cans. His mother's car was untouched, and he grinned at Arabella's expression when she saw it.

"We're too old for all that," he chided as he put her in the car. "Tin cans and soaped windows—my God."

She made a face at him. "Some of us sure grow up too fast," she muttered.

"Not quite fast enough, in your case." He started the car and took off around the back of the church, glancing with amusement at the rear-view mirror where he could see a few friends were just staring after them with astonished faces. "I could very happily have married you at the age of sixteen, but I had a guilty conscience about robbing the cradle."

She was faintly shocked at the admission, not sure if she should even take the remark seriously. But he wasn't smiling.

"Don't believe me?" he asked with a quick glance. "Wait until we get to Galveston. You've got a lot of surprises coming."

"Have I?" She wondered what they were. She had a feeling the biggest one was going to be the wedding night she'd secretly dreaded. Love on one side wasn't going to be enough to get her through that, and she knew it.

He kept music playing until they reached the lovely brick hotel on the beach and checked in. Their room overlooked the beach and Galveston Bay, and it was a remote spot, for all its closeness to town. Sea gulls dipped down on the beach and she watched them wistfully.

"Change into some jeans and a top and we'll walk down the beach," he suggested, sensing her discomfort. "It's a bit cool today for swimming."

"Okay." She hesitated, wondering if he was going to expect her to undress in front of him.

"You can have the bathroom. I'll change in here," he said easily.

She gave him a grateful smile and got her things out of her suitcase. By the time she'd changed into her jeans and a gray pullover shirt, he was wearing jeans and a blue-and-white striped shirt.

"Let's go." He didn't give her time to be self-conscious about sharing the big room with its two double beds. He led her out onto the beach and they spent the afternoon looking for shells and talking. Later they had a seafood supper in a restaurant located in an old lighthouse, and sat on the big deck after dark and watched the ships pass.

By the time they went back into their room, Arabella was relaxed and so much in love that she didn't even protest when Ethan took her in his arms in the doorway and began to kiss her with fervent hunger.

He didn't turn on the light. He closed and locked the door in the dark and picked Arabella up, carrying her to the first of the two beds.

She was lost in his hard, deep kisses, in the caressing movements of his lean hands as he undressed her with slow delight, discovering her body with his lips first, then his hands. She stretched like a cat while he undressed and when she felt the first touch of his naked skin against her own, she gasped with shocked pleasure.

His mouth covered hers then, gentling her. As the minutes began to move faster, as the heat began to burn inside her, as the kisses grew endless and his hands made her shiver and cry out, she forgot her fear and gave him what he wanted. When he moved over her, she welcomed the hard thrust of his body with trusting abandon.

He pushed down and she clung to him. There was a flash of pain, and then it was feverish movement and growing pleasure that finally exploded into an ecstasy that bordered on pain in its sweeping fulfillment.

"No," he groaned when she made a hesitant movement, aeons later. His hands swept her back, hard against him, and he shuddered as he held her there, against his sweat-dampened body. "Stay here."

"Are you all right?" she whispered into his throat.

"Now, I am," he replied. His lips brushed tenderly over her face. "You love me. We couldn't have made love like this out of desire alone," he whispered huskily. "Not with this kind of tenderness."

She closed her eyes. So he knew. It wasn't surprising. That had probably been her biggest fear, that when he made love to her, he was going to realize how much she cared.

Her fingers moved gently in his thick, damp hair. "Yes," she confessed then. "I love you. I always have. I don't think they've invented a cure for it."

"God forbid that they ever should," he whispered back. He cradled her intimately in the curve of his legs with a long sigh. His hand smoothed over her waist, her breast, with slow possession and he laughed. "You're mine," he said with gruff amusement. "I'm never going to let you go now. You're going to live with me and bear my children and we're going to be everything to each other for the rest of our lives."

"Even though you only want me?" she asked sadly.

"I want you, yes," he replied. His hands smoothed her back against him, so that her body could feel the urgent press of his. "I want you to the point of madness and beyond. If it were only desire that I felt, any woman's body would do. But that isn't the case." He held her hips to his. "Not only was there no Miriam, there was no other woman for four years. Is that enough proof of love?"

Her breath caught. She turned in his grasp, her eyes trying to see his through the moonlit darkness. "You love me?"

"My God, with all my heart," he said huskily. "You little blind fool, didn't you know? My mother did. Mary and Matt did. Everyone knew what I felt, including Miriam, so why didn't you?"

She laughed, on fire with the first daring certainty of shared love, belonging. "Because I was a blind little fool! Oh, Ethan, I love you, I love you, I love...!"

That was as far as she got. He rolled her into him and his hands grew quickly urgent, like the hard mouth that had cut off her hasty admission. He moved against her and she moved to accommodate him, and for a long time, they said nothing while their bodies spoke in a new and intimate language of love.

"God knows how I'll share you with the stage," he groaned much later when they were propped up together sharing a soft drink he'd retrieved from the refrigerator in the room. "But I'll manage."

"Oh. That." She grimaced and laid her face against his warm, bare shoulder. "Well, I sort of lied."

"What?"

"I sort of lied," she repeated. "I will be able to use my hand again, and play again, but not like I did before." She sighed, nuzzling her cheek against him with a loving sigh. "I can teach, but I can't perform. And before you say it, I'm not sorry. I'd rather have you than be as great as Van Cliburn."

He couldn't speak. If he needed proof of her love, that gave it to him. He bent and kissed her eyes with breathless tenderness. "Truly, Arabella?" he asked softly.

"Truly, Ethan." She nibbled at his lips and simultaneously set the ice-cold bottom of the soft drink on his warm, flat belly.

His voice exploded in the darkness and he jumped. Arabella laughed with endless delight, anticipating a delicious reprisal.

"Why, you little..." he began, and she could see the smile, hear the loving threat, see the quick movement in her direction.

She put the drink on the bedside table and reached out to him, drawing him to her, accepting her fate with arms that would accept everything life had to offer for the rest of her life. Ethan in her arms. Heaven.

\* \* \* \* \*

# CONNAL

## Diana Palmer

# Chapter One

Because of the date, Penelope knew she wouldn't find him at the barn. That was where he usually was at this hour of the day. Any other time, C. C. Tremayne was always two steps ahead of his men in feeding the animals, especially with the drought that had turned the grass brown and brittle these past few weeks. The drought had been a bad break for her father. Even with the Rio Grande only a few miles away, water was a precious commodity and wells kept going dry, leaving the tanks they filled empty.

West Texas was usually hot in mid-September, but the wind was up and it was unseasonably cold this evening. Penelope had worn a jacket outside, and now she was glad she had. She shivered a little in the late afternoon chill.

It was just beginning to get dark, and Penelope knew that if she didn't get to C.C. before her father did, it was going to mean another nasty quarrel. Ben Mathews and his foreman had been at each other's throats enough in recent weeks and Penelope didn't want any more arguments. Her father always got bad-tempered when money was tight. Things couldn't be much worse right now.

C.C. was drinking. She knew it; it was that time of year again. Only Penelope knew the importance of that day in September in C.C.'s life. She'd once nursed him through a flu and a raging delirium and he'd told her everything. She didn't let on that she knew, of course. C.C.—he was called that, although nobody knew what the initials stood for—didn't like anyone knowing private things about him. Not even the girl who loved him more than life.

He didn't love Penelope. He never had, although she'd worshiped him since she was nineteen and he'd been hired as foreman when her father's oldest hand retired. It had only taken one long look at the lithe, lean, dark-eyed man with the hawkish features and unsmiling face for her to fall madly in love with him. It was three years later, and her emotions hadn't undergone any changes. Probably they never would. Penelope Mathews was pretty stubborn. Even her dad said so.

She grimaced when she saw the light on in the bunkhouse, and it was not even dark. The other men were out riding herd, because calving was in full swing and everybody was in a mean temper during calving. It meant long hours and little sleep, and it wasn't normal for any of the men to be in the bunkhouse at this hour of the day. That meant it had to be C.C., and he had to be drinking. And liquor was one thing Ben

Mathews wasn't about to tolerate on his ranch, not even when it was being abused by a man he liked and respected.

She brushed back her light reddish-brown hair and nibbled on her full lower lip. She had her long, wavy hair in a ponytail and it was tied with a velvet ribbon that just matched her pale brown eyes. She wasn't a pretty girl, but she had a nice figure even if it was a little on the plump side. Not overweight, just rounded, so that she filled out her jeans nicely. Her hair was almost red-gold when the sun hit it, and she had a line of freckles over her straight nose. With a little work, she could have been lovely. But she was a tomboy. She could ride anything and shoot as well as her father. Sometimes she wished she looked like Edie, the wealthy divorcee C.C. dated frequently. Edie was a dish, all blond and blue-eyed and bristling with sophistication. She seemed an odd choice for a ranch foreman, but Penelope tried not to think about it. In her mind, she knew the reason C.C. dated Edie and it hurt.

She paused at the door of the bunkhouse and rubbed nervously at her jeans, tugging her nylon jacket closer against the cold wind. She knocked.

There was a hard thud. "Go away."

She knew the curt, uncompromising tone and sighed. It was going to be a long day.

Her gloved hand pushed open the door and she stepped into the warmth of the big common room where bunks lined the wall. At the far end was a kitchen arrangement where the men could have meals cooked. Nobody stayed here much. Most of the men were married and had homes on the ranch, except

C.C. But during roundup and calving, the new men who were hired on temporarily stayed here. This year there were six, and they filled the building to capacity. But they'd be gone within a week, and C.C. would have the bunkhouse to himself again.

C.C. was leaning back in a chair, his mud-caked boots crossed on the table, his hat cocked over one dark eye, hiding most of his dust-streaked dark hair, his lean hands wrapped around a whiskey glass. He tilted the hat up, peered at Penelope with mocking derision and jerked it down again.

"What the hell do you want?" he asked in his curt drawl.

"To save your miserable skin, if I can," she returned in equally cutting tones. She slammed the door, skinned off her coat to reveal the fluffy white sweater underneath, and went straight to the kitchen to make a pot of coffee.

He watched her with disinterested eyes. "Saving me again, Pepi?" he laughed mockingly, using the nickname that everyone called her. "What for?"

"I'm dying of love for you," she muttered as she filled the coffeepot. It was the truth, but she made it sound like an outrageous lie.

He took it that way, too, laughing even louder. "Sure you are," he said. He threw down the rest of the contents of his glass and reached for the whiskey bottle.

Pepi was faster. She grabbed it away, something she'd never have managed if he'd been sober, and drained it into the sink before he could stagger to his feet.

"Damn you, girl!" he said harshly, staring at the empty bottle. "That was the last I had!"

"Good. I won't have to tear the place apart looking for the rest. Sit down and I'll make you some coffee. It will get you on your feet before Dad finds you," she mumbled. She plugged in the pot. "Oh, C.C.," she moaned, "he's combing the hills for you right now! You know what he'll do if he finds you like this!"

"But, he won't, will he, honey?" he chided, coming up all too close behind her to take her shoulders and draw her back against the warm strength of his lean body. "You'll protect me, like always."

"Someday I won't be in time," she sighed. "And then what will become of you?"

He tilted her worried eyes up to his, and little shudders ran through her body. He'd never touched her except in amusement or at a dance. Her heart had fed just on the sight of him, from a distance. He was very potent this close, and she had to drop her eyes to his lean cheeks to keep him from knowing that.

"Nobody ever gave a damn except you," he murmured. "I don't know that I like being mothered by a girl half my age."

"I'm not half your age. Where are the cups?" she asked quietly, trying to divert him.

He wasn't buying it. His lean fingers brushed back loose strands of her hair, making her nerves sit up and scream. "How old are you now?"

"You know very well I'm twenty-two," she said. She had to keep her voice steady. She looked up deliberately to show him that he wasn't affecting her, but the smoldering expression in those black eyes caught her off guard.

"Twenty-two to my thirty. And a damned young twenty-two," he said slowly. "Why do you bother with me?"

"You're an asset around here. Surely you know how close we were to bankruptcy when you got hired?" she asked on a laugh. "Dad owes a lot to your business sense. But he still hates liquor."

"Why?"

"My mother died in an automobile accident the year before you came here," she said. "My father had been drinking and he was behind the wheel at the time." She tugged against his disturbing hands and he let her go.

She looked through the cabinets and found a white mug that wasn't broken or chipped. She put it down by the coffeepot and filled it, and then she took it to C.C., who had sat down and was rubbing his head with his lean hands at the table.

"Head hurt?" she asked.

"Not nearly enough," he said enigmatically. He took the mug and sipped the thick black liquid. He glared at it. "What in hell did you put in here, an old boot?"

"Twice the usual measure, that's all," she assured him as she sat down beside him. "It will sober you up quicker."

"I don't want to be sober," he said shortly.

"I know that. But I don't want you to get fired," she returned, smiling pertly when he glared at her. "You're the only person on the place except Dad who doesn't treat me like a lost cause."

He studied her smooth features, her soft dark eyes. "Well, I guess that makes us two of a kind, then. Because you're the first person in years who gave a damn about me."

"Not the only one," she corrected, smiling in spite of her feelings as she added, "Edie cares, too."

He shrugged and smiled faintly. "I guess she does. We understand each other, Edie and I," he murmured quietly, his eyes with a faraway look. "She's one of a kind."

In bed, she probably was, Pepi thought, but she couldn't give herself away by saying so. She got up and brought the coffeepot to refill his cup.

"Drink up, pal," she said gently. "The vigilantes aren't far away."

"I feel more steady now," he said after he'd finished the second cup. "On the outside, anyway." He lit a cigarette and blew out a thick cloud of smoke, leaning back wearily in the chair. "God, I hate days like this."

She couldn't admit that she knew why without incriminating herself. But she remembered well enough what he'd said, and the way he'd screamed when the memory came back in a nightmare delirium. Poor man. Poor, tortured man. He'd lost his wife and his unborn child on a white-water rafting trip that he'd had the misfortune to survive. As near as she could tell, he'd blamed himself for that ever since. For living, when they hadn't.

"I guess we all have good ones and bad ones," she said noncommittally. "If you're okay, I'll get back to my cooking. Dad's reminded me that he's due an apple pie. I've been baking half the afternoon."

"You're a domestic little thing, aren't you?" he asked strangely, searching her eyes. "Is Brandon coming to see you tonight?"

She blushed without knowing why. "Brandon is the vet," she said shortly. "Not my boyfriend."

"You could use a boyfriend, tidbit," he said unexpectedly, his eyes narrowing, his frown deepening as he fingered the empty mug. "You're a woman now. You need more than companionship from a man."

"I know what I need, thanks," she replied, rising. "You'd better stick your head in a bucket or something and see if you can get that bloodshot look out of your eyes. And for heaven's sake, swallow some minty mouthwash."

He sighed. "Anything else, Mother Mathews?" he asked sarcastically.

"Yes. Stop getting drunk. It only makes things worse."

He stared at her curiously. "You're so wise, aren't you, Pepi?" he asked cuttingly. "You haven't lived long enough to know why people drink."

"I've lived long enough to know that nobody ever solved a problem by running away from it," she returned, glaring back when his eyes started flashing black fire at her. "And don't start growling, either, because it's the truth and you know it. You've spent years living in the past, letting it haunt you. Oh, I don't pretend to know why," she said quickly when he began to eye her suspiciously, "but I know a haunted man when I see one. You might try living in the present, C.C. It's not so bad. Even at calving time. And just think, you have roundup to look forward to," she added with a wicked grin. "See you."

She started out the door without her jacket, so nervous that she'd given herself away that she hardly missed it until the wind hit her.

"Here, you'll freeze," he said suddenly, and came toward her with the jacket in his hand. "Put this on."

Unexpectedly he held it for her and didn't let go even when she was encased in it. He held her back against his chest, both lean hands burning through the sleeves of the coat, his chin on the top of her head.

"Don't bruise your heart on me, Pepi," he said quietly, with such tenderness in his deep voice that her eyes closed instinctively at the tone. "I don't have anything left to give you."

"You're my friend, C.C.," she said through her teeth. "I hope I'm yours. That's all."

His hands contracted for a minute. His chest rose and fell heavily. "Good," he said then, and let her go. "Good. I'm glad that's all there is to it. I wouldn't want to hurt you."

She opened the door and glanced back, forcing a smile to her lips even though he'd just destroyed all her dreams. "Try some of Charlie's chili peppers next time you feel like a binge," she advised. "The top of your head will come off just as fast, but you won't have a hangover from it."

"Get out of here!" he grumbled, glaring at her.

"If I see Dad, I'll tell him you're getting a snack, before you feed the livestock," she returned, grinning. She closed the door quickly and she heard him curse.

Her father was already home when she got there. He glared at her from the living room, her mirror image except for his masculinity and white hair.

"Where have you been?" he demanded.

"Out counting sheep," she said innocently.

"Sheep or one black one named C.C.?"

She pursed her lips. "Well..."

He shook his head. "Pepi, if I ever catch him with a bottle, he's through here, no matter how good a foreman he is," he said firmly. "He knows the rules."

"He was making himself a snack in the bunkhouse," she said. "I just poked my head in to ask if he'd like some of my...excuse me, *your*...apple pie."

He scowled fiercely. "It's my pie. I'm not sharing it!"

"I made two," she said quickly. "You old reprobate, you'd never fire C.C. You'd shoot yourself first and we both know it, but save your pride and say you'd fire him if it makes you feel better," she told him as she stripped off her jacket.

He finished lighting his pipe and glanced at her. "You'll wear your heart out on him, you know," he said after a minute.

Her back stiffened. "Yes. I know."

"He's not what he seems," he continued.

She turned, eyeing him warily. "What do you mean?"

"You tell me." He stared at the window, where snow was touching the pane under the outside lights. "He drove in here without a past at all. No references. No papers. I gave him a job on the strength of my instinct and his very evident ability with animals and figures. But he's no more a line-riding cowboy than I am a banker. He's elegant, C.C. is. And he knows business in an uncommon way for a poor man.

You mark my words, girl, there's more to him than what shows."

"He does seem out of place at times," she had to admit. She couldn't tell him the rest—that she knew why C.C. was out here on a ranch in the middle of nowhere. But even she hadn't learned from her involuntary eavesdropping during his delirium why he'd left that shadowy past. He'd come from money and he'd suffered a tragic loss, she knew that, and he was afraid to risk his heart again. That didn't stop Pepi from risking hers, though. It was far too late for any warning.

"He could be anything, you know," he said quietly, "even an escaped convict."

"I doubt that." She grinned. "He's too honest. Remember when you lost that hundred-dollar bill out in the barn, and C.C. brought it to you? I've seen him go out of his way to help other cowboys who were down on their luck. He's got a temper, but he isn't cruel with it. He growls and curses and the men get a little amused, but it's only when he's fighting mad that they run for the hills. And even then, he's in complete control. He never seems to lose it."

"I've noticed that. But a man in that kind of control, all the time, may have a reason," he reminded her. "There are other men. Don't take chances."

"You old faker," she muttered. "You're always pushing me at him."

He threw up his hands. "I like him. But I can afford to. You understand what I mean?"

She grimaced. "I guess so. Okay. I'll let Brandon take me to the movies, how about that?"

He made a face. "What a consolation prize," he grumbled. "The poor man's a clown. How he ever got through veterinary school is beyond me, with his sense of humor! He's the kind of man who would show a stuffed cow at a championship cattle show."

"My kind of man, all right," she said fervently, smiling. "He's uncomplicated."

"He's a wild man," he countered.

"I'll tame him," she promised. "Now let me get those apple pies finished, okay?"

"Okay. But I'll take C.C.'s to him," he added gently. "I want to see for myself if he's eating."

She stuck her tongue out at him and went to the kitchen, sighing her relief once she was out of sight.

# Chapter Two

Brandon Hale was a carrot-topped maniac, and in his spare time, he was a veterinarian. Pepi adored him. Probably if her heart hadn't been appropriated by C.C., she might have married Brandon one day.

He came by just as Pepi and her father were sitting down to the supper table.

"Oh, boy, apple pie." Brandon grinned, staring at the luscious treat Pepi had made. "Hello, Mr. Mathews, how are you?"

"Hungry," Ben said shortly. "And don't eye my apple pie. I'm not sharing it."

"But you will, won't you?" Brandon leaned down. "I mean, considering that you need your new calves inspected and that sick bull treated, and those inoculations given, with roundup on the way..."

"Damn, boy, that's hitting below the belt," Ben groaned.

"Just one little slice," Brandon said. "the size of a knife blade..."

"Oh, all right, sit down." The older man sighed. "But I hope you know I wouldn't share it with just anybody. And if you don't stop coming over here at night without a reason, you'll have to marry Pepi."

"I'd be delighted," Brandon said, winking at Pepi from his pale blue eyes. "Name the day, honey."

"The sixth of July, twenty years from now," she promised, passing the corn. "I expect to live a little before I settle down."

"You've already lived twenty-two years," her father remarked. "I want grandchildren."

"You have them yourself," Pepi invited. "I've been thinking about joining the Peace Corps."

Ben almost dropped his coffee cup. "You've what?"

"It would be something to broaden my horizons," she said. Not to mention getting her away from C.C. before she slipped up and bared her aching heart to him. Today had been a close call. He seemed to be suspicious of all the attention she gave him, and worried that he couldn't return her affections. It was getting too much for her. A year away might ease the pain.

"You could get killed in one of those foreign places," her father said shortly. "I won't let you."

"I'm twenty-two," she reminded him with a grin. "You can't stop me."

He sighed angrily. "Who'll cook and keep house and—"

"You can hire somebody."

"Sure." Her father laughed.

That brought home the true situation, and she felt instantly regretful that she'd brought it up. "I won't go right away," she promised. "And don't worry, things will get better."

"Pray for rain," Brandon suggested between bites. "Everybody else is. I've never seen so many ranchers in church."

"I've seen prayers work miracles," Ben remarked, and launched into some tales that kept Pepi's mind off C.C.

After they'd finished off half of Pepi's apple pie, Brandon went out with her father to check the sick bull. "I don't usually do night work when I can get out of it," Brandon told Pepi. "But for an apple pie like that, I'd come out to deliver a calf at three in the morning."

"I'll remember that," she said pertly, grinning.

"You're cute," he said. "I mean that. You're really cute, and if you ever want to propose matrimony, just go ahead. I won't even play hard to get."

"Thanks. I'll keep you in mind, along with my other dozen suitors," she said lightly.

"How about a movie Friday night? We'll run over to El Paso and eat supper before we go to the theater."

"Terrific," she agreed. He was loads of fun and she needed to get away.

"I won't get back until midnight, I guess," her father called out. "After we check that bull down at the Berry place, I want to look over Berry's books before the tax man gets them. Don't wait up."

"Okay. Have fun," she called back. It was a joke between them, because Jack Berry kept books that would have confounded a lawyer. It was almost estimated tax time, and Jack was the ranch's only bookkeeper. They should have hired somebody more qualified, but Jack was elderly and couldn't do outside work. Her father had a soft heart. Rather than see the old man on welfare, Ben had hired him to keep the books. Which meant, unfortunately, that Ben had to do most of the figuring over again at tax time. His soft heart was one reason the ranch was in the hole. He didn't really have a business head like his own father had possessed. Without C.C.'s subtle guidance, the ranch would have gone on the auction block three years ago. It still might.

C.C. She frowned, turning toward the back door. She was worried about him. He hadn't seemed too drunk when she'd gone to check on him earlier, and that was unusual. His yearly binges were formidable. She'd better give him another look, before her father thought to check him out at midnight.

The bunkhouse was filling up. There were three men in it, now, the newest temporary hands. But C.C. wasn't there.

"He was pretty tight-lipped about where he was going, Miss Mathews," one of the men volunteered. "But I'd guess he was headed into Juárez from the direction he took."

"Oh, boy," she sighed. "Did he take the pickup or his own car?"

"His own car—that old Ford."

"Thanks."

It was a good thing she drove, she thought angrily. One of these days she'd be gone, and who'd take care of that wild-eyed cowboy then? The thought depressed her. He wouldn't have any trouble finding somebody to do that, not with his looks. And there was always Edie.

She turned off on the road that led to the border. The official at the border remembered the big white Ford—there hadn't been a lot of traffic across, since it was a weekday night. She thanked him, went across and drove around until she found the white Ford parked with characteristic haphazardness in a parking space. She pulled in beside it and got out.

Fortunately she hadn't taken time to change. She was wearing jeans and a checked shirt with a pullover sweater and boots, just the outfit for walking around at night. She was a little nervous because she didn't like going places alone after dark. Especially the kind of place she was sure C.C. was going to be in. Too, she was worried in case her father came home and needed to ask her anything. Her closed bedroom door might fool him into thinking she was just asleep, but if he saw the pickup missing, he might get suspicious. She didn't want him to fire C.C. He liked the man, but if C.C. didn't tell him why he was drinking—and C.C. wouldn't—then her father was very likely to let him go anyway.

There was a bar not a block away from where she parked. She had a feeling that C.C. was in it, but when she looked inside, there were mostly Mexican men and only one or two young Americans. She walked the streets, peeking into bars, and almost got picked up once. Finally, miserable and worried, she turned and started back to the truck. On the way, she glanced into that first bar again—and there he was, leaning back in a chair at a corner table.

She walked in and went back to the corner table.

"Oh..." C.C. let out a word that he normally wouldn't have. He was cold and dangerous looking now, not the easily handled man of a few hours ago. She knew that her old tactics wouldn't work this time.

"Hi," she said gently.

"If you're here to drag me back, forget it," he drawled, glaring at her from bloodshot eyes. There was a half-empty tequila bottle on the table and an empty glass beside it. "I won't go."

"It's hot in here," she remarked, feeling her way. "Some air might help you."

He laughed drunkenly. "Think so? Suppose I pass out, tomboy. Will you throw me over your shoulder and carry me home?"

That hurt. He made her out to be some female Amazon. Perhaps that was how he thought of her—as just one of the boys. But she smiled. "I might try," she agreed.

He studied her with disinterested brevity. "Still in jeans. Always wearing something manly. Do you have legs, tomboy? Do you even have breasts—?"

"I'll bet you can't walk to the car by yourself," she cut him off, trying not to blush, because his voice carried and one or two of the patrons were openly staring their way.

He stopped what he was saying to scowl at her. "The hell I can't," he replied belligerently.

"Prove it," she challenged. "Let's see you get there without falling flat on your face."

He muttered something rough and got to his feet, swaying a little. He took out a twenty-dollar bill and tossed it onto the bar, his hat cocked arrogantly over one eye, his tall, lithe body slightly stooped. "Keep the change," he told the man.

Pepi congratulated herself silently on her strategy as he weaved out onto the street. He took off his hat and wiped his forehead hesitantly.

"Hot," he murmured. He shook his head, his breath coming hard and heavy. He turned to look at Pepi, frowning slightly. "I thought we were going for a walk."

"Sure," she said.

"Come here, then, sweet girl," he coaxed, holding out his arm. "I can't let you get lost, can I?"

It was the liquor talking, and she knew it. But it was so sweet to have his arm around her shoulder, his head bent to hers, his breath against her forehead. Even the scent of the tequila wasn't that unpleasant.

"So sweet," he said heavily, walking her away from the car, not toward it. "I don't want to go home. Let's just walk the night away."

"C.C., it's dangerous in this part of the city," she began softly.

"My name . . . is Connal," he said abruptly.

That was faintly shocking, to know that he had a real name. She smiled. "It's nice. I like it."

"Yours is Penelope Marie," he laughed roughly. "Penelope Marie Mathews."

"Yes." She hadn't known that he knew her full name. It was flattering.

"Suppose we change it to Tremayne?" he asked, hesitating. "Sure, why not? You're always looking after me, Penelope Marie Mathews, so why don't you marry me and do the thing right?" While she was absorbing the shock, he looked around weavingly. "Aha, sure, there's one of those all-night chapels. Come on."

"C.C., we can't . . . !"

He blinked at her horrified expression. "Sure we can. Come on, honey, we don't have to have any papers or anything. And it's all legal."

She bit her lower lip. She couldn't let him do this, she thought, panicking. When he sobered up and found out, he'd kill her. Not only that, she wasn't sure if a Mexican marriage was binding; she didn't know what the law was.

"Listen, now," she began.

"If you won't marry me," he threatened with drunken cunning, "I'll shoot up a bar and get us landed in jail. Right now, Pepi. This minute. I mean it."

Obviously he did. She gave in. Surely nobody in his right mind would marry them with him in that visibly drunken condition. So she went along with him, worried to death about how she was going to get him home. But she knew that he owned a Beretta and had a permit for it, and she couldn't be sure that he didn't have it on him. God forbid that he should shoot somebody!

He dragged her into the wedding chapel. Unfortunately the Mexican who married them spoke little English, and Pepi's halting Spanish was inadequate to explain what was going on. C.C., she recalled, spoke the language fluently. He broke in on her stumbling explanation and rattled off something that made the little man grin. The Mexican went away and came back with a Bible and two women. He launched into rapid-fire Spanish, cueing first Pepi and then C.C. to say *si* and then he said something else, grinned, and then a terrified Pepi was being hugged and kissed by the women. C.C. scrawled his signature on a paper and rattled off some more Spanish while the little man wrote a few other things on the paper.

"That's all there is to it." C.C. grinned at Pepi. "Here. All nice and legal. Give me a kiss, wife."

He held out the paper, took a deep breath, and slid to the floor of the chapel.

The next few minutes were hectic. Pepi finally managed to convey to the Mexican family that she had to get him to the car. They brought in a couple of really mean-looking young men who lifted C.C. like a sack of feed and carried him out to the parking lot. Pepi had him put in the pickup truck. She handed the boys two dollar bills, which was all she had, and tried to thank them. They waved away the money, grinning, when they noticed the beat-up, dented condition of the old ranch pickup. Kindred spirits, she thought warmly. Poor people always helped each other. She thanked them again, stuck the paper in her pocket, and started the truck.

She made it to the ranch in good time. Her father's Jeep was still gone, thank God. She backed the pickup next to the bunkhouse, where it wasn't visible from the house, and knocked on the door.

Bud, the new hand she'd spoken to earlier, answered the knock. Apparently the men had been asleep.

"I need a favor," she whispered. "I've got C.C. in the truck. Will you toss him on his bunk for me, before my dad sees him?"

Bud's eyebrows rose. "You've got the boss in there? What's wrong with him?"

She swallowed. "Tequila."

"Whew," Bud whistled. "Never thought of him as a drinking man."

"He isn't, usually," she said, reluctant to go into anything more. "This was an unfortunate thing. Can you do it? He's heavy."

"Sure I can, Miss Mathews." He followed her out in his stocking feet, leaving the bunkhouse door open. "I'll try not to wake the other men. They're all dead tired, anyway. I doubt they'd hear it thunder."

"Heavens, I hope not," she said miserably. "If my dad sees him like this, his life's over."

"Your dad don't like alcohol, I guess," Bud remarked.

"You said it."

She opened the pickup door. C.C. was leaning against it, sound asleep and snoring. Bud caught him halfway to the ground and threw him over his shoulder in a fireman's lift. C.C. didn't even break stride; he kept right on snoring.

"Thanks a lot, Bud," Pepi grinned.

"My pleasure, Miss. Good night."

She climbed into the pickup, parked it at the back of the house, and rushed upstairs to bed. Her father would be none the wiser, thank God.

She undressed to get into her gown, and a piece of paper fell to the floor. She unfolded it, and found her name and that of Connal Cade Tremayne on it along with some Spanish words and an official-looking signature. It didn't take much guesswork to realize that it was a marriage license. She sat down, gazing at it.

Well, it wasn't worth the paper it was written on, thank God. But she wasn't about to throw it away. In days to come, she could dream about what it could have meant if it had been the real thing. If C.C. had married her, wanted her, loved her. She sighed.

She put the license in her drawer and she laid down on the bed. Poor man, perhaps his ghosts would let him rest for a while now. She wondered how much of tonight he was going to remember, and hoped he wouldn't be too furious at her for going to get him or for leaving his dilapidated old Ford in Juárez. But with any luck, the old car would be fine, and he could get somebody to go with him to get it when he sobered up. Anyway, he ought to be grateful that she went after him, she assured herself. With winter coming on, it might be hard to get a new job. She didn't want to lose him. Even worshiping him from afar was better than never seeing him again. Or was it?

The next morning, she woke up with a start as a hard knock sounded on her door.

"What is it?" she asked on a yawn.

"You know damned good and well what it is!"

That was C.C. She sat up just as he threw open the door and walked in. Her gown was transparent and low-cut, and he got a quick but thorough look at her almost bare breasts before she could jerk the sheet up to her throat.

"C.C.!" she burst out. "What in heaven's name are you doing!"

"Where is it?" he demanded, his eyes coldly furious.

She blinked. "You'll have to excuse me, I don't read minds."

"Don't be cute," he returned. He was looking at her as if he hated her. "I remember everything. I'm not making that kind of mistake with you, Pepi Mathews. I may have to put up with being mothered by you, but I'll be damned if I'll stay married to you when I'm cold sober. The marriage license, where is it?"

It was a golden opportunity. To save his pride. To save her flimsy relationship with him. To spare herself the embarrassment of why she'd let him force her into the ceremony. Steady, girl, she told herself. The marriage wasn't legal in this country, she was reasonably sure of that, so there would be no harm done if she convinced him it had never happened.

"What marriage license?" she asked with a perfectly straight face and carefully surprised eyes.

Her response threw him. He hesitated, just for an instant. "I was in Mexico. In Juárez, in a bar. You came to get me... We got married."

Her eyes widened like saucers. "We did what?"

He was scowling by now. He fumbled a cigarette out of his pocket and lit it. "I was sure," he said slowly. "We went to this little chapel and the ceremony was all in Spanish... There was a paper of some kind."

"The only paper was the twenty-dollar bill you gave the bartender," she mused. "And if it hadn't been for Bud whats-his-name helping me get you to bed last night, you wouldn't still be working here. You know how Dad feels about booze. You were really tying one on."

He stared at the cigarette, then at her, intently. "I couldn't have imagined all that," he said finally.

"You imagined a lot of things last night," she laughed, making a joke out of it. "For one, that you were a Texas ranger on the trail of some desperado. Then you were a snake hunter, and you wanted to go out into the desert and hunt rattlers. Oh, I got you home in the nick of time," she added, lying through her teeth with a very convincing grin.

He relaxed a little. "I'm sorry," he said. "I must have been a handful."

"You were. But, no harm done," she told him. "Yet," she added, indicating the sheet under her chin. "If my father finds you up here, things could get sticky pretty fast."

"Don't be absurd," he replied, frowning as if the insinuation disturbed him. "You're only a little tomboy, not a vamp."

Just what he'd said last night, in fact, along with a few other references that had set off her temper. But she couldn't let on.

"All the same, if you and Dad want breakfast, you'd better leave. And your car is still in Juárez, by the way."

"Amazing that it made it that far," he murmured dryly. "Okay. I'm sorry I gave you a hard time. Do I still get breakfast?"

She relaxed, too, grateful that she didn't have to lie anymore. "Yes."

He spared her one last scowling glance. "Pepi, you've got to stop mothering me."

"This was the last time," she promised, and meant it.

His broad shoulders rose and fell halfheartedly.
"Sure." He paused at the open door with his back to
her. "Thanks," he said gruffly.

"You'd have done it for me," she said simply.

He started to turn, thought better of it, and went
out, closing the door behind him.

Pepi collapsed on the pillow with a heartfelt sigh.
She'd gotten away with it! Now all she had to do was
find out just how much trouble she was in legally with
that sham marriage.

# Chapter Three

It took Pepi half the next day to work up enough nerve to actually phone an attorney and ask if she was really married to C.C. She had to be careful. It couldn't be a lawyer who knew her, so she called one in El Paso, giving the receptionist an assumed name. She was given an appointment for that afternoon, because the attorney had a cancellation in his busy schedule. She told the receptionist why she wanted to see the attorney, adding lightly that she'd gotten a Mexican marriage and thought it wasn't binding. The secretary laughed and said a lot of people thought that, only to find out to their astonishment that they were very binding in Texas. She reconfirmed the appointment, wished Pepi a nice day and hung up.

Pepi replaced the receiver with a dull thud and sat down heavily in the chair beside the telephone table in the hall. Her heart was beating madly. It would take having the lawyer look at the document to be sure, but it sounded as if his receptionist was right. Legally she was Mrs. C. C. Tremayne. She was Connal Tremayne's wife.

But he didn't know it.

The consequences of her deception could be far-reaching and tragic, especially if he decided to marry Edie. He would be commiting bigamy, and he wouldn't even know it.

What should she do? If she told him now, after having denied it when he'd demanded the truth, he'd never believe anything she said again. He'd hate her, too, for trapping him into marriage. It didn't matter that he'd threatened to land them in jail if she didn't go along. He'd been intoxicated, not responsible for his actions. But she'd been sober. When he asked her why she'd gone through with it, how would she answer him? Would he guess that she was shamefully in love with him?

The questions tormented her. She burned lunch. Her father gave her a hard glare as he bit into a scraped grilled cheese sandwich.

"Tastes like carbon," he muttered.

"Sorry." She'd forgotten to buy cheese at the store on her latest shopping trip, so there had been only enough for three sandwiches. She'd managed to burn all three. All she could do was scrape them off and hope for the best.

"You're been preoccupied all morning," he remarked with intense scrutiny of the bright color in her cheeks. "Want to talk about it?"

She managed a wan smile and shook her head. "Thanks anyway."

He got down another bite of overdone grilled cheese sandwich. "Would it have anything to do with C.C.'s absence last night?"

She stared at him blankly. "What?"

"C.C.'s car was missing all night, and I understand that he had to have one of the hands drive him over to Juárez to collect it this morning." He glared at the remainder of his sandwiches and pushed the plate away. "He was drinking, wasn't he, Pepi?"

She couldn't lie, but it wouldn't do to tell the truth, either. "One of the men said C.C. had a few in Juárez, but on his own time," she added quickly. "You can't really jump on him unless he does it on your time." She warmed to her subject. "Besides that, he only drinks once a year."

He frowned. "Once a year?"

"That's about the extent of it. And please don't ask me why, because I can't tell you." She laid a gentle hand on his forearm. "Dad, you know we owe the ranch to his business sense."

"I know," he muttered. "But damn it, Pepi, I can't have one set of rules for the men and another for him."

"He probably won't ever do it again," she said reassuringly. "Come on, you haven't actually caught him in the act, you know."

He grimaced. "I don't guess I have. But, if I ever do . . . !" he added hotly.

"I know. You'll throw him off the roof." She grinned. "Drink your coffee. At least it isn't burned." She finished hers. "I, uh, have to go into El Paso this afternoon to pick up a package I ordered."

He scowled. "What package?"

"For your birthday," she improvised. That wasn't improbable; his birthday was only two weeks away.

"What is it?" he asked.

"I'll never tell."

He let the subject drop after that, and went back out to work. Pepi washed up and then went to dress for her appointment. Jeans and a T-shirt weren't exactly the best outfit to wear to her own doom, she thought blackly.

She put on her full denim skirt with a blue print blouse and pinned her hair up on her head. She looked much more mature, she decided, although nothing could be done about the freckles on her nose. Not even makeup camouflaged them very well. She did the best she could, adding only a touch of makeup to her face and groaning over her voluptuous figure. If only she could lose enough weight to look like Edie . . .

With a moan, she slipped her hose-clad feet into taupe high heels, transferred the contents of her handbag into the pocketbook that matched the heels, and went downstairs.

As luck would have it, she ran right into C.C. on the front porch. He looked hung over and dusty. His batwing chaps were heavily stained, like the jeans under them and his chambray shirt. His hat had once been black, but now it was dusty gray. He glared down at her with black eyes.

"Brandon's out at the holding corral," he remarked in an oddly hostile tone. "I assume he's the reason for the fine feathers?"

"I'm going into El Paso to do some shopping," she replied. "How's your head?" Better to sound natural, she decided, and she even smiled.

"It was bad enough before I buried it in dust and bleating calves," he muttered. "Come in here a minute. I have to talk to you."

She knew her heart had stopped beating. With a sense of awe, she felt the warmth of his lean, strong hand around her upper arm as he guided her back into the house and shut the door. He let go of her almost reluctantly.

"Look, Pepi, this has got to stop," he said.

"W-what has?" she faltered.

"You chasing me down on my yearly binges," he said irritably. He took off his hat and ran a grimy hand through his sweaty jet hair. "I've been thinking all day about what could have happened to you in Juárez last night. That part of town is a rough place in broad daylight, never mind at night. I told you before, I don't need a nursemaid. I don't want you ever pulling such a stupid stunt again."

"There's a simple solution. Stop drinking," she said.

He searched her uplifted face quietly, scowling. "Yes, I think I might have to. If my memory's as faulty as it was last night . . ."

She had to exert every ounce of will she had not to give anything away. "Your secrets are safe with me, C.C.," she said in a stage whisper, and grinned.

He relaxed a little. "Okay, squirt. Go do your shopping." His dark eyes slid over her body in a way they never had before, and she felt her knees going weak.

"Something wrong?" she asked huskily.

His eyes caught hers. "You kick around in jeans so much that I forget occasionally that you've even got legs." His gaze dropped to them and he smiled in a sensual kind of way. "Very nice legs, at that."

She flushed. "My legs are none of your business, C.C.," she informed him.

He didn't like that. His sharp glance told her so. "Why? Do they belong to the carrot-topped vet already? He acts more like a lover than a friend, despite your constant denials." His expression seemed to harden before her eyes. "You're twenty-two, as you keep telling me. And this is a permissive age, isn't it? No man can expect virginity in a wife anymore."

The mention of the word "wife" made her face pale. But she couldn't let him see how shaken she was. "That's right," she said. "It is a permissive age. I can sleep with a man if I like."

He looked briefly murderous. "Does your father know about that attitude?"

"What my father doesn't know won't bother him," she said uneasily. "I have to go, C.C."

His eyes mirrored his contempt. "My God, I thought you were old-fashioned, in that respect at least."

That hurt. She lowered her gaze to his shirt. "As you keep telling me, my private life is no concern of yours," she said in a tight voice. "You and Edie probably don't play bingo on your dates, either, and I don't make nasty remarks about your morals."

"I'm a man," he said shortly.

She lifted her eyes defiantly. "So what? Do you think being a man gives you some divine right to sleep with anybody you like? If men expect chaste women, then women have the right to expect chaste men!"

His thick eyebrows lifted toward the ceiling. "My God, where would you find one?"

"That's my point exactly. Sling mud and it sticks to your fingers. Now I'm going."

"If you aren't meeting the handsome vet, who are you meeting, dressed like that?" he asked curtly.

"It's just a skirt and blouse!"

"Not the way you fill them out, little one," he said quietly. His eyes made emphatic statements about that before he lifted them back up to capture hers.

"I'm overweight," she got out.

"Really?" He pulled out a cigarette and lit it, but his eyes had hers in a stranglehold and he wouldn't let her avert her gaze.

Her heart raged in her chest, beating painfully hard and fast. Her lips parted on a shaky breath and she realized that her hands were clutching her purse so hard that her nails were leaving marks in the soft leather.

He moved closer, just close enough to threaten her with the warm strength of his body. He was so much taller that she had to look up to see his eyes, but she couldn't manage to tear her gaze away.

The back of his forefinger touched her cheek in a slow, devastating caress. "I thought you were a total innocent, little Pepi," he said, his voice at least an octave deeper. "If that's not the case, you could find yourself in over your head very quickly."

Her lips parted. She was drowning in him, so intoxicated that she didn't even mind the smell of calf and burned hide that clung to him. Her eyes fell to his hard mouth, to its thin chiseled lines, and she wanted it with a primitive hunger. It occurred to her that she could entice him into her bed, that she could sleep with him. They were legally married, even if he didn't know it. She could seduce him. The delicious thought made her breath catch.

Then came the not-so-delicious thought of what would happen afterward. With the experience she was pretty sure he had, he might know that she was virginal, by her reactions if nothing else. Besides that, it might hurt, which would be a dead giveaway. And he didn't know they were married. All sorts of complications could arise. No, she thought miserably, she couldn't even have that consolation. Not even one night to hold in her memory. She had to keep him at arm's length until she could decide how to tell him the truth and what to do about it.

She backed away a little, forcing a smile. "I really have to go," she said huskily. "See you later."

He muttered something under his breath and opened the door for her, his dark eyes accusing as they watched her go. She was getting under his skin. It made him angry that her body enticed him, that he was hungry for her. It made him angrier that she was apparently experienced. He didn't want other hands touching her, especially the vet's. She'd been his caretaker for so long now that he'd come to look upon her with the same passion a wine maker felt for his best vintage. But he'd thought she was virginal, and she'd as good as told him she wasn't. That realization changed everything. He'd placed her carefully off limits for years, but if she wasn't innocent, then he didn't have to worry about his conscience. Odd, though, he thought as he watched her go, she could still blush prettily enough when he looked at her body.

Maybe she wasn't very experienced, despite the red-headed veterinarian's attentions. C.C.'s black eyes narrowed. Brandon didn't have his experience, so that gave him an edge. Yes, it did. He lifted the cigarette to his mouth and smiled faintly as he watched Pepi climb into her father's old Lincoln and drive away.

Blissfully unaware of C.C.'s plotting, Pepi managed to get the car out of the driveway without hitting anything. Her hands on the steering wheel were still shaking from her unexpected confrontation. That was the first time that C.C. had ever made anything resembling a pass at her. Perhaps she should have been less emphatic about her experience—of which she didn't have any. But she'd felt threatened by the way C.C. had looked at her, and her mind had shut down. For one long second she agonized over the thought that he might take her off the endangered species list and start pursuing her himself. But, no, he had Edie to satisfy those needs. He wouldn't want an innocent like herself. And then she remembered that she'd told him she was no innocent. What would she do if he made a heavy pass at her? She loved him to distraction, but she didn't dare let things go that far. If the worst came to pass and they were really married, she could get an annulment without much difficulty. But if she admitted him to her bed, it would mean getting a divorce, and that would take much longer. She couldn't afford to give in to temptation, no matter how appealing it was....

The attorney's office was located adjacent to a new shopping center that had just opened on the outskirts of town. She pulled into a parking spot in front of the adobe facade of the office building and took a deep breath. This wasn't going to be very pleasant, she was afraid.

She went in and produced the document. The attorney took his time looking it over. He was bilingual, so the wording that had sent Pepi crazy trying to decipher with the help of a Spanish-English dictionary made perfect sense to him.

"It's legal, I assure you," he mused, handing it back. "Congratulations," he added with a smile.

"He doesn't know we're married." She groaned. She told him the particulars. "Doesn't that mean anything, that he was intoxicated?"

"If he was sober enough to agree to be married, to initiate the ceremony and to sign his name to a legal certificate of marriage," he said, "I'm afraid it is binding."

"Then I'll just have to get an annulment," she said heavily.

"No problem," he said, smiling again. "Just have him come in and sign—"

"He has to know about it!" she exclaimed, horrified.

"I'm afraid so," he said. "Even if he did apparently get married without realizing it, there's just no way the marriage can be dissolved without his consent."

Pepi buried her face in her hands. "I can't tell him. I just can't!"

"You really have to," he said. "There are all kinds of legal complications that this could create. If he's a reasonable man, surely he'll understand."

"Oh, no, he won't," she said on a miserable sigh. "But you're right. I do have to tell him. And I will," she added, rising to shake his hand. She didn't say when.

Pepi mentally flayed herself for not telling C.C. the truth when he'd demanded it. She'd only wanted to spare him embarrassment, and she hadn't thought any damage would be done. Besides that, the thought of being his wife, just for a little while, was so sweet a temptation that she hadn't been able to resist. Now she was stuck with the reality of her irresponsibility, and she didn't know what she was going to do.

For a start, she avoided C.C. With roundup in full swing, and the men working from dawn until long after dark, that wasn't too hard. She spent her own free time with Brandon, wishing secretly that she could feel for him what she felt for C.C. Brandon was so much fun, and they were compatible. It was just that there was no spark of awareness between them.

"I wish you wouldn't spend so much time with Hale," her father said at supper one night near the end of the massive roundup, during one of his rare evenings at home.

"There, there, you're just jealous because he's getting all your apple pies while you're out working," she teased.

He sighed. "No, it's not that at all. I want to see you in a happy marriage, girl. The kind your mother and I had. Hale's a fine young man, but he's too biddable. You'd be leading him around by the nose by the end of your first year together. You're feisty, like your mother. You need a man who can stand up to you, a man you can't dominate."

Only one man came immediately to mind and she flushed, averting her eyes. "The one you're thinking of is already spoken for," she said tersely.

His eyes, so much like her own, searched her face. "Pepi, you're old enough now to understand why men see women like Edie. He's a man. He has . . . a man's needs."

She picked up her fork and looked at it, trying not to feel any more uncomfortable than she already did. "Edie is his business, as he once told me. We have no right to interfere in his private life."

"She's an odd choice for a ranch foreman, isn't she?" he mused, still watching her like a hawk. "A city sophisticate, a divorcée, a woman used to wealth and position. Don't you find it unexpected that she likes C.C.?"

"Not really. He's quite sophisticated himself," she reminded him. "He seems to fit in anywhere. Even at business conferences," she added, recalling a conference the three of them had attended two years ago. She and her father had both been surprised at the sight of C.C. in a dinner jacket talking stocks and bonds and investments with a rancher over cocktails. It had been an eye-opening experience for Pepi.

"Yes, I remember," her father agreed. "A mysterious man, C.C. He came out of nowhere, literally. I've never been able to find out anything about his background. But from time to time, things slip out. He's not a man unused to wealth and position, and at times he makes me feel like a rank beginner in business. He can manipulate stocks with the best of them. It was his expertise that helped me put the ranch into the black. Not to mention those new techniques in

cattle management that he bulldozed me into trying.
Embryo transplants, artificial insemination, hormone implants...although he and I mutually decided to stop the hormone implants. There's been a lot
of negative talk about it among consumers."

"Negative talk never stopped C.C.," she said,
chuckling.

"True enough, but he thinks like I do about it. If
implants cut back beef consumption because people
are afraid of the hormones, that cuts our profits."

"I give up," she said, holding up both hands. "Put
away your shooting irons."

"Sorry," he murmured, and smiled back.

"Actually I agree with you," she confessed. "I just
like to hear you hold forth. I'm going dancing with
Brandon on Friday night. Okay?"

He looked reluctant, but he didn't argue. "Okay, as
long as you remember that my birthday's Saturday
night and you're going out with me."

"Yes, sir. As if I could forget. Thirty-nine, isn't
it...?"

"Shut up and carve that apple pie," he said, gesturing toward it.

"Whatever you say."

She tried not to think about C.C. for the rest of the
week, but it was impossible not to catch an occasional glimpse of him in the saddle, going from one
corral to the next. He let the herd representatives ride
in the Jeep—representatives from other ranches in the
area checking brands to make sure that none of their
cattle had crossed into Mathews territory. It was a
common courtesy locally, because of the vast territory the ranches in south Texas covered. Her father

ran over two thousand head of cattle, and when they threw calves, it took some effort to get them all branded, tattooed, ear-tagged and vaccinated each spring and fall. It was a dirty, hot, thankless chore that caused occasional would-be cowboys to quit and go back to working in textile plants and furniture shops. Cowboying, while romantic and glamorous to the unknowing, was low paying, backbreaking and prematurely aging as a profession. It meant living with the smell of cow chips, burning hide, leather and dirt— long hours in the saddle, long hours of fixing machinery and water pumps and vehicles and doctoring sick cattle. There was a television in the bunkhouse, but hardly ever any time to watch it except late on summer evenings. Ranch work was year-round with few lazy periods, because there was always something that needed doing.

The advantages of the job were freedom, freedom, and freedom. A man lived close to the earth. He had time to watch the skies and feel the urgent rhythm of life all around him. He lived as man perhaps was meant to live, without technology strangling his mind, without the smells and pressures of civilization to cripple his spirit. He was one with nature, with life itself. He didn't answer to an alarm clock or some corporation's image of what a businessman should be. He might not make a lot of money, he might risk life and limb daily, but he was as free as a modern man could get. If he did his job well and carefully, he had job security for all his life.

Pepi thought about that, and decided that it might not be such a bad thing after all, being a cowboy. But the title and job description, while it might fit C.C., sat oddly on his broad shoulders. He was much too sophisticated to look at home in dirty denims. It was easier now to picture him in a dinner jacket. All the same, he did look fantastic in the saddle, riding a horse as easily as if he'd been born on one. He was long and lean and graceful, even in a full gallop, and she'd seen him break a horse to saddle more than once. It was a treat to watch. He never hurt the horse's spirit in the process, but once he was on its back, there was never any doubt about who the master was. He stuck like glue, his hard face taut with strain, his eyes glittering, his thin lips smiling savagely with the effort as he rode the animal to submission.

The picture stuck in Pepi's mind, and brought with it disturbing sensations of another kind of conquest. She was no prude, and despite her innocence, she knew what men and woman did together in bed. But the sensation, the actual feelings they shared were alien to her. She wondered if C.C. would be like that in bed, if he'd have that same glittery look in his eyes, that same savage smile on his thin lips as he brought a woman to ecstasy under the driving force of his hard, sweat-glistened body...

She went scarlet. Fortunately there was nobody nearby to see her. She darted into the house and up the staircase to get dressed for her dinner date with Brandon.

They went to a restaurant in downtown El Paso, one famous in the area for the size of its steaks and for its view of the city at night from its fourteenth-floor location in a well-known hotel.

"I do love the view from up here," Pepi told Brandon, smiling at him as they were shown to a seat by the huge windows overlooking the Franklin Mountains. The Franklins, in fact, were responsible for the city's name, because the pass that separated the Franklins from the Juárez Mountains to the south was called *El Paso del Norte*—the path of the north. Part of the mountain chain was located in the city of El Paso itself. The only major desert city in Texas, El Paso shared much history with Mexico's Juárez, across the border. Pancho Villa lived in El Paso after his exile from his own country, and historically the Texas city, which sat on the Butterfield Overland stage route in the late nineteenth century had been the site of Indian attacks and a replica of old Fort Bliss marked the former home of the cavalry that once fought the Apaches, including the famous Chief Victorio. Modern day Fort Bliss was the home of the largest air defense center of the free world. Not far from the restaurant where Pepi and Brandon were eating was the Acme Saloon, where gunfighter John Wesley Hardin was shot in the back and killed.

On a less grim note, there was an aerial tramway up to Ranger Peak, giving tourists a view of seven thousand square miles of mountain and desert. There were one hundred parks in El Paso, not to mention museums, old missions, and plenty of attractions across the border in Mexico's largest border city, Juárez.

Pepi had lived near El Paso all her life, and she had the love of the desert that comes from living near it. Tourists might see an expanse of open land nestled between mountain ranges with no apparent life. Pepi saw flowering agave and prickly pear cactus, stately organ pipe cactus and creosote bushes, graceful mesquite trees and the wonder of the mountain ranges at sunset. She loved the desert surrounding the city. Of course, she loved her own home more. The land down near Fort Hancock where the ranch was located was just a bit more hospitable than this, and her roots were there.

"The view from up here is pretty great," Brandon agreed, drawing her out of her reveries. "But you suit me better than the desert and the mountains," he added, his gaze approving her simple mauve dress with its crystal pleats and cap sleeves. Her hair, in an elegant bun, drew attention to the exquisite lines of her face and the size of her pale brown eyes. She'd used more makeup than usual and she looked honestly pretty, freckles and all. But it was her figure that held Brandon's attention. When she dressed up, she was dynamite.

"What will you have to drink?" the waitress asked with a smile, diverting both of them.

"Just white wine for me," Pepi replied.

"I'll have the same," her escort added.

The waitress left and Brandon, resplendent in a dark suit, leaned his forearms on the spotless white tablecloth and stared at her warmly. "Why won't you marry me?" he asked. "Does it have something to do with the fact that I hang out with animals?"

She laughed. "I love animals. But I'm not quite ready for marriage yet." Then she remembered that she *was* married, and her heart dropped. She shifted back in her chair, feeling vaguely guilty at being out with Brandon when she was legally another man's wife. Of course, the man she was married to didn't know it. That made her feel a little better, at least.

"You're an old lady of twenty-two," he persisted. "You'll be over the hill before you know it."

"No, I won't. I haven't even decided what I want to do with my life yet." That was true. She'd never gone to college. Somehow, after she'd graduated from high school, there had been too much to demand her time at home. "I like figures," she murmured absently. "I thought I might take an accounting course or something."

"You could come and work for me. I need a bookkeeper," he said instantly.

"Sorry, but so does Dad. Jack Berry, our present bookkeeper, is hopeless. So is Dad. If I decide to take on bookkeeping, you'd better believe that Dad will scoop me up first. He hates having to redo Jack's figuring."

"I guess . . . Well, well, look at that dress!"

It was unusual for Brandon to be so wickedly interested in what any woman wore. Pepi turned her head slightly to follow his gaze and her heart froze in her chest.

Edie was just coming in the door, wearing a red dress that was cut to the waist in back and dipped in a faintly low V in front. Despite its length, it was an advertisement for her blond beauty, and she drew eyes. Just behind her stood a bored-looking C.C. in a dark vested suit, his hard face showing lines of tiredness from the two weeks of work he'd just put in. Pepi could hardly bear to look at him.

He must have felt her stare because his head turned and even across the room she registered the impact of that level look. She averted her eyes and smiled at Brandon.

"You might as well keep your leering looks to yourself," she said more pleasantly than she wanted to. "C.C.'s pretty possessive of her."

"He's giving you a hard glare. Were you supposed to stay home tonight or something?"

"No. He's probably just tired," she emphasized, trying not to remember the last face-to-face confrontation she'd had with her father's foreman. It made her pulse leap and catch fire just to think about the way he'd talked to her, the things he'd said. She loved everything about him, but if his attentiveness to Edie was anything to go by, the feeling was hardly mutual. She carefully avoided glancing at him again, oblivious to his angry scowl and preoccupied manner while he ate his own supper.

# Chapter Four

If Pepi had hoped that C.C. and his girlfriend would leave without saying anything, she was doomed to disappointment. After he and Edie had finished dessert, he went straight to Pepi's table, dragging the unwilling blonde along with him.

"Well, hello," Brandon said, smiling at them. "How does it feel to finally be through with roundup, C.C.? I'm royally sick of it myself, and I've still got two herds to examine tomorrow."

"It's nice to have a little free time," the older man said quietly. His black eyes were carving up Pepi's face. "I haven't laid eyes on you for two weeks," he told her curtly. "I wondered if you've been avoiding me."

Pepi was shocked by the sudden attack, as well as by the venom in his deep voice. She wasn't the only one. Brandon and Edie exchanged questioning glances, too.

"I haven't been avoiding you," Pepi said, but she couldn't quite meet those eyes with the memory of their last confrontation between them. "You've been out with the men all day and most of the night, just like Dad. I've had things of my own to do, keeping up with the cooking and helping Wiley organize supplies for the chuck wagon."

The Bar M was one of the few ranches that still operated a chuck wagon. The ranch was so big that it wasn't practical to have two dozen men trucking back and forth to the bunkhouse kitchen to be fed. Wiley, one of the older hands, cooked and Pepi helped him keep supplies in.

"You usually come out and watch us work," C.C. persisted, his eyes narrowing.

It was a question, and Pepi didn't want to answer it. She tangled her fingers in her napkin, vaguely aware of Edie's frown as she watched the byplay.

"I'm overweight," Pepi told him belligerently, glaring up at him. "All right? I find it hard to get in the saddle these days. Now are you satisfied!"

"You're not overweight," C.C. said shortly.

"She is, a bit," Edie murmured apologetically, taking C.C.'s arm possessively. "We girls are sensitive about those extra pounds, aren't we, Penelope?" she added with a dry laugh. "Especially when it lands around our hips."

What hips? Pepi wanted to ask, because Edie looked more like a bean pole than a woman with her exaggerated thinness. The older woman's comments had hurt, and Pepi wished she knew why she'd ever brought the subject up in the first place. It had been clumsy and stupid; her usual condition when C.C. came close these days.

"I think Pepi's just right," Brandon murmured, smiling reassuringly at her. "She suits me."

"You angel," Pepi said, smiling at him.

"Why isn't your father with you?" C.C. asked suddenly, his face gone hard at the way Pepi was smiling at the redheaded vet.

Pepi started, her big eyes gaping up at him as if she feared for his sanity. "I don't usually take my father on dates, C.C.," she said.

"Tomorrow is his birthday," he reminded her with faint sarcasm, bristling with bad humor. He hated seeing her with Hale, hated having her avoid him. He felt that it was probably the things he'd said to her that had sent her running, but deeper still was resentment that she was more than likely sleeping with that clown next to her. The thought of Pepi in another man's bed drove him out of his mind. He'd been short-tempered and unapproachable almost the whole time he was working roundup because of the casual way she'd denied being innocent. God knew how many dreams he'd had about relieving her of that condition, and in the most tender way. Now his illusions were shattered, and he wanted to make her as miserable as she'd made him.

"I know tomorrow is his birthday." Pepi faltered. "Brandon and I are taking him to the *Diez Y Seis de Septiembre* parade in the morning. Aren't we, Brandon?" she added, almost frantic. They weren't taking her father anywhere, but she couldn't bear to tell C.C. that all she'd planned was a birthday cake and a nice supper. Not when he was looking at her as if she were public enemy number one and the most ungrateful daughter on earth.

"That's right," Brandon agreed immediately.

Hale, again, C.C. thought furiously. He lifted his chin and looked down his straight nose at her. He spared Brandon a cold, barely civil glance. "I suppose he'll be grateful that you bothered about his birthday."

"What in the world's come over you?" Pepi asked defensively. Was he trying to start a fight, for heaven's sake? She stiffened in her chair, aware of Edie's surprised scrutiny of her escort.

"He's had a hard couple of weeks, that's what," Brandon said with a forced smile, trying to relieve the tension. "I ought to know. I've been out there most days."

"Roundup makes everybody bad-tempered," Pepi agreed. She looked up at Edie. "How are you? I love your dress."

"This old rag?" Edie chuckled. "Thanks. I thought it might cheer up my friend here, but it hasn't seemed to do much for him."

"Oh, hasn't it?" C.C. murmured, diverted at last. He glanced briefly at Pepi before he slid a possessive arm around Edie's shoulders and pulled her close, his eyes warm, his voice deep and sensuous. "Come along, and I'll see if I can't convince you that it has."

"Now there's an offer I won't refuse," Edie murmured huskily. "Good night, Penelope, Brandon."

They murmured their farewells and Pepi refused to watch them walk away. He was her husband. She wanted to stand up and shout it, to drag Edie away from him. They were going off somewhere to be alone, and she knew what would happen; she could see it in her mind. She ground her teeth together.

"Poor thing," Brandon said then, his blue eyes full of concern and sudden understanding. "So that's how it is."

"I've been looking out for him for a long time," Pepi said defensively. "I'm overly protective. I have to stop it. He's not my chick, and I'm not his mother hen. Well, maybe once a year, but only then."

Brandon wasn't buying it. He covered her hand on the table with his own. "If you ever need a shoulder to cry on, you can use mine," he said gently. "And if you ever get over him..."

"Thanks," she said, forcing a smile.

"I guess you know that I can't take you and your father to the parade in the morning?" he added.

She nodded, smiling. "Sorry. I don't even know why I said it. He made me mad. I was going to bake my father a cake, that's all."

"I wouldn't mind helping him eat it, but I'm going to be out all day tomorrow with old man Reynolds's herd," he said ruefully. "I won't be home until after midnight, more than likely."

"I'll save you a piece of cake. Thanks for pulling my irons out of the fire."

"You're welcome." He frowned. "It's not like C.C. to start fights with you in public. Odd that he'd take you to task over your dad."

She couldn't tell him that C.C. had been spoiling for a fight ever since she'd gone overboard and lied about her maidenly condition. Anyway, it didn't matter. C.C.'s opinion didn't bother her. Not one bit!

"Maybe he's just frustrated because he's been away from Edie for two weeks," she said miserably and felt her heart breaking at the thought of how much lost time he could make up for tonight with his blond attachment. . . .

She felt sick. "It's ever so complicated, Brandon," she sighed. "I've managed to get us into a terrible mess, and, no, I can't talk about it. Can we go, please? I've got a headache."

He took her home and she managed to get away without a good-night kiss. C.C.'s appearance had ruined the evening for her. She'd hoped to keep him out of her mind for a little while, but fate seemed to have other ideas.

She hardly slept. She got up with a dull headache and it got worse when C.C. came in smiling and looking like a hungry cat with canary feathers sticking out both sides of his mouth. She didn't need a scorecard to know why he was so smug and content. He'd probably had a hell of a sweet night with Edie, but while she'd always suspected what his relationship with the blonde actually was, her feelings overwhelmed her. She glared at C.C. with eyes that almost hated him, her freckles standing out in a pale, haunted face.

"What do you want?" she demanded testily.

His eyebrows arched. "Coffee, for now. And a word with your father before you and the happy vet take him off to town."

She'd told a bald-faced lie the night before, and now she was standing in the middle of it with nothing to say. Her face slowly flamed scarlet.

His black eyes narrowed. He pushed back the brim of his Stetson and leaned against the kitchen counter, his blue striped Western shirt complementing the darkness of his face and hair and eyes, his powerful leg muscles rippling under tight denims as he shifted his position.

"Are you taking him to the parade?" he asked, his tone less belligerent than it had been the night before.

She shook her head, wiping flour off her hands and dabbing at a streak of it on the denim skirt that she was wearing with a yellow tank top.

"Why did you say you were?" he added.

She glanced at him angrily. "Because you made me sound like a female Jack the Ripper last night, as if I didn't even care about my own father."

His eyes slid down her body and back up again, a visual touch that made her nerves sit up and scream. No man had ever looked at her like that, so sensually that she felt as if he'd stroked her bare breasts. She caught her breath.

He trapped her eyes with his, reading her response in them. So she wasn't immune to him. She might be experienced, but she was vulnerable just the same. A faint smile touched his hard mouth.

"I know you care about your father," he said. "I just don't like the amount of time you spend with Hale."

"Brandon is—"

"A clown," he finished for her, his smile fading. "Too irresponsible and flighty for a woman with your depth. He's probably never satisfied you once."

What he meant was evident in his tone, and she almost dropped the bag of flour in her haste to put it away. She kept her back to him while she made biscuits, hoping he'd go away.

"He makes me laugh," she said through her teeth.

He came up behind her, his body so close that she could feel the heat and strength of it at her back, smell the faint cologne he wore. She tensed all over, waiting for him to touch her, waiting for his lean hands to bite into her waist and jerk her back into his body, for those same hands to smooth up her rib cage to her full, throbbing breasts and cup them. . . .

"What are you doing?" he asked.

Her eyes blinked. He wasn't touching her. She felt his breath on her nape, but he was just looking over her shoulder, that was all. But she was on fire to kiss his hard mouth, to touch him, to hold him against her. She had to clench her teeth to still the feverish excitement he created with his proximity. Perhaps he didn't realize how vulnerable she was, and she wanted to keep it that way.

"I'm making biscuits." Heavens, was that husky whisper really her voice?

"And ham? I like country ham."

"Yes, I know. I'm going to fry it while the biscuits cook. There's coffee on the stove if you want some."

"I noticed."

But he didn't move. She started pinching off biscuits and laying them neatly into the round baking pan in front of her, but her hands were trembling. He was tormenting her. She wanted to scream.

She turned her head helplessly and looked up into his eyes, and all at once she knew. That flicker of mocking amusement in his face was enough to convince her that he was all too aware of the effect he had on her.

"Do I bother you, Pepi?" he drawled, deliberately letting his gaze drop to her full, parted lips. "Surely I shouldn't if Hale is enough for you."

Her breath was ragged. She forced her head back down so that she could concentrate on her biscuits. "Is Edie enough for you?" she countered outrageously.

"When I'm in the mood, anything with breasts is enough for me," he said curtly, angered by her refusal to admit her interest in him.

"C.C.!" she burst out, whirling.

His hands slid past her wide hips to rest on either side of her on the table, effectively trapping her. His gaze was relentlessly probing. "You don't want me to know that you're attracted to me. Why?"

"This isn't fair," she whispered. "I've looked out for you for years, I've done my best to make you comfortable, to help you when I could. Is this any way to pay me back for being your friend?"

He stared at her unblinkingly. "I told you, I don't need a nursemaid. But you've been avoiding me and I don't like it. I want to know why."

"And this is how you plan to find out?" she asked, her voice wobbling a little, because his nearness was devastating to her senses.

"It's the quickest way," he replied. "You've been backing away ever since that day in the hall." His eyes narrowed to glittering slits. "In fact, you've been backing away since that night in Juárez. What did I do to you, Pepi? Did I try to make love to you?"

"No!" she burst out.

"Then what happened?" he asked.

She couldn't tell him. She should, but she couldn't. She lowered her eyes to his broad chest. "You said I could probably throw you over my shoulder and carry you out of the bar," she said dully, repeating the blistering insult he'd thrown at her. "That I was nothing but a tomboy..."

He didn't remember. But he could see the hurt on her face, and that disturbed him. "I was drinking," he said gently. "You know I didn't mean anything I said."

She laughed painfully. "No? I thought people always told the truth when they drank, because they were uninhibited."

He drew in a slow, deep breath. "What else did I say?"

"That was more than enough. I closed my ears to the rest of it."

"And that's why you've been avoiding me?" he persisted, as if it mattered. In fact, it did. He'd been smarting ever since, hurt by her avoidance as he'd rarely been hurt by anything.

She hesitated. Then she nodded.

He bent his head and laid his cheek against hers, nuzzling it gently. The silence in the kitchen grew hot with restrained excitement. She could almost hear her own heartbeat... or was it his? She all but stopped breathing. He smelled of cologne and tobacco, and his cheek was rough and warm where it lay against hers. He didn't try to kiss her, or even pull her against him. But his face drew slowly against her own, and she felt his thick eyelashes against her cheek, her chin, her soft throat, felt the heat of his tobacco-scented breath on her breasts as his forehead rested on her collarbone and she felt the bridge of his nose on the bare swell of her breast where it slowly pushed the fabric out of the way....

"Pepi, where the hell is the newspaper?"

C.C. lifted his head as her father's voice exploded from the hall. He stared down at her shocked face with narrowed eyes in a face like honed steel. He edged away from the table, his lean hands at his sides, and his gaze dropped to the drooping neckline of the tank top, which her cold fingers fumbled to adjust.

She met C.C.'s gaze for one long, shattering instant and then she turned abruptly back to her biscuits with trembling hands and a heartbeat that shook her.

"There you are. Morning, C.C," her father said with a chuckle. "I found the paper," he added, waving it as he went to the table and sat down. "Pepi had already brought it in."

"Happy Birthday," Pepi said with a forced smile. "I'm making breakfast."

"So I noticed. Do I get a cake?"

"Coconut, your favorite, and all your favorite foods for supper," she added.

"C.C., you can come over and help me eat it," he told the younger man.

"I'm afraid not," C.C. replied, glancing at Pepi's rigid spine. "I'm taking Edie to the parade, and then down to Juárez to spend the day shopping."

"Well, you'll enjoy that, I'm sure," Ben said slowly, aware of odd undercurrents in the kitchen.

"Come with us. You, too, Pepi," he added carelessly. "We'll celebrate your birthday in Mexico," he told Ben.

"Great idea! I haven't taken a day off since I don't know when. Pepi will enjoy it, too. We'll do it, then tonight you and Edie can come home with us and have supper, can't they, Pepi?"

She was going to die. She knew she was going to die. Thank God nobody could see her face. "Of course they can," she said through her teeth. "We'll have a lovely time." What else could she say, she wondered. After all, it was Ben's birthday. He was entitled to spend it the way he pleased. But she was still going up in flames at the way C.C. had touched her, and the thought of watching him with Edie all day made her want to run screaming into the yard.

"Just the four of us," C.C. added as he sat down with a cup of coffee in his hand. "Not Hale."

She swallowed. "Brandon can't come anyway. He's going to be working all day and most of the night."

"I thought you liked Brandon," Ben Mathews remarked, eyeing C.C. curiously.

"I do. I just don't like him hanging around Pepi," C.C. replied honestly. He glanced at her rigid back and away. "She can do better."

Ben chuckled. Now the undercurrents began to make sense. He shot a curious look toward his daughter, not missing the flush on her cheeks and the way she fumbled biscuits into the oven. He wondered for a minute what he'd interrupted by bursting into the kitchen. Then C.C. asked him a question about the culled cattle he was selling off, and the moment was forgotten.

The biscuits went fast. Pepi had to grab to get one at all, and the ham and scrambled eggs went even faster.

"You're inhaling it!" she accused them.

"Can I help it if you're the best cook around?" C.C. asked innocently.

"A good cook beats a fashion plate any day," her father remarked bluntly. "Ought to marry this girl, C.C., before she takes her pots and pans elsewhere."

"Dad!" Pepi exclaimed, shattered. She went white with horror, remembering that marriage license in her bureau drawer.

C.C. frowned. That was an odd reaction for a woman who'd been as responsive as she had a few minutes ago. She was acting pretty oddly lately, and he didn't believe it was only because he'd hurt her feelings in Juárez. No, there had to be something more. Something had happened that night, he was sure of it. But what?

"I don't want to get married, to a good cook or a fashion plate," he murmured absently to Ben, scowling as he turned his attention back to the biscuit he was buttering. He missed the expression on Pepi's face.

"Don't you want kids?" Ben asked curiously.

Pepi could have cried when she saw the way that innocent question affected C.C. Her father didn't know what she did about their foreman's past.

"Have another biscuit," she broke in, shoving the plate in her father's face with a scowl.

He was quick, was Ben. He realized instantly that he'd said something he shouldn't. "Well, where's the honey?" he demanded, camouflaging the brief silence. "You've eaten it all, haven't you? It was my honey!"

"It was your apple pie," she threw back. "You ate every bit of it and didn't even offer me any, so you can forget the honey, it's mine!'' She clutched the jar to her breasts and glared at him across the table.

C.C. was touched by her attempt to protect him, even now. He watched her quietly, thinking how attractive she was, extra pounds and all. Come to think of it, she didn't look overweight. She looked just as a woman should, all soft and rounded and sweet. He liked her freckles and the way her hair caught fire and burned like bronze and honey in the sun. He liked the way she talked, the way she smelled. He liked a lot of things about her. And if it hadn't been for the tormenting memories, for the wounds of the past, he might have considered marrying her. But no, marriage wasn't something he coveted. It was a part of life he'd already experienced. Despite his jealousy of Hale, the other man would probably be better for Pepi than he would.

He never should have touched her. Now he was going to have to undo the damage he'd just done by losing his head before Ben walked in. He'd have to play up to Edie to throw Pepi off the track, to make sure she didn't get any ideas about him. Friendship was all he had to offer, and the sooner he made that clear to her the better. But he was going to have to keep his emotions under control to accomplish that. She went to his head, more so every day. He'd said and done things that he'd never meant to; he'd deliberately made passes at her. He couldn't understand his loss of control, or his sudden fascination with Pepi. Perhaps the long hours and hard work of the past few weeks were telling on him. He frowned and studied his cooling coffee. Maybe what he needed was a vacation. God knew he hadn't taken one in three years. He might go

back to Jacobsville, Texas, where he was born, and
visit his three brothers who were running the family
business in his absence. He might go and try to face
the past, if he could.

"I said, when do you want to leave?" Ben asked
him for the second time.

"About nine-thirty," he said, tossing down the rest
of his coffee. "We don't want to get there too late for
the parade."

"Are you sure you want both of us along?" Pepi
asked hesitantly.

He got up and glared at her. "It's your father's
birthday. Of course I'm sure. Edie and I will enjoy
having company." His eyes narrowed. "After all,
we're alone most of the time. As we will be tonight,
when I take her home. I don't mind sharing her occasionally."

Ben chuckled, but Pepi felt as if she'd been slapped.
Coming so close on the heels of C.C.'s ardor, it was
painful to be reminded that he belonged to someone
else. She got up and began to clear the table absently.

C.C. went out the door without looking back. He
hated hurting her. He never should have touched her.

Pepi took her time dressing. She'd thought about
wearing one of her colorful Mexican dresses for the
parade, with their lavish embroidery so delicate
against the bone-white cotton and lace. But if Edie was
going along, she might as well not bother to look
feminine. Beside the blonde, she felt like an oversized
tank.

She put on gray slacks and a bulky khaki top, tying
her hair back in a severe ponytail. She looked terrible, she thought as she saw her reflection, defiantly

leaving off makeup as well. Good. That would show C.C. Tremayne what she thought of him!

It did. He scowled at the sight of her, no less than her father had when she'd come downstairs.

"What the hell happened to you?" C.C. demanded. He'd changed, too, into a very becoming yellow knit designer shirt and tan slacks, a creamy Stetson perched on his black hair.

"What do you mean? I look the way I always do," Pepi defended.

"You didn't look like that last night," he said accusingly.

"Last night, I dressed up for Brandon," she said, staring back at him. "You have Edie to dress up for you," she added meaningfully.

C.C. shifted his eyes uncomfortably. He'd deserved that. "Ready to go, Ben?" he asked the older man, who was dressed casually himself.

"Just let me get my hat." He glanced at his daughter and scowled. "You could have worn that Mexican dress, just for me. I thought it looked just right for a fiesta."

"It doesn't fit," she lied, averting her gaze from C.C. "Besides, I look like a hippo in it...."

"You don't look like a hippo," C.C. said angrily. "My God, will you stop harping on your weight? You're just right. At least you look like a woman. People don't have to stop and guess when you walk by!"

Pepi stared at him with raised eyebrows. He glared at her and turned away just as Ben joined them.

She wondered if she was ever going to understand him. He was acting so completely erratic these days, like a man in love. She sighed. Probably it was just a matter of time before he and Edie tied the knot, despite what he'd said at the breakfast table about not wanting to marry again. She turned, picking up her purse on the way out the door. Anyway, why would he look twice at her with someone as beautiful as Edie on his arm?

Edie was waiting in C.C.'s Ford, looking bored and irritable.

"Finally!" she muttered. "It's hot out here!"

"Sorry. I had to find my hat," Ben mumbled as he put Pepi into the back seat and climbed in beside her.

"I didn't mean to sound like that, Ben," Edie purred, all smiles when C.C. climbed in under the wheel and cranked the car. "You know we're delighted to have you, and Pepi, with us today. Happy Birthday!"

"Thanks," Ben said. He glanced at his daughter's quiet, sad face. She sat stiffly beside him, staring blankly out the window. He was beginning to get the picture about the way she felt. If she wasn't in love with C.C., she was giving a good imitation of a woman who was.

"Well, on to the parade," Edie mused, checking her makeup in her compact mirror. "Want to borrow a lipstick, Pepi? I didn't realize I'd rushed C.C. that much."

"I'm not wearing any," Pepi replied, "but thank you."

Edie glanced at her and then shrugged.

The parade was colorful and there was a crowd. The *Diez Y Seis de Septiembre* celebration was the annual observance of Mexico's independence from Spain—

Mexico's Independence Day. Pepi always enjoyed the music and the floats, and the carnival atmosphere, but today she was preoccupied. She put on a happy face for her father's benefit, hoping he wouldn't see through it. But C.C.'s obvious interest in Edie was killing her. He had a possessive arm around the blonde, and once he bent and kissed her hungrily in full view of Pepi and the rest of El Paso.

Pepi turned away to buy a pinwheel from a passing vendor, glad for the diversion. She handed it to her father, deliberately keeping her eyes away from C.C.

"Happy Birthday, Dad," she said gently and smiled. "I've got your present at home. I thought you could have it with your cake after supper."

"That will be a nice touch." He patted her shoulder. "Sorry about this," he murmured, nodding toward an oblivious C.C. and Edie. "I should have refused."

"No, you shouldn't. It's your birthday." She smiled. "It's for the best, you know. I was wearing my heart out on him. It's just as well that I have to face how he really feels. Dreams are sweet, but you can't build a future on them."

"You've been different lately, Pepi," her father said surprisingly. "Is there anything you want to tell me?"

"A lot." She turned her eyes toward C.C. "But, first I have to tell him something. I should have told him before, but it's not too late. The minute we get home I'll make it all right. Then," she said with a rueful smile, "I'm going to need a shoulder to cry on, I think."

"You aren't in trouble, or anything?" her father asked hesitantly.

She laughed. "Not the kind you're thinking, no." She sighed and watched the parade. "It will be all right," she said, trying to convince herself. "It's just a little thing. Just a minor inconvenience."

She hoped C.C. would see it like that. She had to tell him today, before she lost her nerve. He and Edie were getting involved, anybody could see that. She couldn't, in all good conscience, let him face a bigamy charge because of her own stubborn pride. Tonight, she'd tell him the truth, and hope for the best.

# Chapter Five

They went past the border guards for the day trip into Mexico with no problem at all. The car was stopped, but Pepi knew why. The border guard, a rather squatty young man, had spotted Edie and asked her instead of C.C. what they were going to do in Juárez.

Edie ate up his attention, tossing her blond hair and laughing as she told him they were going shopping. He waved them through with flattering reluctance, still eyeing Edie, while C.C. chuckled softly under his breath. Edie did love to make a conquest. She seemed to enjoy letting C.C. know that she could attract other men quite easily.

Watching the woman, Pepi could have sworn that C.C. knew exactly what she was up to. He seemed so cynical about women, as if he knew them inside out and couldn't care less. She happened to glance at him then, and saw that bitter, half-mocking smile on his sensuous mouth. Before she could look away, he caught her eyes. It was like lightning striking. She had to drag her gaze away.

C.C. drove while Edie leaned over the back seat of his big Ford and talked animatedly to Ben. Pepi shook her head. Even her father wasn't immune to Edie's flirting. He was grinning like a Cheshire cat.

It wasn't a long drive and minutes later, they were in Juárez. And it was only thanks to C.C.'s experience that they found their way around—Juárez was impossible with a map, and worse without one.

The city was deliciously Mexican. They browsed through the endless markets and Edie pleaded until C.C. bought her a ridiculously expensive turquoise necklace. Pepi would have been easier to please. If C.C. had handed her a pebble from the ground, she'd have slept with it under her pillow for the rest of her life. But her tastes were simpler than Edie's—she only wanted C.C.

Down the street was a magnificent cathedral, and near that was a small boutique. Edie exclaimed at the display in the window, and noticed that they honored her charge card.

"I'll only be a few hours," she told C.C., tiptoeing to kiss his lean cheek. "Penelope, want to come along?" she called to Penelope, knowing full well that the younger woman had little interest in fancy clothes and didn't possess a charge card. She'd never gone further afield than the small town she grew up in; Edie knew that, too.

"No, thanks," Pepi said amiably. "I'd rather sightsee."

"Good," her father said. "You can keep me company. C.C. seems to be in another world."

He did, and when Pepi saw where his dark eyes were riveted, she felt her stomach sink. He was mentally retracing his steps the night he got drunk, she was sure of it! His eyes went from the bar down the street to a small chapel—the chapel where he'd drunkenly forced Pepi to stand in front of a priest.

"Well, well, a wedding chapel," Ben murmured. He glanced down at Pepi. "For a man who isn't interested in getting married, he does seem to find it fascinating, doesn't he?"

Pepi had a sick feeling when she saw C.C. jam his lean hands into his pockets and start toward the chapel. She moved forward instinctively to try to divert him. And just as she reached him, oblivious to her father's surprised expression, the two Mexicans who'd helped her bundle up C.C. and get him to the truck that night came sauntering out of the wedding chapel. Perhaps they were related to the priest . . .

Don't say anything, don't recognize him, please, she prayed, both her fingers crossed.

They did recognize him, though, and broke into wide grins. *"Felicitaciones,"* they laughed. *"¿Como quiere usted vida conjugal, eh? ¡Y alla esta su esposa! ¿Hóla, señora, coma 'sta?"*

"What?" Ben burst out, overhearing the conversation.

Pepi buried her face in her hands. "What did they say?" she asked through her fingers.

"They're congratulating him on being married!"

Ben didn't say another word. Rapid-fire Spanish exchanges led to an ominous silence, and seconds later, a furious C.C. was towering over her. He took her by both shoulders and shook her, hard, ignoring Ben's dazed presence.

"What the hell do they mean, congratulations on my marriage?" he demanded, his deep voice cutting and sharp. "You lied to me! We were married here that night, weren't we? Weren't we?"

"All right, yes," she whispered. "I didn't know it was legal," she tried to explain, her eyes big, tearful and anguished. "C.C., I didn't know it was legal!"

"You're married?" Ben burst out.

"Not for long," C.C. said, all but throwing Pepi away from him, as if the touch of her burned his hands. "My God, of all the low, contemptible, underhanded ways to get a husband! Get a man drunk and drag him in front of a minister, and then keep it a secret! You knew I'd never marry a plain, plump little schemer like you if I was sober! You're nothing to look at, and you're more man than woman the way you dress and act. It wouldn't surprise me if you told Hale every move to make when you get him in bed!"

"C.C., please," she pleaded, aware of the attention his loud, angry voice was attracting.

He seemed to realize that they were on display. "I'll get Edie. We're leaving, right now," he told Pepi. "The sooner this farce ends in an annulment, the better."

"You got him drunk and married him?" Ben asked, shaken by the revelation.

"He got drunk and threatened to land us in a Mexican jail if I didn't," she said heavily. "I didn't think it was binding anywhere except in Mexico or I'd never have gone through with it. You know what the criminal justice system is like down here, it's as slow as molasses. We could have spent weeks or months in jail before you could have managed to get us out...."

"I know that! What did he mean about you sleeping with Hale?" he demanded.

"I don't sleep with Brandon. I just let C.C. think it... Well, to throw up a smoke screen, I guess. Dad, it's such a mess! I had the best intentions... and on your birthday!" She burst into tears. "I should have said something, but I was scared. I thought I could get a quiet annulment, but the lawyer said he'd have to know...!"

Ben held her while she cried, awkwardly patting her back until a fire-eyed C.C. joined them with Edie in tow.

"What's the matter with Pepi?" Edie asked.

"Don't ask," Ben said heavily. "We have to go."

"Okay," she shrugged, eyeing the younger woman curiously. "Gosh, Pepi, are you sick?"

"If she is, she damn well deserves to be," C.C. said furiously. "Let's go."

Edie didn't dare question him. Pepi cried silently and Ben sat by helplessly while they got out of Juárez into El Paso and on the road to the ranch.

C.C. was out of sorts the whole way back home. He smoked in silence, letting Edie prattle on until she got disgusted with him and turned up the radio. Lost in thoughts of her own, Penelope just leaned back with her eyes closed, oblivious to the worried look on her father's face.

Instead of going to the ranch, C.C. stopped by Edie's apartment, escorted her to the door and left her there without a word. He didn't say another word all the way home. He didn't speed, or drive recklessly. Penelope wondered at his control. Even when he was furious, and she knew he was right now, he never lost that iron control. She wondered if he ever had.

Back at the ranch, C.C. headed for the stables the minute he parked the car, and Pepi felt sorry for any poor soul who was in there undefended. C.C. in a temper was a force to behold. Presumably he was going to work off some steam before he started on her again. She couldn't even blame him for being so angry. She should have told him in the very beginning. It was her own fault.

"Suppose you tell me the whole story?" her father asked while she made coffee in the kitchen.

She did, all about C.C.'s once-a-year bender and the reason for it, about the way she'd sobered him up—or thought she had—and the way she'd trailed him to Juárez and wound up married to him.

"The bottom line," she said, "is that I think he comes from money, despite the work he does here. He might think I deliberately maneuvered him into marriage for mercenary motives."

"C.C. knows you better than that," Ben scoffed.

"He knows the ranch hasn't been paying and that I don't have a job and my future looks pretty insecure," she said. "It isn't, but it looks that way. And I'm reasonably sure he knows that I'm attracted to him."

"Attracted, as in head over heels in love with?" her father mused.

She shook her head. "No, thank God, he doesn't know that." She jammed her hands into her slacks pockets with a heavy sigh. Her eyes were red-rimmed from crying. "It's not the end of the world. We can get an annulment pretty easily, and I'll even get a job and pay for it. Maybe someday he'll forgive me, but right now I guess he'd like to strangle me and I don't blame him. I just hope he doesn't tell Edie. I wouldn't like her to be hurt by it."

"What about you?" Ben asked angrily. "You're hurt by it, and it's his own damned fault. If he'd stayed sober...!"

"Dad, he loved his wife. I guess he's still grieving for her. Remember how you felt when Mom died?" she added.

He got a faraway look in his eyes. He sighed. "Yes, I can understand that. Your mama was my world. We were childhood sweethearts and we lived together for twenty-two years. I could never find anyone to measure up to her, so I never remarried. Maybe he feels like that."

"Maybe he does," she agreed.

He hugged her warmly and let her go. "Try not to brood. It will all pass over. C.C. will blow off steam and come to terms with it, and you'll get it worked out. I hope," he mused on a chuckle. "With times as hard as they are, I need to keep C.C.'s mind on business, with all due respect to you."

"Ever thought of selling shares in the property?" she asked seriously.

"Yes, I have. Or taking on a partner," he added. He glanced at her. "You wouldn't mind if I did that?"

"Of course not. I don't want to lose it, either," she added gently. "You do whatever you have to."

He sighed, looking around the rustic, spacious kitchen. "Then I think I'll do some discreet advertising. God knows, you can't go much longer without a new wardrobe," he added with a mischievous wink.

"Forget about my wardrobe," she returned. "I don't care what I wear. Not anymore," she added, turning back to see about the coffee.

"There's still Hale," he said, trying to comfort her as best he could. Her pain was tangible.

"Yes, there's still Brandon. He's taking me to a cattleman's association dinner next Wednesday night," she said. "He's a nice man, don't you think?"

He studied her quietly. "Sure he is. But you don't love him. Don't settle for crumbs, honey. Go for the whole meal."

She laughed. "Old reprobate," she accused. "You do have a way with words."

"You have a way with food," he countered. "Will you hurry up and get some supper fixed? I'm starving!"

"Okay." She went back to her pots and pans. From the kitchen window, she could see the bunkhouse. C.C. came out suddenly, dressed in, of all things, a suit. He walked toward the house, big and lean and elegant, and she washed the same dish four times while she waited for the step at the kitchen door. C.C. never went to the front. He was too much like family. But right now he was her worst enemy. The suit bothered her. Was he quitting? She felt her heart stop beating momentarily while she brooded. Did he hate her that much . . . ?

He came in without knocking, letting in a chilly burst of wind. Penelope shuddered.

"It's getting colder out there," Ben said to ease the sudden tension.

"Colder than you know," C.C. said. He had a smoking cigarette in his hand. He lifted it to his thin lips, glaring at Pepi. "I'll be away until early next week. I've got some personal business to see to. Including," he added icily, "getting an annulment underway. I want that marriage license, Penelope."

She wiped her hands on her apron, not looking at him. "I'll get it," she said in a subdued tone, and ran for the staircase.

Her hands trembled as she took the piece of paper out of her bureau drawer and looked at it. C. C. Tremayne. The name on the license said Connal Cade Tremayne. Connal. She'd never called him anything but C.C. Until that night in Juárez, she didn't know what the initials stood for. Now she said the name to herself and grieved for the dreams contained in that simple page of words. If only things had been different, and they'd married because he loved her.

She took one long, last look at the license and carried it back downstairs.

C.C. was waiting for her at the foot of the staircase, alone. His black eyes bit into her face, but she wouldn't meet them. She held out the paper in trembling, cold fingers until he took it and then she jerked her hand back before it touched his. She could imagine that he'd welcome her touch about as much as leprosy right now.

"I'm sorry," she said huskily, staring at her boot-clad feet. "It was just—"

"Just an outsize crush that got out of hand," he returned icily. "Well, it backfired, didn't it? You're underhanded and scheming and probably a golddigger to boot."

Hot tears stung her eyes. She didn't answer him. She edged past him and went into the kitchen, barely able to see the floor as she went back to the pots and pans on the stove.

He clenched the license in his lean hand, hating himself, hating her. He was taking the hide off her, and he knew he was being unreasonable, but she'd tricked him into marriage when he was too drunk to know what he was doing. He'd thought better of her. She had no right to land him in this predicament. He'd taken Edie out, he'd ... And he was married! What if he'd decided to take Edie to a minister? He'd have been committing unwitting adultery and bigamy all at once!

"She's paying for it," Ben said quietly, joining the younger man in the hall. "Don't make it any worse on her. She didn't do it deliberately, regardless of what you think."

"She should have told me," he returned curtly.

"Yes," Ben agreed. "She should have. But she didn't know how. She didn't think it was legal. And to give her credit, she did call an attorney about a quick, quiet annulment. But she found out she'd need your signature for that."

"Did you know?" C.C. demanded.

Ben shook his head. "Not until today. I thought she was in some kind of trouble, but I had no idea what it was."

C.C. stared at the paper in his hand with angry, troubled eyes. Marriage. A wife. He couldn't forget Marsha, he couldn't forget her determination to go down that river with him. She'd always been headstrong, hell-bent in her own way. He should have insisted, especially since she was sick so often and dizzy. He hadn't known she was pregnant. It had been horrible enough to have to identify her body, but to know that she'd been carrying their first child...

He groaned aloud. He'd all but killed her. His wealth had been tied to hers, a joint venture that had paid off in the embryo transplant science. He'd been too sickened by the accident to take up the reins again, leaving his oldest brothers in charge and the younger one to help while he went in search of peace of mind. He'd found it here. He'd enjoyed helping Ben build up a ranch that had been headed for receivership. He'd enjoyed Pepi's bright, undemanding company. And now she'd stabbed him in the back. He had to get away, from her and the memories she'd brought on him again.

"Where are you going?" Ben asked. "Or is that a question I shouldn't ask?"

"What do you mean?"

Ben shrugged. "Pepi said she thought you probably came from money. You blurted a lot out to her that time you were delirious and she nursed you. She thought maybe you'd been punishing yourself for your wife's death and that's why you stayed here." C.C. didn't answer. Ben lifted an eyebrow. "Whatever the reason, you're welcome here if you want to come back. I'm grateful for all you've done for me."

C.C. felt doors closing. Ben was talking as if he wasn't coming back. He glanced toward the kitchen, but Pepi was not visible there. He felt a sudden shock of panic at the thought of not seeing her again. God, what was wrong with him?

He folded the marriage license. "I don't know what I'm going to do. I might go home and see my people. I need to make an appointment with a lawyer about this," he added, fingering the paper. Odd how it seemed more like a treasure than an unwanted legal tie.

"Well, if you decide not to come back, I won't blame you," Ben said wearily. "Not much hope for this place, and we both know it. You've got us in the black, but cattle prices are down and I had to go in the hole for more equipment. I'm getting too old to manage, anyway."

That didn't sound like Ben. C.C. scowled. "My God, you're barely fifty-five!"

"Wait until *you're* fifty-five and say that," Ben chuckled. He held out a hand and C.C. shook it. "Thanks for giving me a shot at keeping the place. But you've got your own life to live." His eyes narrowed. "Maybe it's time you faced your ghosts, son. I had to do that, when I finally came to grips with my drinking problem and the fact that it cost me Pepi's mother. I survived. So will you."

"Marsha was pregnant," C.C. said curtly.

Ben nodded. "That's the worst of it for you, I imagine. You're a young man, C.C. Comparatively young, anyway. You can have other children."

"I don't want children. I don't want a wife," he said angrily, shaking the marriage license. "Least of all one I didn't choose!"

In the kitchen, Pepi heard his words, and tears rolled silently down her cheeks. She remembered what he'd said to her in Juárez, about her being plump and plain. It certainly wiped out all the former compliments he'd given her, about being womanly looking. Now he just thought she was fat. She wished she could crawl in a hole and die.

Out in the hall, Ben could imagine Pepi's pain. He herded C.C. toward the front door instead of the back one, to spare Pepi any more anguish.

"Take a few days," Ben suggested. "You've had two hard weeks of roundup and you haven't had a real vacation in over three years. Some time off is just the thing."

C.C. relaxed a little. "I guess I do need it." He stared at the folded license and involuntarily, his eyes went back down the hall. He'd been harder on Pepi than he probably should have been. He frowned, remembering what he'd said to her. She was little more than a child in some ways. He was beginning to wonder if her so-called experience wasn't just a figment of her imagination. The way she'd reacted to him in the kitchen that morning hadn't been indicative of sophistication. Could she have lied about that, too?

His jaw clenched. He'd never be able to trust her again. If she'd lie to him once, she'd do it twice. God, why had she done this to him?

"Go on," Ben said gently, wary of new explosions. "I can handle things until you get back. Or until I have to look for a new foreman. I won't pressure you."

He frowned, thinking about something Ben had said. "You said she knew I had money."

Ben grimaced. "Yes, I did. And she was sure you'd think the marriage was because of it." He shook his head. "You're doing your damnedest to paint her evil through and through, aren't you, son?"

C.C. blinked. Was he? He moved restlessly. "I'll be in touch. Sorry to leave you in the lurch like this. God knows, it's not your fault."

"It's not Pepi's, either," Ben said enigmatically. "When you want to know the whole story, you might ask her side of it. But cool down first. And have a safe trip."

C.C. started to say something, but he closed his mouth. "Take care of yourself. Happy Birthday," he added, withdrawing a small package from his breast pocket. "I wish it could have been a happier one."

"I'm getting a whole coconut cake," Ben reminded him. He grinned. "Nothing makes me happier than not having to share it."

C.C. chuckled softly. "Okay. See you."

"Yes. I hope so," Ben added under his breath when the younger man had gone. He opened the package. It was a tie tack with a gold maverick head. He grinned. Leave it to C.C. to pick something he really liked.

He went back into the kitchen, hesitant about approaching Pepi. But she was calm enough, dishing up supper.

"Ready to eat?" she asked pleasantly. Only the faint redness of her eyes attested to her earlier misery.

"Sure. You all right?" Ben asked.

She nodded. "Right as rain. There's just one thing. I don't want to talk about it. Ever. Okay?"

He agreed. And she was her old self, on the surface at least. What Ben couldn't see was the agony under her calm expression, the pain in her heart. She was sure she didn't love C.C. now. A man who could be that cruel didn't deserve to be loved, and it was his fault anyway. He was the one who'd forced her to get married. But he made it sound like she'd trapped him! Well, they'd see about that when he came back again. He'd never have to worry about having her heart at his feet ever again!

She served her father his favorite foods for supper and gave him his present—a new pipe and a special lighter for it—with a huge slice of coconut cake. She pretended to be happy, and hoped he wouldn't see the truth. She didn't want to spoil the rest of his birthday.

"There's just one thing you might think about," he said before she went up to bed later. "A man who's caught against his will isn't going to give in without a fight."

"I didn't catch—!" she fumed.

"You aren't listening. I mean a man who's fighting his own feelings, Pepi. I think he's got a case on you, and he doesn't want to face it. He won't take it lying down. He'll give you hell until he accepts it."

She knew better than to let herself dream again. She couldn't take another disappointment in love. "I don't want him anymore," she said bluntly. "I should have married Brandon in the first place. At least he doesn't yell at me and accuse me of things I didn't do. He's fun to be with and even if I don't love him, I like him. I sure as hell don't like C. C. Tremayne!"

"Don't marry one man trying to forget another one," Ben cautioned. "It'll only hurt Brandon and yourself."

She sighed. "I guess so. But I might learn to love him. I'm going to do my best to love him. I hope C. C. Tremayne never comes back!"

"God forbid. If that happens, the ranch will go under," Ben chuckled.

She threw up her hands and climbed the staircase.

But she didn't sleep. She wondered if she ever would again. She felt sick all over, hearing C.C.'s angry words every time she closed her eyes. Eventually she gave up even trying to go to sleep. She got up and cleaned the kitchen until dawn, an exercise that proved adequate to take her mind off C.C.—for two minute stretches, at least.

By the time Ben had finished his breakfast, she was dressed for church. He didn't say a word. He went and put on his suit and they drove to the little Methodist church five miles down the road.

When they got home, with Pepi still brooding and withdrawn, Brandon Hale's car was parked at the front steps. She got out of her father's car and ran to Brandon as fast as her legs would carry her.

Ben, watching, frowned. Trouble was sitting on the horizon, and he wondered where this new complication was going to land them all.

# Chapter Six

Brandon gaped at Pepi when she told him what was going on. They'd just finished a sparse lunch and her father was bringing the coffee tray into the living room where they were sitting.

"You're married?" Brandon groaned.

"Not really," she said quickly. She fingered her skirt while she gave him the details. "So, you see, it's just legal on paper, and only until I can get it annulled."

"C.C. knows, I guess?" Brandon persisted.

"Boy, does he know!" Ben Mathews muttered. He brought in a tray with three cups of black coffee on it. "If any of you want cream, you can go get it," he added as he put it down on the coffee table in the early American decor of the living room.

"Well, what did he say?" the younger man asked.

"You couldn't repeat it in mixed company." Ben sighed.

"He was furious," Pepi volunteered. She stared at her skirt. "I guess I can't blame him. He doesn't know the whole story, and I was too upset to try to make him listen. It doesn't matter anyway," she said miserably. "He said he sure didn't want to be married to somebody like me."

"He was in shock," Ben said stubbornly, staring at her averted face. "A man has to have time to adjust to news like that."

"How long will an annulment take?" Brandon asked.

"I'll find out in the morning. I'm going to see our attorney," Pepi told him. "Maybe it won't take long. Heaven knows, C.C. will do his best to rush it through. I hope I don't have to have the marriage license," she added, frowning. "C.C. took it with him."

"Where'd he go?" Brandon asked.

"¿Quien sabe?" Ben shrugged.

"At least it's not a real marriage," Brandon said gently, patting Pepi's soft hand in her lap. "You scared the life out of me."

"Well, it's definitely not real, so you can relax," Pepi said. "Drink your coffee, Brandon. Then we can go riding. I need to get out of the house."

"Good idea," Ben seconded. "And I can start on the books."

"It's Sunday!" she protested.

"I know that. I'll eat my cake while I work on them. That will make it all right. Besides," he chuckled wickedly, "we went to church first."

She threw up her hands and went to change into jeans and a T-shirt.

Brandon stayed until late, and Pepi was glad of his company. She hardly slept that night, and early the next morning she went to see the family attorney.

Mr. Hardy was sixty and very abrupt, but under his bespectacled, dignified manner, he was the best friend that the Mathews family had ever had.

"Don't have the license, hmm?" he murmured when Pepi had told him the whole story. "No matter. I'll go ahead and draw up the papers for the annulment. Have C.C. come in and sign them Friday. Meanwhile, don't worry about it. Just one of those things. But if I were him, I'd keep away from liquor from now on," he added dryly.

She smiled. "I'll try to make sure he does that," she replied gently.

There, she told herself later, it was done. The wheels were in motion. In no time, she'd be plain old Penelope Mathews again, not Penelope Tremayne. The thought depressed her. She'd wanted so badly to keep the name, to have the marriage real and wanted. But C.C. had made no secret of his feelings on the matter, or of his patent disgust with the idea of Pepi as a wife. She wondered if she was ever going to be able to forget the wounding things he'd said to her.

On an impulse, she stopped by the local department of labor office to see what kinds of jobs were going for women with minimum typing skills. Fate was kind. There was a receptionist's job open with a local insurance agency. She went over to inquire about it, and was hired. She was to start on the following Monday, a week away—on the condition that their valued receptionist, who'd just had a baby, stuck to her decision not to return. They couldn't refuse her if she wanted her job back, and they promised to call Pepi if she wasn't needed.

Well, if that didn't work out, she'd find something else, she promised herself. There was just no way she could stay on the ranch now that this fiasco had occurred. Every time she saw C.C., it would rip her heart open. And if he made fun of her, or taunted her about the almost-marriage, it would be unbearable. Probably he still hated her. That might make it easier. Ben needed him, so she couldn't demand that he be fired. She'd just have to find a graceful way out of the dilemma for all of them. Despite the hurt, she loved C.C. more than her own life. She could leave the ranch and find a room in El Paso, and a job. That way her father could have his very necessary foreman and she could have peace of mind. Besides, Brandon lived in El Paso. He'd look out for her. She might even marry him. He was kind and he cared about her. Surely that was better than living alone.

By Wednesday afternoon, C.C. still hadn't come back. Wednesday night, Brandon took Pepi to a cattleman's association meeting with him. It was a dinner meeting, and Pepi enjoyed not only the meal but the discussion about range improvement methods that followed it.

She'd worn a new mustard-colored rayon skirt with her knee-high lace-up Apache moccasins and a Western-cut patterned blouse. Her reddish-brown hair was around her shoulders for a change, and she'd put on enough makeup to embellish her face. She looked pretty, and Brandon's interest was echoed by several single men present.

Her drooping spirits got quite a lift. She smiled and talked and laughed, and by the time they left the meeting, she was relaxed and happy.

That mood lasted until they got to the front porch and Brandon bent to kiss her good-night. Before he reached her lips, a coldly unapproachable C.C. sauntered into the light from the darkened corner where he'd been sitting.

"Oh, hello, C.C.," Brandon said hesitantly. He raked a hand through his red hair, glancing worriedly at Pepi's suddenly white face. "I'll call you in the morning, Pepi. Good night!"

He darted off the porch. Pepi watched him go so that she wouldn't have to look at C.C. One glimpse told her that he was wearing a charcoal-gray suit with a pearly Stetson, and that he looked dangerous. Smoke from the cigarette in his lean fingers drifted past her nose as Brandon waved and drove out of the yard.

"Where have you been?" he asked, his deep voice accusing.

"I've been to a cattleman's association meeting, C.C.," she replied, moving unobtrusively away from the threat of his powerful body. She turned and went into the house, leaving C.C. to close the door behind them.

"No word of welcome?" he asked sarcastically.

She didn't look at him. She couldn't bear to see the expression in his eyes. She started toward the staircase, but he reached out to catch her arm.

Her reaction caught him off guard. She jerked her arm away from his lean hand and backed against the staircase, her wide, dark eyes accusing and frightened.

His thin lips parted on a sharp breath. "My God, you're not afraid of me?" he asked, scowling.

"I'm tired," she said, averting her face. "I just want to go to bed. Mr. Hardy says you can come in and sign the annulment papers Friday," she added. "I started proceedings and I'll pay for them. You won't have to be out a penny. Is Dad in his study?"

He frowned as he lifted the cigarette to his lips. "He's over at the bunkhouse, talking to Jed. I don't want you seeing Hale while you're legally married to me."

She hesitated, but it wasn't really much to ask. And she was too tired to argue with him. "All right, C.C.," she replied dully. "Maybe the annulment won't take too long."

His eyes narrowed to angry slits. "In a hurry to put Hale's ring on your finger?" he asked.

"I don't want to fight with you," she said quietly, meeting his gaze with an effort. It disturbed her, the way he was looking at her. It made her heart race, her knees tremble under her. "I've got a job," she told him. "I start Monday. Then I'll look for a room or something in El Paso. You won't... You won't have to worry about running into me all the time around here."

"Pepi!" he said huskily.

She whirled. "Good night, C.C.!"

She ran all the way upstairs and into her room, closing the door with hands that trembled, with tears running down her pale cheeks. So he was back. Back, and spoiling for trouble. That didn't bode well for the future.

She got into her gown, washed her face, and climbed into bed with a long sigh. She was reaching for the bedside light when her door suddenly opened and C.C. came in, closing it behind him.

Pepi froze with her hand out, all too aware of the way the almost transparent green gown she was wearing outlined her body, left the upper curve of her breasts bare. With her hair around her pale shoulders, she looked very soft and feminine, and C.C. was getting an eyeful.

"What do you want?" she asked uneasily.

"To talk," he replied. He pulled up a chair beside the bed and dropped into it. There were new lines in his face, and he looked as tired as she felt. He'd discarded his suit coat and tie and rolled up the sleeves of his exquisite cotton shirt, its neck unbuttoned to his collarbone. Dark curly hair peeked out between the loose buttons and Pepi had to force her eyes back up to his face. She didn't like being reminded of his vibrant masculinity. She wasn't his type, and he didn't want her. She had to remember that.

"About the annulment?" she asked hesitantly. She sat up against her pillow, demurely pulling the sheet over her breasts, an action that C.C.'s faintly amused eyes didn't miss.

He watched her hungrily. The days he'd been away, a lot of things had been settled in his mind. He'd brooded about his own situation until he'd given some thought to Pepi's. That was when he'd realized how much he owed her. She'd been the best friend he had, ever since he'd come to the ranch. But he'd repaid her loyalty by hurting her, making her feel unwanted. Now he had to put things right, if he could. Perhaps telling her the truth about his past might be a good first step. If she understood him, she might be able to forgive the things he'd said to her before he left.

"No," he said after a minute. "I don't want to talk about the annulment right now. I want to tell you about me." He leaned back in the chair and crossed one long leg over the other. "I was born in Jacobsville, down near Victoria," he began, watching her while he lit a cigarette and fished for an ashtray on the dresser. He grimaced as he emptied jewelry out of it and put it in his lap. "I have three brothers, two older, one younger than I am. We're in the cattle business, too, except that we deal in purebred cattle—Santa Gertrudis. Our land came from one of the early Spanish land grants, and we've always had money."

She watched him, astonished at the revelation.

"I got married years ago. I was getting older, I was lonely," he shrugged. "I wanted her. She was my age, and a wild woman from the word go. We both liked dangerous sports, like shooting the white water." His fingers clenched on the cigarette, and there was suddenly a faraway, tormented look in his dark eyes. "She went everywhere with me. But that weekend, I wanted to get away. She had this tendency to smother me; had to be with me every minute, night and day. After the first few weeks we were married, it got so I couldn't stand and talk to one of my brothers without having her in my pocket. She was insanely jealous, but I hadn't realized that until it was too late. Well, I signed up for a rafting trip down the Colorado and went without her. But when I got to the river with the rest of the group, she was there waiting. We argued. It didn't do any good. She was hell-bent on going." He took a draw from the cigarette. "The raft capsized on a bad stretch and she went under. We searched for the better part of an hour, but by the time we found her, it was too late." He looked straight at Pepi, his eyes cold. "She was three months pregnant."

"I'm sorry," she said quietly. "That must have been the worst of it, for you."

He was surprised at her perceptiveness, although God knew why he should have been. Pepi always managed to see things that other people missed. "Yes, that was the worst of it," he confessed. "I was never able to find out if she knew about her condition, or if she didn't care. She was a free spirit. She wasn't really suited to marriage. If she'd stayed single, she'd probably still be alive."

"I'm a fatalist," Pepi said, her voice gentle. "I think God chooses when we die, and the circumstances."

"Perhaps you're right. But it's taken me three years to come to grips with it. I inherited her estate, and she was as wealthy as I was. That was one reason I came here, started over again from scratch with your father. I wanted to get away from money and see what I could do by the sweat of my own brow. I inherited most of what I had. It's been fun, making my own way."

"It's been a lifesaving experience for us," Pepi said. "We owe you a lot. And you were a mystery to us, but you always seemed to fit in very well."

"Except for one day a year," he mused sadly. "Every year on the day it happened, I go a little crazy.

I didn't know how much I wanted a child until it was too late."

She searched for the right words to comfort him. "C.C., you're still young enough to marry again and have children," she said hesitantly.

His eyes narrowed. "But I am married, Pepi. To you."

She felt her cheeks stinging with heat. She averted her wounded eyes to the coverlet. "Not for long. Mr. Hardy said an annulment would be no problem at all."

"I'd like to know what happened that night," he said after a minute.

"Not a lot. You were stinking drunk in a bar in Juárez. I went in to get you out, you made a lot of insulting remarks, and then you said since I seemed to be forever nursemaiding you, I might as well marry you. In fact, you threatened to land us in jail if I didn't."

His eyebrows arched. "I did?"

"You did," she muttered. "I wasn't sure what to think. You were pretty loud and you sounded serious to me. Mexican jails are easy to get into and hard to get out of. I had visions of us languishing down there for months while Dad went nuts trying to get us out."

"My God! Why didn't you tell me that?"

"You didn't want to listen," she replied doggedly. "You were too busy telling me what an underhanded little golddigger I was!"

He sighed angrily. "I know plenty about golddiggers," he said defensively. "Until I married, I fielded them like baseballs."

"You never had to field me!" Pepi returned. She glared at him from the depths of her feather pillow. "I looked after you when you needed it and I liked to think we were friends, but that's all it was," she lied, salvaging what she could of her pride. "I never wanted to marry you!"

His dark eyes narrowed as he turned that statement over in his mind and examined it. He didn't believe her. She'd been vulnerable to him before he'd hurt her pride so badly. If any feeling was still there, he might be able to reach it if he was careful, and slow.

"I remember telling you once that I had nothing left of love in me," he said. "It felt like that, for a long time. I got numb, I think, because of the guilt. I wouldn't let myself feel."

She lowered her eyes to his chest. "Yes, I can understand that," she said gently. "But I was never any threat to you, C.C."

"Weren't you?" he mused, smiling faintly. "You were the most caring little thing I'd ever met. You mothered me. Funny, how much I enjoyed that after a while. Apple pie when I was broody, hot stew when I was cold, unexpected things like puff pastries in my saddlebags when I went out to roundup. Oh, you got under my skin, Pepi, right from the beginning. The miracle is that I didn't realize how far."

"You don't have to baby me," she muttered, glaring at him. "What you said when you found out we were married was the truth. It was honest. I always knew you wouldn't want a fat frump like me...."

"Pepi!"

"Well, I am one," she said doggedly, her fingers clenching in the cover. "Ugly and overweight and country to the bone. Dad used to say that you were sophisticated enough for a debutante, and he was right. Edie's just your style."

He leaned back in his chair. "Edie doesn't want a house in the country and two or three kids," he said quietly.

So that was it. He couldn't have Edie, so he might be willing to settle for second-best—for Pepi. She lowered her eyes. She'd wanted him for so long that she was almost ready to take him on any terms, even on the rebound. But she couldn't forget the things he'd said about her, and to her.

"You might be able to change her mind," she said.

He scowled, watching her. "I don't want to change it," he said surprisingly. "Pepi, we're married."

She colored. "That isn't a hurdle. I told you, I've already seen Mr. Hardy. All you have to do is sign the papers on Friday and he'll get the annulment underway."

He felt that statement to his bones. He shifted in the chair, his gaze on her flushed face. "You haven't considered the options. Your father is still just barely operating in the black. I could put the ranch back on its feet for good. You might find a few things that you wanted, too. After all, I'm rich."

"I don't care about your money," she returned, her pale brown eyes accusing. "I like having food in the house and a roof over my head, but I couldn't care less about how much money I've got, and you know it!"

His breath sighed out roughly. "Is it Hale?" he demanded. "Is he why you're in such a rush to get an annulment?"

Her eyes dilated. "*You're* the one who was demanding a speedy end to the marriage!"

"Yes, well, I've had second thoughts." He uncrossed his legs and sprawled, one hand loosely grasping the almost-finished cigarette as he stared at her. "If I'm already married, I won't have to fend off potential brides, will I?" he added.

She sat up straight in bed. "Now, you listen here, C.C., I'm not going to become a human sacrifice to save you from the altar! Marrying you sure wasn't my idea!"

"You could have called my bluff," he reminded her, his dark eyes faintly twinkling. "Why didn't you?"

"I told you! Because I didn't want to spend the rest of my life in a Mexican jail!"

"If I was drunk enough to pass out, I was too drunk to cause much trouble," he continued. "Besides, I didn't have a gun."

She drew up her knees angrily and clasped her arms around them. "You've got all the answers, haven't you?"

"Not quite all," he said. "But I'm getting there." He took his time, stabbing out his cigarette in the ashtray. "You said once that you and Hale were lovers. Are you?" he asked, lifting his eyes back to hers.

She gave him a wary look, hoping he hadn't seen through the lie. If he thought she and Brandon were close, it might keep him at bay until she could decide how to cope with this newest complication. "That's none of your business."

"The hell it's not. You're mine."

Electricity danced through her veins, but she didn't let him see the reaction in her eyes. "No, I am not.

You're only married to me because of an accident. That means Brandon is none of your concern."

He got up with deceptive laziness and put the ashtray back on the side table. "I'm making him my business." He paused at her bedside, narrow eyes assessing, threatening. "You aren't sleeping with him again," he said shortly. "And no more dates, either. From now on, you'll stay at home where you belong."

Her eyes opened wide. "Who do you think you are?" she demanded.

"Your husband," he said, "*Mrs*. Tremayne."

"Don't call me that," she grumbled. "It's not my name."

"Oh, yes, it is. And you can forget that annulment. I won't sign the papers."

"But, you have to!" she said helplessly.

"Really? Why?" he asked, and looked interested.

"Because it's the only way to get rid of me!"

He pursed his lips and let his eyes slide over her. "Do I want to do that? After all, you've been looking out for me for the past three years, through thick and thin. You're a treasure, Pepi. I don't intend giving you up to the redheaded vet. You can tell him I said so."

"I don't want to be married to you," she yelled.

He lifted his eyebrows. "How do you know that? I haven't made love to you yet."

She went scarlet. Her fingers grasped the covers in a death-grip and she stiffened when he took a step closer to the bed, her eyes as wide as saucers in her flushed face.

He shook his head and made a clicking sound with his tongue. "My God, if you keep up this attitude, it's going to be damned hard for us to have children together."

"I won't have children!" she whispered.

"Well, not like that," he murmured, grinning. "You *do* know how women get them?"

"Sure," she said hesitantly. "From the hospital."

"That comes later," he reminded her. He smiled. "Afterward."

That slow, meaningful smile made her nervous. "I don't want to sleep with you," she told him.

"We won't sleep," he promised.

"Will you get out of here!"

Before he could reply, the bedroom door opened suddenly and her father glanced from one of them to the other, scowling. "For God's sake, what's all the yelling about?"

"I've been explaining the facts of life to Pepi." C.C. shrugged. "She thinks babies came from the hospital. Did you tell her that?"

Ben looked flustered. "Well, not exactly... Look here, what are you doing in her bedroom?"

"We're married," C.C. reminded him. He produced an envelope. "The marriage license is in here."

"But you don't want to be married to her," Ben returned. "You said so. You went off to get an annulment."

"I changed my mind. She's a good cook, she's nice looking, and she doesn't have any bad habits. I could do worse."

"I could do better!" Pepi shouted, red-faced. "You get out of here, Connal Tremayne! I'm getting that annulment, and you can go to hell!"

C.C. exchanged an amused glance with Ben. "I suppose you taught her to swear, too?" he asked the older man. "For shame!"

"She taught me," Ben said defensively. "And I don't think she wants to say married to you, C.C."

"Sure she does!" he replied. "It's just going to take a little time to convince her of it. Meanwhile—" he threw an arm across the older man's shoulder "—I want to talk to you about some improvements I have in mind for the house and the ranch."

"Don't you listen!" Pepi raged. "He's trying to buy us!"

"I am not!" C.C. said indignantly. "I'm trying to overcome your objections. Your father wouldn't mind a partner, I'll bet. Especially when it's his own brand-new son-in-law. Right, Dad?" he added, smiling with crocodile intensity at the older man.

"Right, son!" Ben agreed, grinning back. "I hadn't thought about that," he mused to himself. "I'll finally have a son of my own!"

"Are you both forgetting something?" Pepi asked haughtily.

"I don't think so," C.C. replied.

"I'm not staying married to you!" she told him. "I'm getting an annulment."

"Don't worry, Dad," C.C. told Ben encouragingly. "She has to have my cooperation for that, and I'll never agree. Imagine a woman hard-hearted enough to try to get rid of a man even before the honeymoon!"

"Say, that's right, you haven't had a honeymoon," Ben agreed.

"C.C. can go on the honeymoon by himself," Pepi said. "I hear it's nice in Canada this time of year. Don't they have grizzly bears up there . . . ?"

"We don't have time for a honeymoon just now," C.C. replied easily. "We've got too much work to do fixing up the ranch. First, I thought we'd get a contractor over here and let him look at the house. I'm inviting my brothers up from Jacobsville to talk to us about getting one or two Santa Gertrudis seed bulls . . ."

"Stop!" Pepi held up her hand. "I won't agree to this!"

"What do you have to do with it?" C.C. asked innocently. "Your father and I are going to be partners."

"Dad, you can't let him do this," she pleaded with her parent.

Ben lifted his eyebrows. "Why not?" he asked.

"She's only frustrated," C.C. said, leading the older man out the door. "A little loving will put her on the right track in no time."

"You try it and I'll crack your head with a tire iron!" she raged.

C.C. grinned at her from the doorway. "I do like a woman with spirit," he murmured.

"Will you please leave?" she said, admitting defeat. "I want to go to sleep."

"You might as well. Maybe it will improve your mood," he said as he closed the door.

"Improve my mood," she muttered, glaring at the closed door. "First he insults me, then he storms off in a snit demanding an annulment and now he wants to go partners with Dad. I will never understand men as long as I live!''

She put her head under the pillow. But despite her best attempts, it was early morning before she finally got to sleep.

# Chapter Seven

It wasn't at all unusual for C.C. to have breakfast with Pepi and her father, but in recent months he'd kept very much to himself. Even so, Pepi wasn't surprised to find him sitting in the dining room with her father when she came down to breakfast. She was surprised to find food on the table, waiting for her, right down to a fresh pot of coffee.

"Shocked, are we?" C.C. murmured dryly, his dark eyes sliding possessively down her body, clad in jeans and boots and a white blouse with a yellow knit pullover sweater. "Think men are helpless, do we?"

She glanced around, looking to see how many people he was talking to.

"Cute," he chuckled. "Sit down and eat, before it gets cold."

She took the chair across from him, next to her father. Her gaze went restlessly from C.C. in working clothes—denim and chambray—to her father in a suit.

"Are you planning to be buried before the end of the day, or are you going somewhere?" she asked Ben.

"I'm going to the bank to pay off the note on the place," he said hesitantly.

"With what?" she cried.

"We can talk about it later," C.C. interrupted. "Eat your eggs."

"With what?" she persisted, glaring at her father. He looked guilty. Her eyes went to a smug C.C., leaning back like a conqueror with his shirt straining over a muscular chest and broad shoulders while he watched her. "You did it. You gave him the money to pay off the note, didn't you?" she demanded.

"He's my father-in-law," C.C. said easily. "Not to mention my partner. We're having the papers drawn up today. Your father is seeing about it while he's in town."

"You aren't going with him?" she asked warily.

He shrugged. "We've got a new shipment of cattle coming in. Somebody has to be here to sign for them and oversee the unloading."

"New cattle?" She knew her eyes were bulging. "What new cattle?"

"Some heifers to add to our replacement heifers, that's all," C.C. assured her. He grinned. "But we're going to have two purebred Santa Gertrudis bulls. My brothers are coming up tomorrow."

"There are more like you?" she wondered aloud, recalling his vague reference to them the night before.

"Three," he reminded her.

"God help us all. Are they married?"

His dark eyes narrowed. "One of them is. The youngest. The older two are still single, and don't get any ideas. You've already got a husband."

"Only until I can get your signature on a document," she replied sweetly.

"And hell will freeze over, first," he returned.

"Can't we save the arguing for later?" Ben moaned. "I want to enjoy my breakfast."

"He's got a point. Have some salsa."

She gave up. She spooned the brilliant red salsa over her eggs and savored the spicy flavor they gave the perfectly cooked scrambled eggs. The bacon was neatly done, too, and the biscuits were even better than her own.

She frowned at C.C. She knew that he, like most of the men, could whip up a meal when he had to. But this was beyond the scope of most men who weren't professional chefs. "You cooked all this?"

"Did I say that?" C.C. asked innocently.

"Well, no..."

"Consuelo did it," Ben told her. "We thought you might like a late morning, what with all the excitement last night."

"Excitement," she muttered. "First he wants an annulment and now he doesn't want one."

"Let's just say that I came to my senses in time," C.C. said lazily, smiling at her over a forkful of eggs. His gaze went to her full lips and lingered there, before it slid back up to catch and hold hers. "I know a good thing when I see it."

Her heart went crazy. It wasn't fair, to do this to her. "Why do you need me to ward off prospective brides?" she managed in a husky tone.

"Because I'm going to start a small branch of the family business over here," he replied. "Most people in southeastern Texas know the Tremayne properties. Pretty soon they'll know them in El Peso, and I'll be on the endangered species list. That's where you come in. If I have too many money-hungry women after me, all I have to do is produce my sweet little wife to ward them off."

"I'm not sweet and I'm not little." She put down her fork. "I'm plain and fat, you said so."

His jaw clenched. "I said a lot of things I regret," he replied. "I hope you're not going to spend the next twenty years throwing them in my face every time you get hot under the collar."

She stared at him until she had to drop her eyes to her plate in self-defense. That level, unblinking stare of his had backed down grown men in a temper. She shifted under it. "You said you didn't want to get married."

"I didn't. But it's something of a *fait accompli*, now, isn't it?"

"A what?" she frowned.

He lifted an eyebrow. "It's French. It means an accomplished fact. You don't speak French, I gather. I do. I'll teach you. It's a sexy language. So is Spanish."

She cleared her throat and sipped coffee. "I don't have a facility for languages."

"A few words won't hurt you. Especially," he added softly, "the right kind of words."

She knew what he was insinuating. Her gaze went helplessly to his face and slid to his thin, firm mouth. She'd always wondered how it would feel on hers, but in three years he'd never really kissed her, unless she counted a peck on the lips under the mistletoe that time, and that was as impersonal as a smile. She'd dreamed and dreamed about his arms around her, the pleasure of having him kiss her in a fever of passion. Of course, she wasn't the kind of woman who inspired passion in men. Edie was.

Edie. She thought about the other woman and felt uneasy all over again. She had a pretty good idea what C.C. had seen in Edie and she wondered if he planned to continue that relationship. The marriage was by no means a real one. He could claim that Pepi had no right to tell him what he could and couldn't do, and he'd be right. They were only married in name.

She put down her fork, her appetite gone. If only he loved her. If only he'd married her voluntarily, and not because of a drunken rampage.

"What's the matter now?" her father muttered, watching her expression change. "You look like the end of the world."

"I couldn't sleep," she said defensively.

"Dreaming about me." C.C. grinned.

She glared at him. "I was not!"

"That's right, Pepi, fight it. But I'll win," he added quietly, getting to his feet to stare down at her. "And you know it."

She didn't understand his new attitude, or that look in his dark eyes, either. She looked up at him helplessly.

"All at sea, aren't you, little one?" he murmured. "Well, it's going to take some time, but you'll get the idea eventually. See you later, Ben." He tossed down the rest of his coffee, retrieved his Stetson from the counter and slanted it across his eyes. "Why don't you come down to the loading dock and watch us move the cattle in?" he asked Pepi.

It was the first such invitation he'd ever extended to her, almost as if he'd welcome her company. She didn't know how to respond to it, so she hesitated.

"Suit yourself," he said on a heavy sigh. "If you change your mind, you know where I'll be."

He went out the door and Pepi exchanged a puzzled glance with her father.

"What's going on?" she asked him.

"Damned if I know, except that he's sure done a hard about-face," Ben replied. "I can't say I'm sorry, in one respect. This land has been in our family since just after the Civil War. I'd hate like hell to lose it, because of my own financial incompetence."

Pepi knew how much the ranch meant to her father, and she felt a twinge of guilt for putting up a fight when C.C. was the answer to all his problems. But he was the root of all hers.

"How do you really feel about this?" Ben asked quietly.

She fingered her coffee cup. "I think he's just making the most of a bad situation," she said. "Or maybe he feels that getting an annulment would be a reflection on his masculinity." She shrugged. "Maybe it's even what he said, to keep prospective brides off his back when his monied background gets around. But how I feel about it is uneasy. He's too smooth about it for a man who was ranting and raving like a madman when he found out what happened in Juárez."

"He was away for several days," Ben said thoughtfully. "Maybe he came to grips with it then."

She remembered what C.C. had told her about his wife, and she wasn't sure about that. He'd mentioned wanting a family, that Edie didn't. He could just be thinking about how easily Pepi could be cast in the mold he wanted—housewife and mother and cook, somebody in the background of his life, somebody he could walk away from without his emotions being involved if the marriage dissolved for any reason. She knew he didn't love her. He'd made that all too obvious already. He might want her. She wasn't even sure about that, because he only let things show on his face that he wanted people to see. He might be playing a game. He might be getting even.

"You're doing it again," Ben observed. "Brooding," he added when she frowned with curiosity. "Stop brooding. Live one day at a time and see what happens."

She wanted to argue, but there was really no reason to. "Okay," she said easily. "I've got a job," she said.

"A what?"

"A job. Well, I've almost got a job," she amended. "There's one going in El Paso, if the receptionist who just had a baby doesn't come back." She told him about it, puzzled by his worried look. "What's wrong with my having a job?" she demanded.

"You've got enough to do around here," he muttered. "I'll have to give up my apple pies and cakes if you go to work. Who'll take care of me?"

Her eyebrows arched. "But, Dad, I can't stay at home forever!"

"Could if you stayed married to my new son-in-law," he said curtly. "No reason why you shouldn't. He's a great catch. Rich, good-looking, smart..."

"...hardheaded, autocratic, unreasonable..." she amended.

"...and best of all, he likes kids," he concluded firmly. "I like kids. Would have had more than just you if we could have, you know. Nothing in the world I'd enjoy more than a houseful of grandkids."

"Great. When I get free from C.C. and marry Brandon, we'll make sure you have lots. All redheaded," she said with a smug grin.

"I don't want redheaded grandkids!" he raged.

"Too bad," she sighed, finishing her breakfast. "Because I'm not going to spend the rest of *my* life helping C.C. ward off women."

"Hasn't it occurred to you that he might have other reasons for wanting you to stay with him?" her father asked after a minute. "More personal reasons than he's given?"

She searched his face. "You mean because of his wife, and the baby?" she asked.

He nodded. "Hard for him, losing her like that, and her pregnant at the time. I can see why he's haunted. I know all about guilt, sweetheart, I felt it for years because I was drinking the night of the wreck that killed your mother. I learned finally that you can't live in the past. You have to shoulder your mistakes and regrets and go on. He's learning that. Maybe he's ready to start over, too."

"Maybe he is, but it's not enough, Dad," she said wearily. "I can't be just a healing balm in his life, you know? I have to be loved, wanted, needed."

"He needs you, all right, we've all seen that over the years," Ben reminded her.

"Sure. Good old Pepi, keeping him out of trouble, making sure he wears his raincoat, watching over his meals... but that isn't what he needs, Dad. He needs a woman he can love. Edie would be a better choice than I am, at least they've got a relationship of sorts. C.C. and I—well, he's never even kissed me," she muttered with a faint flush.

"You might ask him to, then," Ben said with a twinkle in his eyes. "Just to sample the goods, so to speak."

She went redder and lowered her brown eyes to her plate. "I don't want to kiss him, I don't know where he's been."

"You won't know what you're missing until you try," he said. "After all, you've lived like a saint for the past few years, despite the best efforts of the red-headed vet."

"You didn't tell C.C. that!" she exclaimed.

"He figured it for himself," he said easily. "C.C.'s been around. Even a blind man could tell that you haven't. You blush too much."

"I'll dot my face with rice powder and wear a mask over my eyes from now on, that's for sure!" she grumbled. "Men!"

"Now, now. We only want what's best for you."

"And the fact that he can get the ranch out of debt is like icing on the cake, huh?"

He smiled placatingly. "I won't say no. This land is a legacy. We'll hand it down for years to come now, and the history that goes with it. John Wesley Hardin slept in this very house. A Comanche war party raided the ranch and killed one of the cowboys. The cavalry used to bivouac on the bottoms on its way to various campaigns toward the Pasa del Norte and back. Yes, girl, this land is full of history. I'd like your kids to inherit it."

She reached out and lightly touched his wrinkled hand. "I understand that. But marriage seems to be hard enough when you love someone. When you don't..."

"But you do," Ben replied knowingly. "I've seen the way you watch him, the way you light up when he comes into a room. He doesn't see it because he's not looking. But the fact that he doesn't want an annulment gives you hope, doesn't it?"

"He doesn't want it for the right reasons," she moaned. "Any woman would suit him, don't you see?"

"No, I don't." He tugged his pocket watch out by its gold chain and looked at it. "And I don't have time to make you see it right now, I'm late. Won't be in for lunch, so don't worry about me. C.C. mentioned he might be in for it, though."

"I'll be sure I leave him something on the table," she muttered.

"Now, now. Is that any way to treat the man who's getting your worried old father out of debt?"

She grimaced. "I guess not. All right, I'll try to look suitably grateful. Now if you'll excuse me," she added, getting up to stack the dishes, "I've got some chores to do. And I'm not giving up that job, either," she tossed over her shoulder. "If they hire me, I'm going!"

Ben threw up his hands and went toward the door.

Pepi did the dishes and cleaned the house. All the while she was thinking about C.C.'s impromptu invitation to come out to the loading docks and watch them process the new heifers. He'd probably be through long before lunch, and he hadn't pressed his invitation. But she went, anyway, riding lazily down the unpaved ranch road toward the loading docks; the wooden chutes down which arriving cattle were driven into the ranch's only fenced pasture.

As she rode, her mind was comparing this valley land with the mostly desert country farther to the northwest, toward El Paso. The desert country around El Paso was deceptive. Beautiful, in its stark way, and its barren appearance only disguised a multitude of life, animal and plant. The prickly pear cactus could inflict enough hairy thorns to keep a man busy with tweezers and a flashlight for the better part of an hour, but it put forth some of the most elegant blossoms of any desert plant. The rain kindled more blossoms, so that the desert came alive with them. Even the tough mesquite tree put out its own heavenly bloom. Animal life abounded, and not just rattlesnakes and lizards. There were other stretches where only the creosote bushes grew, spreading like miniature orchards, with no vegetation nearby because of their toxic root secretions, which killed any vegetation that tried to grow up around them. After a rain, their pungent, spicy smell was a treat to the senses. Old pioneers made medicines and glue out of them.

But where the Mathews ranch sat, near the site of old Fort Hancock, southeast of El Paso in Hudspeth County, the Rio Grande was close enough to make the area fertile and there was plenty of grazing land for the cattle. The U.S. Army had situated a number of forts along the Rio Grande in the mid and late 1800s in accordance with the settlement of the southern boundary of Texas against the Mexican border. The United States accepted responsibility for stopping Indian attacks across the border, so a number of forts were located along the river. One of those was Fort Hancock, named for General Winfield Scott Hancock. Pepi had played on the site of it on trips with her parents, the eternal history buffs. They'd known every point of historical interest in the area, which was why she knew about the Salt War, provoked by the salt deposit at the base of Guadalupe Peak, which resulted in some fierce gun battles between people who thought the salt should be free and others who argued the advantages of private mineral rights. She knew about the Indian hot springs on the Sierra Blanca road, and nearby Fort Quitman, another of the early forts—although no real ruins were left of it, only an adobe scale model on private land.

As a girl, she used to wander around those historic spots imagining war parties of elegant Comanche warriors on horseback—the best light cavalry in the world, they'd been called. She could imagine men on long cattle drives, and Mexican bandits like Pancho Villa, and Apache and Yaqui raiders. Her imagination had kept her from brooding about being an only child.

Pepi wondered if C.C. liked history. She'd never asked him. She frowned as the mare picked up her pace as they approached the bottoms near what they privately called Mathews Creek, a tributary of the Rio Grande. This area was known to flood when the spring rains came, otherwise it was the haunt of such creatures as pronghorn antelope and white-tailed deer. Her father occasionally allowed hunting on his land, but only if he knew the people involved. Since man had killed off most of the predators that once kept the browsing animals in check, man now had to arrange a less natural way of reducing the number of antelope and deer. Otherwise they overgrazed the land and threatened the survival of the cattle and even themselves.

She felt her heart climb into her throat when she saw the big trucks still unloading new stock, because C.C. was straddling the fence supervising the operation. He must have sensed her approach, because he looked straight at her. Even at the distance, she could see the smile.

He jumped down from the fence and moved toward her, lean and rangy and dangerous. She wondered if there had ever been a man like him. He was certainly the stuff her dreams were made of.

"So you decided to join us," he mused. "Well, come on down."

She swung out of the saddle and fell into step beside him, the reins loosely in her hand. The mare followed noisily behind them.

"That's a lot of cattle," she mentioned when they'd tied the mare to the fence a little farther along.

He glanced down at her. "It takes a lot of cattle to make a living these days," he reminded her. "Especially for ranchers like your father and me, who aren't taking shortcuts."

She frowned. "Shortcuts?"

"Hormone implants, super vitamins, that kind of thing."

"Didn't I read in Dad's market bulletin that some foreign countries were refusing to import cattle with hormone implants that make them grow faster and bigger?" she asked.

He grinned. "Did your homework, I see," he mused. He lit a cigarette and pushed back the brim of his battered tan Stetson. "That's right. People are becoming more health conscious. We have to raise leaner beef in more natural ways to fit the market. Even the pesticides we use on our grain is under fire."

"Not to mention branding," she murmured, darting a glance upward.

"Don't get me started," he began gently. "It isn't cruel, but it is necessary. A freeze-dried brand won't last or be visible after a year or so. Even a burnt brand fades after the cattle shed their coats a few times. Ear tags can be removed. Hot branding is the only way a rancher can protect his investment and mark his cattle. Anything less is an open invitation to rustlers to come and wipe us out."

"I can hear the giggles now. Rustlers, in the space age."

"You know as well as I do that rustling is big business, even if they do it with trucks instead of box canyons," he muttered. "Damn it, we're under the gun from every side these days. People may have to choose between meat and tubes of food paste one day, but until they're willing to pass up a juicy steak, some concessions are going to have to be made."

"I still don't think they ought to torture animals unnecessarily," she said doggedly. "Not just out of curiosity, or to make cosmetics safer for women."

He chuckled. "You and your soft heart. You'd make pets of all my steers and name the chickens, wouldn't you? A hundred years ago you'd have starved to death. And I'll remind you of a time when children died by the thousands or were crippled by endless diseases. How do you think the researchers found cures for those diseases?"

"By using animals for their experiments, I guess," she said uneasily.

"Damned straight. And a hundred years ago, if you couldn't kill an animal, you starved." He stared out over the range. "Cruelty is a part of life. Like it or not, you and I are predators, animals. Man is just a savage with the edges smoothed over. Put him in a primitive environment with an empty belly, and he'll kill every time."

"Can we talk about something less violent?" she asked. "Are your brothers like you?"

He turned, staring down at her appreciatively, from her loosened reddish hair to her rounded figure in jeans. "Evan is," he said finally. "He's the eldest. We look alike, although he's more reserved than I am. Harden is closest to my age, but he's blue-eyed. My youngest brother is Donald—he got married just before I left to come here. Nice girl. Her name is Jo Ann."

"Are your parents still alive?" she asked.

"Our father died when we were just boys. Mother's still around, though." He hooked his thumbs in his wide leather belt and looked down at Pepi. "Her name is Theodora," he said, his gaze falling to Pepi's mouth. "If we have a daughter, I'd like to name her after my mother. She's a special woman. Gritty and capable and loving. She'd like you, Penelope Mathews Tremayne.''

She felt her face going hot. He was much too close, and the threat of that lean, fit body made her nervous. She shifted away a little, but he moved with her, his smile telling her that he knew very well how he affected her.

"I'm not a Tremayne for long," she said defensively.

"For as long as I say so, you are," he murmured. "Marriage isn't something to be taken lightly. If you didn't want to marry me, you should never have let me convince you to do into that Mexican wedding chapel."

He had a point there, but she couldn't admit it. She stuck her hands into her pockets to keep them still. She couldn't get her eyes up past his shirt. It was blue-checked, Western cut, and drawn taut across that broad expanse of chest. She could see the shadow of hair under it. She'd seen him without his shirt once or twice, but only from a distance. She couldn't help wonder what he looked like up close, and when she realized what she was thinking, her face flamed.

He lifted an eyebrow. "My, my, aren't we unsettled?" he mused with a slow smile. "Want me to take it off, Pepi?" he drawled softly.

Her eyes shot up to his, glanced off them and darted away to the cattle. Her heart almost shook her with its beat and her mouth went bone-dry as she searched for poise. "I was . . . admiring the color," she stammered.

"You were undressing me, you mean," he said casually, lifting the cigarette to his mouth. "Why don't

you?'' he murmured. ''We're married. I don't mind if
you touch me.''

She actually gasped and started to move away, but
he caught a long strand of her hair between his hard
fingers and stayed the movement effectively.

''Don't run from me,'' he said, his voice deep and
slow, carrying even over the bawling of the cattle and
the shouts of the nearby cowboys who were unloading them. A big cattle trailer had been backed in,
shielding them from the men with its bulk. ''It's time
you faced up to the reality of our situation.''

''Our situation would resolve itself if you'd agree to
an annulment.'' She choked out the words.

His hand moved, tangling in her hair. He turned
her, lifted her face to his with the pressure of it, and his
dark eyes had an odd, new glint in their narrowed
depths. ''Annulments are for people who can't work
out their problems. You and I are going to give this
marriage a chance, starting now, here.''

''We're what . . . C.C.!''

His mouth covered her startled cry. He didn't re-
lent, even when she twisted and tried to fight him. He
threw the cigarette in the dirt and his free arm gathered her up against the length of his hard-muscled, fit
body. The warm strength of it weakened her will.
Slowly she became aware of her hands gripping his
muscular arms frantically, her breathing almost stifled. Then she began to feel the slow warmth of his
mouth against her own, the sensual movements growing gentler and more insistent by the second.

Brandon had kissed her. So had other boys. But it
had been nothing like this. She barely felt the hot sun
on her head or heard the noise around them or smelled

the dust. She hesitated in her struggles for an instant and gave in to the steely arm around her back. He moved her closer, and she shivered a little with the newness of letting a man hold her like this, in an embrace that was nothing short of intimate.

His mouth lifted, brushed, touched the corners of hers as he felt her resistance slackening. She melted into him unexpectedly and his cheek drew slowly against hers, lifting fractionally so that he could see her eyes. The dazed pleasure in them made him hungry. Soft, pale darkness under those long, thick lashes, pierced with curiosity and need.

"The . . . men," she managed halfheartedly.

He turned her just fractionally, so that she could see that they were shielded from view by the cattle trailer. "What men, little one?" he whispered. His mouth settled on hers like the brush of a butterfly's wing. Lifted. Teased. "Slide your arms under mine," he murmured as he nibbled her lower lip. "Come close."

She obeyed him helplessly, sinking into a sweet oblivion that throbbed with new sensations. Her hands flattened against his shoulder blades. Odd, she thought dazedly, how well they fit together, despite his superior height.

"Kiss me, Mrs. Tremayne," he whispered, coaxing her lips apart.

She went under. His mouth was gentle, and then not gentle. She moaned as the pressure and insistence grew to shocking hunger, and she felt her legs begin to tremble against the hard pressure of his.

He let her go unexpectedly and drew back, his jaw clenched, his eyes strange and glittery. "Wrong time, wrong place," he said huskily. He took a slow breath and surveyed his handiwork, nodded as he saw the unmistakable signs of arousal. "Yes, you want me," he said under his breath. "That's a start, at least."

She swallowed. Her lips felt bruised and when she closed them, she tasted him. She wanted to ask him why, but he took her hand and tugged, pulling her along with him.

"These are Herefords," he said as if nothing at all had happened. "You know that we cross Brahman cattle with shorthorns to produce Santa Gertrudis. Well, this is another kind of cross," he said, and proceeded to give her a refresher course in cattle breeding.

She listened, but her eyes were all over his face, and her body was burning.

He lit a cigarette while he talked, and once he smiled down at her in a way that made her heart beat heavily. They seemed to have crossed some new bridge, quite unexpectedly, and she felt a sense of excitement that she'd never anticipated. Even when he had to leave her to go back to work, and she was riding home again on the mare, the excitement lingered. She only wished she knew where they were headed together.

As she gazed at him, drinking in his sharp features, his dark complexion and lithe, muscular build, she wondered what a child of theirs would look like.

The thought embarrassed her and she dragged her eyes away. There would be plenty of time for that kind of curiosity later, if and when things worked out between them.

# *Chapter Eight*

Life got more complicated very quickly. Brandon came by to see Pepi the next morning, a little hesitant because she was still technically married to C.C. Brandon didn't quite understand what was going on. Pepi had told him that the marriage was a mistake, but C.C. was glaring daggers at him from across the living-room coffee table, and he felt like a buck under the sights of a marksman.

"I, uh, thought we might take in a movie tomorrow night, that is, if C.C. doesn't mind," Brandon added quickly.

Pepi hadn't seen C.C. until Brandon showed up, but here he sat, self-appointed chaperon, and the way he was watching Brandon made her nervous.

C.C. leaned back in his chair and smoked his cigarette with arrogant self-confidence. "Pepi is my wife," he told the younger man. "I don't think married ladies should date other men. Just a little quirk of mine," he added with faintly dangerous eyes.

Brandon's eyes widened. "I thought . . . Pepi said," he faltered, glancing at her and finding no help, "that it was all a mistake."

"It might have started that way," C.C. replied. "But Pepi and I are determined to make the most of our unfortunate situation. Aren't we, Penelope?"

She looked at him uncertainly. She hadn't felt like herself since the day before, when C.C. had kissed her with such passion. He was backing her into a corner, and she couldn't see the way out.

"Now, look here, C.C.," she began.

He smiled at her lazily. "Connal, sweetheart, remember? Her memory comes and goes, poor little squirt," he told Brandon.

"It does not!" she raged at him. "I never forget anything!"

"Just a few minutes ago, you forgot you were married." He shrugged. "Can't blame a man for worrying when his own wife forgets her own wedding."

Pepi fumed while Brandon shifted uncomfortably in the chair. He looked as if his world was coming down around his ears. "I wanted to have another look at those two heifers with the parasites," he told C.C., changing the subject. "How are those calves that we're treating for scours?"

"They're better," the older man replied. "But I'd feel easier if we had more time to watch them. We've had a lot of sick cattle. I don't like it."

"Might not hurt to check the graze," Brandon suggested. "They may be getting into something toxic."

"I had the same idea." C.C. nodded. "I'm going to have those tanks checked today, too. There may be something leaching into the water supply."

"Just thank your lucky stars we aren't up near the Guadalupe Mountains, where the salt flats are," Brandon murmured dryly.

"I do, every day." C.C. got to his feet. "I'll walk you out. We've got company coming today, so I don't have a lot of time to spare. I'll let Darby go with you to see about the calves."

Pepi didn't like the expression on his face. She jumped up. "I'll go, too."

C.C. lifted an eyebrow, but he didn't say anything. Pepi went out behind Brandon, who was looking more than a little flustered.

They walked toward the barn, where Darby, the wizened little wrangler, was working. C.C. left Brandon with him and came back to where Pepi was waiting and watching. He took her arm and led her around the corner of the house, where his Ford sat by the deserted bunkhouse a few hundred yards from the back barn.

"Where are we going?" she asked.

"To the airport to meet my brothers, have you forgotten?" he asked conversationally.

"Yes, I guess I had," she said. "But I didn't know I was going with you to get them," she added meaningfully. "I'm not properly dressed. . . ."

"You look fine to me," he murmured, his eyes approving the long denim skirt she was wearing with her high-topped moccasins and a pullover knit blouse. "I like your hair down like that."

"Does it really matter how I wear it?" she asked coolly. "After all, it won't make me any less fat."

His breath stilled. He caught her hand and turned her toward him, his black eyes quiet and steady on her face. "I regret saying that most of all," he told her, "because you please me exactly the way you are. I wanted to hurt you." He looked down at her small hand in his. "God help me, I said things I never meant to. It was a shock, and not a very pleasant one at the time. I didn't know the circumstances, if that's any excuse. I don't expect you to get over it very soon. But maybe the wounds will heal in time. I have to hope so, Pepi."

Her pale brown eyes fell to his thin, sensuous mouth and lifted again to meet his eyes. "We were friends," she began. "I wish we could be again."

"Do you?" He moved a little closer, his expression as much a threat as his taut, fit body. "After yesterday, I doubt either of us is going to be able to settle for just friendship." His eyes fell to her soft mouth. "I want you."

She moved back a step, her face mirroring her indecision. "You want Edie, too."

He frowned. "In the same way you wanted Hale?" he probed suspiciously. "Some suitor, rushing out the door without you. I'd have laid my head open with a stick and taken you off to safety if I'd been him."

"I'd like to see you lay your own head open with a stick," she muttered.

He chuckled. "That wasn't what I meant." He lifted his chin and, with one eye narrowed, he looked down his nose at her. "Did you want him, little one?" he asked very softly. He let go of her hand and lifted his, knuckles down, to her collarbone. He trailed it slowly over the fabric, the sound of it loud in the stillness of early morning, his eyes assessing her sudden color, the rustle of her breath.

"C.C...." she whispered uncertainly, but she didn't try to move away.

"It's all right," he said quietly. "I'm your husband."

She couldn't think, which was just as well. The back of his hand moved down ever further, over the knit blouse to the swell of her breast—back and forth with delicate tenderness, until she felt as if her whole body was on fire. Her breath caught in her throat; she was burning with need.

As if he sensed her hunger, his forefinger bent and he brushed it down to her nipple, making it go suddenly hard and exquisitely sensitive. She gasped audibly.

He saw the heat in her cheeks and felt her faint shudder with a sense of shocking satisfaction.

"It was a lie," he said curtly. "You haven't had Hale. You haven't had a man at all."

She couldn't deny it. But she couldn't move, either. He was casting a spell over her. She loved the pleasure his touch was giving. She was getting drunk on it, in fact.

He glanced around them, frustrated and hungry to teach her more than this cursory lesson, but there were damned cowboys everywhere, coming out of the woodwork, and any minute they were going to be heading for that back barn. His brothers were due in thirty minutes. He wanted to throw something.

He looked back down at Pepi, his hard face showing new lines. "This will have to do, for now," he said huskily. He slid his free hand under the thick fall of her hair and lifted her mouth. "God, it hurts...!" he groaned.

She didn't understand. His mouth settled on hers in soft, teasing movements and his hand went slowly under her breast to lift its soft weight while his thumb slid roughly over the taut nipple.

"Oh!" she groaned against his mouth, but it wasn't pain that dragged the sound out of her, and he knew it.

"Open your mouth," he ground out at her lips.

She fit her lips to his and lifted her arms around him, shivering, trying to get closer to that expert hand on her breast. But all at once, he moved both hands to her hips and jerked.

Her shocked exclamation went into his mouth. He moved her thighs in a quick, sharp rotation against his aroused body and then put her away from him just as roughly.

"No," he said shortly when she tried, dazed, to move back into his arms. "Come on," he said, catching her arm to pull her along with him toward the car.

His hand was rough on her soft flesh, but she hardly felt it. She was shaking all over. So that was what it felt like to make love. She was sure there was a lot more to it, like having their clothes out of the way. Her skin went hot and she sighed huskily at the thought of C.C.'s lean, hard hands on her naked body.

"Miss Experience," he bit off, glaring down at her. "My God, why did you lie to me?"

"I thought it would make me less vulnerable," she said without thinking.

His eyes darted from her swollen, parted lips back up to her shocked face. "You look less vulnerable, all right," he said mockingly.

"You needn't make fun of me, C.C.," she whispered. "I can't help the way you make me feel."

He opened the passenger door of the Ford and stood aside to let her get in. "I'm not making fun of you," he replied. "If you want the truth, it arouses me like hell to have you cave in when I touch you."

She looked up at him, her pale brown eyes curious and a little afraid. He seemed very adult and worlds ahead of her in experience. "What you...did to me," she asked hesitantly, trying not to stammer. "Does it feel like that, in bed?"

His heart stopped beating. Then it went wild, and his body strung him out. He searched her soft eyes in a silence that throbbed with promise.

"Why don't you come to me tonight, and I'll show you?" he asked quietly.

Her eyes widened until the pupils seemed to blot out their color. "You mean...sleep with you?" she whispered.

He nodded. "The bunkhouse is empty, now that we're through roundup. You're my wife," he added, feeling the words all the way to his toes. "There's no shame in it, Pepi," he added when he saw her hesitation. "It would only be the consummation of our wedding vows." He lifted her hand and drew its palm hungrily to his lips. "Until you sleep with me," he added huskily, "we're not legally married. Did you know that?"

"No. I mean, no, I didn't," she faltered. The look in his eyes was melting her ankles. She could hardly stand up. It was hard to remember that he didn't love her. She had to try to keep that in mind, but it was difficult to keep anything in mind with his eyes piercing hers like that.

"Afraid of it?" he asked quietly.

"Yes, a little," she whispered.

"I'll be careful with you." He drew her hand to his chest and pressed it there, palm down, so that she could feel the powerful beating of his heart under his shirt.

"It will hurt," she blurted out.

"Maybe," he agreed. "But you won't care."

She searched his eyes curiously.

"You may find bruises on your hips tomorrow because I was rough with you on the way here," he replied, his voice deep and slow. "I didn't intend to be that rough, but you were fighting to get back into my arms afterward, not to get out of them."

Her lips parted. She'd forgotten the steely bite of his fingers into her soft flesh. "So it's like that," she whispered.

"Yes. It's like that. A fever that burns so wild and so high, you can't even feel pain through it." His face hardened. "I'll make you so damned hungry for me that you won't care what I do to you."

"But, what about Edie...." she whispered painfully.

He framed her face in his hands and bent to kiss her forehead with breathless tenderness. "Edie was a pleasant, and a very innocent, diversion," he whispered, sliding his cheek against hers so that his breath was warm at her ear. "I haven't slept with her."

"But...you must have wanted to," she began again.

He lifted his head, and his dark eyes searched hers slowly. "Pepi, I don't really understand why, but maybe the guilt made it difficult for me to deal with relationships. I...haven't wanted sex since Marsha died. At least, not until yesterday."

"You wanted me," she whispered with growing wonder.

"Oh, yes, I did," he said with undisguised hunger. "I still do, more every day." His eyes slid down her body and he drew her against him, his lean hands on her shoulders. "Do you want to give me a baby?" he asked.

It was the first time anyone had asked her that. She felt her body burning with heat, and she knew her freckles were standing out like crazy in her face. "Now?" she asked uncertainly.

"If you don't want to get pregnant, I'll have to do something to prevent it," he explained gently.

"Oh." She averted her eyes. "Well, I...I don't know." Things were moving fast. Almost too fast. She felt hunted.

"Don't look like that," he said, his voice almost tender as he tipped her face up to his eyes. "You don't have to, if you don't want to. I'm in no hurry. We've got the rest of our lives. If you want to spend some time getting used to me first, that's all right. I'll never rush you."

"C.C.," she said softly, and she smiled at him. "You're a nice man."

"That's what I've been trying to tell you. It's just that I haven't quite tried to prove it, yet," he added with a smile full of self-mockery. "And my name is Connal."

"Yes. Connal." She reached up hesitantly and paused, but he caught her fingers and drew them to his face, letting her trace his dark eyebrows, his straight nose, the hard curve of his thin mouth.

"We'll take one day at a time," he assured her solemnly. "No pressure."

"Thank you."

He smiled and put her in the car, sliding in beside her with apparent good humor to start the engine.

She fastened her seat belt and studied his profile hungrily. "Connal?" she asked.

He glanced at her and lifted an eyebrow.

"Do you...I mean, is a child important to you?" she asked quietly.

He frowned. She made it seem as if he wanted her because she could bear him one. He wasn't certain what to say to reassure her. She'd said that she wasn't in love with him, although she was certainly attracted to him. God knew, he didn't want to frighten her off.

"Eventually, yes," he compromised. "Don't you want children?"

"Yes, I do," she said huskily, meeting his eyes. "I want them very much."

His chest began to swell. He hoped against hope that someday she'd want them because she loved him. But it would take time, he reminded himself. He mustn't be impatient.

He didn't say anything else. He nodded and turned his attention back to the road.

The airport was crowded, and Pepi clung to C.C.'s lean hand on the way through the crush of people.

"Everybody decided to come on the same day," he mused, moving aside with her to let the embarking passengers get by. For a brief moment, they were alone in the corridor. He chuckled and drew her along with him, his spurs "making music" as the cowboys like to call it.

"I'd forgotten what spurs sounded like," she murmured.

"I forgot to take them off this morning," he recalled. "Back in the old days, the Mexican spurs were so big that vaqueros had to take them off just to walk," he replied. "God knows how their mounts survived."

"You use spurs when you help break horses," she reminded him.

He smiled down at her. "Sure I do. But you know we use special spurs that don't break the skin or injure the horse's hide. To a horse, it's like being tickled. That's why he jumps and sunfishes."

Her hand felt very small and helpless in his. It wasn't a feeling she'd have liked with another man, but with C.C. it seemed very natural.

She looked down, marking the size of her foot and his. He had big feet, too, but they suited him because he was so tall.

"I don't have big feet," he remarked, accurately reading her mind.

"Did I say anything?" she protested.

He chuckled. "You didn't have to. There they are!" he said suddenly, looking over the crowd in front of them. "Evan! Harden!"

Two men who looked very much like C.C. moved toward them. They weren't wearing working clothes, though. They were in suits. The taller man had on a pearl-gray vested suit with a matching Stetson. He was huskily built, but certainly not overweight. He looked like a wrestler, with dark eyes and dark hair and complexion that was even darker than C.C.'s. The other man was only fractionally shorter, dressed in dark slacks with a white open-necked shirt with a sports jacket. He wore a black Stetson at a cocky angle over his equally black hair, and when he came closer, Pepi noticed that his eyes were a pale, glittery blue under thick black lashes. He had a leaner look than Evan, and a wiry frame that was probably deceptive, because he looked as fit as C.C.

C.C. greeted his brothers and then drew them to where Pepi stood waiting awkwardly, her uncertainty evident in her nervous face.

"Evan, Harden, this is my wife, Penelope," C.C. introduced her, sliding a casual but possessive arm around her shoulders.

"She looks just the way you described her," Harden murmured dryly, extending a lean hand. His pale blue eyes assessed her and gave nothing away. "You're a rancher's daughter, I gathered."

Penelope nodded. "I grew up around horses and cattle," she said quietly, and smiled nervously. "Hereford cattle, of course," she added. "I guess our stock will look pretty mangy to you by comparison with your purebred Santa Gerts."

"Oh, we're not snobs," Harden murmured. He stuck his hands deep in his pockets and glanced at C.C. "Except when it comes to Old Man Red."

"The foundation sire of our herd," Evan added. He extended a hand the size of a plate and shook Pepi's with firm gentleness. His dark eyes narrowed. "You look threatened. No need. We're domesticated, and we've had our shots."

Pepi's rigid stance relaxed and she laughed, her whole face lighting up. Evan didn't smile, but his dark eyes did, and she felt at home for the first time.

"Speak for yourself," Harden drawled, and his blue eyes were briefly cold. "The day I get domesticated you can bury me."

"Harden is a card-carrying bachelor," Evan mused.

"Look who's talking," Harden replied.

"Not my fault that women can't appreciate my superior good looks and charm," the eldest Tremayne shrugged. "They trample me trying to get to you."

Pepi laughed with pure delight. They were nothing like she'd imagined.

"Come on. You can fight out at the ranch," C.C. said. He took Pepi's arm.

"Pity you had to walk off with Penelope before she got a look at us," Evan said, shaking his head. "I'm a much better proposition, Pepi. I still have all my own teeth."

"That's true," Harden agreed. "But only because you knocked out two of Connal's."

"Fair trade," Connal returned. "I got three of his."

"It was a long time ago," Evan said. "We've all calmed down a lot since then."

"C.C. hasn't been very calm lately," Pepi murmured. "I thought he was going to murder me when he found out we were married."

"Served him right for getting drunk," Evan said curtly. "Mother would lay a tire tool across his head for that."

"Oh, Pepi threatened to," C.C. chuckled. "Still a tee-totaller, I see, Evan?"

"He carries it to sickening extremes," Harden murmured. "Justin and Shelby Ballenger will never invite him to another dinner party. He actually got up from the table and carried the glass of wine the waiter accidentally poured back to the kitchen."

C.C. burst out laughing. "Well, Justin never was much of a drinker himself, as I recall. Not in Calhoun's league, anyway."

"Calhoun's gotten as bad as Evan," Harden told him. "He doesn't want to set a poor example for the kids, or so he says."

"Alcohol is a curse," Evan said as they reached the car.

"My father will love you," Pepi said, grinning up at him.

When they got to the ranch, Ben seemed to take to Evan even before he knew about the eldest brother's temperance stance. But he was less relaxed with Harden. In fact, so was Pepi. The blue-eyed brother moved lazily and talked lazily, but Pepi sensed deep, dark currents in him.

The men talked business while Pepi whipped up a quick lunch, but the brothers only stayed for two hours and had to catch a plane right back to Jacobsville. Pepi didn't ride with C.C. to take them to the airport, though. She had a call from her prospective employer just as they were going out the door, and she waved them on to take it.

The insurance company's receptionist had decided that she did want her old job back. They were very apologetic, and promised to let Pepi know the minute they had another opening. She was disheartened, but it was probably just as well.

"We're going to get a bull." Ben Mathews was all but dancing as he told her. "One of the new crop of young bulls out of Checker. Remember reading about him in the trade paper? He's one of the finest herd sires in years!"

"And his progeny cost plenty, I don't doubt," Pepi said. "C.C.'s going to fund the addition, I gather."

"He's a full partner," Ben reminded her. "And we're all in this to make the ranch pay, aren't we?"

"Yes, I guess we are. How do you like his brothers?"

"Oh, Evan's a card. He's very obviously the financial brains of the outfit. Knows his figures."

"And Harden?" she added.

He sat down in his chair and crossed his legs. "Harden is a driven man. I don't know why, but he strikes me as a bad man to have for an enemy. He's charming, but underneath it, there's a darkness of spirit."

"A deep kind of pain," Pepi nodded, "and a terrible anger."

"Exactly. I hope we'll be doing most of our business with Evan. He's more like C.C."

"He's more like two of C.C.," Pepi laughed. "I wonder what the other brother looks like, the one who's married?"

"Just like C.C. and Evan, from what I gather. Harden's the odd one, with those blue eyes. He doesn't really favor the others very much."

"Probably a throwback to another generation, like Aunt Mattie who had dark-haired parents and was a blonde."

"No doubt."

"My job didn't come through," she said after a minute. "They don't need me."

"Then why don't you do some bookkeeping and typing for the ranch?" Ben asked. "Connal said we're going to have to keep proper books now, and there'll be a lot of correspondence. He was going to hire somebody, but you're a good typist and you aren't bad with figures. We can keep it in the family."

"I guess I could," she said. "I like typing."

"You can talk to Connal when he gets back."

She cleaned up the kitchen and made an apple pie. By the time she took it out of the oven, Connal had returned.

"Did they get off all right?" she asked him.

"Like clockwork." He paused by the counter where she was placing a cloth over the pie. "For supper?" he asked hopefully.

She smiled at him shyly. "Yes. I like your brothers," she said.

"They liked you, too. Evan was particularly impressed."

"Evan is easier to get along with. Harden . . ." She hesitated. "He's . . . different."

"More different than you know," he said quietly. He moved closer, taking a strand of her hair in his fingers and twirling it around one. "How about supper and a movie tonight?"

"I have to get supper for Dad," she said, hesitating.

"We'll take him with us," he chuckled.

"On a date?" She lifted her eyebrows. "He'd love that. Besides, this is his checkers night with old man Dill down the road. No, I'll fix something for him before we go. He won't mind."

"If you're sure." He sighed heavily, watching her. "Pepi, how would you feel about moving into a house with me?" he added, frowning.

"But... but what about Dad?" she asked.

"Consuelo can cook and clean for him. She could go on salary. And there's a house, the Dobbs house. They moved back East last month," he reminded her. "Your father was renting them the house. It's small, but it would be just right for the two of us."

She couldn't cope with so much at once. Things were happening with lightning speed, and her mind was whirling.

"You mean, live with you all the time," she faltered. "Even at night?"

"That's the general idea," he replied. "A wife's place is with her husband."

"You didn't want a wife. You said so..."

"...with alarming repetition, yes, I know," he finished for her. "Will you try to understand that I've changed my mind? That marriage is no longer the terror it was for me?"

"Well, yes, I'll try. But you didn't have much choice about ours, did you?"

He let go of her hair. "Not much," he agreed. "But looking back, I wouldn't have wanted to marry anyone. Surely you realized that?"

"You were pretty adamant about it," she nodded. "I just wish we'd gone about things in the normal way. I'll always feel that you were trapped into a relationship you really didn't want."

"So were you," he replied. "But the thing we have to do now is make the most of it. An annulment would disgrace us both, Pepi, especially your father. Now that he and I are in partnership, the best way to cement it is to make the marriage a real one."

"Is it what you really want, Connal?" she asked worriedly.

"Of course it is," he said.

She couldn't help feeling that he was only saying that to put her at ease. It would hurt his pride to get an annulment. People might think he wasn't enough of a man to fulfill his wedding vows. Too, he might still have in mind using her to ward off other contenders for his hand in marriage.

"Could I have a little more time?" she asked hesitantly.

He stared down at her. After the afternoon, he'd thought she'd be immediately receptive to his advances, but perhaps she'd had too much time to think and she'd gotten cold feet. The last thing he could afford to do was to rush her.

"Okay," he said after a minute. "You can have a little more time. But you and I are going to start doing things together, Pepi. If we don't live together, we're at least going to start acting like married people in public."

"That's all right with me," she said. But afterward, she worried about Edie. Had Connal told her about his marriage? And was his relationship with Edie really as innocent as he'd said it was?

## Chapter Nine

Connal took her to the same exclusive restaurant in El Paso where she'd gone with Brandon the night before her father's birthday. She was wearing a plain gray jersey dress with a pretty scarf, her hair down around her shoulders, and Connal had told her that she looked delightfully pretty. Even if he was lying, it was exciting to go on a real date with him, to have his dark eyes possessive on her face as they walked to their table.

He looked elegant in a dinner jacket and dark slacks, his white silk shirt a perfect foil for his dark complexion and darker eyes and hair. Pepi loved to look at him. She thought that in all the world, there couldn't be a more handsome man.

He seated her and then himself, and she smiled at him until a movement caught her eye and she saw Edie sitting at a nearby table all alone, staring pointedly at Connal.

"I'd better have a word with her," he told Pepi, his eyes narrowing. "I won't be a minute."

He got up and went to the other table, smiling at an Edie who became suddenly radiant. The blonde was wearing a simple black sheath dress cut almost to the navel in front, and Pepi despaired of the way she probably compared to the sophisticated older woman.

She couldn't tear her eyes away from them. They did look so right together, and despite C.C.'s determination to make the most of a bad situation—their marriage—she felt guilty and ashamed that he'd had to be trapped into marrying her when he'd have been so much better off with Edie. Pepi was just a country girl. She had no sophistication. She didn't even know how to choose the kind of clothes that were proper for a place like this. Inevitably she was going to be a dismal disappointment for a man like Connal, who was born to wealth and high society.

Edie's face suddenly went rigid. She stared at Pepi blankly for an instant, and then with quickly concealed rage. Her attention went back to C.C. and she seemed to come apart emotionally. She started crying.

C.C. got her up out of her chair and put a comforting arm around her as he led her gently out of the restaurant.

Obviously he'd told her about the marriage. Did he tell her, Pepi wondered, that it had been a forced one, and not of his choosing? Was he going to take her home now or get her a cab?

Ten minutes passed and Pepi grew more upset as she realized he'd more than likely driven Edie home. He'd comfort her, surely. Maybe more than that. He and Edie were close, even if they weren't lovers. Or had he stretched the truth about that, too?

The waiter hovered and Pepi went ahead and ordered soup du jour and a chef's salad. It was all she had any appetite for.

She'd just finished when C.C. came back, his expression telling her nothing as he sat down across from her.

"Is she all right?" Pepi asked quietly.

"Not really, but she'll do. I should have picked a better place to tell her," he said shortly. "God, I never expected that kind of reaction."

"She's been your only steady date for a long time," Pepi said with downcast eyes. "It's understandable that she had hopes of her own."

C.C. hated scenes. It brought back unpleasant memories of times when Marsha had put away too many cocktails and did her best to embarrass him. She'd never succeeded. Neither had Edie, but it touched off his temper.

"Women always have hopes," he said with cold bitterness. "Of course, not all of them are fortunate enough to catch a man drunk and drag him into a Mexican wedding chapel."

Pepi closed her eyes. She shouldn't let him get to her like this. Despite his ardor, his desire for her, underneath there was always going to be resentment that he'd been less than sober when he signed the marriage license. He was never going to let Pepi forget, either, and what kind of life was that going to be for either of them?

"I wouldn't exactly call it fortunate," Pepi replied without looking at him.

"Thank you," he replied acidly. "I can return the compliment."

The waiter came and C.C. ordered a steak and salad. He sipped the coffee he'd ordered and glared at Pepi. It wasn't her fault, he knew, but he was furious at Edie's theatrics and Pepi's meek acceptance of his bad humor. He wanted a fight, and he couldn't seem to start one. If Pepi continued to knuckle under like this, marriage was going to be impossible for her.

"Nothing to say?" he prodded.

She tightened her fingers around the water glass. "What would you like to hear?" She lifted the glass, her pale brown eyes glittering with dislike. "Or would you prefer something nonverbal but just as enlightening?"

His eyes began to twinkle. "Go ahead. Throw it."

She glanced around at the elegant diners surrounding them and thought better of it. There were some priceless antiques decorating the place. With her luck she'd hit something irreplaceable and land them in debt for years. She put the water glass down.

"It's not my fault," she said coldly. "You're the one who threatened to shoot up Juárez."

"And you knew I didn't have a gun," he countered.

"No, I didn't," she returned. "Dad told me once that you have a Beretta and a license to carry it. I had no way of knowing there wasn't one in your pocket, and I wasn't about to frisk you."

"God forbid," he said with mock horror. "Imagine having to touch a live man like *that*!"

"Cut it out," she muttered, reddening.

"You are a greenhorn and a half, aren't you?" he mused. "Don't know how to kiss, don't know how to make love, wouldn't dream of touching a man below the belt . . ."

"Stop!" She glanced around quickly to make sure nobody had heard him, her face beet-red. "Somebody might hear you!"

"So what? We're married." His eyes narrowed. "Till death do us part," he added mockingly.

Her own eyes narrowed and she smiled sweetly. "In that case, do check your bed at night, dear man. I'll see if I can find a couple of rattly bedmates for you."

"One of your ranch hands did that, the first night I was here," he recalled, grinning at her shock. "Didn't they ever tell you?"

"Somebody put a live rattlesnake in your bed?" she gasped.

"Indeed they did," he replied. "Fortunately they'd defanged him first, but it was an interesting experience."

"What did you do?"

"You didn't hear the gunshot, either, I gather?" he mused.

"You shot it?"

"Uh-huh," he agreed. "Right through the head, the mattress, and the bunkhouse floor."

"Poor old snake," she said.

He gave her a hard glare. "Aren't you the one who leaped up onto the hood of a truck from a standing start when one came slithering past your foot this summer?"

"I didn't say I liked them," she emphasized. "But I think it's horrible to kill things without reason. What could the poor thing have done to you—gummed you to death?"

"You're forgetting I didn't know he'd had his fangs pulled."

"Oh. I guess not."

The waiter brought his meal and he ate it in silence, noticing that Pepi's eyes wandered back to the window and the sharp, dark outline of the mountains in the distance. She was brooding, and he felt bad that he'd attacked her without reason.

"I suppose Edie was angry?" she said, fishing.

He finished the last bit of his steak and washed it down with steaming black coffee. "That's an understatement. She had a lot to say when I told her how our marriage had come about."

"Including advising you on the quickest way to have it annulled, I imagine?" she asked miserably.

"I told her we couldn't get an annulment," he murmured dryly.

"But, of course we can," she said without thinking. "We haven't—" She broke off, gasping.

He watched her eyes widen when she realized what he was saying.

"You didn't tell Edie that?" she burst out.

"Why not?" His black eyes probed hers. "Regardless of how they got said, I consider marriage vows binding. That means I don't have women on the side. As for what we haven't done yet, you'll sleep with me, eventually. You're as hungry for it as I am. Maybe even hungrier. I remember how I ached before my first time. And I wanted Marsha so much that I couldn't sleep at night.''

Neither could she, but she wasn't about to admit that to him. She lowered her eyes to the table. "I suppose your first wife loved you?" she asked idly.

"She loved the idea of my money, just like the ones who come after her, up to and including Edie," he replied with a cynicism that shocked Pepi. He looked at that moment like a man who'd known every conceivable kind of woman and trusted none of them.

"Did Edie know who you were?" Pepi asked.

He nodded. "Through a mutual friend. So you see, it wasn't love eternal on her part. She enjoyed a good time and eating in the best places. But she'll find someone else. There are plenty of well-heeled bachelors around."

"Are you as cynical as you sound?" she asked.

"Every bit," he replied narrowly. "Even Marsha married me as much for what I have as what I was. She told me she couldn't endure being married to a man who worked for wages. She was pretty and I wanted her. But long before the accident, I regretted marrying her."

Would it be that way with Pepi, too, she wondered. Would he be that resentful of her? He already disliked the way they'd been married.

"You must have missed her, though," she said gently.

"I missed her," he agreed. "I missed the child more. God, it was hard living with that! If I'd had any idea, any idea at all that she was pregnant, I'd never have let her in the raft. But she was too possessive to let me go alone. There were two other women in the rafting party, and she'd convinced herself that I wanted both of them."

She studied his hard face. "Didn't she know that you aren't the kind of man who'd forsake any vow he made?" she said after a minute.

His head came up and his dark eyes glittered into hers. "If you believe that, why did you look so accusing when I came back from taking Edie home? Were you picturing me in bed with her?"

She blushed. "There's a big difference between taking a vow voluntarily and taking one when you're out of your mind on tequila," she said with wan pride. "You didn't get married out of choice, this time." She picked up her napkin and stroked the embossed design. "It's not going to work, C.C.," she added wearily.

"Oh, hell, yes, it is," he said tersely. He finished his coffee. "I'm still in the adjustment stage, that's all. Until recently I thought of you as Ben's tomboy teenage daughter."

So that was it. Probably she still acted like one, too. But it was beyond her abilities to pretend a sophistication she didn't have.

"Or your nursemaid," she mused, smiling a little. "That's what you said in Juárez, that since I was always playing nursemaid, we might as well get married so I'd have an excuse."

"You've always looked out for me," he said quietly. "I never thought of you in a physical way, Pepi. It was as much a shock for me as it was for you that morning in the kitchen when your father interrupted us," he added, his eyes glittery under his thick lashes.

She averted her gaze. She remembered, too. It had been the sexiest kind of lovemaking, but he hadn't even kissed her.

"If things had happened naturally," he continued, his voice deepened, "it wouldn't have affected me the way it did."

"They wouldn't have happened naturally, and you know it, C.C.," she told him, her eyes a little sad as they met his. "You'd never in a million years have wanted somebody like me. I guess if this hadn't come up, you'd have married Edie eventually."

"Didn't you hear a word I just said, about why Edie kept going out with me?" he asked irritably.

"Edie loves you," she muttered. "I'm not blind, even if you're trying to be. She genuinely cared about you. No woman is completely mercenary, and there's a lot more to you than just the size of your wallet."

He lifted an eyebrow. "Really? Name something."

"You're kind," she said, taking the sarcasm at face value. "You don't go out of your way to start fights, but you'll stand your ground when it's necessary. You're fair and open-minded when it counts, and you have a lot of heart."

He stared at her. "I thought you didn't care enough about me to want to stay married to me?" he murmured, touched by her opinion of him.

"And I'll remind you again that you're the one who wanted the annulment and went storming off in a snit to get it," she shot back. "I still don't understand what changed your mind while you were away."

"Evan did," he said after a minute. "He accused me of running from commitment." He paused to light a cigarette, staring absently at his lighter before he re-pocketed it. "I guess in a way he was right. I couldn't bear the thought of another Marsha, another possessive woman smothering me. I couldn't bear the thought, either, that tragedy could repeat itself, because I was still working out the guilt I felt over Marsha's death. Evan said that I should keep you, if you were brave enough to take me on," he added, staring at her quietly. "He thought you sounded like exactly the kind of woman I needed. And maybe he was right, Pepi. The last thing you are is possessive."

She could have laughed out loud at that! Of course she was possessive; she loved him. But he obviously didn't want a woman who cared deeply about him. He wanted a shallow relationship that would allow him to remain heart-free and independent, and she couldn't settle for that.

"All the same, I'm not sure I can handle this," Pepi confessed. "You'll never get over the fact that it was an accidental marriage. Even a few minutes ago, when you were upset about Edie, you threw it up to me."

"Haven't you been doing the same thing, about what I said to you before I left to visit my brothers in Jacobsville?" he countered.

She shrugged. "I guess I have. But we're two pretty different people, C.C., and I won't ever get used to a rich life-style or high society," she said honestly. "I'm not a social animal."

His face went hard. "You don't think you can live with me as I am?"

"I could have lived very well with my father's foreman, who was just an ordinary working man," she replied. "I'm made for cooking and cleaning, for taking care of a house and raising a family. I'm just not cut out for society bashes, and no matter how hard you try to change me, you'll never get the country out of me."

He lifted his chin, his eyes narrowing on her face. "Do I strike you as the kind of man who lives from party to party?" he asked.

"You've been hiding out for three years," Pepi reminded him, "living a life-style that probably wasn't a patch on the one you left behind. I don't know anything about that side of your life at all."

"Would you like to?" he asked. "We could go to Jacobsville and visit my family for a few days."

She hesitated. Harden intimidated her, but she liked Evan well enough. "What's your mother like?" she asked.

He smiled. "She's like Evan," he replied. "She's dry and capable and easy to like. She'll like you, too."

"Harden doesn't like me," she said.

"Harden doesn't like women, sweetheart," he said gently. "Despite the fact that he's got a face like a dark angel and the charm to match, he's the original woman-hater."

"Then it wasn't just me," she said, a little relieved.

"It wasn't. He hates our mother most of all," he added quietly. "That's why he doesn't live at home. Evan does, because it's too much of a burden for Mother, but Harden has an apartment in Houston, where our offices are located."

She wanted to follow up on that, but it probably wasn't the best time to start probing into family secrets.

"I guess we'd have to stay in the same room?" she asked worriedly.

His dark eyes searched hers in a warm silence. "Yes."

"Twin beds?" she asked hopefully.

He shook his head.

"Oh." She toyed with her fork, going warm all over at the thought of sleeping with him.

"Want to back out?" he challenged softly.

She lifted her eyes to his and hesitated. Then she gave in, all at once. She loved him. If he wanted to try to make their marriage work, this was the first step. He seemed adamant about not getting an annulment, and she didn't really want one, either.

"No," she said. "I don't want to back out."

His face tautened and he seemed to have a hard time breathing. "Brave words," he said huskily. "Suppose I have more in mind than sharing a pillow with you?"

She gnawed on her lower lip. "That's inevitable, isn't it?" she asked hesitantly. "If we stay married, I mean."

He nodded. "I won't settle for a platonic marriage. I want a child, Pepi," he added, his voice deeper, slower as he stared into her eyes.

She stared at her hands, neatly folded in front of her on the table. "I'd like that. I'm just a little nervous about it, that's all. Most women these days are experienced."

"You can't imagine what a rare and exquisite thing a virgin bride is to me," he said quietly. "Your innocence excites me, Pepi. Just thinking about our first time makes my knees go weak."

It made hers go weak, too, but she didn't think she should admit it. Her eyes glanced off his and away again. "When did you plan for us to visit your family?" she asked instead, changing the subject.

"Tomorrow. My mother wants to meet you. It wouldn't hurt to let her see that I haven't let history repeat itself."

"As if you had much choice." She sighed. "Oh, C.C., I'm so sorry I got us into this mess," she groaned, meeting his dark gaze levelly. "I didn't know what to do. Edie or somebody like her could have coped with it better."

"Edie or somebody like her would have been laughing like hell at my predicament and adding up the settlement all at the same time," he replied. "They wouldn't have flayed themselves with attacks of conscience."

"Wouldn't you like to get an annulment, anyway?" she asked him. "Then, you'd have the right to choose..."

"Is it the damned redheaded vet after all?" he shot back, suddenly dark-faced with rage. "Well, is it?"

"What do you mean?" she faltered, staggered by the venom in the attack.

He leaned forward, his eyes like black fires burning in his lean face. "You know what I mean. He's in love with you. Was it mutual? Is he why you're so single-minded about that annulment, so you can dump me and marry him?"

"Brandon did ask me to marry him, but..." she began.

"But you did your Florence Nightingale act and followed me to Juárez," he said angrily. "Well, don't hold your breath until I let you go. We're married, and we're staying married. And I'd better not catch Hale hanging around you, either!''

She gaped at him. "That's not fair!" she tossed right back. "Even if it wasn't a conventional marriage, I take my vows seriously, too!"

"Do you? Prove it," he said tersely.

"Prove it?" she echoed blankly.

"You know where the bunkhouse is," he said with a mocking smile.

She averted her angry face. He'd told her that before and she'd refused, asked for time. Now here he was rushing her again, and it felt almost as if he were requesting something horribly immoral. She couldn't help her reticence. She still didn't feel married to him.

"So you still have cold feet?" he taunted. "All right, then. Save your pride. But you'll sleep with me when I take you to visit my family. You gave your word."

"Yes, I know," she said huskily. She folded her napkin neatly and laid it beside her plate. "Could we go now?"

"Of course." He got up and pulled out her chair, pausing to look down at her with troubled dark eyes. "You're going to fight me every step of the way, aren't you?" he asked deeply. "You'll never forget the things I said when I found out about the marriage license."

"It wasn't any surprise, C.C.," she replied, looking up at him with quiet pride. "I always knew I wasn't your type of woman. You even warned me once, that morning I came to make black coffee for you when you were hung over. You said you didn't have anything to give and told me not to break my heart over you. There was no need to worry. My heart isn't breaking." That was true. It had already been broken by his cold indifference.

He let out a rough sigh. He'd closed all his doors and now he didn't know how to open them again. All he knew was that if he lost Pepi, there wouldn't be much left of his life.

He paid the bill and led her out to the car. He didn't say anything, driving quickly and efficiently down the long road paralleling the Rio Grande until they were on the turnoff to the ranch. It was wide open country here, and deserted most all the time.

Pepi sat beside him in a rigid silence, toying with her purse. There was a tension between them that disturbed her. Despite his apparent unconcern as he drove, smoking his cigarette without talking, she sensed that he was boiling underneath. Maybe Edie had upset him and he couldn't get over having lost her. She didn't take his remarks about Brandon seriously, because he had to know she wasn't crazy about their vet. Besides, if he'd been jealous, that would mean he cared. And he'd already said he didn't.

She leaned her head back with a faint sigh, anxious to be home, to get this turbulent evening into the past where it belonged.

But C.C. suddenly pulled off into a small grove of trees, their outline dark against the night sky, and cut off the engine.

She opened her eyes and looked at him. In the pale light from the half moon, his eyes looked glittery and dangerous.

"Afraid?" he asked softly.

"N-no," she faltered.

He put out his cigarette and unfastened first his seat belt, then hers. He took the purse out of her hands and laid it on the dash. With deft sureness, he lifted her body across his legs and eased her head back onto the hard muscle of his upper arm.

"Liar," he said quietly, searching her oval face. "You're scared to death. Physical love isn't something to be afraid of, Pepi. It's an exquisite sharing of all that two people are, an intimate expression of mutual respect and need."

He sounded more gentle than he ever had, and some of her apprehension drained away. She rested her cool hand on his dinner jacket as she searched the hard face above hers. Once she'd dreamed of lying in his arms like this, being totally alone with him and wanted by him. But so much had happened in the meantime that it seemed somehow unreal.

"Do you really want me, that way?" she asked, her voice sounding strained and high-pitched.

"You greenhorn," he murmured. He shifted her so that her belly lay against his, and he rotated her hips sharply, letting her feel what happened to him almost instantly. He heard her gasp and felt her stiffen against him. "Does this answer your question?" he asked outrageously, and his steely hand refused to let her draw away from the stark intimacy. "Would you like to know how many years it's been since a woman could turn me on this fast?"

Her fingers clenched on his dinner jacket, but she stopped trying to pull away. The feel of him was drugging her. Her own body began to betray her, reacting unexpectedly to the evidence of his need and lifting closer to it.

He caught his breath. "Pepi!" he ground out.

She felt him tremble with a sense of wonder. She watched his face and repeated the tiny movement of her hips. Yes, he liked it. She could tell by the way his jaw tautened, by the sudden catch of his breath, the stiffening shudder of his body against her.

"Do you . . . like that?" she whispered shyly.

"Yes, I like it!" he groaned. He bent, his free hand tangling in her thick, soft hair, the other going to the base of her spine to hold her even closer. "Do it again, baby," he whispered against her lips. "Do it again, hard . . . !"

His mouth invaded hers. She felt the sudden sharp thrust of his tongue and her body arched as his hand went under the skirt of her dress and up against her stocking-clad leg. He touched her inner thighs, his mouth teasing now, nibbling at her lips while his hand slowly discovered the most intimate things about her trembling body. She couldn't even protest. She loved what he was doing to her.

His hand withdrew and went up her back to the zipper of the dress, to loosen it before he did the same thing with the catch of her lacy bra.

"Don't be afraid," he said softly when she tried feebly to stay the downward movement of his hands. "I want to look at your breasts, Pepi. I want to touch them."

She trembled all over with the words, her eyes lost in his. She gave way, and the dress fell to her waist along with the thin wisp of lace that had hidden her from his rapt stare.

He held her a little away from him, and his dark eyes feasted on her nudity in the dim light. She could feel the tension in him. He didn't move or speak for the longest time, and as she watched, her nipples began to harden under that piercing stare. She didn't understand the contraction, or the way her body arched up faintly, as if enticing him to do more than look.

"It isn't enough, is it, little one?" he asked tenderly. His hands slid under her bare back and he bent his dark head to her body. "You smell of gardenias, Pepi," he whispered. His lips touched the silken swell of her breast, lightly brushing it, and she shivered. He liked that reaction, so he did it again, and again, working his way around, but not touching the hard nipple. Pepi's hands clenched against his chest and she felt her body beginning to throb in a new and scary way.

"C.C.," she moaned. "Please…it aches so! Make it…stop!"

One lean hand slid up her rib cage to tease at the outside edge of her breast. His lips teased some more, until she actually shuddered with the need and began to beg him.

"Sweet," he breathed roughly. And his mouth suddenly opened, taking the hard nipple inside, closing on it with a warm, slow suction that made her cry out. It was like a tiny climax. Her hands tangled convulsively in his hair and she wept, gasping as the pleasure went on and on and on.

"Oh, God…!" he ground out, shocked at her capacity for lovemaking. If she could be this aroused when he'd barely touched her, he could hardly imagine how it would be in bed, with her naked body under his, her long, elegant legs enclosing him, holding him, welcoming him as a lover.

"Connal," she whispered shakily. Her lips touched his forehead, his closed eyes, trembling. "Connal, please. Please."

"I can't," he bit off, lifting his head. He could barely speak, his lean hand unsteady on her breast where it rested like a brand of fire while he looked down at his handiwork. "Not here."

"No one would see us," she moaned.

"I can't take the risk," he said heavily. He pulled her to him, wrapping up her bare breasts against the silky fabric of his dinner jacket, rocking her. "Anyone could drive up here, including the county police," he murmured at her ear. His lips brushed her earlobe. "I don't want anyone to see you without your clothes except me. And when we go all the way, I want it to be in a bed, not the front seat of a car."

She shivered, nestling closer. "Does it feel like this, when you go all the way?" she asked huskily.

"Yes," he breathed at her ear. "But it's much more intense." He bit her earlobe and his hands smoothed over her bare back with slow sensuality. "Has Hale seen you like this?" he whispered.

"No," she whispered back. "Nobody has, except you."

He lifted his head and looked down at her, making a meal of her bareness. He touched her nipple, very gently, and watched it harden, felt her shiver. His eyes caught hers. "Much more of this," he said roughly, "and I'll take you sitting up, right here. We'd better go home."

Her body exploded with heat as he lifted her back into her own seat. "Could we do it, like that?" she asked hoarsely.

His face tautened and for one insane instant, he was tempted. "Yes, we could." He banked down the fires. "But we're not going to. We're married. We don't have to make out in cars. Here, sweetheart, let me help you."

He forced himself to control the singeing need in his body as he put her bra and dress back in place, delighted with her headlong response and the certainty that their marriage had a chance after all.

"I don't want to stop," she whispered.

"Neither do I. But we'll wait a while, all the same," he said curtly. He searched her face. "Before we both get blinded and sidetracked by intimacy, I want a little time for us to get to know each other. We'll go see my family and we'll do some things together. Then we'll sleep together."

She was stunned. That had to mean he cared a little, it had to! "I'd like that, Connal," she said.

He smiled at her. "Yes. So would I." He started the car and waited until she fastened her seat belt to drive off. But he held her hand the rest of the way home.

# Chapter Ten

Pepi and C.C. left the next morning for Jacobsville. Ben waved them off, muttering something about not knowing how he was going to keep from bursting with all that freedom and being alone with the apple pie Pepi had baked him that morning.

She hadn't been sure what to pack, so she put in her finest clothes and hoped for the best. None of her things were very expensive. She had a feeling that where she was going, they'd look like rags. But she didn't say that to C.C. He was suddenly very distant as he drove.

"You're not having second thoughts, are you?" she asked hesitantly. "About taking me to meet your mother, I mean?"

He glanced at her, astonished. "Why should I?"

She shifted and glanced out at the flat horizon. "Well, C.C., I don't know a lot about fancy place settings and etiquette, and I stayed up half the night worrying about what would happen if I got flustered and spilled coffee on her carpet or something."

He reached over and found her hand, entwining her cold, nervous fingers with his strong, warm ones.

"Now, listen. My mother is a ranch wife. She's as down-to-earth as your father, and she doesn't have one of those houses that get featured in the designer magazines. If you spilled coffee she'd just point you toward the kitchen and tell you where she keeps the spot remover. Fancy place settings aren't necessary, because Jeanie May cooks such great meals that nobody cares about formal etiquette once they get to the table. The only real hazard is going to be my brother Harden, who'll go off into a black study at the thought of having to help entertain you."

"Who hurt him like that, made him so bitter?" she asked.

He glanced at her. "Well, you'll hear it sooner or later. Better you hear it from me. About a year after Evan was born, my mother and father got a separation. During that time, she met and fell in love with another man. There was a brief affair. Her lover was killed in Vietnam and she came back to my father finally because he kept pleading with her. She was pregnant with Harden, so Dad adopted him. But Jacobsville is a small town, and inevitably, Harden found out the hard way that he wasn't Dad's son."

"And he blames your mother."

"That's right, he does. Despite the fact that she's a pillar of the community now, Harden can't forget that she took a lover while she was still legally married. He can't forgive her for making him conspicuous, an outcast as he calls it."

"But your father adopted him, doesn't that count for anything?" she asked.

He shook his head. "Harden has the most rigid views of any of us. He's an old-line conservative with Neanderthal principles." He glanced toward her with a rueful smile. "I'd bet you that he's still a virgin. I don't think he's even had a woman."

Her eyes widened. She remembered Harden's astonishing good looks, his physique, his rugged personality. Harden a virgin? She burst out laughing. "Not nice," she accused. "Teasing me like that."

"I'm not teasing, as it happens, I'm serious," he replied. "Harden is a deacon in the church and he sings in the choir. In fact, there was a time when he seriously considered being a minister."

"How old is he?"

"Thirty-one."

"A year older than you?" she asked.

He nodded. "Mother and Dad had a rather physical reunion when she came home. They were happy together, but I don't think she ever really got over the other man. And despite the fact that Harden hates her, he's her favorite even now."

"Forgiveness is a virtue," she said. "I guess not everybody is capable of it, but I'm sorry for your mother."

"You won't be, when you meet her. She's spunky. Like you."

She leaned her head back and smiled at him, her eyes faintly possessive. Memories of the night before streamed back to fire her blood and lingered in her pale brown eyes.

He stopped at an intersection and looked back at her, his own eyes kindling with what he read in that level stare.

"Remembering?" he asked huskily.

"Yes," she whispered.

His breath came more quickly, his brown sports shirt rising and falling roughly over his broad chest. His gaze went down to her breasts under the pale green shirtwaist dress she was wearing and lingered there. "You were like warm silk under my mouth," he bit off.

She gasped.

His eyes lifted back to hers and time stopped. "This isn't the place," he said tightly.

"No."

He glanced around and behind them. Not a single car in sight. "On the other hand, what the hell," he murmured and threw the car out of gear. "Come here."

He snapped open her seat belt and pulled her to him, his hard mouth crushing down over hers in a fever of ardent need. She circled his head with her arms and held on for dear life, giving him back the kiss hungrily. Her body throbbed with need of him, her mouth shaking as his tongue penetrated it insistently.

He dragged his head up at the distant sound of a big truck coming closer and spotted it in the rearview mirror. "Obviously he's not a married man," he muttered, putting a radiant, breathless Pepi back in her seat and buckling her in. "Damn it." He put the car in gear again, his hands slightly unsteady on the wheel, looked both ways and pulled out onto the highway.

He glanced at her hungrily. "Tonight, I'm going to have you. One way or the other, the waiting's over."

Her lips parted on a rough breath. "Are the walls very thin?" she asked hesitantly.

"We'll be in a room away from the others," he said curtly. "You can scream if you want to, nobody will hear you."

"I...I can't seem to be quiet when you start touching me," she said gently. "I lose control."

"So do I," he replied tersely.

She flushed. He made it sound very intimate and she wanted him. Her body blazed with the need, even now.

He glanced at her. "Baby, if you don't stop looking at me like that, I'll park the damned car and make love to you on the roadside," he threatened huskily.

"Anywhere," she said shakily. "Oh, Connal, I want you so much, it's like a fever."

His jaw tautened. He actually shivered. His eyes went to a small crossroads where a motel was situated. Without thinking, he pulled off and cut the engine. "Do you want me enough?" he asked, staring at her.

The fever was so high that even her shyness didn't faze it. "Yes," she whispered huskily, flushing.

He got out, went inside the office and came out with a key. He didn't say another word until they were in the room, with the door locked.

"Do you want me to use anything?" he asked before he touched her.

She knew what he was asking. She loved him. If a child came of this, it would be all right. He wanted one desperately, she knew.

"No," she said, going close to him. "Don't use anything."

He drew her slowly to him, already so aroused that his tall, fit body was shaking. "I don't know how long I can hold out," he breathed at her lips. "But I'll try to arouse you enough to make it bearable. And later, afterward, I'll make it up to you if I lose control."

She didn't understand what he was saying. His hands were on the buttons of her dress and she stood very still, letting him peel the clothing from her body until she was totally nude.

Her skin felt blazing hot. She was shy, and the way he was looking at her burned her, but it made her proud, too, because his pleasure in her body was evident in the glitter of his black eyes and the tenderness of his smile.

He jerked back the covers on the big double bed and picked her up, putting her down gently against the pillows. Then he set about removing his own clothing.

Pepi had seen pictures of naked men, but nothing had prepared her for the sight of Connal without clothing. He was magnificent, all lean hard muscle and black, curling hair. Aroused, his body was faintly intimidating and she held her breath when he came toward her.

"Don't panic," he said gently as he slid onto the bed beside her. "By the time we start, you'll be ready for me. Your body is like a pink rosebud, all silky and tightly furled. I'm going to open the petals, one by one, and make you bloom for me." He bent his mouth and took hers, very softly. One lean hand slid down her rib cage to her hips and over her thighs and back up to tease around her breast.

The embarrassment and shyness faded as he began to touch her, his fingers delicate and deft and sure on her untaught body. He lifted his head and looked at her, watched her reactions as he feathered caresses over her taut breasts, down her flat belly, to that place where she was most a woman. He touched her there and she shivered and tried to get away.

"No," he whispered tenderly, kissing her eyes closed. "This is part of it. You have to give yourself completely, or I could hurt you even without meaning to. I want to show you how it's going to feel. Relax, little one. Give me your body."

His lips coaxed lazily, and she gave in to the slow, tender probing of his fingers, shivering as she permitted the extraordinary intimacy. Her body reacted to him with headlong delight, arching and throbbing as he made it feel incredible sensations with his deft touch.

"It won't even be difficult for you," he whispered, smiling against her mouth. "Now it begins, little one. Now..."

The kiss grew deeper, invasive. His hand tormented and then began to move with a slow, torturously sweet rhythm that made her lift and tremble with each touch. She gasped and then little cries began to purr out of her. She reached for him, her nails digging into his upper arms as the pleasure built beyond anything she'd ever dreamed.

He smiled through his own fierce pleasure at the look on her face. His head bent to her breasts and he took one into his mouth with the same rhythmic movement his fingers were teaching her. All at once, she began to convulse.

And at that moment, he lifted his body completely over hers, nudging her long, shivering legs aside, and thrust down with one fierce, smooth movement.

She cried out, her eyes meeting his at the instant he took possession of her. But she didn't draw back, even at the faintly piercing pain that quickly diminished in the face of a slow, anguished pleasure that fed on itself and grew and grew with each sharp, downward movement of his body.

Somewhere along the way, his taut face became a blur, and she shuddered into oblivion just as she heard his hoarse cry and felt the deep, dragging convulsions of his body.

She opened her eyes at last, feeling new, reborn. Her skin was damp and cool. So was his. He was lying over her, dead weight now that the passion had drained out of him, and her arms enfolded him tenderly, holding him to her. She moved and felt him move with her, awed by the fusion of her female body with his male one, with the devastating intimacy of lovemaking.

"Did it hurt very much?" he asked at her ear, his voice drowsy with pleasure.

"No." Her arms contracted. "Do it again."

He chuckled. "I need a few minutes," he whispered. "Men aren't blessed with the capacity of women."

"Really?" She looked into his eyes as he lifted his dark, sweaty head. "You cried out."

"So did you," he said lazily. "Or don't you remember?"

"It all sort of blurred at the last," she replied. Her eyes mirrored her awe. "I hope I get a baby," she whispered. "It was so beautiful."

His face tautened and to his astonishment he felt his body react to the words with sudden, sharp capability.

She gasped. "Connal! You said—"

"Never mind what I said," he bit off against her mouth. His arms caught his weight and he began to move hungrily. "Help me this time," he whispered, and taught her how. "Yes, like that, like...that," he gasped, shivering as the wave began to catch him all over again. Impossible, he thought while he could. His teeth clenched. He could feel her eyes on him. She was...watching him...and he was so caught up in the fevered need that he didn't even mind. Her body, soft like down, silky, hot, absorbed him into it, holding him...

He arched, hoping against hope that she was still with him as he felt the sensation blind him with pleasure.

"Are you all right?"

He heard her voice and managed to open his eyes. She was above him, now, her face concerned, her pale brown eyes curious and gentle.

His heart was still slamming wildly against his chest. He could barely breathe. He pushed back his damp hair and drew her mouth down to his, kissing her tenderly.

"Yes, I'm all right," he whispered.

"You looked scary," she managed. "Like you were being killed. And you cried out..."

He laughed wearily. "My God, honey, why do you think the French call it the little death?" he asked. He drew her hand to his mouth. "You look the same way," he added, smiling. "I watched you, the first time."

"Oh." She colored a little. "I watched you, the second."

"Yes, I know." Hid dark eyes held hers. "It's all right," he said when she looked faintly guilty. "Total intimacy is a gift, something that two people share. Don't be embarrassed by anything you say or do when you're with me like this. I'll never ridicule you with it. I want you to feel completely uninhibited when we make love, as free to take me as I am to take you."

Her eyes widened. "Could I?"

"Well, not right now," he murmured ruefully.

"I didn't mean right now. You'd let me?"

He frowned slightly. "Of course I'd let you. You're my wife."

"And you...won't mind if I get pregnant right away?" she persisted.

"I told you I wanted a child," he said simply. His dark eyes narrowed. "They say a woman can tell at the instant of conception," he murmured.

She smiled down at him gently. "I don't think I can," she said. The smile faded and she traced his thin lips with a trembling forefinger. "Connal, what if I can't give you a child?" she asked worriedly. "Will you want a divorce...?"

"No!" He dragged her down to him and kissed her roughly. His eyes blazed at her. "It isn't a conditional marriage," he said firmly. "If you can't, it won't matter, so stop thinking up things to worry about."

"All right." She relaxed against him, sighing with pleasure as she felt the crisp hair on his broad chest tickling her breasts. She laughed softly and moved deliberately from side to side. "That feels good," she whispered.

"Yes, indeed, it does," he murmured, indulging her. "But you've had enough for one day. You're much too new to the art for long sessions in bed."

She opened her eyes and stared across his hair-covered chest to the window beyond. "Connal, it's addictive, isn't it?" she asked lazily. "Once you know what it's like, you want it more every time."

"Yes." His arms contracted. "No regrets?"

"Not even one," she whispered. She closed her eyes and nestled closer, smoothing one of her long legs against his powerful, hair-roughened one. "I ache."

"So do I," he confessed. "But we have to stop."

She sat up, her eyes slow and possessive on his body, openly curious. He watched her with evident amusement as she learned him by sight.

"I've never seen a man without his clothes before," she said.

"I'm glad. You won't be able to compare me unfavorably with anyone else," he mused.

She laughed. "As if anybody could compare with you," she murmured. "You're beautiful, Connal. You're just beautiful."

He sat up and kissed her warmly. "Men aren't beautiful," he said firmly, and got up to dress.

"Handsome, then. Physically devastating." She stretched hugely, enjoying the way his eyes slid over her appreciatively. "I used to think about being with you, like this, but it was always night and the lights were out."

"What a shock you were in for," he said dryly.

She stood up, smiling at him. "It was a very nice shock, actually," she said.

He pulled her gently into his arms and kissed her. "I hope I gave you half as much pleasure as you gave me," he whispered. "The fact that you came to me a virgin is something I'll treasure all my life."

She hugged him fiercely. "You make me glad that I waited," she murmured. "None of my friends did. They used to make fun of me."

"I never will," he said, tapping her gently on the nose. His eyes were brilliant with some inner feeling. "Get your clothes on."

"Fancy telling a woman that," she sighed. "And after she's given you everything she has."

"Oh, I'd keep you like that forever," he murmured, tracing her soft lines with his eyes. "But people are bound to stare if you go out like that."

"I get your point." She put her clothes on again and brushed her hair. Connal was waiting when she came out of the bathroom.

"Is this dress all right?" she asked worriedly. "I won't look too out of place, will I?"

He tilted her face up and kissed her. "You look just right, Mrs. Tremayne."

"I like the way that sounds," she whispered, thinking that it would be even more special if he loved her as much as she loved him. But he'd been gentle, and he must care for her a little to have been so tender.

"Legally mine," he murmured. His eyes darkened. "So don't give Evan any ideas."

Her face mirrored her shock. "I've only seen him once," she began.

"He thinks you're the berries," he replied. "And he's a lonely man. Don't encourage him."

"I noticed you didn't mention Harden. Don't you want to protect him, too?"

He ignored the sarcasm, shocked by his own possessiveness, his sudden sharp jealousy. "Harden's immune. Evan isn't."

"Listen here, C. C. Tremayne, just because I liked sleeping with you is no reason to accuse me of being a loose woman...!"

"Point one," he said, covering her lips with a firm forefinger, "I am not accusing you of anything. And point two, what we just did together had nothing, not a damned thing, to do with sleeping."

"Ticky, ticky," she returned.

He searched her eyes slowly. "I've never had it like that," he said curtly. "Not with anyone. Not so bad that I cried out and damned near fainted from the force of the pleasure when you satisfied me. I don't know that I like losing control that savagely."

She felt a fierce pride that she'd done that to him, and her eyes told him so. "Suppose I make you like it?" she whispered huskily.

His heart began to thunder against his ribs all over again at her sultry tone. "Think you could?" he challenged.

She moved closer, her finger toying with one of the pearly buttons at his throat. "Wait and see," she said softly. She reached up and teased his lips with hers, a fleeting touch that aroused without satisfying.

He watched her go to the door with a feeling of having given up a part of himself that he was going to miss like hell one day. She knew how he reacted to her, and that gave her a weapon. She enjoyed lovemaking, that was obvious, but she'd said she didn't love him. If she ever realized how hopelessly in love with her he was, she'd have him on the end of a hook that he'd never get free from. He almost shivered with apprehension. Accidental marriage or not, he wanted this woman with blind obsession. Whatever happened now, he wasn't going to give her up.

They drove the rest of the way to Jacobsville in a tense silence. C.C. smoked cigarettes until Pepi had to let down a window in self-defense. He seemed nervous, and she wondered if it was coming home that had him in such a state, or bringing her here. Despite his denials, she wondered how she was going to be received by his family. He was used to wealth and society people, and she wasn't. Would they even accept her?

He drove past a huge feedlot, through the country and down a long winding paved road until he reached an arch that boasted a sign that read Tremayne.

"Home," he murmured, smiling at her. He sped down the driveway in the Ford, while Pepi clenched her hands in her lap and hoped that she could cope. There were white fences on either side of the driveway, and far in the distance sat a white Victorian house with a long porch and beautiful gingerbread latticework. There were flower beds everywhere, and right now assorted chrysanthemums were blooming in them.

"It's beautiful," she said, her eyes lingering on the tall trees around the house.

"I've always thought so. There's Mother."

Theodora Tremayne was small and thin and dark, with silver hair that gleamed in the sun. She was wearing jeans and a sweatshirt with an apron. She rushed out to meet them.

"Thank God you're home," she said, hugging Connal. "You must be Pepi, I'm so glad to meet you." She hugged Pepi, too, before she turned back to her tall son. "The sink in the kitchen is stopped up and I can't find Evan anywhere! Can you fix it?"

"Don't you have a plumber's helper?" Connal asked with a wry smile.

"Of course. What do you want with it?" she asked blankly.

"She had a flat tire on the wheelbarrow," he told Pepi.

"Go ahead, blurt out all the shameful family secrets at once!" Theodora raged at him. "Why don't you tell her about the mouse under the sink that I can't catch, and the snake who insists on living in my root cellar?"

Pepi burst out laughing. She couldn't help it. She'd been so afraid of some rich society matron who'd make fun of her, and here instead was Theodora Tremayne, who was nothing short of a leprechaun.

"I'm glad to see you have a sense of humor, Pepi," Theodora said approvingly. "You'll need it if you have to live with my son. He has no sense of humor. None

of my sons do. They all walk around like thunder-
heads, glowering at everybody.''

"Nobody glowers except Harden,'' C.C. said defensively.

"He's enough,'' Theodora said miserably. "He gets
worse all the time. Well, come in and fix the sink, son.
Pepi, do you like ham sandwiches? I'm afraid that's
all I could get together in a hurry. I've been out helping Evan and the boys brand new calves and things are
in a bit of a mess.''

She went on mumbling ahead of them. Connal
caught Pepi's hand.

"No more worried thoughts?'' he asked with an
amused smile.

"None at all. She's a treasure!'' she said.

He slid his arm around her and hugged her close.
"She isn't the only treasure around here,'' he whispered, and bent to kiss her.

Pepi went inside with him, her feet barely touching
the floor. She wondered if she wouldn't float right up
to the ceiling, she was so happy. He had to care a little. He just had to!

## Chapter Eleven

But Connal's earlier warmth seemed to disintegrate as the day wore on. He fixed his mother's sink, leaving Pepi to help a flustered Theodora set the dining-room table.

"I'm so glad he's coming out of the past," Theodora told the younger woman with sincere gratitude. "You don't know how it's been for us, watching him beat himself to death over something he couldn't have helped. He came to see us, occasionally, and there were phone calls and letters. But it's not the same thing as regular contact."

"We never knew anything about his past; Dad and I, that is," Pepi said. "But C.C. always had class. You couldn't miss it. I used to wonder why he buried himself on a run-down place like ours."

"He speaks highly of your father," Theodora said.

"And he, uh, had a lot to say about you, too, the last time he was here."

Pepi blushed, lowering her eyes to the plate she was putting on the table. Thank God she knew where the knife, fork and spoon went, and it wasn't one of those elaborate settings that she couldn't figure out. "I guess he did," she answered Theodora. "He was furious when he left the ranch. I didn't blame him, you know," she said, lifting quiet brown eyes to the other woman's face. "He had every right to hate me for not telling him the truth."

Theodora searched those soft eyes. "He's hurt you badly, hasn't he?" she asked unexpectedly. "Does he know how you feel?"

The blush got worse. Pepi's hand shook as she laid the silverware. "No," she said in a whisper. "If he even considers it, he probably thinks I'm in the throes of physical attraction. And for right now, it's safer that way. I'm not convinced that I can ever be the kind of wife he needs. You see," she added worriedly, "I'm not sophisticated."

Theodora impulsively went around the table and hugged her, warmly. "If he lets you get away from him, I'll beat him with a big stick," she said forcefully. "I'll go and bring in the sandwiches and call the boys in. Don't look so worried, Penelope, they won't take any bites out of you!" she said with a grin.

Pepi sat down where Theodora had indicated, and a minute or so later, the older woman came back with a huge platter of sandwiches, closely followed by her three towering sons.

"Hello, again," Evan said warmly, seating himself beside Pepi. "What a treat, having something pretty to look at while I eat," he added, with a meaningful glance toward his brother Harden.

Harden lifted a dark eyebrow, glancing with cold indifference at Pepi. "I've told you before, if you don't like looking at me while you eat, wear a blindfold."

"God forbid, he'd probably eat the tablecloth!" Theodora chuckled. "Sit down, Connal, don't dither."

"Yes, ma'am," he murmured, but his smile wasn't reflected in his eyes as he glanced with open disapproval at Evan sitting beside Pepi.

"Say Grace, Harden," Theodora said.

He did, and everyone became occupied with sandwiches and coffee preparation. Evan told Pepi about the ranch and its history while Harden ate in silence and Theodora quizzed Connal about his future plans.

Pepi couldn't hear what Connal was saying, but she did feel the angry lash of his eyes. She wondered what she'd done to make him so cold toward her. Could he be regretting that impulsive stop at the motel? She flushed a little, embarrassed at the memories that flooded her mind. She still ached pleasantly from the experience. But perhaps it was different for a man, if he didn't love a woman he slept with. Connal had wanted her with a raging passion, she couldn't have mistaken that. But afterward he might have regretted his loss of control, the lapse that had turned an accidental marriage into a real one. He might be having second thoughts about Edie even now. He looked odd, too. Very taciturn and quiet. Pepi knew that mood very well. It was the one that caused the men to keep well away from him, because when he got broody, he got quick-tempered, too. Pepi hoped he wasn't spoiling for a fight with her.

"I always wanted a sister," Evan murmured dryly. "What I got was Connal and Donald and...him," he shuddered as he glanced at Harden.

Harden kept eating, totally impervious to the insult.

"You won't get through his hide with insults," Theodora told her son. "I tend to think he thrives on them."

"You should know," Harden told her, his blue eyes as cold as the smile he bent on her.

"Not now," she told him firmly. "We have guests."

"Family," Evan corrected.

"Yours, not mine," Harden said with a pointed glare at his mother. "No offense," he added to Connal.

"You plan to carry the vendetta to your grave, I gather," Theodora muttered.

"I've got to get back to work," Harden said, rising. "I'll see you tonight, Connal."

He walked out, lean and lithe and arrow-straight, without a backward glance.

"Now that the company has improved, what do you think of our quaint little place?" Evan asked Pepi.

She replied automatically, her mind on the awkward conversation that had gone before. If this was any indication of how things were going to go for the duration of her visit, she wasn't at all sure she wanted to stay.

But it got better, without Harden's difficult presence. Evan took her in hand before Connal could protest and drove off with her in the ranch Jeep.

"What about Connal...?" she asked uneasily, glancing back to where he stood with Theodora glaring after them.

"Now, now, all I have in mind is a little brotherly chat," Evan replied, and the teasing was abruptly gone. As he glanced at her without smiling, she saw in Evan the same steely character that had intimidated her first in C.C. and then in Harden.

He pulled the Jeep off on the side of the ranch road when they were out of sight of the house, and cut the engine. "Edie called here this morning, looking for Connal," he said without preamble.

"Oh. I see." She studied the broad, leonine features quietly. He and Connal looked alike. Although Evan's hair was more brown than black, he had the same piercing, unsmiling sternness as his brother.

"I don't think you do," Evan replied. "Edie isn't the kind of woman to take a rebuff lying down. She didn't believe him when he told her he was married. She thought he was being tricked by a fake license, and she told me so."

She sighed heavily. "Well, it's easy enough to check, you know," she said.

"Undoubtedly. I did, when Connal showed us the license." He smiled ruefully at her glare. "No offense, child, but he stands to inherit a hell of a fortune when Mother passes on. He's not exactly a poverty case now, and I didn't know you from a peanut when he came storming in here waving that damned license and cursing at the top of his lungs."

"But Connal said it was you who changed his mind about staying married to me," she faltered.

He leaned back against the Jeep door, big and elegant-looking for a cattleman, his Stetson pushed back over his broad forehead. "Sure I did," he mused. "One of these days I'll let you read what my private detective said about you. You're the kind of woman mothers dream about finding for their sons. A walking, talking little elf with domestic skills and a gentle heart. In this oversexed, undercompassionate generation, you're a miracle. I told Connal so. Eventually he began to realize that he could do a lot worse."

"I wonder." She sighed.

"Edie doesn't seem to agree, so watch out," he cautioned sternly. "Don't let her spring any surprises on you. Forewarned is forearmed, right?"

"Right. Thanks, Evan."

"Connal deserves a little happiness," he said tersely. "He never had much with Marsha, and she couldn't bear to have him out of her sight five seconds. It's time he stopped beating himself to death."

"I think so, too," she said gently. "I'll take good care of him, Evan." *If I get to,* she added silently.

He smiled almost tenderly. "I gather that you've been doing that very well for the past three years," he said, his deep voice warm with affection. "We'd better get back. I thought you ought to know what the competition was up to so there wouldn't be any unexpected surprises."

"I'll watch my back," she promised.

Evan drove her around the ranch and pointed out herd sires along the way. He seemed to have a phenomenal memory for their names, because he never seemed to draw a blank. He was in a jovial mood for the rest of the way home.

But Connal was in a furious one when they got there. He gave his brother a glare that would have fried a defenseless egg, and the one he bent on Pepi made her feel like backing away.

Theodora pretended not to notice the tension. She herded them into her four-by-four and they drove into Jacobsville to get some more supplies for roundup.

She seemed to know everyone. Pepi lost her nervousness as she was introduced to several people at the hardware store, including a harassed young woman herding three small children through the aisles, followed by a tall blond man.

"The Ballengers," Theodora told Pepi, "Abby and Calhoun. That's Matt... no, it's Terry... and that's Edd," she said, trying to identify each child.

"You've got it just backward, Theodora," Calhoun drawled. "Terry, Edd and Matt."

"Between your kids and your brother Justin's children, I can't keep the names straight!"

"And Justin and Shelby have another one on the way," Calhoun chuckled. "Shelby's sure this one is going to be a girl."

"After two boys I can understand her determination," Theodora replied.

"We gave up," Abby sighed. "I like boys and I'm tired of the maternity ward, not to mention never being able to get one word in edgewise. They'd trample my dead body to get to their Daddy."

"They sure would, but I still love you," Calhoun murmured and kissed her forehead warmly.

She melted against him, almost visibly a part of him. Pepi felt a twinge of sadness that she might never know that kind of devotion. Apparently desire was all she aroused in C.C., and the way he was acting, he might not even feel that anymore. His lean face was as hard as if it had been carved out of granite, and he didn't move a step closer to Pepi when she was introduced as his wife. It was hard to pretend that everything was fine, that she was divinely happy, when her heart was breaking.

Later, Theodora took her on a tour of Jacobsville, named after Shelby Ballenger's family, and pointed out the huge Ballenger feedlot and the old Jacobs's home, now owned by a new resident. Back at the ranch, Theodora produced photo albums, while the men went out to check on the progress of the branding.

There was little conversation over the supper table. The pert, gangly cook made some acid comments about the enormous male appetites and grinned on her way back to the kitchen.

"She's been here for so long that she owns the kitchen," Theodora explained merrily. "She loves clean platters after a meal."

"She's a wonderful cook," Pepi mused.

"I hear you make wonderful apple pies," Evan commented dryly.

"I don't know about that," Pepi said shyly. "My dad seems to think they're pretty good, because he sure hates sharing them."

"I don't blame him." Evan glared at Harden and his mother. "I hardly ever get my fair share of any dessert around here."

Theodora's eyebrows arched. "Penelope, his idea of a fair share is two-thirds of the pie."

"I'm going seedy, anybody can see that," Evan protested. "Wasting away from starvation..."

Pepi laughed delightedly, her eyes twinkling at Evan, who was sitting beside her.

Across the table, Connal wasn't laughing. He was tormenting himself with that smile and reading all sorts of ridiculous ideas into it. She'd been attracted to Evan since the first time she'd seen him, and today she'd gone off with him all too willingly. Now she was hanging on his every word. He was losing Pepi. If all she'd felt for him was a sensual curiosity, now that he'd satisfied that, she might have no interest left in him. God, what if she fell in love with Evan? His face contorted and he averted it quickly, before anyone saw his anguish.

After supper, Theodora produced a new video as a special treat, a first-run comedy that Pepi had been dying to see. But her enthusiasm quickly waned when C.C. left in the middle stating that he needed to make a few business calls.

Pepi excused herself shortly thereafter and went toward the study, hoping to have it out with C.C. But he wasn't there. With a leaden sigh, she went out the front door, pulling her sweater closer around her, and sat alone on the steps to look out over the dark horizon.

The door opened and closed. Expecting, hoping, that it was C.C., she got to her feet. But it was Harden.

Of all the men she'd ever met, he made her the most nervous.

"Am I intruding?" he asked quietly.

"No. I . . . just wanted a little air," she stammered. "I'd better go back in now."

He caught her arm, very gently, and held her in place. "There's no need to be afraid of me," he said softly. "None of my vendettas, as Theodora calls them, involve you."

She relaxed a little when he let her go and lit a cigarette.

"Connal's been watching you all night," he said after a minute. "Brooding. Did you argue before you came here?"

"No," she said, glad of the dark because she blushed remembering what they'd done before they came here. "We were getting along better than we had in some time, in fact. Then when we got here, he closed up."

"About the time you went off with Evan," he suggested.

"Well . . . yes."

"I thought so."

"But that was so Evan could tell me about the phone call," she said, puzzled.

He moved into the light from the windows, frowning. "What phone call?"

"There's this lady C.C. used to go around with," she said wearily. "Edie. Evan says she called here looking for C.C. because she thinks I faked the marriage license."

"Sour grapes, I expect," he mused. "Did you tell Connal why you went off with Evan?"

"I haven't had a chance. He seems to be avoiding me. I guessed maybe he was having second thoughts, again. He was sure mad when he found out the marriage was valid," she said, grimacing. "I thought he'd never speak to me again as long as he lived. Then when I agreed to an annulment and started the wheels turning, he showed up again and said he didn't want one." She threw up her hands. "I don't know what he wants anymore. Maybe he's missing Edie and angry because he's stuck with me."

"Maybe he's jealous," he murmured dryly. "I see that thought hadn't occurred to you," he added when she gaped at him.

"C.C.'s never been jealous of me," she faltered. "My gosh, he never wanted me. Well, not for a wife, I mean . . ." She averted her red face when she remembered who she was talking to.

Harden actually laughed, the sound deep and pleasant in the night air. "He's a man. And it does rather go with marriage."

"I suppose so," she murmured. "But he doesn't have any reason to be jealous of Evan. I always wanted a big brother, you see."

"And Evan is a teddy bear, right?"

"Well, yes . . ."

"That particular teddy bear has some nasty fangs and a temper you're better off not knowing about," he advised. "He likes you, but Marsha wouldn't come near the place because of him. He hated her from head to heels and made no secret of it."

"But he's so nice," she said.

"You're not doing business with him," he chuckled. "Evan's deep. Just don't put too much stock in that boyish charm. I'd hate to have you totally disillusioned when he throws somebody over a fence."

"Evan?" she gasped.

"One of the new men took a short quirt to a filly and drew blood. Evan heaved him over the fence and jumped it himself. The last we saw of the man, he was tearing through the blackberry thicket like a scalded dog trying to outrun Evan."

She was beginning to get a good idea of what the Tremayne men were really like. She whistled silently. "My, my, and here I thought you were the terror of the outfit." She grinned.

"Oh, I'm right down the line behind your husband and Evan."

"And Donald, is that his name, the youngest?"

"Donald puts Tabasco Sauce on his biscuits," he replied. "And I have personally seen him skin men at five feet when he's angry."

"I don't know that I want to be related to you savages," she said, tongue in cheek.

"Sure you do," he replied. "Once you get to know us, you'll feel right at home. Any woman who'll take on Connal has to be a hell-raiser in her own right. God knows Jo Ann is, or she'd never have lasted three years with Donald."

She laughed. "I can't wait to meet them."

"They're away for two weeks on business, I'm sorry to say. Another time."

"Yes." She glanced toward the front door. "I suppose I'd better go and try to find my husband."

"That's a step in the right direction. Good night, Penelope."

"Good night, Harden," she replied, smiling as he went down the steps and out to his car. He was nice. Like the rest of C.C.'s family.

She said good night to the others and went upstairs, wondering if she could work up enough nerve to seduce her own husband.

# Chapter Twelve

It was barely ten o'clock, but when Penelope got to the room where Connal had taken their suitcases, it was to find him already in bed and apparently asleep.

She hesitated. The lamp by the king-size bed was on, but the bare chest half-covered by the plaid sheet was rising and falling regularly.

"Connal?" she asked softly, but he didn't answer.

With a long sigh, she got out her gown and took it into the bathroom to put it on. This was not the night she'd envisioned, and her courage failed her when she walked back into the bedroom minutes later wearing the long green nylon gown.

She climbed slowly into bed beside him, gave his dark head and his hair-covered muscular chest a long look, and resignedly turned out the light.

But she couldn't sleep. She tossed and turned, remembering so vividly the ardor she'd shared with C.C.

only hours before. Her body had never ached so when she'd been unawakened. Now she knew what desire was, and she felt it so acutely that it was almost pain.

"Can't you sleep?" he asked, his voice deep and clear, not muffled with drowsiness.

"Not very well," she said. She lay on her side, looking toward the dark shape that was his head. Dim light from the safety lights by the barn shone in through the curtains. "I guess it's because I'm not used to sleeping with anyone," she added.

"Neither am I, just lately." He reached out and drew her slowly against him. Her hand came in contact with his bare hip and she realized belatedly that he wasn't wearing pajamas.

He felt her stiffen unexpectedly and chuckled under his breath. "You saw me nude just this morning," he reminded her. "And I saw you. Is it still such a shock? Or is it just that I'm the wrong man?" he added sarcastically.

"The wrong man?" she echoed.

"You've been hanging on Evan all day," he said. His hands smoothed up her body, his thumbs edging out to rub against her sensitive nipples. "Are your marriage vows uncomfortable all of a sudden?"

"C.C., that's not true," she said quietly. "I like Evan very much, but I haven't been hanging on him."

His fingers bit into her sides. "I wouldn't really expect you to admit it. Maybe I can't even blame you. One way or another, I got us into this mess."

A mess. He was admitting that it was that, in his eyes. Her heart plummeted. "I thought you were making a phone call. I went looking for you," she said, making a clean breast of it.

"I made it up here," he said. "I had to call Edie."

Her heart stopped beating. She wanted to hit him. So Evan's warning had been right on the money, had it? That woman wasn't going to give up, and if C.C. had no qualms about calling her from his family home, then he must have misgivings about breaking off with her in the first place.

Connal felt her go rigid and his heart jumped. That was the first hopeful sign he'd ever had that she might care a little for him. God, if only it were true!

"Nothing to say?" he chided.

She ground her teeth together. "I think I can sleep now," she said through them.

"Can you?" He moved the covers away and while she was dealing with that unexpected action, his lips came down squarely over her breast, taking the nipple and the fabric that covered it into the hot darkness of his open mouth.

The cry that tore out of her throat was music to his ears. He shifted and while his mouth made intimate love to hers, he stripped the gown down her trembling body and his hands relearned its soft, sweet contours with a lazy thoroughness that had her moaning in his arms.

"Can I have you without hurting you?" he whispered at her ear, his breath as hot as the body threatening hers.

"Yes," she whimpered. Her nails bit into his shoulders, tugging at them, her legs already parting to admit him, her body lifting to meet the fierce, heated descent of his. "Connal...!"

"Take me," he ground out against her mouth as his hips thrust down in one long, invasive movement.

She whimpered under the sharp pleasure, clinging to him as his body enforced its possession with increasing urgency. "Don't stop, Connal, don't... stop...!"

His mouth bit at hers. "You're noisy," he breathed huskily. "I like it. I like the way you feel, the way you taste. Tell me you want me."

"I...want...you!" She could barely get the words out. He was killing her. The pleasure was too sweet to bear and she was going to die of it.

She said so, her voice breaking as he fulfilled her with savage urgency, finding his own shuddering release seconds later.

She couldn't stop trembling. She clung to his damp body, frightened by the force of the satisfaction he'd given her.

He felt tears against his cheek and lifted his head. His heartbeat was still shaking him, his arms trembling as they supported him above her. He couldn't see her face, but he could feel the convulsive shudders of her body, feel how disturbed she was from the grip of her hands.

"Don't be afraid," he whispered. "We went very high this time. Give yourself time to come down again. It's all right." His fingers smoothed back her damp hair and he kissed her eyes closed, kissed her cheeks, her trembling mouth in a warm, soft silence that gradually took the fear away.

"You said . . . I was noisy," she whispered.

"Didn't I say that I liked it?" he murmured. He bit her lower lip gently. "Touch me."

He guided her hand to him, and smiled when she hesitated shyly.

"We're married," he said. He opened her fingers and spread them, pressing them slowly against him. "You won't hurt me, if that's why you're so tense," he whispered. He kissed her gently and in between kisses, he guided and coaxed and in soft whispers, explained to her everything she needed to know about a man's body.

The lesson was sweet and lazy and slow, and as her eyelids began to fall drowsily, he joined her body tenderly, intimately, to his and pulled her over him to cradle her softness on his strength. Incredibly, she slept.

They went home the next day. Connal was less rigid, and seemed perfectly happy all the way back to the ranch. But he was preoccupied again by the end of the day, and he didn't mention sharing her bed that night.

It became a routine for several days. He was friendly enough, even affectionate, but he didn't touch her or kiss her. He did watch her, with brooding, narrow eyes as if he couldn't decide what to do.

She was still worried about the phone call he said he'd made to Edie, and if his desire for her had waned because of the other woman.

"What's going on between you and my new son-in-law?" Ben Mathews finally demanded one morning in the kitchen after breakfast.

"What do you mean?" she hedged. She had her hair in a ponytail and she was wearing a sweater and jeans and scuffs, less than elegant attire. C.C. hadn't even come in for breakfast for the second time in as many days.

"I mean, you and Connal are married, but you don't act like it," he said bluntly. "And ever since you came home from his family's ranch, you've both gone broody. Why?"

"He called Edie," she said quietly. "I don't know if he's looking for a way out or trying to make me get a divorce. He hasn't said. But he's not happy, I know that." She glanced at him, hoping to forestall any more personal questions. "Don't you have to be in El Paso at eleven for a meeting?" she asked.

"Yes, I do, and I'm going any minute. Why not an annulment?"

She blushed and put her hands back in the warm, soapy dishwater. "For the obvious reason," she said demurely.

"Then if that's the case, why aren't you living together? There's a furnished house going spare, if that's the problem."

She felt tears stinging her eyes. "It's more than that."

"What?"

She dropped a pan and in the ensuing noise, nobody heard C.C. come in the front door and down the hall. He was standing right outside the door, about to make his presence known, when he heard Pepi's choked voice.

"I'll tell you what," she wept. "He doesn't love me. He never did, and I didn't expect it, you know. But I had hoped . . ."

Ben pulled her gently into his arms and held her while she cried. "You poor kid," he sighed, patting her back comfortingly. "I don't guess you ever told him you were dying for love of him?"

Connal felt his body go rigid with the shock. He couldn't have moved if his life had depended on it.

"No, I never told him," Pepi sobbed. "Three years. Three long, awful years. And we got married by accident, and I knew he wouldn't want somebody plain and tomboyish like me, but oh, God, Papa, I love him so much! What am I going to do?"

Connal moved into the room, white-faced, his dark eyes blazing. "You might try telling him," he said harshly.

Ben let her go and moved away, a smug grin on his face that he quickly hid from them. "I'm late. Better be off. See you kids after lunch."

They didn't even hear him leave. Connal was still staring at her with an expression she could barely see through her tears.

"Oh, mother!" she wailed. "Why did you have to stand out there and listen!"

"Why not?" He moved closer, catching her arms and jerking her close, his bat-wing chaps hard and cold even through her jeans, like the tan checked Western shirt her hands rested against. "Say it to my face. Tell me you love me," he dared, his taut expression a challenge in itself, giving nothing away of his own feelings.

"All right. I love you!" she burst out. "There, are you satisfied?" she raged, red-faced.

"Not yet," he murmured in a low, sexy tone. "But I think I can take care of that little problem right here..."

His mouth settled on hers in slow, arousing movements. It had been so long. Days of polite conversation, tormented lonely nights aching for what had been. She went wild in his arms, pressing close against him, welcoming the intimate touch of his hands on her breasts, their pressure at her thighs as he moved her urgently against his hips.

"Just a minute," he whispered gruffly, as he locked the door.

His hand then went to the chaps. He stripped them off and threw them on the floor, his hands going to her blouse and then her jeans. Somehow he managed to get them off along with the scuffs she'd been wearing instead of boots. He sat down in the chair at the kitchen table and pulled her over him.

There was a metallic sound as his belt hit the floor and the rasp of a zipper. He pulled her down on him, watching her eyes as she absorbed him easily, quickly.

"Forgive me," he whispered jerkily. "I can't wait."

"Neither can I," she whispered back, meeting his lips halfway. "I love you, Connal," she whimpered as he moved under her.

"I love you," he said huskily. "Oh, God, I love you more than my own life...!" He heard her shocked gasp and said it again and again, his hands insistent, demanding as he rocked her, lifted and pushed her in a rhythm that eventually shook the floor and the heavens.

She trembled uncontrollably. So did he. The explosion they'd kindled had all but landed them on the floor. He laughed huskily, lifting his head to meet her wickedly amused eyes.

"So much for new techniques borne of desperation," he murmured. "Now let's go upstairs and do it properly."

Hours later she nestled her cheek against his damp chest and opened her eyes. "We really ought to get dressed. Dad will be home eventually."

He kissed her forehead lazily. "I locked the door, remember?"

"So you did." She sighed, loving the new closeness they were sharing. "Harden said you were jealous of Evan."

"I was. Blind jealous, of him, of Hale, of any man who came near you. All these years together, and I didn't know that I loved you. Evan knew it instantly. And when I realized it, it was almost too late to stop you from getting an annulment." He shook her gently. "God, you've led me a merry chase! Even our first time, I was convinced that you were just curious about sex. I didn't think you gave a damn about me except physically."

"I've loved you since the first time I saw you," she whispered. "You became my world."

His arm tightened around her. "You were mine, too. It just took a while for me to realize it. Until that happened, I said some pretty harsh things to you. I hope in time you'll be able to forget them. I was running as fast as I could. It's taken me a long time to get over Marsha, but I think I have. I had to be whole again before I had anything to offer you. I had to stop being afraid of commitment, and it wasn't easy."

"Dad said that. I wasn't so optimistic. I thought you hated me."

"Wanted you, not hated you. And resented it like hell. Eventually you stayed on my mind so much that I burned from morning till night wanting you. It's becoming an obsession."

"Wanting isn't loving."

He chuckled. "I know that, too, but you have to admit, it's a big part of it." He kissed her closed eyelids. "I'd die for you, Penelope," he whispered huskily. "Will that do?"

"Oh, yes." She nuzzled her head against his chin. "Why did you call Edie?"

"I thought we'd come to that," he said, and grinned. "Evan told me what she was up to, so I phoned and told her that my marriage was perfectly legitimate and furthermore, I was desperately in love with my wife. I don't think we'll hear any more from her."

She lifted up, searching his face while he made a meal of her breasts with his eyes. "That's why Evan took me riding, to warn me that she'd called, looking for you!"

"Well, I'll be!" he burst out, diverted. "And he never said a word."

"Harden said you were jealous," she murmured dryly. "That gave me the first hope I'd had."

"How do you think I felt that night we spent together when you grumbled about Edie?" he laughed softly. "God, I'll never forget the way we made love then!" he whispered at her temple.

"Neither will I." She looked down into his eyes, her own fever kindling as she stared at him, her body tautening visibly. "Connal..." she whispered, her voice shaking.

His jaw tautened. He caught her waist and lifted her over him, pulling her down on his hips. "Yes," he whispered. "I need you, too. Again, little one."

"I don't think I can, this way..." she hesitated.

"Yes, you can," he said huskily. "I'll teach you. Like this, Pepi..."

She was shocked to discover that she could, indeed, and it was a long time before she was able to get up and dress afterward.

"Shy little country girl, hmmm?" he mused as they sat in the dining room sipping coffee and eating apple pie. "What an about-face!"

"It's the company I'm keeping," she murmured. "And we have a problem."

"You're pregnant?" he asked hopefully.

"That isn't a problem, and I may be but I don't know yet," she said. "I mean, we're married, but I don't have a wedding ring."

He grinned and pulled a box out of his jeans pocket. "Don't you?"

He held it out and she opened it, producing a beautiful set of rings—one with a big diamond, the other a gold band with inlaid diamonds that matched it.

"It's lovely," she said huskily. "But where's yours?" She glared at him. "You're wearing a ring, Connal Cade Tremayne. I won't have every lonely spinster in south Texas trying to trespass on my preserves!"

"Well, well," he murmured dryly. "Okay. We'll go into town and buy me one."

The front door slammed and her father came walking into the dining room, stopping suddenly. "My God!" he wailed.

"You noticed my rings, did you?" Pepi grinned.

"Tell him that we're moving into the vacant house this afternoon, that'll unfreeze him," Connal dared.

"We are," she told her father. She frowned. "What's the matter with you? Aren't you happy that our marriage is going to work out and Connal and I are going to live together and you're going to have grandchildren at last? Aren't you happy about all that?"

"Of course I am, Pepi," he groaned. "It's just..."

"Just?" Connal prompted.

"Just?" Pepi seconded.

"Damn it," he raged, slamming his hat down. "You've eaten my apple pie!"

Several weeks later, Pepi made him a present of three freshly baked pies and the news that he was going to become a grandfather. She told Connal after-

ward that she wasn't sure which of her presents made
him smile the widest.

* * * * *

## MILLION DOLLAR SWEEPSTAKES (III)

No purchase necessary. To enter, follow the directions published. Method of entry may vary. For eligibility, entries must be received no later than March 31, 1996. No liability is assumed for printing errors, lost, late or misdirected entries. Odds of winning are determined by the number of eligible entries distributed and received. Prizewinners will be determined no later than June 30, 1996.

Sweepstakes open to residents of the U.S. (except Puerto Rico), Canada, Europe and Taiwan who are 18 years of age or older. All applicable laws and regulations apply. Sweepstakes offer void wherever prohibited by law. Values of all prizes are in U.S. currency. This sweepstakes is presented by Torstar Corp., its subsidiaries and affiliates, in conjunction with book, merchandise and/or product offerings. For a copy of the Official Rules send a self-addressed, stamped envelope (WA residents need not affix return postage) to: MILLION DOLLAR SWEEPSTAKES (III) Rules, P.O. Box 4573, Blair, NE 68009, USA.

## EXTRA BONUS PRIZE DRAWING

No purchase necessary. The Extra Bonus Prize will be awarded in a random drawing to be conducted no later than 5/30/96 from among all entries received. To qualify, entries must be received by 3/31/96 and comply with published directions. Drawing open to residents of the U.S. (except Puerto Rico), Canada, Europe and Taiwan who are 18 years of age or older. All applicable laws and regulations apply; offer void wherever prohibited by law. Odds of winning are dependent upon number of eligibile entries received. Prize is valued in U.S. currency. The offer is presented by Torstar Corp., its subsidiaries and affiliates in conjunction with book, merchandise and/or product offering. For a copy of the Official Rules governing this sweepstakes, send a self-addressed, stamped envelope (WA residents need not affix return postage) to: Extra Bonus Prize Drawing Rules, P.O. Box 4590, Blair, NE 68009, USA.

SWP-S795

# WESTERN *Lovers*

Stories by your favorite top authors with
romantic Western settings and lots of cowboys,
babies, reunited lovers, marriages of convenience
and much more!

In July, look for these great titles:

**CARVED IN STONE** by Kathleen Eagle
*"Ranch Rogues"...hard to tame, but easy to love!*

Sexy Sky Hunter is a full-blooded Sioux as rugged
as the Rocky Mountains he calls home. And when
he meets Wyoming newcomer Elaina Delacourte,
he's determined to give her some lessons about the
land...and love!

**SOMEONE WAITING** by Joan Hohl
*"Hitched in Haste": They bargained for marriage
but not for love!*

Royke Larson wanted a child and a wife was only a
means to that end. But saying "I do" with sultry
Stacy had him thinking less about a marriage of
convenience and more about a marriage of *forever!*

Don't miss each and every WESTERN LOVERS
title...all you love in romance—and more!

WL795

# As a Privileged Woman,
## you'll be entitled to all these *Free Benefits.* And *Free Gifts,* too.

To thank you for buying our books, we've designed an exclusive FREE program called *PAGES & PRIVILEGES*™. You can enroll with just one Proof of Purchase, and get the kind of luxuries that, until now, you could only read about.

## *B*IG HOTEL DISCOUNTS

**A privileged woman stays in the finest hotels.** And so can you—at up to 60% off! Imagine standing in a hotel check-in line and watching as the guest in front of you pays $150 for the same room that's only costing you $60. Your *Pages & Privileges* discounts are good at Sheraton, Marriott, Best Western, Hyatt and thousands of other fine hotels all over the U.S., Canada and Europe.

## *F*REE DISCOUNT TRAVEL SERVICE

**A privileged woman is always jetting to romantic places.** When <u>you</u> fly, just make one phone call for the lowest published airfare at time of booking—<u>or double the difference back!</u>  PLUS—

you'll get a $25 voucher to use the first time you book a flight AND <u>5% cash back on every ticket you buy thereafter through the travel service!</u>

# *F*REE GIFTS!

**A privileged woman is always getting wonderful gifts.**
Luxuriate in rich fragrances that will stir your senses (and his). This gift-boxed assortment of fine perfumes includes three popular scents, each in a beautiful designer bottle. <u>Truly Lace</u>...This luxurious fragrance unveils your sensuous side. <u>L'Effleur</u>...discover the romance of the Victorian era with this soft floral. <u>Muguet des bois</u>...a single note floral of singular beauty.

YOURS FREE!

$50 VALUE

# *F*REE INSIDER TIPS LETTER

**A privileged woman is always informed.** And you'll be, too, with our free letter full of fascinating information and sneak previews of upcoming books.

# *M*ORE GREAT GIFTS & BENEFITS TO COME

**A privileged woman always has a lot to look forward to.** And so will you. You get all these wonderful FREE gifts and benefits now with only one purchase...and there are no additional purchases required. However, each additional retail purchase of Harlequin and Silhouette books brings you a step closer to even more great FREE benefits like half-price movie tickets... and even more FREE gifts.

*L'Effleur*...This basketful of romance lets you discover L'Effleur from head to toe, heart to home.

*Truly Lace*...
A basket spun with the sensuous luxuries of Truly Lace, including Dusting Powder in a reusable satin and lace covered box.

*Complete the Enrollment Form in the front of this book and mail it with this Proof of Purchase.*

## PROOF OF PURCHASE

Offer expires October 31, 1996

BR-PP3

**MONTANA Mavericks**™

Stories that capture living and loving
beneath the Big Sky, where legends live
on...and mystery lingers.

This July, don't miss the exciting conclusion with

## COWBOY COP
### by Rachel Lee

Clint Calloway's orderly life turned chaotic after he
learned of his true parentage—and discovered his
explosive desire for the gorgeous rookie assigned as his
new partner. Dakota Winston was dangerous, all right,
and the last distraction Clint needed—because he was
on the verge of breaking the biggest case that ever hit
Whitehorn, Montana....

Only from **V** *Silhouette*® where passion lives.

MAV12